A Guarded
Heart

Laura Langa

A GUARDED HEART
Copyright © 2021 by Laura Langa

ISBN-13: 978-0-578-86711-3

Cover design by: Karri Klawiter

For Brooke and Alex, my little loves

·CHAPTER 1·

"Physical Therapy, this is Elaine." Elaine balanced the handset between her ear and shoulder, scratching notes onto the scrap piece of office paper she held against the wall.

"Ms. Ritter, hi," said a young female voice. "Uh. My name is Zoe. I'm calling from the childcare room. I'm new. There's, um, been an incident with Colton."

Painful pinpricks rippled rapidly over her skin. "Is he okay?" *Please tell me he's okay. Please tell me he's safe.*

"He was playing with another kid, and . . . well, I mean, it was an accident, but policy states—"

"Is he *okay?*" Her voice dominated the small charting room. Adrenaline coursed through her veins, rushing to the outermost parts of her body as if creating a shield to protect her. The transition from fear to anger was so fast, Elaine almost never saw it coming.

On the other end of the phone, Zoe inhaled sharply. "He's, um, been bitten by another child, and I need you to—"

"I'll be right there." Elaine slammed the phone on the receiver and swung down the hall to the therapy gym. Though she'd just finished with her last patient, some of her coworkers were still completing their appointments.

"Everything okay?" Leslie stood from a crouched position next to her patient who was prone on the gym mat, completing his four-way straight leg raises.

Her cadence hitched slightly—everything rode on her continuing to make a good impression at this clinic. Six months ago, Elaine had transferred from the free-standing physical therapy clinic where she'd worked for the last two and a half years to this one—the outpatient clinic attached to the main hospital. She'd put in the transfer request because she'd heard gossip that the hospital clinic supervisor would be retiring soon and hoped that already being familiar with this clinic's workflow and the fellow PTs would improve her chance at securing the promotion.

Elaine smoothed out the tension around her eyes and forced a neutral expression. "Childcare called me about an incident with Colton."

"Oh, okay." Leslie gave an understanding look, having twin boys herself. "You're done for the day, right? Why don't you take your purse with you? I'll clean up your treatment area."

Elaine's lips softened as a grateful exhale left her tight lungs. "Thank you. That'd be great."

"Sure thing. We moms need to stick together." Her coworker grinned back. "Have a good weekend. I'll see you Monday."

Throwing her crossbody purse over her shoulder, Elaine strode down the main corridor of Edwards Memorial. It took less than two minutes to get from the clinic to the onsite childcare facility provided for hospital employees. During those seconds, Elaine tried to ignore the drumming voice in her head. The one that told her she wasn't doing a good enough job. The one that said it was her responsibility to keep Colton safe, and she didn't have the liberty of failure. Reminding her that she was all Colton had left.

Her toes clenched in her black sneakers as she stopped behind the little half gate that kept the kids securely in the daycare area. "Hello . . . ? Zoe?"

As her gaze scanned the large, brightly colored room, the scent of Play-Doh and baby wipes accosted her nose. Her blond-haired boy was missing from the crowd. So was Mrs. Harris, the older woman who ran the childcare center. "Anyone?"

Every nerve-ending stood at attention, ready to react, almost waiting for someone to challenge her, so she could unleash a torrent of fury on them. She drew a deliberate breath as the deep rumble of a man's voice drew her attention to the small office to the right.

Racing through the door, she asked, "Where's Mrs. Harris?"

"She's, uh, hold on a minute, I'm talking to the other parent," Zoe mumbled.

Elaine felt as if a tendon had snapped in her neck. *Enough.* She needed to see Colton. To see his careful blue eyes look into her own. To know he was okay. And she needed that *now.* "I will not hold on. You told me my son was hurt, and I want to know what is going on now!"

The young woman, perched lightly on the end of the desk, flinched and leaned back.

"Well?" Elaine asked impatiently, taking another step forward.

The man she'd heard from the hall, but had been so focused on Zoe she hadn't yet seen, cleared his throat. "I'm sure she will be able to explain everything as soon as we all take a breath."

The office was so cramped it genuinely surprised her to find him standing there in his well-tailored suit. He looked so put together and comfortable, as though this whole interaction was beneath him. Elaine's already tight muscles strained at the sight of him.

"Did you just tell me to *calm down?*"

His composure wavered. "I think we—"

A rushed breath left her nose. "I will not calm down when some *animal* has hurt my son, and I want answers."

"Technically, the bite didn't break—" Zoe offered.

The man leveled his gaze. "No child is an animal."

She hissed through her teeth, "The one who bit my son is."

His orderly, restrained demeanor instantly evaporated. "Look, *Crazy*. We were trying to figure out what happened in a calm manner before you came in here yelling and calling names."

"I'm calling names? You just called me crazy"—she looked him up and down—"you lousy suit."

His face flushed then recovered so rapidly, it was barely noticeable, but she'd seen it. Attuned from years of watching for subtle cues, she noticed his hands unconsciously clench then release. That word had struck a nerve.

"What did you just call me?"

"I don't know how things stand in your world, *Suit*,"—she emphasized the word and was rewarded with a grimace—"but in civilized society, people don't bite each other."

"They're children! It was probably an accident. How do I know your son didn't attack my daughter, and she bit him in self-defense?" He pointed a finger at her.

A sharp breath whipped into her lungs. "My son would *never*—"

"How am I supposed to believe that when you came in here yelling? Your son clearly has a dysfunctional, unhinged, hothead of a mother. The apple doesn't fall far from the tree."

Her mouth opened, prepared with a cutting retort, when the sweet, soft sound of Colton's "Mama?" sounded from beyond the door.

The relief flooding her body was immediate and overwhelming. A short exhale left her lips as all of her taut muscles threatened to relax simultaneously. She swallowed against the insurmountable emotion swelling in her stomach and tossed words in Zoe's direction. "I'm taking my son home."

Reaching over the metal half-gate, she picked up Colton, clutching his small body. As she held his warm frame firmly to hers, his comforting scent filled her nose. *Breathing. Alive. Thank God.* Elaine blinked against the tears threatening at the corners of her eyes as she carried him through the double doors toward the parking garage.

·CHAPTER 2·

Tilting her face toward the waning sun, Elaine let out a breath, allowing the remaining tension in her muscles to dissipate. She'd fully inspected Colton's skin once they were inside the safety of her ten-year-old, beat-up sedan, but saw no marks. The bite must not have been an aggressive one since it hadn't bruised or broken his skin.

Drilling her son for details had also been fruitless, even after bribing him with an early fast-food dinner of chicken nuggets and fries. Since he didn't tend to elaborate on his day, she wasn't surprised when he gave his typical one-word answers.

Unease rippled over her intercostal muscles, and she rubbed at her ribs to alleviate it. She'd overreacted at the childcare area, chewing out that dad. His child had made a small mistake. Kids made mistakes. Hell, adults made mistakes—she'd just exemplified that with her poor behavior.

A groan left her mouth as Elaine leaned into the park bench. *Why do I always react first, then think later?* By twenty-eight, she should've outgrown this habit.

The near-constant coastal breeze blew her hair back over her shoulder as she let her head tilt skyward. This early October day was actually a little crisp, necessitating the cardigan over her work polo, but Elaine knew early fall in Virginia could be fickle. Tomorrow, it could just as easily be eighty-five degrees and humid or pouring rain. Six, half-dozen, and all that.

The rustling of green oak leaves above her added a calming whisper to the chorus of children's playful shouts. The relaxing combination soothed the flush that always lingered under her skin after her anger left. Elaine took her first deep breath since she'd received Zoe's call as she lowered her gaze to the playground.

Colton darted from the base of the slide and began quickly climbing the stairs. Pressing her right thumb hard into her aching palm, she rubbed while keeping visual tabs on her son. Several of her patients today had required manual therapy, and giving massage took a toll on her hands.

A small smile laced her lips as she watched Colton slip off the slide and start to spin tight circles. The edges of his unzipped hoodie splayed out almost as wide as his outstretched arms while his too-long blond hair whirled away from his scalp. His mouth gaped open in a wide grin, a joyous "wheeee" accompanying his movement.

Moments like this made all the worry over the last two years fade away. Moments like this grounded her and let her believe that maybe—just maybe—she was doing a good enough job. Maybe she was enough for Colton.

Another deep breath left her lungs.

Her momentary reprieve was immediately interrupted when she noticed *him*.

Curly, unruly brown hair flopped over the professional digital camera completely obscuring his face. He was wearing a weathered bomber jacket over beat-up jeans and dusty boots as he crouched, undeniably taking pictures of her son.

All her muscles automatically tensed, ready for another fight.

Standing, she eyed the other parents, noting their locations if she needed help, before moving to tower over him. "What are you doing?"

The camera fell from his face as he glanced up. "Oh, hey. Is that your son?" He gestured the camera toward Colton.

She jammed her hands on her hips. "Answer my question."

He rose quickly, the beaded bracelets around his wrist clacking with this movement. "I'm a photojournalist—"

"So because you're a photojournalist, you think you can take pictures of children without parental consent? How do I know you're not a pedophile?"

"Oh, no. You misunderstand." He winced before turning the LCD screen on his camera toward her. "I can assure you, I would have approached you for consent if these turned out. I just hadn't had a chance to check them before you came over."

On the miniature screen, Colton was a whirling blur of happiness. The inner essence of her son was easily observable in the quickly captured photo. Not the nervous, quiet version he usually showed the world, but the happy, secure one that came out in fits and spurts. She saw all of this, even though the features of his face were completely blurred. The man in front of her must have done something with the exposure when he took the shot.

"Between assignments, I shoot artistic portraits for my own portfolio. Sometimes, I get caught up in framing the right shot, and your son was in such a peak moment of activity that I had to capture it. I truly meant him no harm."

He continued to click through pictures. "I just returned from Sri Lanka where I was working on a freelance piece on burial rites."

He paused at a particularly beautiful photo of a wrinkled woman wrapped in a colorful sari. Her hair was pulled away from her tearful face as her eyes stared straight out of the camera and into Elaine's soul.

"Do you have your phone on you?"

Elaine looked from the camera to his face, noticing that his body had inched closer to hers while she was engaged with the photos. His earthy, masculine scent reached her nose. Another nervous thought washed over her, and she checked for Colton. Seeing her son going down another slide, she pulled her phone from her back pocket.

"Look up BrentJacobs.com." He leaned back and let his camera fall to his side.

Colton was happily climbing the rock wall as she pulled the page up on her phone. It was a professional website with magnificent pictures matching the ones he'd shown her and a photo of the man in front of her, smiling. The menu bar boasted different photo collections and a page for publications, which included *The New York Times*.

She took one more peek at her son and felt her guard begin to slide away. "So not a pedophile?"

"Not a pedophile." A grin hit the corners of his mouth.

"Okay," she said, as her shoulders lowered.

"Let's start over." He extended his right hand. "I'm Brent. Nice to meet you." Now that he was no longer a threat, Elaine noticed warm brown eyes smiling over three days of stubble.

"Elaine." She let her hand be engulfed in his large grip.

"I really am sorry for startling you." This time perfect teeth glinted from beneath the flirty twist of his lips. "Though you looked like you could have taken me down with your eyes alone, mama bear." His gaze ticked to her lips briefly before returning to her eyes.

Elaine felt the shift in his demeanor, and her body instantly clicked into awareness.

Every day she tried to be the best mother for Colton, uncertain if she was failing or succeeding, but there were two things Elaine *knew* with unwavering confidence she excelled at—her job and playing men's games.

And Brent wanted to play.

Little did he know he was going to lose.

Elaine barely suppressed the corner of her mouth from tugging up.

Half a breath was all she needed to assess Brent—artistic, devil-may-care, well-traveled, confident, flirty, likely a lot of trouble, but guaranteed a lot of fun. Just her type. She'd never wanted anything serious even *before* she'd unexpectedly gone from fun-loving aunt to insecure adoptive mother.

Crossing her arms across her chest, she tilted her head to the side. "It's a natural instinct to protect your child from predators." Letting go of her arms, she strode back to her bench.

As she expected, Brent followed. "Good thing I'm not a real threat."

She gave a noncommittal hum as she sat.

He gestured to the seat. "May I join you?"

"Sure," Elaine answered, her eyes checking again for Colton.

Brent sat a respectful distance away from her and crossed a dusty boot over his knee. "So you know what I'm doing when I'm not badly impersonating a pedophile." He paused when a surprised laugh burst from her lips. "What's your chosen profession?"

Her smile was genuine as she answered, "I'm a physical therapist."

"I bet you are expecting me to tell you all about the crick in my back," he said playfully.

Come on, Brent. You can do better.

"That's exactly what I was expecting."

Though most people did it without a gleam in their eye, it was a natural course of action once people learned about her occupation. Usually, she suggested some stretches or strength training exercises. A good deal of ailments could be fixed with PT, though she wasn't a miracle worker.

He leaned forward and rubbed his lower back exposing the expanse of his chest as his jacket gaped open. "I'll have to try harder to be more original."

Unconsciously, her eyes flicked over him. "You can *try*."

Brent relaxed his arm along the edge of the bench, his hand carelessly dangling behind but not touching her shoulder. She watched him glance at her naked left hand before focusing back on her face. "Would you like to go to an art opening with me?"

Even though they had been undeniably toying with each other, shock subtly resonated through her. She got asked out all the time—at the gym, in the hospital cafeteria, out with her best friend, Jodi, on the rare occasions Elaine could secure a sitter, but never when she was with Colton. Usually, when she mentioned she was a single mother, whoever had asked went running.

Elaine searched his face for malice. "An art opening?"

"Thursday. A friend of mine is a glass artist. She's opening her latest installation at a gallery downtown." The smile he held was disarming. "I'd love for you to come with me."

"Mama! I'm thirsty." Colton ran up short of breath before noticing Brent. Once he did, he moved himself around the side of the bench, so she was physically between the two of them.

A slow breath left her lungs as she glanced at her son. Reality came back to her in pulses. Flirting at the park was fun, but Colton was her life. She needed to focus.

"Hey, buddy." Brent gave a friendly wave.

Colton's blue eyes slid to hers, but he didn't say anything. Instead, he draped his body on hers sideways, watching Brent though stolen glances.

"Colton, this is Mr. Brent," she said, rubbing her son's soft shoulder with her hand.

He peeked again at the man next to her on the bench and then bolted off toward the slide.

"He can be shy," she offered and then internally chastised herself. She shouldn't label him like that. The worry she felt over her son stemmed more from her insecurities as a mother than from who he was.

"Some of the most intelligent and successful people are introverts," Brent said, as if it was unconcerning.

That small kindness pulled at her stomach, and she felt her body slump a bit as it softened.

"I just realized I asked you out without knowing if you have someone to watch Colton. Would dinner at a place with a play structure be better for you?"

Years of practice at keeping her face expressionless worked to her advantage as she turned to assess Brent again. His gaze only reflected sincerity.

She left his question unanswered, swallowing away the lump in her throat. "What kind of glass does your friend do?"

His eyes volleyed between hers for a breath before he answered, "Kiln casting that she assembles with other non-glass items in a really unique mixed-media sort of way." He began speaking with his hands, as if laying out a sculpture. "She'll use glass for a portion and then other objects like wood, wire, or plastic for the rest." He let out a low chuckle. "Really, it's easier to see than to describe."

Having seen the second biggest glass art collection on the East Coast at the art museum in downtown Norfolk, Elaine knew a fair amount about the medium. She and Jodi had attended several of the museum's performance art events.

She nodded along as the next question left her lips. "What time is the opening?"

The devilish charm he'd concealed through their last few exchanges came back in full force. "Eight-thirty, but you've got to try this great Ethiopian place beforehand. I was thinking I could pick you up around seven?" He caught her gaze and held it.

Jodi probably wouldn't mind giving up her Thursday night so Elaine could have a little non-mommy time. Colton was usually so sleepy in the evenings that she could get him to bed at six forty-five before Jodi even came over. Then he wouldn't worry about her being gone—he'd be none-the-wiser when he woke up the next morning.

She let out a breath through pursed lips. "I don't know. It's a school night."

Excitement flashed through Brent's pupils. "I promise to have you home before midnight . . . or whenever your curfew is."

"How about you pick me up at seven-fifteen and give me your number, so I can text you my address later," she said, pulling her phone from her back pocket.

He gave her a broad smile that resonated down her arms and legs before he rattled off the digits.

Rising to stand, he said, "I'll see you Thursday."

She leaned back casually against the bench as she replied, "See you then."

Her eyes found Colton near the monkey bars before Brent called out from behind her, cupping his hands around his mouth to shout over the distance. "Oh, and Elaine . . . wear pants."

Brent turned and walked his sexy body to the street where he pulled a helmet from the back of a vintage looking motorcycle trimmed in chrome and burnt orange. He revved the engine and gave a wave before heading toward the main road.

Elaine laughed as he sped away.

Oh yes. This is gonna be fun.

·CHAPTER 3·

Nate barely managed to trap the shout threatening to rip from his throat as he bolted up in bed. Cool air from the AC vent pricked at the droplets spreading in an even sheen over his now-exposed chest and back. He shivered reflexively while grabbing for his forehead, rubbing the space between his eyes as the nightmare slowly evaporated.

The worst scenes of his life faded away as consciousness gradually returned.

When he swung his legs out of bed, the room spun, and he had to put his hands on his knees to regain control. The darkened room continued on its circular path as the green digital numbers of his alarm clock multiplied. One by one, each iteration laid on top of the previous one until the numbers revealed it to be a little after two in the morning.

He would've been sleeping soundly if his glass of scotch the night before hadn't turned into three. Or was it four? It wasn't good if he couldn't remember. He attempted to clear his mouth of the cotton that seemed to line the insides of his cheeks.

Nate had woken up drunk yesterday as well, but being alone on the hardest day of the year had necessitated his alcohol consumption the night before. His brain had logically reasoned he could have twenty-four hours to wallow before having to come back to reality. Twenty-four hours and that was it. Twenty-four hours before all the responsibilities started piling up again.

He'd sobered up enough to drive to the cemetery in the late afternoon, but once he'd left the gravesite, he'd just numbly gone through the motions for the rest of the day. The problem was that once darkness hit, last night's beer had turned into something stronger.

Remorse seeped out of his stomach and slowly crawled up his esophagus until it flooded the back of his throat.

I shouldn't drink like that. I should be better.

His intestines twisted and revolted against the self-inflicted poisoning while his head maintained a steady pounding. After slipping from bed, he went to his bathroom to crush chalky antacids in his teeth and drink as much water as he could hold.

His feet took him to the bedroom at the end of the hall where his daughter slept soundly in her twin bed, surrounded by four stuffed animals. Ten more held vigil, watching over her with beady plastic eyes from their perch on her headboard. The soft snoring sound she made, its tone and volume the same whisper it had been since the day she was born, always brought him comfort.

Tonight, though, the sound of Addie sleeping couldn't counteract her features—her dark tumble of hair strewn across her pillow, those striking blue eyes tucked away beneath flickering, dreaming eyelids, the goodness that radiated from her as if it was a simple attribute you could have, like freckles. All those things pulled at Nate's shoulders until he felt as if he were folding upon himself. All those traits were Sarah's.

Times like this, when Addie was in bed the same way Sarah had been, still shocked him. His brain knew he was looking at his tiny daughter and not his late wife, but his body still responded as it had that day four years ago. Heart galloping, he pushed his palm hard against his chest as a sharp inhale involuntarily filled his lungs, causing Addie to twist in her sheets.

Mentally telling himself to get a grip, Nate froze and focused on the truth in front of him, not the image in his mind. Addie let out a soft, sleepy moan and began snoring louder than she had before. The simple sound of her breathing sent a shudder of calm through his weary body. With the tension loosening between his brows, he bent to lightly brush a kiss to her forehead before leaving.

Once back in his own bed, he tossed against the dampened sheets and willed himself to sleep. It shouldn't be this hard. Every year he told himself it would get better, but he'd been wound tight for days. He'd even unnecessarily yelled at another employee after work on Friday, which was completely unprofessional given that he was the hospital's administrator.

Nate never lost his temper—never—not when he was tied down with bureaucratic nonsense, or when the many personalities of the many different professionals he had to deal with clashed, not even with Addie when she was misbehaving.

But that woman, unrelenting and ridiculous, had crawled right under his skin in a fraction of a second.

He'd felt smugly self-righteous in his actions, a completely foreign sensation, until he'd recognized the unmistakable shadow of fear streak across her face. When the woman had left, he'd learned Addie had accidentally bitten her son while pretending to be a tyrannosaurus.

This failure stacked heavily atop the crushing weight of all his past mistakes as he stared vacantly at the ceiling. Nate covered his face with his arms, and eventually, slumber crept up like a subtle seductress and mercifully took possession of him.

The alarm clock didn't have a chance to bleat as his human alarm clock woke him two minutes before six. A small, not-so-gentle hand to the face accompanied, "I'm hungry, Daddy." His daughter stood beside the bed in pink butterfly pajamas holding a stuffed triceratops. Nate's mother had given her the dinosaur at her fourth birthday party on Saturday, and it was instantly Addie's favorite toy.

"Daddy. I'm hungry," she said again. Her bright eyes shone wide awake like only a child's can first thing in the morning.

Even though his impulse was to push the reset button on the world, he reached his arms out and plucked his daughter from the ground to playfully toss her on the bed. She burst into laughter as she flew over him in an arch of happiness, which efficiently dissolved most of the lingering negativity in his brain. Addie was the best thing to have ever happened to him.

"Snuggles and kisses first." He laid a half-dozen sloppy kisses on her hair and face while hugging her.

Addie squealed, pretending not to love her father's kisses, before pushing at his jaw. "Too scruffy."

"Oh yeah?" He loosened his arms and ran his hand over his morning stubble. "Let's see how scruffy you are."

Addie tilted up her chin for examination while smiling, enjoying their morning game.

"I think you are scruffier."

"No Daddy! My face is smooth."

"Let me double check."

She jutted her chin out a second time, and he ran the back of his knuckles against it. "So it is." He planted one last kiss on her forehead before releasing her. "What are we having for breakfast?"

"Waffles." She jumped up on the bed and bounced a few times. "But Dino-sa-nore is having leaves."

It was adorable that even though she could fully communicate all her needs to him, she still mispronounced some words.

"Waffles for you, leaves for Dinosaur, and coffee for Daddy. Got it."

Nate got out of bed and pulled pajama pants over his boxers and a shirt from the nearby dresser. He could smell his Sumatran roast percolating from downstairs and decided coffee was just the thing he needed to get rid of his relentless headache.

"I'm so glad it's Monday." Addie sang at top volume as she stomped down the stairs. "Monday! Monday! Monday!"

He held his temple. "Quiet feet, Addie."

She ignored him, swinging into the kitchen and opening the freezer to get the toaster waffles for him. Taking the box from his exuberant daughter, he put two waffles in the toaster before pouring himself a large cup of coffee.

"You know what the best part about Monday is?"

There is no best part to a Monday.

Nate took a big draw from his mug in an effort to ingest enough caffeine to be able to match Addie's natural zest for life. "What?"

"I get to play with Cole." She swung her stuffed animal in circles.

Addie had been going on about her "new best friend" Cole for months since he'd started attending her daycare. Nate wondered if he shouldn't reach out to the boy's parents to schedule a playdate or something—not that he'd ever done that before. Just like he hadn't thought to invite other kids to Addie's birthday party.

When she'd sweetly asked if friends could come to her next birthday, Nate had felt a boulder push down his spine. They'd always had family birthday celebrations for her, but now that she was getting bigger and making friends with children her age, he should have thought to invite other kids. He'd kneeled before her and promised that next year, she could invite anyone she wanted.

The toaster popped in completion, pulling his thoughts back to his kitchen, and Nate gave the waffles a light coating of peanut butter and honey before placing them on a plate at the table. When Addie sat and started eating like a starving velociraptor, he cleared his throat.

Blazing blue eyes flitted up and realized their mistake. "Thank you, Daddy."

"You're welcome."

He sat beside her with his coffee but didn't bother to make his usual spinach, mushroom, and Swiss omelet—his insides were still too angry. Pulling his phone from his pajama pants pocket, he opened the first of forty-eight emails that had arrived in his inbox since he'd checked it after the party Saturday afternoon.

"Cole's favorite color is green, and my favorite color is green." Addie managed around a mouthful of waffle.

Nate let out a long sigh, exhausted already, and it wasn't even six-fifteen.

◊◊◊

The clattering of weighted plates moving on and off chrome-cap barbells only exacerbated the persistent thumping in his skull. Gritting the back of his teeth, Nate exhaled and pushed the heavy bar away from his chest. The muscles in his body revolted over being used since he had lubricated them with alcohol instead of water.

"I wasn't sure we were meeting this morning." Tyler's words still carried a slight echo of his teenage emigration from South Africa.

Nate had let Addie dawdle at home instead of sticking to their Monday routine. When he'd arrived fifteen minutes ago, Tyler had already been halfway through their weight training workout. Part of him knew he'd stalled because of what his friend would ask, but he didn't want to talk about it today. Not right before work.

"I texted you last night when we landed, but I didn't hear anything," Tyler said. "I would've been happy to come over and hang with you."

Nate sat up on the bench. "I didn't see it until this morning." Had he seen the message last night, he would have taken his friend up on his offer. Then maybe he wouldn't feel like complete garbage this morning.

Tyler eyed him as if trying to decide if he was telling the truth before adding weight to the bar and lying down to do his set. "Are you okay?"

The familiar scent of the antiseptic cleaner the hospital used wafted from the hallway every time the gym door opened. He usually didn't mind it, but today the smell turned his stomach. Nate positioned himself to spot. "Yeah, I'm fine." If he said it out loud enough, maybe he'd believe his own words.

Tyler completed his set in silence, and the noises of those working out around them were suddenly too loud in Nate's ears. "How was your trip?" he asked, changing the subject.

His friend considered him for a moment and then answered, "It was a nice getaway. There was so much going on every night, and Ibiza was really scenic. Chloe took a bunch of pictures."

"I'm glad you had a good time." He hadn't meant to, but his voice came out clipped. He *was* glad his friend had had a good time. Truly. But before, Tyler had always been with him on the anniversary of Sarah's death, and this was the first year Nate had been left to deal with it alone.

Tyler finished his set and stood. "I've got rounds in twenty minutes, so I've got to shower. We should talk. Or get drinks or something."

Internally, Nate winced. The last thing he needed was more alcohol.

Avoiding his friend's dark piercing eyes, he started racking weights. "I'm good, really. I'll see you Friday morning."

Nate didn't look up, and a long pause settled over the sound of treadmill belts spinning.

"I won't be able to meet you Friday morning. I'm on long call that day, and we're understaffed, so I'll probably end up staying overnight," his friend said.

Nate remembered that Tyler's internal physician's group was temporarily understaffed, as two of their doctors were out on maternity leave. Last week, he'd coordinated with the group's medical director to make sure there were no coverage issues that would affect the hospital.

"No problem. I'll just skip the day."

When Nate glanced up, Tyler had his dark, muscular forearms crossed over his chest with a disapproving look on his face.

With an intentional exhale, his friend released his arms to his sides. "Or you could take the spin class they offer at three forty-five. It's a tough class, but you'll feel great afterward. It might be a good way to get out some . . . negative energy." Tyler gulped from his water bottle and wiped the edge of his mouth. "Just make sure to show up early. It's always packed."

Negative energy? Tyler was starting to sound like Chloe, his yoga instructor girlfriend.

"Thanks for the tip. I might do that," he said.

"I'll see you next Saturday, then? You're still coming over with Addie?" Worry was starting to etch into the creases at the corner of his eyes.

Nate grinned in an attempt to soothe his friend. "Yeah. We'll definitely be there." He rarely missed one of Tyler and Chloe's big family cookouts on their three-acre farm property.

"Good." Tyler's body visibly relaxed. He turned, taking one step toward the locker room before rotating back to clap a large hand on Nate's shoulder. "I know this is hard. I'm here if you need me."

Nate's muscles tensed on their own as he willed his body not to react. He couldn't get into this when he was supposed to be in the office in less than a half hour. "I'm okay," he reiterated.

Tyler muttered something unintelligible before he squeezed Nate's shoulder. "Okay."

Watching Tyler walk away, Nate silently chided himself for being so stilted with the one person who really knew what his life was like. It wasn't Tyler's fault Chloe had surprised him with an amazing last-minute getaway.

Nate took one step forward and then stopped. There'd been enough incidents over the last few days—he didn't need to add falling apart before work to the list. He would tell Tyler the truth some other time.

Picking up a thirty-five pound dumbbell, he started reps of bicep curls. In five minutes, he'd have to take his own shower and get dressed for his workday. Right now, he needed to blow off just a little more steam. The rest of his day needed to go smoothly.

·CHAPTER 4·

Brent pulled his motorcycle sharply to the left as he wove around a slow-moving Jeep. With the movement, Elaine tightened her grip around his ribs. A grin laced his lips as he leaned back slightly to further the connection between their bodies while accelerating down the HOV lane.

When he'd picked her up at her apartment complex, she'd heeded his warning of wearing pants and doubled down. The black, skin-tight faux leather pants tucked into heeled ankle boots showed off every incredible curve of her legs. She'd paired them with a flowy white T-shirt, a green cropped jacket, and a few long chain necklaces. Her rich brunette hair had been loose over her shoulders, and Brent hoped the wind was making a complete mess of it right now. It would give him an excuse to smooth it out over dinner.

Her outfit this evening was a departure from the cardigan, polo, slacks, and sensible black sneakers she'd had on at the park. Brent understood that was her work attire, and this was date attire, but it was something more. There was an intensity she carried with her tonight that he'd caught a glimpse of the day they'd met—a confidence that was intoxicating.

The ride ended much too quickly as he pulled into a parking spot in front of the restaurant. He made a mental note to take the long way when dropping her off later. Cutting the engine, he allowed her to swing off the bike before he dismounted.

"I haven't ridden on a motorcycle in a long time," she said, pulling off her helmet.

"I like to feel the forces of air resistance and acceleration pulling at me when I travel, if I can. Makes me feel like I'm more involved in the world around me rather than passing it by." He sent his best grin her way as he put his helmet on the bike.

Her head tilted with a glint in her eye. "Must be cold in the winter."

"I have a car too. Driving this is just a lot more *fun*." Allowing a smirk to fully spread across his face, he pointed to the restaurant. "Shall we?"

Keeping her eyes locked on his, an almost evil grin tugged at her mouth as she elongated her spine and used her hands to shake out her hair. When she lowered her arms with a roll of her neck, her hair fell in a nearly perfect cascade down her back.

Damn.

After a hard blink, Brent forced his feet away from her and toward the restaurant. He caught a hint of jasmine when she breezed by him as he held open the door. It immediately transported him to the French Quarter in spring. Her scent was almost as distracting as the coy glance she flicked up at him as she strode past.

Once they were seated on the small wooden stools around the woven mesob, she asked, "What made you want to be a photojournalist?"

"When I was little, I noticed that I saw the world a little differently than other people. It wasn't until high school when I took photography as an elective that I really started to appreciate the talent required to capture a good photo. My parents, being more traditional, insisted I major in journalism as well as photography in college—"

Their waiter arrived with waters and set them on a small wooden table next to their mesob before they placed their order.

"I started freelancing and made connections within the journalism world right after graduation. I enjoy the travel that usually accompanies my assignments, but now I'm trying to concentrate on my art. I'd like to be able to stop freelancing and focus solely on my artistic goals."

Having just turned thirty, he needed to finally prove he could make it alone on his photography. That he didn't need the money his mother transferred into his account every month to help pay the bills.

He was certain the breakthrough he'd been waiting for was just out of sight. It was something he could taste in his mouth. He couldn't describe it, but he *knew* something was going to change soon.

"Your photos are quite good. I'm sure you could make the switch," she said before taking a sip of water.

He arched an eyebrow. "You looked at my photos?"

She leaned back slightly on her stool. "You showed me your camera screen at the park, remember?"

Brent was hoping to catch her admitting she'd perused his web page, maybe even searched online for him, but she only said, "I don't have an artistic bone in my body, but I can appreciate the work of others."

"Everyone can be artistic. Your medium might just not be as easily observable." He moved a fraction, so his knees were touching hers across the tiny table—she didn't adjust her body.

A *Yeah right* look tugged on her eyebrows. "Unless you count the broken bodies of other people as a medium, I highly doubt it."

"See, there you go." He leaned forward, gesturing with his hands. "You heal others and put their bodies to rights. That *is* an art form."

The breath from her exhaled scoff blew over his fingertips, and the heat that hovered just below his collarbones intensified. Brent was seconds away from reaching for her knee, shoulder, wrist—anywhere—when the waiter placed their meal in front of them.

He hid his disappointment at the interruption with an uptick of his lips. "Why did you choose to be a physical therapist?" Ripping off some flatbread with his hands, he used it to pick up a little shiro.

Elaine dug into the food, signaling she'd eaten this cuisine before. He'd hoped to impress her with new experiences like a motorcycle ride and unfamiliar food, but so far, nothing had surprised her.

"I was a bit of a nerd growing up, and science came easy to me. I had some experience watching PTs when I was a teenager, and it seemed like a great job, helping people recover from different injuries or surgeries.

"It's so rewarding to help a person get back to who they used to be, or sometimes even better than they were before therapy." She took a small bite and swallowed. "Plus, it's something that would always be around."

Her word choice struck him as odd. "Always be around?"

She shrugged casually before grabbing another mouthful. "Healthcare is always in demand."

This was adding a layer to the picture forming in his mind—worldly, passionate, practical. He liked the idea of her taking care of herself and not needing anyone else. A sort of badass strength emanated from her that was sexy as hell.

Before he could respond, she asked, "Do they serve alcohol here?"

He smiled. "No, but there's a wine bar up the street, and this makes for a quick meal."

"Perfect."

That twist of her lips was seriously hampering his focus.

◊◊◊

After finishing dinner and a glass of wine each, they walked the rest of the way to his friend Umi's art opening. Elaine didn't seem to mind him winding his arm around her trim waist to help her navigate the uneven sidewalk. A constant gust blew from the harbor, kicking up her hair and making it impossible for him to ignore her incredible scent.

As they approached the small crush of people standing outside the gallery, he leaned his lips close to her ear. "Let's say 'hi' to Umi first and see if she's free to talk to us."

Chill house mix pulsed into the street through the open gallery door as he looked for his friend. Brent found her next to her smallest piece, champagne glass in hand. Her black hair was buzzed on one side of her head, pixied and dyed neon yellow on the other. She was wearing black combat boots, cut up green canvas pants, a cropped knit tank, and her iconic red cat eyeglasses.

"Umi!" he called out as they headed over.

"Brent, you devil," she said, giving him a fierce hug. "I didn't know you were in town."

After Umi released him, he placed his hand on the small of Elaine's back. "Umi, this is my friend, Elaine."

Elaine put her hand out to shake. "Nice to meet you."

Umi wrapped her into a tight hug. "Any friend of Brent's is a friend of mine."

Elaine seemed only a little startled before she smiled widely. "Your work is amazing."

"Thank you. It's a labor of love." Umi sighed affectionately as she glanced around the room.

Brent's gaze followed Umi's, taking in all the different pieces she'd created before settling on the one beside them. The glass cast of a child's head was incredibly detailed, down to her cherubic smile and twin pigtails. The neck and arms of the girl were formed from chicken wire and her dress was a high-necked bodice made of broken eggshells over a white feather skirt. Her legs, cuffed socks, and Mary Jane shoes were another detailed glass cast. Laid at her feet was a newspaper nest containing a single blue glass egg.

"They're all incredible," he agreed. "I was hoping you'd have a minute to explain the collection to us."

"I'd love to." She started to discuss the piece in front of them.

They were fortunate enough to receive a tour of half of the pieces before more friends arrived and pulled Umi away.

"How do you know Umi?" Elaine asked after they'd ambled through the remaining exhibit.

"A photography friend introduced me to her a few years back."

They passed a small table of snacks and drinks at the back of the gallery, and he grabbed them each a glass of champagne. Unexpectedly, another artist and friend of Umi's that Brent hadn't talked to in a while showed up to grab a drink. As he caught up with the man, Elaine easily joined in the conversation.

When she laughed at a joke his friend made, the impulse to capture her large smile as her head tilted back in amusement was visceral. Elaine was undeniably gorgeous and therefore a perfect model, but it was moments of genuine human emotion that were his favorite to capture. Being caught at a moment like this without his camera made his eyes twitch at the missed opportunity.

When the man left them alone in the back of the gallery, he asked, "What do you think?"

"I think you live in an interesting world," she mused, draining her glass as her eyes flowed over the room.

He'd meant about Umi's collection but continued with her train of thought. "This is only half of it. This is the best half. Where you get to create your art and put it out into the world. When your friends come and join you in the celebration of what you've accomplished. This is the part I want to live in all the time. The creative half." He took a gulp of champagne. "The other half is endless layovers, being perpetually jet-lagged, sleeping on dirt floors, trying to follow a story, not eating for a few days, and having to barter your shirt for a bottle of water in a foreign country."

She glanced up and then *chuckled*. "Am I supposed to feel bad for you?"

Something in the way she laughed pulled at him.

Setting his mostly full glass down on a nearby table, he focused fully on her black-lined umber eyes. "Do you?"

"No." Elaine held his gaze as one side of her mouth lifted. "I have the feeling that regardless of what you go through, in the end, you always get what you want."

Brent freed her of her glass and set it aside, standing straight in front of her. The muscles of his neck and chest tightened. "Do I?" he challenged.

"Yes."

She wasn't touching him, but she didn't have to. He noticed the heat searing from her body from a foot away. Feeling the olive skin of her arms under his fingertips would be incredible right now, but this game was much too fun.

Cocking his head to the side, he asked, "What do you want, Elaine?"

"My own—" Her mouth slackened as her answer died on her tongue. Her eyes flicked to his chest for a beat before returning to his with their searing tease. "A ride through the wind."

After an extended ride home, where he made sure to weave a bit causing her to cling tightly to his body, they ended back at her apartment complex. It was one of those where all the doors exited to the outside, and the grouped two-story buildings were separated by a bit of green space.

He took her hand and led her to the picnic table near an iron pedestal grill where he'd picked her up earlier. At eleven o'clock on a Thursday, the complex was silent except for the sounds of those still awake within the building nearby.

Without asking permission, he picked her up and settled her on top of the table. He left his hands on her waist and cheered internally when she wove her slender fingers up the arms of his jacket before settling them over his biceps.

"Did you enjoy yourself tonight?" he asked, gazing into her unreadable eyes. The dim lamplight of the complex cast her face in an amber glow, but her eyes were so dark it was hard to discern their exact expression.

"Did you?" she answered with a question, the quality of her voice hitting all the right spots in his body.

He allowed himself to inch a fraction closer to her mouth. "Other than not impressing you at all, I did."

Elaine laughed and tossed her hair back like she had at the art gallery. An impulse thrummed strongly between his shoulders—normally he was content with seeing, but right now he needed to touch. He released her waist with his right hand and pulled a few loose strands of hair past her neck, holding them just in front of her shoulder. Even though his eyes were trained on his hand, he heard her expectant intake of breath.

"I'd like to see you again." He leaned back but kept rubbing the lock between his fingers.

A slight pause preceded, "Would you?"

"I'm heading out of town tomorrow. I've got a meeting with *The Post* in D.C. tomorrow afternoon and then another one with a gallery owner in New York on Monday. I plan on staying in Manhattan for the week to tie up some loose ends, but I could be back by next Saturday. Would you happen to be available?"

This time her pause sent a slight alarm through his temples. His instincts weren't usually incorrect, but he had to admit she had him so mystified that perhaps he'd misread her.

Or maybe her situation. Though Brent had always liked kids, he'd never dated a single mom before.

"If going out at night is too much, we could always meet at the park again. I'll bring coffee and chocolate milk."

Her controlled inhale was as audible as her exhale.

When he glanced at her, her mouth slowly curled into a sly grin. "I think I could make Saturday night work."

Triumph soared in his chest as his eyes fell to her lips. "I was hoping you'd say that."

Those dusty-rose lips twisted higher. "Don't you always get your way?"

He let confidence creep into his voice as he moved his hand to weave through the hair at the nape of her neck. "Yes."

Firmly pulling her mouth to his, Brent felt her press forward with the same urgency radiating through his body. Her knees separated when he leaned onto them and then snuggly held his torso. Heat seared him as her tart tongue traced the edges of his lips before his dove straight between hers.

Winding his left arm around her body, he pulled her even closer to him as her hands pushed up over his shoulders and plunged into his hair. The gasp that escaped his mouth couldn't be stopped as her tongue spun fervent circles around his. He was about to weave his hand under the back of her thin shirt when he heard rustling nearby.

"*Ahem.*"

Brent glanced up to find an elderly man with a flat cap and a cane staring at them. Elaine dropped her hands to his chest as she turned toward the voice.

"You two mind taking that inside?"

Elaine leaned her forehead onto her hands and snorted.

At least one of us finds this funny.

Lifting her head with a sigh, she turned to address the man on the sidewalk. "Sure. Sorry, Walter."

Brent blinked at the woman whose legs were still hugging his waist.

"Walter" seemed to be just as perturbed to be addressed by her as he was to happen upon the two of them. "Elaine, is that you? Are you okay?"

She barely contained a laugh. "Yes, I'm fine."

The old man scoffed, as if unconvinced. "I've got my cane, young man, and I'm not afraid to use it."

Elaine pushed off the table to stand, putting a very undesirable distance between them. "I was just saying goodnight to my date. I'm completely fine."

The man in the cap gave Brent a spitfire once-over and seemed to accept her answer. "All right then."

"'Night, Walter," she said.

The old man shuffled back in the direction of the nearby apartment building, stealing hostile glances at Brent over his shoulder.

As soon as Walter was out of earshot, she said quietly, "My next door neighbor. He can be a bit overprotective."

"I'd say." Brent watched the man throw a final glare his way before going through his front door.

"He means well." Her tone softened.

Finally alone again, he let his eyes focus on the woman before him. His attention centered on the fullness of her kiss-swollen lips and how he was much too far away from them.

"I should probably head inside." Her lips were perfect, but the words were all wrong.

"You did warn me it was a school night," he admitted with a teasing grin.

She laughed in that way that he was really becoming attached to hearing. "I'll see you next Saturday."

Her smile dropped as an intensity shifted over her face. Taking hold of the collar of his jacket, she pulled his face down to hers. His nerve endings popped at the blissful sensation of her lips pushed to his. She drove her free hand through his hair behind his head and gripped tightly as she casually tasted his mouth once more. When she let go, she flicked her eyes down in a false show of shyness before fixing them intently on his. "'Night."

Elaine let her gaze drag as she turned before walking the short distance to her front door. Distracted by the way the light bounced off the reflective surface of her pants as she sauntered away, he barely managed to call "Goodnight" after her.

She gave a little finger wave as she let herself in her apartment, and he stood frozen for a solid ten seconds before he turned to head to his motorcycle.

"Whoa."

·CHAPTER 5·

The high Elaine felt walking through her front door immediately vanished upon seeing her pajama-clad son nestled on Jodi's lap. Her friend's light brunette waves draped over Colton's shoulder like a protective curtain as she rubbed his back, whispering soothing words.

After silently bolting the front door, Elaine quickly crossed the short distance.

"He had a nightmare." The almost imperceptible rasp that always accompanied Jodi's words was more pronounced with her hushed tone.

Colton raised his face from Jodi's chest, a blanket impression running down the center of his left cheek. "Mama?" His little fist pushed residual tears from his sleepy eyes. "Where'd you go?"

Elaine's stomach gnarled as she reached for her son. "I went to see a friend. I'm sorry I wasn't home when you woke up."

Colton slung his warm arms around her neck, and she rocked him back and forth like she had done when he was a baby. When he nestled his head onto her shoulder, she inhaled the familiar lavender scent of his bath wash. Normally the best smell in the world, the delicate scent only intensified the guilt brewing in her gut.

Kissing his soft hair, she let out a breath. "Let's get you back to bed."

When Elaine reentered her small living room, Jodi was sitting cross-legged on the couch hunched over a sketchbook, several others scattered over the nicked coffee table. Her ink-stained fingers were putting the finishing touches on a crosshatch portrait of Colton. Like the many others she'd drawn, it was perfect. Jodi had captured his innocence but also the uncertainty in his eyes with a fine-tipped black pen.

Funny how both of the artists in Elaine's life were using her son as a muse.

"That's beautiful, Jo."

"Thanks." Her friend paused as she looked up before pulling another sketchbook closer and flipping through some pages. "I'm working on a contrasting theme. Pictures of little kids next to these."

Jodi leafed through sketches of very downtrodden adults. Just like the one of Colton, each was absolutely stunning and incredibly detailed. The tiny black marks on the paper added a roughness to the worn lines and creases on the faces of her subjects. Heaviness settled in Elaine's body when Jodi stopped at a drawing of a particularly disheveled middle-aged woman holding a paper bag-covered liquor bottle against her forehead.

Snapping the book closed, Jodi started stacking them. "How was your date?"

Oh, right. Her date.

With hard memories of the past tensing the muscles in her jaw, her enjoyable date felt like an apparition.

"Good." She let her suddenly weary body collapse onto the lumpy cushions near her friend.

Jodi exhaled a short breath through her nose before playfully pushing on Elaine's leg. "*Details*, Elaine."

"Right, sorry."

"What gallery did you go to?"

"Art Culture."

"Wow. Good for them." Jodi leaned back against the armrest.

Since Art Culture was one of the larger galleries outside of the Chrysler Museum downtown, it was one of the best places to show artwork. Jodi had shown partial collections at Commune Community a few blocks away, in addition to single pieces here and there at local restaurants, but never a full collection. Perhaps this new set of drawings would be what her friend needed to fully break into the art scene.

"Yeah, and she had the whole bottom floor." Elaine kicked off her boots.

"That's impressive." Jodi's light brown eyes widened. "What was the artist's na—never mind." She waved a hand in front of her. "I'm focusing too much on the art. Tell me about the guy."

A wicked smile tugged at her lips. "He was as nice to look at as the art."

Jodi laughed loudly before hushing herself and looking at Colton's closed door.

Pulling herself up to watch for movement, Elaine let out a breath when the door remained silent and unopened. Colton had always been a light sleeper.

Her son's drawings and half-filled coloring pages covered the white door, which was surrounded by white trim and white walls. A throbbing pulsed under her breastbone as she thought about the possibility of being able to move out of this apartment to a place she owned, being able to take Colton to the paint store and let him pick whatever color he wanted, being able to finally build him a home. As her gaze flitted from the white water-damaged popcorn ceiling to the long white wall separating her apartment from her neighbor's, her eyes relaxed as they rested on Jodi's drawing of her and Colton.

Gratitude swelled as she turned to her friend. "Thank you again for watching Colton tonight."

"Don't even start." Jodi began placing her sketchbooks and pens into her shoulder bag. "I love watching Colton. Besides, I was mostly sketching, which I would have been doing in my own apartment two hundred feet away anyway. You needed a night out." She leveled a gaze at Elaine. "I could tell."

A laugh bubbled up in response. "It was that obvious?"

"Um, yeah."

"Tell me how you really feel," she joked.

"I always do." Her friend smiled.

That was one of the best things about Jodi. She never lied. She never sugar-coated. She told you exactly what she thought and saw. The same perceptive eyes she used to find and draw the slightest detail—an overlooked acne scar, a slight unevenness in a smile, a barely asymmetric nose—also noticed emotions as if they were pen marks on your face. It made Jodi one of the best art therapists at Norfolk Children's Hospital.

"Our weekly pizza hangouts with Colton are fun, but you needed some *adult-only* evening time." Jodi arched an eyebrow. "So this guy . . ."

"Brent."

"Brent the photographer."

"Yes."

"Was he a vapid pile of testosterone like most guys?" Another grin laced Jodi's lips.

"Actually, no. He was interesting and charismatic, though at times a little cocky—"

"So just your type, then?" Jodi interjected.

A chuckle escaped her lips. "Basically."

"Are you going to see him again?" Jodi's asked.

"Yeah. Next Saturday."

Her friend didn't hide her shock. "Oh, wow, a second date."

"It's not that big of a deal." She rolled her eyes.

Jodi snorted. "Please. You 'one and done' guys all the time. What makes this guy so special?"

"There's nothing wrong with dating guys who are never going to meet Colton. Never going to be part of this." She waved her hand around her small apartment, somehow trying to visually represent their lives with a swoop of her arm. "Have a nice meal, get to feel like an independent adult for a few hours, maybe get in a good make out, and then done. I was planning on kicking Brent to the curb, but he offered for our second date to be at the park *with* Colton."

Something had softened inside her when Brent had offered that. Almost immediately, the desire to know the sexy, artistic man, who undoubtedly wanted her, intensified.

"That's not a bad thing. Eventually, you were going to meet a guy who didn't mind that you were also a mom." Her friend's eyes filled with understanding—Jodi was the only person who knew Elaine's whole story.

She lifted a shoulder. "Yeah, I guess."

"Maybe just be open-minded with this one?" Jodi's raspy voice was soft. "Not all men are bad."

Elaine nodded. That was true, but the good ones were rare and hard to find. The only man she'd ever trusted had been her sister's husband, Chuck. The man who had fiercely loved Rose and had protected them both. The man who had died defending people he didn't even know deployed in active duty combat overseas when Rose was eight months pregnant. After years of trying for a child, it had been unimaginably cruel that Chuck had never met the son who looked exactly like him.

The sounds of people talking loudly outside penetrated the apartment walls as Jodi said in a playful tone, "Tell me you at least got your make out session."

As Elaine's mouth curled up on its own, the tension she'd been holding in her jaw released. "Walter *might* have caught us on the picnic table by the grill."

Jodi choked on her laugh, using one hand to stifle the sound while pushing Elaine's leg with the other one. "That's my girl."

Elaine's grin widened before Colton's "Mama?" pulled her attention to his open bedroom door.

"I'll go," Jodi said, slinging her bag over her shoulder while crossing the room to Colton. She knelt to give him a hug and a kiss. "Go to bed, cutie."

"Kay, Auntie Jo," he yawned.

As Jodi let herself out and locked the front door with her key, Elaine swooped her son up again. She wrapped her body around his tiny one and snuggled with him on his bed. Before long, Colton's soft breathing dominated the star-patterned, nightlight-illuminated room.

That's when memories assaulted her—some good but mostly ones that brought a sheen of wetness to her eyes.

Moving back in with a desolate Rose to help her prepare for Colton's birth without her husband. Being the second person to hold his wiggly newborn body. Fumbling along with Rose through their mourning while also learning how to care for an infant. How she had always felt nervous and unsure learning to care for Colton, but Rose always seemed to instinctively know the right thing to do. How beautiful it was to see her loving sister with the child she had wanted for so long—how even on the saddest days, Colton always brought her joy. The pride Elaine had felt being able to help her sister financially so that even with Chuck gone, Rose could do what she wanted—take a leave from her job as a bank teller and stay home with Colton full time.

Elaine tightened her grip around Colton's body and drew in a deep inhale. At the time, she'd felt so grateful she'd been able, in some small way, to balance out all the years Rose and Chuck had taken care of her. But two years later, when Elaine had had to confirm that the still, lifeless person on the hospital gurney was her sister prior to being ushered to collect Colton from the social worker, Elaine knew that time between Rose and Colton had been precious.

That's what had made living after it so much harder.

"Mama? Mama?"

Elaine heard her nephew's cries as he wandered all around the small townhouse looking for Rose, but couldn't raise her head. She was balled on her sister's bed, pillow gripped to her chest so hard her knuckles paled, her breath heaving to the point of hyperventilation.

The pillow was losing Rose's smell.

Elaine knew somewhere deep in her bones that this would be the first to go, then it would be the memory of her voice, or the particular way her face twisted when she ate something sour, or the way she'd snort when something was really funny. You couldn't hold all the memories of a person in your mind forever. Eventually, you forgot.

It had only been six days, but they had been the hardest of Elaine's life. She should have expected her upbringing or Chuck's loss to have been some sort of perverse training for this, but nothing could have prepared her for losing the person she'd loved more than anything.

A loud, violent sob racked from her chest as her body shook.

She was so alone.

It took her several minutes to realize she wasn't the only one in the room crying. Colton stood next to the bed holding his small blue blanket in one hand and reaching up to her with the other. Dragging herself to the edge, she pulled his tiny body into hers and folded herself around him.

"Mama?" He kept asking. "Mama?"

"Mama's gone." Her voice cracked.

"Lane?" He shifted around so they were facing—his wet, swollen eyes torturing her.

"Yeah, bud?" Tears fell through her words.

Then Colton's chubby little hands pulled at her shirt until his face was buried in it. "Mama."

Elaine's chest throbbed as if it had been cracked open, and she was bleeding all over the unmade bed.

For the rest of that first year, a lot of transitions happened. She legally became Colton's mother. They moved from her sister's Navy-appointed townhouse to a little apartment. Her name slowly morphed from *Lane* to *Mama*. But the thing that stayed the same was that every night they slept like this, woven around each other, needing each other equally.

Colton never returned to the carefree child he'd been with Rose, but he became calmer. He was still more cautious and quiet, but every time he reached for her with a questioning "Mama?" and she returned with a warm embrace and kisses, he seemed more secure. As much as the sting of being called that word had hurt Elaine's heart initially, knowing she could never be the mother Rose would have been, she also knew that Colton needed her. No matter what, she was going to try to be the best mother to him because Rose couldn't.

Elaine leaned forward until she could press her lips against Colton's hair in a delicate kiss. "I love you," she whispered. Slowly, moving by degrees, she slid from the bed.

When she reached the threshold, she paused with a sigh before gently closing her son's door.

·CHAPTER 6·

Nate rolled his neck as he walked toward the cycling room at the back of the gym. After the maelstrom of a day he'd had, he'd only managed to get to class a mere five minutes before it was supposed to start. Stepping through the threshold, it became obvious Tyler hadn't been joking when he'd said it was a popular class. There was only one bike left open, and he weaved his way from the back of the room to secure it, putting his water bottle on the holder part of the handlebar.

The man behind him pushed a black metal piece under the ball of his cycling shoes into his pedals with an audible click. Nate examined the pedals of his own bike, flipping them over to find fabric cages for his tennis shoes on the opposite side.

"Need help with your bike, Suit?"

Her question sent twin emotions pulsing down his already tight shoulders as he attempted to stymie his reactive irritation. That *word*. He hated that word. Unfortunately, his brain only registered her light tone and the innocent awkwardness in her dark brown eyes after he gruffly responded, "I'm sure I can manage."

Her jaw visibly tightened as her gaze hardened.

Idiot.

He'd just figuratively slapped her olive branch to the ground and stomped on it.

"Look, I didn't—"

She held up her hand. "You know what? Never mind—"

"If you're new, you need to have the bike sized to you," the woman on the bike next to him interrupted. The pedaling woman had a physique suggesting she'd completed a triathlon the day before.

When Nate glanced back to the woman in front of him, her arms were crossed tightly across her chest.

"I think we—" he tried again.

"Do you want help or not?" her voice snapped.

Unfamiliar pettiness bloomed under his skin. "Fine, yes. I've never been to a spin class before."

The evil smile that lifted her lips could almost be described as a sneer. She showed him how to size his bike to his frame and then how to tighten the cages to his shoes, though not without completely insulting his intelligence and manhood.

When she strode away, everyone who was still standing got onto their bikes. There wasn't a single empty bike. It dawned on him the second before she grabbed the microphone from the front sound system and put the headset around her neck and over her mouth.

She's the instructor.

"Welcome to The Joy Ride." She easily mounted and clipped into the bike on a raised platform facing the class. "I'm Elaine." To this, she received no less than twelve whoops and hollers from the room.

Her lips curled into a slightly wicked grin. "Who's ready to work?"

After a quick warm-up, Nate learned how hard a spin class really was. She was constantly calling out for them to add a gear or go faster, and all his male pride had him doing exactly as he was told and making sure the speed of his legs matched hers. They were working through a series of seated and standing climbs on what seemed like an impossibly high gear when she shouted, "Come on, guys! It's not supposed to be easy!"

Even though she was tough, she was also very encouraging, which was why he could see she had such a following. Calling out about which muscles to use and something about pedal strokes—that went over his head—was peppered with repeat commands like "push," "faster," and "dig."

After the longest seated sprint of his life, the piano introduction of an older song led to a much-desired instruction. "Take off all your gear. Let's cool down."

The fit woman next to him exhaled. "Oh, thank God."

Nate was glad he wasn't the only one who thought the class was hard as hell. He'd sweated completely through his gym shorts and T-shirt.

As "Apologize" played loudly through the room's speakers, his shoulders tensed toward his ears before he intentionally pushed them back down. It was juvenile how he had behaved at the beginning of class. He'd planned to do what the song title dictated the next time he saw her, not snap at her over one stupid word.

After going through a series of stretches, Elaine wished the class a good weekend and took off her mic. Nate dismounted right before the triathlete handed him a cleaning wipe and started wiping down her bike. He mumbled thanks, observing his own very wet bike. After thoroughly cleaning it, he grabbed his water bottle, intending to catch Elaine before she left the class. Only she wasn't in the room anymore.

He followed the flow of either very tired or very excited cyclists—depending on their fitness levels—out of the back of the room into the larger multipurpose weight room. Nate looked around to see if she was anywhere else in the gym but came up empty again. Acid bubbled up to the back of his throat as he grabbed his gym bag from the locker room. His legs felt tired and heavy trudging toward the childcare area to pick up Addie.

But as soon as he walked through the double glass entry doors into the brightly painted room, he was rewarded with black bike shorts and a sweat-soaked blue racerback. The ends of Elaine's wet ponytail stuck and unstuck to the top of her bare shoulder as she moved her head.

"What do you mean you're not open tomorrow?" Her voice was shrill as she questioned Mrs. Harris, the manager.

"Ms. Ritter," the older woman said with the same patient voice she used to speak to screaming toddlers all day. "I sent the email out two months ago. This weekend, we will be closed so that new flooring can be installed.

"We are finally replacing this carpet with more durable, easy to clean floors. It will be better for the children, and we will be able to keep things more germ-free. We will be open on Monday as usual, but unfortunately this weekend, we are closed."

Elaine muttered to herself while tapping at her phone, looking for the email. A blond-haired boy darted toward the little half-gate they used to keep the children corralled during the day, and Mrs. Harris opened it for him. He gave Elaine a big hug before looking up at her face with a frown.

"Do you know anyone who would be available to watch Colton? Anyone who does babysitting on the side? I can't miss work tomorrow, and my friend who usually helps me with childcare just went out of town today."

At that moment, Addie saw him and ran to the gate. "Daddy! Daddy! Daddy!"

His daughter flung her outstretched arms over the top railing as Elaine glanced over her shoulder, her dark brows furrowed in further frustration at his sheer existence behind her.

"Are you ready for her, Mr. Brennan?" Mrs. Harris said through a laugh.

"Let her loose." He grinned back at the sweet woman.

Addie rushed to him, quickly hugged his legs, said "eww" to his sweatiness, and then bounded over to the little boy. She stopped just before him and gave him a delicate hug. "Bye, Cole."

"His name is Colton," Mrs. Harris said to his daughter. "Not Cole, remember."

"Oh ya. Saw-dee, Colt." She gave him another embrace. "I like being your friend."

"Me too." He gave her an adorable hug back and waved as she skipped away.

"That's Cole?" When Nate looked up, he could see Elaine was as surprised by the exchange as he was.

"You're friends with her?" she asked her son.

The boy raised his bright eyes to his mom's face and nodded, his hair bobbing as he did.

"BFFs!" Addie added while she swung from Nate's hand, using the term she'd heard on one of the girly cartoons he let her watch on the weekends so he could have a few moments to himself.

"Oh, yes. They play so nicely together all the time." Mrs. Harris smiled at the children. "I was surprised to hear about Addie biting Colton when I was out last Friday, but we talked about it, and she knows better than to play like that again. Don't you, love?"

"Uh-huh," his daughter answered dutifully.

"I'm glad it was just a play-bite, and that she didn't really hurt him. I had her apologize on Monday morning, and both of them have been right as rain ever since. I'm sincerely sorry I wasn't here during your conference." Her apologetic eyes focused on each parent in turn. "Actually, since I have both of you here, would you mind signing the incident form? It seems Miss Zoe forgot."

They exchanged a glance as Mrs. Harris brought up a piece of paperwork. It wasn't that Miss Zoe forgot. It was that the two of them had screamed at each other and then stormed out of the building before it could be signed.

"Of course." He stepped forward and signed where she pointed an age-spotted finger.

"Sure." Elaine added her signature to the form as well.

"You two have a good weekend." Mrs. Harris filed the paper before leaning to peek behind them.

Nate turned to notice the line of other parents waiting to pick up their children. They both gathered their kids' backpacks from the cubbies and walked out of the double doors before Elaine swore under her breath.

"Hold on, bud, we have to go back and finish talking to Mrs. Harris."

"Actually, Elaine . . ." He stood in front of her. "It's Elaine, right?"

She seemed too tired to even try to sneer at him and nodded instead.

"I wanted to talk to you about last Friday. The way I behaved was completely inappropriate. I know it's no excuse, but I'd had a really rough day at work after not a lot of sleep, and I unfairly took it out on you.

"Addie should have never bitten your son, and we talked a lot about how that's not how we should treat anyone. I realized in giving that lecture to her, I had not set a good example by blowing up at you. And then today . . ." He didn't want to explain why that word made his skin crawl. "I should have apologized as soon as I saw you at the beginning of class. I'm sorry it took this long."

Elaine exhaled slowly as her shoulders softened. "Thank you for your apology. I shouldn't have reacted the way I did, either. I just tend to be a little overprotective of him at times." She glanced at her son who clutched her hand, leaning firmly against her side.

"I understand. No one wants anything bad to happen to their child." Addie held Colton's other hand, telling him which outfits of the people walking by she liked best. Occasionally, a description would lay a shy smile on the boy's lips. "They do seem to get along well."

"Yes," she agreed.

Something about the tender way she watched their children and the fact that she was a fellow single parent in need triggered his desire to help. All day long, he fixed problems, and he could solve this one right now while simultaneously making his daughter extremely happy.

"Why don't you let Addie and I make amends for last week?" Her gaze flicked up as he continued. "We would be happy to have Colton over for an extended play date at our house tomorrow."

"Oh, I couldn't—" she started.

"I overheard your conversation with Mrs. Harris—by accident. We would be happy to have him over while you work tomorrow. It seems like the kids would enjoy each other's company, and if you were just going to ask for a sitter who would be new to him anyway, at least at our house he'd have a friend."

Addie whispered something into Colton's ear and they both giggled.

Elaine's focus drifted toward their children. "Are you sure?"

"Absolutely. It would be our pleasure."

Elaine's eyes blinked to his with such tender vulnerability that his breath stopped in his chest. The two seconds her gaze held his felt like an eternity before she glanced back to the kids. They were now swinging their hands and softly singing the daycare center's "Goodbye Friends" song.

Nate felt his lips open on their own as he exhaled.

"Okay." She jostled her gym bag and searched in her purse to find her phone. "What's your address . . . um . . ."

"Nate," he said, extending his hand. "Nate Brennan."

Her eyes held their previous strength as she took his hand with a firm grip. "Elaine Ritter."

Giving her his address and phone number, she saved the information in her phone. They discussed what time and a few more logistics before Addie picked up on the adults' conversation.

"Is Colt coming to play tomorrow?" She beamed at Elaine.

Nate noted the apprehension in her voice as she said, "Yes."

"Yiphoo!" Addie jumped and gave Colton a big hug.

"Yiphoo!" her son echoed.

The laugh that captured Elaine must have taken her by surprise. "Yiphoo?" she asked the kids in general.

"Addie still mixes up some words," Nate offered.

His daughter was thoroughly explaining all the different toys they could play with tomorrow as Elaine spoke again. "Seven fifteen's not too early?"

"This alarm clock gets up at six whether or not it's the weekend." He nodded to his daughter.

"Same story," she sighed. "I miss sleeping in."

"Me too."

They stood quietly in a brief moment of parental camaraderie.

"Okay, bud, say goodbye to your friend. We'll see her tomorrow at her house. Thank you again for your help." She directed the last sentence to him.

He swooped up Addie onto his hip. "We'll see you both tomorrow."

Elaine nodded as Colton yelled, "Bye. Bye, Addie!"

As Nate headed down the hallway to the VIP surface-level parking lot, he felt lighter and less burdened than he had before attending the spin class. A chuckle rippled free of his mouth.

"What is it, Daddy?" Addie asked from her monkey grip on his side.

He was certain if he admitted that Tyler had been right, that he did feel better after the exercise, it would be the first thing Addie would tell Tyler the next time she saw him.

Of course, maybe it wasn't just the exercise.

"Nothing." Nate kissed the loose hairs at Addie's temple and pushed open the door to outside.

·CHAPTER 7·

Striding out of the monstrous Washington Post building, Brent headed in the direction of his favorite artisan coffee shop, seeking a shot of caffeine. Not that he needed it. He was vibrating all over, buzzing from his good fortune.

He'd taken this meeting as a favor to his friend, Mark, the former *New York Times* writer, now a political writer for *The Washington Post*. Brent liked Mark; he was a hardworking man and incredibly straightforward with what he wanted. They had worked together on countless assignments before, and Brent was happy to do another one—his last, hopefully.

Minutes after his meeting with *The Post*'s editor, he'd been in the lobby when he'd gotten the call that had him punching his fist into the air, all while trying to keep his voice calm and professional.

Things had been stagnant for too long, but now everything seemed hyper-focused. Light played off street signs and the stone corners of buildings in new and captivating ways while fall leaves dotted his perspective with saturated hues of orange, red, and brown. A fast pulse thrummed under his collarbone as the crisp air pulled at the collar of his jacket.

He pushed into the warm coffee shop with an energetic breathlessness that had him smiling and paying for the coffee for the woman behind him just to share some of that zeal with someone else. After sitting down with his steaming hot Americano, the need to tell someone brimmed in his chest. The timestamp on his phone read six forty-five.

There were countless people he could text, but his fingers brought up her contact, and before he could think too much about it, he thumbed out a quick message.

Brent: *Hey*

He drummed his fingers on the table while he waited. Then he started looking at his predecessor's photographs. He'd seen them before. *Everyone* had seen them. Getting this job would mean national exposure on a level that even working for some of the top newspapers couldn't touch.

Elaine: *Hi*

A grin spread over his lips as he licked at the remaining coffee from his last sip.

Brent: *How's my wind rider tonight?*

She responded right away.

Elaine: *Tired. I rode the non-motorized version of your bike today*

Brent: *Cycling around town?*

Based on her incredible legs and fit body, he wouldn't doubt she was a cyclist.

Elaine: *I teach spin Tuesdays & most Fridays after work*

He began typing something about how that tracked with how sexy she was but deleted it before sending it. Yesterday, she'd liked a cat-and-mouse approach better. Not that he minded. He was quite fond of a good chase.

Brent: *Ahh I see*

Elaine: *How did your meeting go?*

She'd remembered. Beautiful *and* thoughtful. He was liking this woman more and more.

Brent: *It was fine*

The assignment was simple: travel with Mark to Terlenitsi, a tiny country in Central Europe, capture photo documentation of the Prime Minister's corruption, and be the first to notify the world. Just a normal Tuesday in Brent's life. The one good thing was there were potential tiebacks to fat cats in this very city, which meant not only foreign but national implications. A story like that would likely require a photo spread, so not only would he get his photo credit on the byline, but he'd be paid well.

Brent: *But it was the call I got afterward that's A-FREAKING-MAZING*

Elaine: *So nothing exciting today, gotcha*

A laugh ripped from his lips, and a couple at the table next to him looked over. Giving them his best smile and a lifted shoulder, he returned his attention to his phone.

Brent: *I got great news on a potential photography gig that would be exactly what I want to be doing. I don't want to say anything about it yet, but maybe I can clue you in on our next date.*

He'd said gig like it was taking pictures of engaged couples. Creating iconic portraits of some of the country's most famous celebrities and musical artists could hardly be considered a "gig." He paused for a split second before his thumbs typed one more line.

Brent: *It's going to be so great for me*

The sounds of the coffee shop pulsing with energy infiltrated his mind as he waited for her response. Three little dots hovered, then disappeared, then hovered again. His eyes tightened at having to wait to hear from her, and he looked out at the shop to distract himself. Focusing on the contrast of the sharp lines of the navy and white chevron design painted on the wall across from him, he heard his phone ping with her answer.

Elaine: *You always get your way, don't you?*

Brent's lips tugged up as his mind automatically replayed the scene from last night. How she had asked the same question of him before he'd pulled her perfect dusty-rose lips to his mouth. His skin immediately grew warm, remembering her kiss.

Reed: *Hey man, are we still meeting at Huai Kha at 7:45?*

His friend's text came up over the screen as he was thinking of a witty response to Elaine. Quickly, he clicked over to Reed's message and confirmed dinner. Seeing it was seven thirty-five, he needed to start walking. Switching screens, he answered Elaine.

Brent: *We'll see, won't we*

She sent an eye-roll emoji and he chuckled.

Brent: *I've got to meet the friends I'm crashing with for dinner. Talk to you later, gorgeous*

He stood to put his paper cup in the grey trash bin.

Elaine: *Night*

Craving flicked like flames at the memory of how she'd said goodbye to him yesterday.

As he walked down the sidewalk, his mind wandered over what he knew about Elaine—she was smoking hot, she was a single mom, she was a physical therapist, she'd been on a motorcycle before, she ate Ethiopian food like it was PB&J, she seemed completely comfortable with spontaneity, she had an eye for good art, and she taught a spin class.

It became apparent he hadn't done a good job of finding out more information about her last night. His focus had been on making a good impression and seeing how much of his body could casually touch hers. The fact that she was still such a mystery to him only enticed him more. On a whim, he pulled his phone from his pocket and dialed her number. She picked up on the second ring.

"I thought you were going to dinner with friends?" She spoke in a hushed voice that sounded like purring.

It made him stop mid-step, imagining her whispering into his ear. He shook his head, and a curl bounced into his temple. "I am. I realized I could walk and talk. What's your favorite book?"

She laughed a quieted version of that laugh of hers, and he could see her tilting her head back in his mind. "What is this? An interrogation?"

He went for it. "I just realized I was so distracted by your physical beauty last night that I didn't pay enough attention to your inner beauty. Allow me to use the journalist side of my brain to ask a few questions."

For a quick pause, all he heard was silence. He stepped around a couple pushing a stroller on the sidewalk.

"*A Tree Grows In Brooklyn*. What's yours?"

The flowing relief that she answered him allowed his lips to stretch into a wide smile. "*The Negative*." He clarified, "By Ansel Adams."

"That makes sense," she said.

So she knows something about photography. Ansel Adams was a big name, but he wasn't as ubiquitous as da Vinci or Monet.

Keeping his momentum, he memorized her first answer quickly and asked another question. "Favorite food?"

"We're really doing this?"

"*Elaine*." His roguish grin was lost to the D.C. sidewalk. "How am I supposed to learn about you if I don't ask questions?"

Her slight huff of irritation only made his heart pulse faster as he waited patiently. Patience was an important trait in a good photographer. Sometimes, it took a long time for a subject to present the perfect frame to you.

She sighed. "Mexican."

"Was that so hard?" he teased, tucking his left hand in his jeans pocket. "Favorite—"

"If I am going to answer these questions like I'm at a firing squad, then you'd better answer them too." Her voice was playful as she interrupted him.

"Fair enough. Italian. Good Italian, preferably in Italy. I spent a few months there right after college."

"Post-college backpacking through Europe?"

"Something like that," he admitted.

After graduation, he'd followed his foreign exchange student girlfriend back to her hometown of Florence only to find her parents weren't too happy about their relationship. When an ultimatum had been raised, she'd chosen her family over him. Heartbroken and low on cash, he'd hitchhiked his way to Rome and stayed longer than he should have, sulking over his misfortune.

The time hadn't been completely wasted, however, as he'd used it to fine-tune his use of natural light, capturing photo after photo of the gorgeous people of Rome, and his palate, eating some of the most delicious food on the planet.

"Don't try to slow down my momentum with your own questions," he chastised playfully, and a flash of luminosity streaked through his veins when she laughed again. "Favorite dessert."

"Hmmmm . . . Dark chocolate. Yours?"

Brent was glad he was doing this over the phone. Too much of his attention would have been on her humming lips if they'd been talking in person. He was fairly certain he wouldn't have made it to his second question if given the opportunity to feel those lips on his again.

"Brent?" Her voice filled the empty space he'd created by daydreaming.

"Any kind of pie."

That laugh of hers felt like it was tapping at his sternum, stealthily trying to get in. "That's specific."

He blinked, forcing his feet to continue on their trek. "I'm serious. If it has pie crust on the outside, I don't care what's inside." Actually, his absolute favorite was the apple pie his mother made at Christmas, but he'd loosened his standards to whatever pie he could get any other time of the year. "Favorite movie?"

Only ambient street sounds filled his ears again.

After a few breaths, she said, "You can't judge. It was my favorite to watch when I was in high school."

"I promise not to judge," his voice rang with a sincerity that surprised him.

"*The Proposal*."

Despite his previous moment of earnestness, he laughed—*hard*.

"You said you wouldn't judge!"

"I'm not judging." He stifled his laughter as he heard another huff of air.

It was good to see she had a bit of a girly side. So far, he had only seen seriousness, strength, and sensuality. Not that he didn't like those qualities, but it was nice to know that if he brought her flowers, she wouldn't pitch them into a trash can for being anti-feminist and anti-earth. And he was speaking from experience—artists could be a temperamental bunch.

"Ryan Reyolds does it for you, huh?" he needled.

"Betty White is a national treasure," she countered.

"Hey, Brent." Brent hadn't realized how close he was to the restaurant. His friend Reed stepped in front of him, and wrapped him a one-armed hug, much to Brent's surprise.

"Reed, what's up?" He spoke into his friend's shoulder.

"Sounds like you've found your friends," Elaine said.

Brent pointed to his phone and took a few steps back from Reed, turning to face the street. "Yeah. You get a reprieve from my question arsenal for now."

"Thank God," she joked.

The smile on his face pulled higher. "I've got to go, but I'll see you next Saturday."

"'Night, Brent."

She didn't confirm, but there was no way he wasn't seeing her again.

"Bye."

Hanging up his phone, he grinned at it before turning to see Ayann and Chris now standing next to Reed.

"Gentlemen." He walked over to his friends. "I can't thank you enough for putting me up tonight. Dinner is on me."

His friends greeted him with man-hugs or back pats before they entered the restaurant. Brent could feel the change in his life happening. Things were finally going to be different. He had a chance at an amazing job, a new girl, and was surrounded by old friends. What more could he want?

·CHAPTER 8·

Elaine sighed when she stopped in front of the two-story, single-family home wrapped in grey siding. Naturally, it had a beautiful white-railed front porch and sat on a good-sized but not ostentatious lot with two mature trees out front. She could only imagine a large backyard behind it as well.

Glancing at the special mirror she had under her rearview mirror to see Colton, she assessed his mood. He seemed curious but not nervous, which was good. She was feeling enough trepidation for the both of them.

"You ready for your playdate with Addie?" she asked with too much enthusiasm.

"Yup." An easy grin pulled at his mouth.

"Yup" had been his new favorite word, and he'd used it instead of "Yes" for the last few weeks. He frequently said it while nodding his shiny, straight blond locks.

After they gathered his backpack—filled with his favorite toys—and his lunch box, they started up the walkway to the house. Elaine took a deep settling breath and rang the doorbell. The thumping of feet that undeniably belonged to a four-year-old preceded a man's voice telling her to step back so he could open the door.

Addie was still wearing purple polka dot pajamas and a mess of bedhead, but Nate was dressed and, by the smell of him, freshly showered. He looked comfortable in jeans and a dark green T-shirt with no shoes.

"Hey," he said to her before squatting down to her son's level. "Hi, Colton. Remember me? I'm Addie's dad, Mr. Nate. We're very excited that you get to play with us today."

Colton lifted his large plastic Tyrannosaurus Rex in response. "This is T. rex."

"I like him." Nate's lips curled into a small smile.

Addie grabbed Colton's hand. "I have lots of dino-sa-nors. Let me show you, Colt."

As the two kids raced down the hall, Elaine's gaze followed them inside.

"Would you like a full tour before you leave?" Nate asked.

She followed him down the short hallway, glancing over the family pictures in matching frames—Nate's arms wrapped around the very pregnant belly of a gorgeous, dark-haired woman; the woman's tired but bright blue eyes smiling with a wrinkly newborn baby in her arms; a toddler Addie standing next to grandparents near a riverbank.

The elegant, unpretentious decor continued throughout the house into the clean and well-appointed kitchen. Everything about his house screamed *home*. Actually, it didn't scream—it gently sighed with contentment. A sagging breath involuntarily left Elaine's lips.

Yesterday the hospital clinic supervisor position had finally been posted, and she'd sent in her application. If she was selected, the increase in salary would make her plans for next year easier. Then she could afford a little townhome with a small yard in the back for Colton, preferably in this school district.

"No, thank you. Your house is lovely, and I'm sure it's very safe." She glanced around to see child locks still on all the kitchen cabinets. Doctors were generally very cautious parents. "Thank you for doing this on such short notice. I really appreciate it."

He maintained his professional demeanor as he waved her off. "Does he have any allergies? Does he still nap? Anything else I should know about?"

"No allergies." She rolled her eyes at the second question. "He hasn't napped since he turned three. He needs help wiping when he goes potty, and I packed his lunch. He can be a picky eater." She held out Colton's Incredible Hulk lunchbox and backpack. "He has some of his favorite toys in here, in case he gets a little homesick. He can be a bit shy and quiet at times, but he's a good boy."

Nate took both. "We'll keep him busy. Addie's got a whole dinosaur hunt planned for him in the backyard."

"Colton would love that." She stepped toward the window. A small swing set with a slide was tucked beneath a tree in the corner of the gorgeous, grass-filled yard. "My only complaint with the childcare center at the hospital is that there's no outside play area for them."

"I agree," he said, leaning against his kitchen island.

Elaine glanced at her watch. They'd arrived a little early to give Colton time to adjust to the new surroundings, but she needed to get going to make the drive to the hospital. "I should be going. I just want to give him a kiss before I leave."

Nate pushed off the counter. "They're probably in the playroom."

Following him up a half-staircase, she saw that the large room over the garage, painted a bright, cheerful blue, was completely filled with toys. A kid-sized kitchen stood along one side of the room, and a miniature closet hung with princess dresses leaned against another wall. Neatly organized cubbies filled the third wall, with a child-size table and two chairs under a double window, allowing the morning sunlight to stream through.

"Wow," she rasped, before she could stop it.

"Mama!" Colton ran to her wearing a pink capelet with spikes down the spine ending in a spiky tail. "I'm a stegosaurus."

Addie was busy at the play kitchen, humming and pulling out all the plastic vegetables and setting them in front of a large half-circle of dinosaur figurines on the carpet.

"That's really cool, bud." She smiled at how his eyes simply beamed. "It looks like you're going to have a good time here today. Mama has to go to work now. Can I give you a kiss?"

He flung his little arms around her legs and kissed her thigh.

With a widening grin, she picked him up and smothered kisses into the nook of his neck and the top of his head. "I love you. Be good for Mr. Nate, and I'll be back this afternoon."

Nate followed her to the front door to see her out.

"I should be back just after four."

"No problem. We'll be here all day." He opened the front door.

"Okay." Nervousness began to snake through her chest, and she pinned her shoulders back to suppress it. "Thank you again."

"It's the least I could do," he said. "You have my number. If you want to call just to chat with Colton when you get a break, feel free."

She let out the breath that'd sat trapped in her lungs. "Okay. I will. Thank you."

Nate's reassuring nod allowed her to turn and walk toward her car.

◊◊◊

It wasn't twenty minutes after four when she arrived back at Nate's house, but closer to five-thirty. She'd texted him to let him know her appointments were running long and received a simple "no prob" in response.

When she was finally able to pry herself from the antiseptic-smelling building, she'd caught every red light on the way here. At the last one, she'd let out a deep-throated groan and rested her head on the steering wheel. The moment's peace had been shattered when the driver of the car behind her had lain on their horn, alerting her to the fact she'd missed the green light.

Her appointments today had been completely over-scheduled—as they had been for the last six months. When she'd first started working at the hospital clinic, she'd been shocked to see it in such a disorganized mess. Glen, the current supervisor, had one foot out the door of retirement and had basically stopped doing his job. Trying to prove her value early on, Elaine had helped clean and organize the center's main gym to be more conducive to their workflow and offered to help cover shifts whenever it was needed. She was only supposed to have one Saturday shift a month but had volunteered to help cover today to show she was a team player.

Elaine rang Nate's doorbell and stood for what felt like a full minute before her muscles started to tense. Her body already ached from all the passive range-of-motion exercises she'd done with her patients that day. She was pulling her phone from her purse when laughter floated up from behind the house. The gate to the fenced backyard swung into the yard when she clicked it open.

Addie and Colton were running in different directions, squealing and giggling as Nate loped after them. His arms were tucked tightly to his ribs and his fingers were waving like little claws. After intentionally keeping behind them a few paces, he easily picked up Addie in his left arm and then swooped up Colton in his right arm. He ran a bit, carrying the two delighted children by their bellies, before stopping to pretend to eat them with a hungry "Omnomnomnom."

Seeing Colton's carefree, open laugh in Nate's arms smacked the air from her lungs. She'd always known her skills as a mother were lacking, that she was never going to be as good a mother as Rose, but this was another thing Colton was missing—a male figure in his life.

Her grip tightened around her purse strap as her forearms flexed.

Colton saw her first. "Mama!"

Nate bent to release both children safely to the ground, his shoulders stretching under his snug T-shirt. Addie ran quickly behind Colton who jumped into Elaine's arms, full of joy. When his body hit hers in a tight gripping hug, the tension in her spine lessened a little.

"We were playing dina-sa-nors," Addie said, spinning the skirt of her dinosaur-print dress.

"I see that." Elaine glanced up to find Nate in front of her, his hazel eyes still lit up from playing with the kids. His easygoing and happy demeanor was such a departure from the orderly, focused man she'd previously seen. She blinked, trying to ignore the fact that Nate was actually quite attractive when he was relaxed.

"Mr. Nate's the best T. rex." Colton's cheerful face diverted her attention.

She kissed his flushed, pink cheek. "I'm so glad you had a good day."

"I did. We made crafts." He squirmed in her arms, and the minute she put him down, he sprinted toward the deck.

"Oh ya! You'll see." Addie's braided pigtails bounced as she took after him.

Nate's steady presence drew her focus. "Crafts too?"

The slow smile spreading across his mouth was surprisingly charming. "It keeps them busy."

By the time they made it up the deck steps, the two kids were already back outside with dinosaurs made from paper plates and construction paper in their hands. The excited children were talking at the same time, explaining their individual design and color choices as they all shuffled inside. The delicious aroma of chili instantly made Elaine's stomach growl.

Exhaustion hit her full force when she realized she was going to have to drive home and make something for dinner. If she'd been smart, she would've put something in her slow cooker like the one steaming on the kitchen island. A loud beep rang into the room before Nate pulled up his shirt to silence the kitchen timer clipped to his front jeans pocket.

The scent of freshly baked cornbread chased Elaine up the stairs as Colton tugged her along to see the dinosaur town they'd built in the playroom. When she followed the bubbling, jabbering kids back down the stairs a minute later, she found Nate leaning against the island, frowning at his phone and typing away. Something in her loosened, seeing him return to his serious state.

Elaine cleared her throat as she gathered her son's belongings. "I can't thank you enough for watching Colton today. Are you sure I can't pay you?"

His head popped up. "Oh. Ah, no." He pocketed his phone. "You're welcome."

"Colton, go potty, so we can drive home," she instructed the same moment Addie asked, "Can you stay for dinner?"

Colton ran into the hallway bathroom, and Elaine leaned over to address Addie, glancing out of the corner of her eye at Nate. "No. I think we should probably be heading home, but thank you for the invitation, Addie."

"*Please*." The little girl drew out the word and clasped her hands in front of her chest, obviously used to working her blue eyes to her advantage.

"I wouldn't want to intrude on your family dinner. Isn't your mommy coming home soon?"

"My mommy's in heaven," the girl said matter-of-factly.

"Oh." Elaine stood up straight, suddenly at a loss for words.

"I'm sure Miss Elaine and Colton want to have dinner at their house tonight." As Nate ran his left hand through his short brown hair, she took in for the first time that he wasn't wearing a wedding ring.

Colton bounded back into the room with a double-footed jump, landing in place beside her. "Ready!" Colton's shoes were on the wrong feet, but she didn't want to take the time to remedy that and instead helped him into his backpack.

Awkwardness hovered in the room until Addie gave Colton a huge hug and a sloppy kiss on the cheek with a loud *mmwah*. Colton groaned and frantically wiped his cheek, causing Elaine and Nate to dissolve into surprised laughter.

"I guess that's better than biting," she teased.

Nate's smile faded, and she was caught off-guard at the disappointment of its absence. In the short course of ten minutes, her perspective on him had completely shifted.

"I'm sorry again about that and how I reacted last week." His eyes focused on her with earnest regret—the centers a sunburst of golden brown circled by green—before he directed his gaze at his daughter. "We only bite food, right, Addie?"

"Yes, Daddy," came her sweet reply as she started chasing Colton around the kitchen island.

Nate was watching the kids giggling around the island when he took a large step forward, so they wouldn't run into him. The sound of little feet filtered into Elaine's brain as she froze—his movement had unintentionally obliterated the personal space between them.

He glanced up and his eyes widened. "Sorry," he said, but then paused as if trapped by her gaze. His chest rose and fell in a deeply drawn breath.

The suspended moment broke when he took a large step back, and Colton ran smack into Nate's leg, comically bouncing to the floor. Addie pulled on Colton's arms as he struggled to get up, looking like an upended turtle with his backpack on.

Nate picked up her son and set him on his feet. "How about we get you and your mama home?"

Knowing she'd already overstayed her welcome, Elaine quickly said her thanks and ushered Colton to the car. Only once her son was softly singing along to his favorite kids music CD as she drove did Elaine allow herself to wonder if she'd imagined that tense, intimate moment in Nate's kitchen.

·CHAPTER 9·

"Nana!" Addie sprinted through the front door, and as Nate closed it, he tried not to let the tension that always accompanied this house seep into his shoulders.

The bright afternoon light streamed in the high foyer window and refracted through an ornate Schonbek chandelier. When Addie shrieked with excitement from the other room, Nate assumed his mom had probably bought her another toy, even though the playroom could hardly contain all the ones she'd received for her birthday. Taking a deep breath, Nate rubbed the back of his neck as he passed the designer-decorated sitting room on his way to the kitchen.

"Hey, Nate."

All the pressure that had been building in his body instantly relaxed as he crossed the room to hug his kid brother. "Jay."

"Daddy!" Addie bounced around the two men's legs. "Daddy, Unky J's here! Unky J's here!"

Nate chuckled. "I see that, sweetheart."

"Addison, darling, I know it's exciting, but please don't screech," his mother instructed in a crisp voice before looking at him with a quick smile. "Hello, Nathaniel."

"Hi, Mom."

His mom was collected, as always, in her chinos and crisp white oxford. A Hermes scarf was tied perfectly around her neck, and her hair was an immobile bob that artfully framed her face.

"When did you get in?" Nate asked his brother.

"Apparently last night, but he decided to stay in a hotel instead of here," she said, disapproval strategically peppered into her words.

"*Mom*." His brother crossed to her, giving an *I'm sorry* face and placing a hand on her shoulder. "I was severely jet-lagged and knew I would just be sleeping it off anyway. Once I was awake, showered, and presentable, I came right over."

Jay had kept to the Brennan dress code of slacks and a collared shirt, matching Nate's attire. God forbid they visit their parents' house in jeans and a T-shirt.

His brother's charm worked on their mother, as it always did, and she squeezed his hand on her shoulder. "Well, you are staying here tonight." She raised her eyebrows as much as Botox would allow.

"Yes, ma'am."

"Are you flying home tomorrow?" Nate leaned against the Carrara marble countertop. His brother lived and worked in Manhattan, but would often fly through for a day on his way back if he'd been overseas.

Their mother huffed as she busied herself pulling vegetables from the refrigerator.

"Yes, unfortunately, midday, but not until after I have brunch with Mom." His brother winked at their mother, and her face instantly melted into a genuine smile. "And you, princess . . ." He left Mom's side to sweep Addie up on his hip. "I heard you had a birthday recently. How old are you now? Ten?"

Addie giggled. "Four."

"You can't possibly be four. You're too mature. You must be ten," Jay play-mocked.

"No, Unky J." She shook her blue eyes at him as a little smile lifted her lips.

"Oh. Well, good, because the gift I bought wouldn't make sense for a ten-year-old." He carried her over to his luggage in the hall, picking up a stuffed Paddington Bear complete with blue duffle and red hat. "I also bought you some Paddington books, so your daddy can read them to you before bed."

"Thanks, Jay," Nate said before addressing Addie. "Sweetheart, say 'thank you.'"

His daughter was too busy hugging her new bear to notice he'd spoken to her.

"Addison, say 'thank you' to your uncle," his mother instructed.

Nate never understood why he, and by extension his daughter, were always addressed by their full names, but his brother got to be called by his nickname. It was just one of the many discrepancies in the way the two men were treated. The standards Nate was held to never seemed to apply to his younger brother.

He supposed it was because though he and his brother looked pretty similar—both with medium brown hair, brown eyes, and the same build—his brother's face strongly resembled his mother's. Between his parents, she was more joyous and relaxed. Nate had inherited his father's stern face and serious temperament. His father was perpetually giving his mother whatever she wanted, and Nate surmised that some of that trickled down to her male carbon copy.

Lifting her head to grin at Jay, Addie said "thank you" before wiggling free and running out of the kitchen. She was probably headed to her bedroom here to add the bear to the rest of her toys.

"It was very nice of you to bring her something back from London. How was your business trip?" Mom asked.

"Very successful." His brother put his hands in his pockets as he rocked back on his heels.

After a few seconds of stilted silence, Nate asked, "Do you need any help preparing dinner?"

"No, thank you. Though I'm fully aware you could prepare this meal better than me"—her lips lifted into a broad smile—"you two should catch up since your brother will only be here a short while."

Nate had always cooked the meals when Sarah had been alive because he had a nine-to-five job, and her hours varied widely, with her being an ICU physician. What had started out as necessity eventually bloomed into a hobby he enjoyed immensely. Though his mastery of French cuisine wasn't as useful now that his only dining companion preferred frozen toaster waffles to boeuf Bourguignon.

"Great idea, Mom." Jay ushered him out of the kitchen to the nearby butler's pantry and opened the cabinet. "Let's crack open Dad's good bourbon and have a drink before dinner."

"Now, *that's* a great idea," Nate agreed, finding two highball glasses.

Once they were outside with the door shut, his brother blew out a breath. "I always forget how being around them makes it feel like all the air is being sucked out of your lungs."

"They're not that bad," Nate said before he took a swig.

Jay widened his eyes as if to say, *Yeah, okay,* before he took a large gulp. "I can't thank you enough, dear brother, for procreating and thereby forcing them to move from Connecticut to be closer to you and Addie here. It saves me these weekly torture sessions."

"You know my life has only existed to make yours easier." Sarcasm dripped into his words on its own volition.

His brother was smart and let that go. They settled into two Adirondack chairs overlooking the expansive yard and drank in silence.

Nate decided to break the strained stillness since he only saw his brother a handful of times a year. "How's Sloane? Is she still performing in *Hamilton?*"

Jay had always dated a wide variety of interesting and incredibly attractive women. He went through a stint of dating only models before stating they weren't "intelligent enough" for him. Two years ago, he'd started dating Sloane—a vivacious and charismatic actress who seemed to love Jay no matter what he did.

"Yeah, she's hoping to move up from the company next year," his brother said.

Naturally, their parents had been thrilled with Jay's connection to the theater and enjoyed prime orchestra seats whenever they visited their youngest. But had Nate dated an actress before marrying Sarah, they would have staged an intervention on his behalf.

"That's exciting for her," he said.

His brother shrugged and took the last long draw from his glass.

Nate's fingers tightened around the textured curve of his armrest. Jay often took for granted relationships that would've made Nate's day. He let his eyes float to the sky until the bones in his neck popped before he consciously relaxed his grip. It wasn't Jay's fault Nate's dating life had recently sputtered into nonexistence—that the last time he'd kissed a woman was before his breakup with short-term girlfriend, Olive, five months ago.

"How was Addie's birthday?" Jay's voice interrupted Nate's thoughts. "Did she have a good time?"

Safe ground. Addie was always a neutral topic they both could discuss. For as cavalier as he was in his other relationships, Jay was very engaged as an uncle.

"She did. Mom even rented a pony and put triceratops horns on its head, so Addie could 'ride on a dinosaur,'" Nate said, using finger quotes.

His brother choked on a laugh. "You're kidding."

"No, dead serious."

"I'm glad she had a good time. Addie deserves whatever she wants," he said with a broad smile. "That girl is happiness personified."

"She is," Nate agreed with a matching grin. "And energy."

His brother chuckled again. "True."

As if they had summoned her by talking about her, Addie burst through the back door and ran over to them, her yellow tulle skirt updrafting with each bound.

"Unky J, play soccer with me." She pulled on his arm with her full thirty-five pounds.

"Anything for you, princess." His brother rose, and she dragged him into the grass area of their parents' yard before running off to the large basket tucked near the house, where various outdoor toys were stored.

Nate finished the last gulp from his glass and set it on the table between the two chairs. He watched them kick the ball back and forth before his gaze settled over the water beyond them.

When his parents had relocated to Norfolk after Addie was born, they'd bought this property on the river. It was more than they needed—six bedrooms on a one acre lot, which had its own grass tennis court, dock, and boat lift—but they'd always had more than they needed. The home was professionally cleaned and gardened. Most days a chef prepared their meals, though on family Sundays, his mother preferred to cook their dinner herself.

Part of him felt guilty that his parents had moved away from the city to help him raise Addie, but he couldn't imagine doing

it alone. His mom had always been there for him. She often kept
Addie for overnight sleepovers, so he could date, go out with
Tyler, or just exist in his house without someone needing him.

Seeing Elaine struggle when she'd had no one to turn to had
pulled hard at his chest. He'd been more than happy to help her
to take a little bit of the pressure off, if only for a few hours. He
understood more than anyone what it meant to be both
Mommy and Daddy. Stiffness pulled at his shoulders, and he
rolled his neck to try and dispel it.

When it didn't work, he stood and took the glasses inside.
The delicious smell of sauteed chicken and vegetables greeted
him as soon as he was through the threshold. He found his
mother standing over the eight burner range, browning butter.

Putting the glasses in the dishwasher, he asked, "Can I set
the table?"

She tossed a grin over her shoulder. "That would be
wonderful."

Nate was laying out the family china in the dining room
when his thoughts returned to Elaine, though this time he
didn't focus on the similarity of their parenting situations. This
time, his mind replayed the surprised but engaged look of her
dark brown eyes when they had been mere inches from him in
his kitchen. How her muscles had seemed frozen along with her
breath between parted lips.

"Nathaniel." His father's presence in the ornate archway
leading from the hallway interrupted his memory.

His body stiffened on its own. "Dad."

"Jay is here," his father spoke dryly, as if Nate was missing
something.

Nate held in a sigh as he laid down the silver fork in his hand. Pinning his shoulders back, he rose to his full height. "I know. We were just catching up outside before Addie asked him to play soccer."

His father nodded for a moment. "Good."

Nate rigidly held still as he waited. It was better to wait to be spoken to in Dad's presence.

"Good," his father repeated before shuffling down the hall.

Nate closed his eyes for an extended blink before returning to his task. Even at thirty-three, he still felt like he was twelve when he was around his father. He suspected most grown children occasionally felt the same when surrounded by family, everyone falling back into well-worn roles like wagon wheels into ruts.

When he'd finished setting the table with English precision, his eyes wandered to the oak dumbwaiter tucked artfully into the corner. After striding to the crystal decanter, he poured himself another stiff drink; he'd need it to make it through dinner.

·CHAPTER 10·

As the radio song tapered off, the morning show host spoke over the final chords with his deep baritone, "TGIF, everybody."

"Do people even say that anymore?" a female disc jockey asked with a laugh.

Elaine cut the engine, silencing their inane banter. She didn't care if people didn't say it anymore; she felt it. Fridays were always the hardest to drag herself out of bed. *She* was glad the workweek was over, even if no one else was.

Especially since she had a date Saturday night.

After seeing how happy Colton had been with Nate last weekend, she'd decided it was time to give dating an honest try. So when Brent had texted her on Tuesday just to say hi, she'd answered. And not with coquettish half-answers, but authentic answers. It was daunting trying to be open for the first time, but since then, they'd touched base with a few texts every day.

While holding Colton's hand, she led him across the parking garage and into Edwards Memorial Hospital. They were halfway down the busy main corridor when her phone sounded with its guitar string *plunk plunk* tone notifying her of a text. Using her free hand to retrieve it from her purse, her lips pulled up on their own when Brent's icon flashed over the screen.

Brent: *Hey gorgeous*

She typed while walking.

Elaine: *Morning*

Colton began tugging on her arm, and glancing up, she saw a familiar boisterous four-year-old pulling Nate into the childcare area forty yards ahead of them. The plunking sound drew her attention to her phone again.

Brent: *I hate to do this, but I need more time to finish up my work here. I'm going to have to cancel tomorrow. Could we meet up next weekend instead?*

Her shoulders slumped as she used one to push through the daycare center's glass door.

Elaine: *Sure*

Brent: *You're the best*

Colton's hand ripped from hers as he dropped his backpack on the ground before running to the half-gate. Nate was talking to Mrs. Harris, and Addie had her little arms outstretched to Colton through the bars.

"Um, bye. Love you too," she murmured as she picked up his bag and hung it in his cubby.

Seeing the two children hugging despite the metal between them, Nate broke into the same warm laugh that had bounced between the planks of his backyard fence last weekend. The already bright and noisy play area seemed a little merrier with its addition.

"Good morning, Elaine."

"Morning." She managed to sound semi-chipper.

"Daddy! Can Colt come over tomorrow? Please, please, please?" Addie begged.

Nate glanced at Elaine quickly before answering, "We can't have Colton over every Saturday, sweetheart."

"Could we go, Mama?" Colton slid his eyes up as he hugged her leg.

"Mr. Nate said 'no,' bud." She pulled her face into a sympathetic look.

"I wasn't saying 'no.'"

"Oh." The short word was almost a breath as she looked up to find his hazel eyes focused on hers. His green-striped oxford, solid hunter-green tie, and charcoal-grey tailored suit seemed to intensify the whirl of green in his irises. For a moment, he looked as calm and relaxed as he had been running barefoot through the grass.

"Would you two step aside just a bit?" Mrs. Harris asked politely, letting Colton through the gate. Both children jumped up and down sing-yelling, "Playdate! Playdate!"

Nate sidestepped as he spoke. "I was giving you an out in case you have other plans."

Their kids had vanished from beyond the gate into the corner of the large playroom—well out of hearing range. She'd be *the bad parent* if she said "no" now. "I'm sure you've got a busy weekend."

"I do have plans with friends in the afternoon, but if you'd like to come over and let them play for a few hours before lunch, that would be fine with me." He brushed his hand over the front of his suit jacket before securing it in his pocket.

In the time Elaine had been Colton's mother, she'd never been on a single playdate. Rose had taken him places—to the park, to the library for storytime, to other moms' houses. But with working full-time and zero close friends who were also parents, it just wasn't something Elaine had ever considered. She'd always assumed Colton got enough socialization with kids his age at daycare.

"Okay, sure," she said. "That would be great."

Nate's lips tugged up slightly. "Anytime after seven."

◊◊◊

Elaine looked over the menu boards of the hospital cafeteria and made the decision she always did. After adding a rainbow of vegetables to the heaping amount of lettuce and spinach on her plate, she got in line for some chicken tenders.

Stepping behind a nurse in scrubs, she recognized the suited man's voice at the head of the line as he ordered roast chicken, broccoli, and mashed potatoes. Nate happened to glance right as he received his lunch, catching her eye.

"Elaine." He stepped beside her as she received her requested chicken from the cafeteria worker. "I'd ask if you were stalking me, but you don't seem like the type." The right side of his mouth kicked up.

She exhaled an awkward chuckle. "No, definitely not. Though I do think it's funny I've been working here for six months, and until a week ago, I'd never run into you. Perhaps you're stalking me."

They stepped to the center of the room to be out of the way of the other hospital staff and visitors getting their lunch from the various food stations.

"I can assure you that I'm not. Unrelated, you should know I'll no longer be taking your spin class this afternoon, so you won't get the wrong idea."

"You were going to take my class today?" She kept the surprise from her voice, considering she'd tried to torture him through physical exertion the last time he'd attended.

"I was, but I think now it would just be awkward. Don't you?" That slow smile spread across his lips.

The movement pulled her gaze to them, and she found her eyes lingering a second longer than was professionally appropriate before turning toward the long line to pay. "Don't let me get in the way of your personal fitness goals."

He chuckled as he stepped in line behind her. "I'm not a fan of changing my calendar once it's set, but I can always run on the treadmill to get my cardio."

Given that Nate emanated order, his statement didn't come as a shock.

She put her tray on the counter near the register and decided to poke. "Sometimes you have to break out of your comfort zone, Suit."

"*Elaine.*"

The sadness that stretched into the vowels of her name stole her inhale. She turned to see weariness slackening his downturned mouth and the light that had been present in his eyes a moment ago extinguished. She'd done that. She'd done that with one word. *Why?*

"Please don't call me that."

She tugged at the collar of her hospital-logo embroidered polo, her fidgeting useless against the acid building in her belly. "Oh, okay. I won't."

His eyes flicked to the floor as he seemed to cave into himself. Everything she'd ever known of Nate was gone.

"Ma'am," the cashier called out.

"Sorry." She turned and swiped her badge to pay for lunch before waiting for Nate to pay for his.

"I'll see you tomorrow morning. I've got to work through lunch today." He'd regained his usual strong posture, but his lips were in a firm line.

"Sure. Bye."

He nodded a goodbye as she stood for a minute near the napkins and forks, giving him the chance to get out of the cafeteria before she carried her lunch back to the clinic.

Good job, Elaine. Way to piss off the dad of Colton's only friend.

In the break room, she sat next to Leslie who was almost finished with her turkey and sprout sandwich.

"I know that look," her coworker said before lowering her voice. "What did *you-know-who* do today?"

Leslie was asking if their supervisor, Glen, had screwed up something, and to be fair, he had been screwing a lot of things up lately. Elaine didn't want to get into her new and floundering parenting friendship with Nate. If that was what it was. It was more like a playdate-buddy, single-parent commiseration.

"Oh, luckily nothing today." She gave a *we're on the same team* expression with a raise of her eyebrows. "It's just that Colton got up a lot last night," she lied.

"It gets better. Soon he'll be sleeping through the whole night, and then before you know it, he'll be running away from your kisses and wanting nothing to do with you." She sighed wistfully, pushing a few wayward strands of her fiery hair back into her french braid. "Give your sweet boy a snuggle for me tonight."

According to her friendly colleague's daily stories, Leslie's eleven-year-old twin boys had decided they no longer needed their mama as much as they used to.

"I will." Elaine smiled.

Leslie patted her hand before standing to put away her lunch box. "Do you think you can help me this afternoon?"

She covered her large bite of salad with the back of her hand. "Sure."

"*You-know-who* gave me two patients with herniated disks, and I haven't cared for that diagnosis since PT school eons ago. I know you are good with spinal cases, so maybe you could give me some pointers on current best practice." Her coworker filled her bottle at the water cooler in the corner.

"Actually, my next two are knee replacements. Do you just want to swap?"

Leslie had specialized training in leg injuries, and usually, those appointments were scheduled with her.

"That would be great," she said before blowing out a dismissive breath. "Glen used to schedule us to our strengths. I don't know why he stopped. It's so frustrating. I've been working at this clinic for three years, and it always ran smoothly until nine months ago."

Elaine hummed noncommittally over her mouthful of chicken. After lunch, she'd look over the schedule and talk to her old supervisor and mentor, Cora, for advice on how to fix it.

"Thanks for rescuing my day." Leslie's lips lifted. "I'm glad you transferred here."

"Me too." Elaine found herself smiling as wide as her coworker.

Leslie stopped just outside the door. "Oh, I almost forgot. Madison mentioned in passing that you are a cyclist. My husband and I host a group ride on Sunday mornings—if you want to join. This week we are doing the Dismal Swamp trail. It's an out-and-back, so a little boring, but an easy seventeen miles. We usually do it twice."

Elaine carefully kept the mournful twinge she felt at the base of her spine from showing on her face. Her mind flashed to the birthday present Rose had given her a few months before she'd died—a used but nicely repaired road bike. It had been her sister's way of encouraging Elaine to take a chance on a goal she'd always wanted to accomplish.

After those first long rides, Rose had been there with encouragement, ibuprofen, and an ice pack. Once Rose died, Elaine couldn't bring herself to get back on the bike. The idea of finishing a ride and not being able to have a long, leisurely chat with her sister over the hot breakfast Rose would make for them both sat like a heavy stone in her stomach. After the move, the bike had sat untouched against the naked white wall of her apartment for a year until she'd finally sold it.

"Thanks for the invite, but I don't actually own a bike." She lifted a shoulder.

"Oh. No problem. If you ever want to venture outside, you're always welcome." Leslie grinned.

Elaine was careful that her smile appeared genuine. "I'll keep that in mind."

·CHAPTER 11·

After closing the door to his office, Nate slumped into the chair behind his desk and pushed his lunch aside. When Elaine had called him a suit that first time, or even in the cycling room before he realized she'd done it teasingly, he'd responded in anger.

With good reason.

His father had weaponized that word, using it to chastise him for choosing to attend a Master of Healthcare Administration program instead of reapplying to medical school for the third time. *You're choosing to be a useless, paper-pushing suit instead of someone who actually makes a difference?* The pièce de résistance of his father's tirades had always been reminding Nate that his wife was a doctor, but he wasn't.

Though they'd met in college during a pre-med lecture series, Sarah had never thought less of Nate when he'd found he actually preferred the business side of medicine and decided to be a hospital administrator. She had actively argued with his father whenever the issue arose at family dinners. When it came time for her to apply for ICU residencies, she'd suggested she only apply *outside* the tri-state area, prompting their move to Virginia.

Nate let his elbows rest on the desk as his hands bracketed his head. He stared at his keyboard, taking intentionally slow breaths and ignoring the sour taste in his mouth.

The problem was his father had been right.

He *had* been useless.

He *hadn't* made a difference.

And because of that, Sarah was gone.

Because he hadn't fought Sarah when she'd pushed for an early discharge after Addie's birth. Because he'd believed Sarah when she'd said she was "just tired" as she became winded climbing the stairs to their bedroom. Because he'd been blissfully cooking dinner, so ecstatic that they were finally a family, when the most important woman in his life had stopped breathing while taking a nap. Because when he'd brought a bawling Addie into the bedroom to nurse, he couldn't remember his First Aid training. Because he'd shaken Sarah and screamed for help before his brain could function enough to call 911. Because it was only after a paramedic picked a crying Addie up off the floor by the window that he had remembered his newborn daughter.

The phone on his desk rang, but that last image of Sarah, dark hair fanned over her pillow, snuggled into a sleep she would never rise from, refused to dissipate from his mind.

On its fourth ring, he cleared his throat, picked up the receiver, and heard himself answer, "This is Nate Brennan."

◇◇◇

Nate rolled the edge of his beer bottle against the lacquered wooden bar top in a repetitive circular pattern. The motion left sloppy condensation curves glinting in the dim light of the upscale bar. The crushing weight between his shoulders had him craving something much stronger, but he was trying to pace himself tonight. He was only here because Tyler had insisted.

As soon as he'd left the office, he'd discarded his suit jacket and tie, loosening his collar and rolling back his sleeves. All afternoon he'd wanted to rip the tie from his neck; it had been trying to steal the air from his throat. Now the beer was beginning to loosen some of the stiffness he felt in every muscle, but it still wasn't quite doing the trick.

His phone buzzed in his pants pocket.

Tyler: *Handoff is taking forever. I'm sorry. I'll be another 20 min*

Nate: *No prob, take your time*

The defeated breath that left his lungs took the last of his fight with it. He drained the dregs of his beer, ignoring his growling empty stomach.

"Another one?" the bartender asked on his way back from delivering two martinis to the middle-aged women seated at the end.

"Actually, can I have a double Bulleit on the rocks?"

"You got it," he said, turning to grab a highball glass.

Nate tented his hands while he waited and pushed the crevice between his brows into his fingertips. The ubiquitous sour-acid stench of the bar crept into his nose as the bartender placed a new black paper napkin and his drink in front of him.

"Thank you," he said without raising his head.

His mind reviewed his history with Tyler—meeting years ago when Sarah had introduced them after a shared residency rotation, how Tyler had quickly become his workout partner and closest friend, and how Tyler had continued to be an irreplaceable support system after Sarah's death. Even though his friend was a physician and Nate wasn't, he'd never felt inferior. Tonight, however, that intrusive thought kept repeating itself on a loop as he swallowed mouthfuls of bourbon.

By the time Tyler arrived with his apologies forty minutes later, Nate was nearly finished with his second double.

"Don't worry about it." Nate leaned back as he regarded his friend, now slightly hazy through the blurry lens of the alcohol. "You've got important things to do. Important *life-saving* things. Good for you!" He raised his glass in a toast.

The bar was noisier now, the din of other happy patrons slowly chipping away at what was left of Nate's functioning brain.

Tyler's eyebrows pulled down as he spoke. "Are you drunk?"

"Nope. No, no, no." He set his glass down harder than he intended, and a bit sloshed onto his hand. "I'm good. I'm good."

"What'll it be?" the bartender asked Tyler while Nate shook liquor off his fingers.

"I'll take your IPA on draft." He sat sideways on his wooden high-back stool, facing Nate. "So let's talk about this."

"Talk about what?" When Nate glanced left, the snap of his neck made his vision swim a bit.

"You're drinking again." Tyler stared pointedly at his highball glass.

"So are you." He nodded to the beer the bartender had just delivered.

"That's not what I mean, and you know it."

Nate shrugged and took a big draw from his glass, staring straight ahead.

Tyler sighed. "I should have been with you that weekend." Nate felt his friend's hand on his shoulder. "I'm sorry."

"It's okay," Nate whispered.

"No. It's not okay. *You're* not okay."

The warmth of his friend's hand on his shoulder and his kindness were almost too much to take. He didn't deserve to be comforted. This was his fault. It was his fault that he was alone. It was his fault Addie didn't have her mother to raise her. If he'd been a doctor, had noticed the symptoms of Sarah's impending pulmonary embolism, he might have been able to call 911 before she died, not after.

Warm tears had dripped onto his exposed forearms before he realized he was crying—publicly—in a *bar*. His father would be mortified if he could see him now. Not that it mattered. Of all the people he'd disappointed in his life, of all the times he'd never been enough, he'd let down his beautiful wife the most.

"I failed Sarah." He nearly choked on the words.

"*Nate . . .*"

"No." He pulled away from Tyler, swinging rapidly into indignant anger. "It's my fault. It's my fault she's dead."

The bartender's head snapped up.

"Why don't we go outside and get some air?" His friend glanced around the room.

"I'm fine." Nate drained the last of his drink and set the glass down with a hard clunk. "Can I get another?"

Tyler threw down his credit card. "Ring me up for his and mine."

"I can pay for my own drinks. I may not be a doctor, but I make six figures, same as you." He fumbled for his wallet, dropping it to the floor. As he bent down, he misjudged the distance between his head and the wooden chair next to him, smacking his forehead on the seat. "Damn it!"

Nate grabbed his ringing head as he watched Tyler's dark hand swipe his wallet from the ground. Next thing he knew, his friend's arm was firmly around his shoulders, pulling him to the door.

"Wait. My drink . . ." He looked back, but the bartender was already cleaning up his discarded glass, Tyler's untouched beer, and pulling a paper slip from a checkbook.

Tyler walked him to the parking lot and opened the hatch to his crossover. "Sit down." He pointed to the hatchback before ducking into the driver's side and returning with a bottle of water. "Drink this," he said, sitting next to him.

Nate took the bottle of water but didn't open it. The image of Sarah's sleeping face kept flashing behind his eyes every time he closed them. It was becoming physically painful to blink.

"You did not fail Sarah—" Tyler began.

"I did. If I had been better. Smarter. If I'd made it into medical school, I could have seen it coming. I could have *done something.*" He forcefully spat out the last two words, as if he could spit out the bad taste in his mouth. "Instead, I failed her."

"Nate," his friend said in a measured voice. "You not being a doctor didn't kill Sarah—a massive PE did. There was nothing you could do. There was nothing *I* could have done if I'd been there. Even if you'd watched her collapse in front of you, you still couldn't have saved her. Sometimes, there's nothing we can do." He took a deep breath with a loud exhale. "Sometimes, people just die."

Nate said nothing but took a sip from the water bottle.

"Have you thought this the whole time? For the last four years?" Tyler asked.

Nate didn't answer, just stared straight ahead and tried not to blink. The vision in his head was why he redid his CPR training every year instead of every two years, as the certification required. He never wanted to be caught unprepared again.

Tyler swore under his breath and muttered something in a language Nate didn't understand before leaning into his line of vision. "We are going to talk about this right now. You cannot go on like this. Do you understand me?" Sincerity etched the subtle creases around his eyes.

Nate met his friend's dark brown irises and nodded.

"You cannot blame yourself for what happened to Sarah. You cannot blame yourself for something that was completely beyond your control."

They sat listening to the sounds of the busy street for a few breaths as Nate failed to come up with a response.

"Tell me it wasn't your fault," Tyler insisted.

His muscles flinched at the idea of making his mouth form those words. Words he still wasn't ready to believe.

"Nate." His friend's voice was stern.

Rubbing the back of his neck, he parroted Tyler's words. "It wasn't my fault."

"What wasn't your fault?"

He blinked slowly. "I can't."

"Okay. Fine. Right now, just listen to me tell you the *truth*. What happened to Sarah wasn't your fault. There was nothing you could have done. You cannot go on blaming yourself, using alcohol to mitigate the guilt you shouldn't even be feeling."

Silence stretched between them again.

"I've never said anything before because I never thought it was my place . . . but Addie needs to be with you on the anniversary of Sarah's death."

Nate's mother had insisted it was macabre for him to take Addie with him, saying Addie's birthday would always be tainted by her mother's death, even though her mother *had* died the day after she was born.

Nate swallowed a large mouthful of water. "We visit at other times. It's not like she's never been to Sarah's grave."

He typically took Addie in the summer on Sarah's birthday. Usually, his daughter bounded over to the opulent headstone and dropped a kiss on it before explaining why she'd picked out the flowers she brought.

"Yes, but *you* need Addie with you on the anniversary. Not the other way around." He paused. "Do you two talk about Sarah?"

Nate's spine crumbled as he mumbled, "Sometimes."

He kept pictures of her in the house, and Addie knew her mother had died unexpectedly and had loved her very much, but mostly they didn't talk about Sarah. He assumed as Addie got older, she would ask more questions, but for now she was more interested in toys and what dinosaur dress she was going to wear than in who had brought her into the world.

Tyler's voice lightened. "Think of it this way. There was nothing humanly possible you could have done to prevent Sarah's death, but you are in complete control of her memory. You both have to move on and live your lives, but you can remember her together. I think it will be better for you."

Nate found himself nodding before Tyler's hand found his shoulder again. "Is your mom keeping Addie overnight, or are you going to pick her up?"

"Pick up." He took the last gulp of water.

"Text your mom, and let her know you'll be late. I'm going to fill you with food and more water until you're sober enough to drive. Okay?"

Crushing the empty plastic bottle in his hands, Nate agreed with a resigned exhale. "Okay."

·CHAPTER 12·

Pork fat slipped over Brent's tongue as he licked his lips. This fusion restaurant in Brooklyn was complete perfection, from the decor to the light fixtures to the acoustics, everything had been executed flawlessly. As a person who noticed small details, he appreciated the time and energy the restaurateurs had taken to curate the space.

The raucous table of twelve called for their guest of honor, Cosmo, to make a speech about his achievement. The inebriated blond-haired painter stood with the help of his partner, Clark. Cosmo and Clark were quite a pair of opposites on a regular evening, but since this was Cosmo's celebration, he was wearing more color than usual, topped off with cherry cheeks from all the wine. Cosmo leaned to give his carefully coiffed partner a kiss on the head, and several of his beaded necklaces clicked against the large glass table. "Thanks, honey."

Brent watched Clark carefully for the exact moment he would covertly wipe the slobbery kiss from his forehead with his black cloth napkin, half wishing he'd pulled up his camera in time to capture it.

"I couldn't have done this without the full support of my wonderful partner. My rock . . ."

Brent half-listened to the slightly sloppy speech, observing the faces of their friends as they watched Cosmo. He pulled his camera from his lap and shot a few close-ups of the couple and their friends. No one batted an eye when he did—they were used to him photographing them, even in the middle of dinner. Only his friend Hazel cheekily winked a wing-tipped eyelid when the lens centered on her.

He was flipping through the pictures on the LCD screen, pleased with his quick work, when Clark raised his glass, offering a final toast to his partner. Everyone followed suit as they celebrated his upcoming full showing at the best art gallery in Chelsea. Brent forced his lips up before taking a large gulp of his wine, trying to ignore the slight tightness at his temples and the dryness at the back of his throat.

Setting his glass down, he used his free hand to rub at the side of his jaw. This was wonderful for Cosmo—he surely had earned his moment in the sun. Brent tried to rejoin the table conversation, but the more he ignored the sensations pushing at him, the more they exacerbated. When a spot like a flash blinked over his vision, he excused himself from the table.

After pressing through the backdoor, he weaved through the garden seating area and escaped out a low metal gate to the alley. He'd hoped that he'd be able to sit at his friend's celebration silently brimming with pride at having already taken his meeting with the famous producer, but now that his appointment had been pushed back another week, an uneasy headache kept throbbing behind his eyes.

Even outside in the fresh air, a persistent agitation followed him. Brent pulled his phone from his pocket and saw he'd missed a call from his mother. Since it was 10:34 p.m., he'd wait until tomorrow to touch base with her. Looking for something to distract himself with, he clicked through his text messages.

The sound of digital ringing was in his ear before he realized he'd dialed her number.

"Hi," Elaine answered, almost as a question.

He was doing this all wrong. He was probably coming across as desperate. But he *was* desperate. He was desperate to change his status quo. Everyday he woke up with a restlessness even his extensive travel couldn't cure. His life felt stagnant and heavy, as if he were carrying chains around. He was trapped in a set of roles and rules that didn't make sense to him anymore.

But then he'd met Elaine, and her quick humor and unpredictability wiped the slate clean. He never knew for certain how she'd respond to him, and it was insanely addictive. Sometimes, she'd be sly and evasive and other times, completely honest.

And if he kept this nonsense up, he was going to scare her off.

"Hey," he drew out the word for effect, infusing calm he didn't feel. "Elaine. I'm sorry. I was trying to call my friend Ethan, and I tapped your contact by mistake."

"Oh." Her statement was short, and he thought he heard disappointment breathed into it.

Brent moved away from the clamor of the restaurant toward the sidewalk where it was quieter. "But while I've got you, are you free for a minute?"

When she spoke again, she was fully composed. "Are you sure you don't need to get a hold of Ethan first?"

"A bunch of us are going out, but I can remind him later." He was bending the truth. They were going out after dinner, but Ethan was seated at the table he'd just abandoned.

"I'll talk on one condition." She paused. "I will not be answering rapid-fire questions."

A laugh escaped from his mouth. She always made this so easy. Why couldn't everything be this easy? "I promise no cross-examination this time."

"Good."

He sent a friendly grin at a group of women walking past as he stepped toward a tree in the sidewalk. "I wanted to say I'm sorry about canceling tomorrow. I was invited to dinner with an influential gallery owner to discuss my work."

"That sounds like a big opportunity," she said.

"It is," he agreed. *Though not as big as the other one.* He picked at a bit of bark on the trunk in front of him. "Hopefully, she'll be interested enough to want to show some of my work. We'll see."

"Don't sell yourself short, Brent. You don't seem like the humble type."

He found himself laughing as a taxi rattled by. "I have a nagging sensation that you can see right through me. What's next, you detail all my hang-ups?"

"Perhaps you weren't listening, I said I was a *physical* therapist."

"Oh, I was listening," he said, running his free hand through his curls. "I distinctly remember the *physical* part."

The millisecond pause before she hummed a response meant his comment had landed just as he hoped it had. Suddenly, he wished he was driving back to Norfolk tomorrow instead of staying in the city.

"I appreciate you being so flexible with me," he added. "My lifestyle can sometimes seem strange because I'm here one day and gone the next, always traveling between locations."

"That sounds routine to me. My sister's husband was in the Navy—constantly coming and going based on his orders."

"Navy, huh?"

"Yeah." The word elongated, as if she was stretching while saying it. "I've lived near a base my whole life."

"Near a base. So you're not originally from here?" he asked, pushing his hand into his jacket pocket.

There was a slight pause on the phone, and he heard her exhalation. "No. I was born and raised in San Diego. I moved here after I graduated from high school, when my sister's husband was reassigned to Naval Station Norfolk."

A sadness rang in her voice that made Brent's throat throb. He swallowed the trapped saliva in his mouth and decided against the follow-up question he wanted to ask, opting instead to try to make her smile. "So if you've always lived near a base, you must like a man in uniform. That doesn't bode well for a scruffy looking artist like me."

A breathy chuckle sounded in his ear, and victory sang in his veins.

"That was my sister's preference, not mine," she corrected.

"And what's your preference?" He let his words drip with suggestion.

"Oh, I don't know." Her voice held a lighthearted flippancy.

A roguish grin laced his lips. Damn, it was fun to play with her. "Let me guess. Someone who looks like Betty White."

This time, her laugh was so loud and careless, it felt like flashbulbs were igniting in his chest.

Cosmo staggered out of the front door of the restaurant, followed by the rest of his friends. Ethan held his camera in one hand and lifted it aloft when he saw Brent on the sidewalk.

"I've got to go." The words reluctantly fell from his mouth. "Thanks again for being so great about everything. I'll make it up to you next time I see you."

A flirty exhale preceded, "You promise?"

"Absolutely." The confidence that usually surged through his body felt fully restored as he answered. "I'll text next week to firm up details for our date."

"Sure. Talk to you then," she said lightly.

His lips curved high as he spoke, already anticipating her response. "Goodnight, Elaine."

"'Night." Her word was a short, resonant melody before the call disconnected.

Brent grinned at his phone before taking a few large steps to catch up with his friends.

·CHAPTER 13·

The minute Nate's front door opened, Colton sprinted down the hall with an ecstatic Addie.

"Would you like some coffee?" Nate asked as a hello.

Elaine quickly assessed his eyes, which seemed tired and dark-circled but not angry. She'd been expecting some tension this morning after their interaction in the cafeteria yesterday, but his question was delivered in a friendly way.

Her toes unclenched in her knock-off Toms. "You don't have to ask. The answer's always 'yes.'"

"That kind of morning, huh?" He turned, walking to the kitchen. "Same here."

That was another reason that despite her trepidation over this playdate, they were still here. There was no way she was going to disappoint Colton when his little body had trounced her out of sleep at five forty-five, radiating with happiness and asking if it was time to go to Addie's house. Though it was only eight o'clock now, she couldn't have made Colton wait any longer.

The beautiful, soothing tones of Ella Fitzgerald's voice floated softly through the kitchen, along with the smell of coffee. Nate was in the corner, pulling two mugs from a cabinet.

Elaine allowed herself a minute to look around and wonder what it was about this house that made her so comfortable. Maybe it was the warm-toned paint colors or the way the sunlight streamed through the large windows facing the backyard. Whatever it was, she wanted to replicate it when she finally bought her own place.

"Do you take anything in your coffee?" He took the carafe off the coffeemaker and filled the first cup to the brim.

"Milk and sugar, if you have it," she said, before humming along to one of her favorite songs. Running her hands over the cool granite island countertop, she softly sang the verse about fireflies.

"I've got both." He placed a mug in front of her before turning to the fridge.

Once doctored with the right amount of milk and sugar, she sampled her coffee and let a contented sigh pass over her lips. Some of life's biggest pleasures were the littlest ones.

"I love this song." Elaine wrapped both hands around the steaming mug. "I had a thing for swing music when I was in high school."

Well, Rose was the one who'd had a thing for swing music first. During its small resurgence in San Diego when her sister was a high school senior, Rose would go dancing with her girlfriends—all dressed up in vintage-looking dresses with red lipstick and pinned up hair. Dancing with her friends at the club *Forte* was how Rose had met Chuck.

Nate leaned back against the counter opposite her. "You know she was from Newport News, just across the bridge."

"No, I didn't know that." She drank her coffee before slipping into whisper-singing again, this time about strolling and shadowboxing in the dark.

"You have a beautiful singing voice," he said.

You should have heard Rose's.

The memory of her and her sister singing at the top of their lungs, riding in Chuck's car as he sternly pretended not to love it, flashed through her mind.

It had been a perfect July beach day. After roasting in the sun and playing in the salty surf all day, Rose had leaned over to crank up her favorite song. Chuck had teased her about her taste in music, but when Rose had gathered his hand in hers, he'd simply brought Rose's fingers to his lips with a smile. Later that week, they'd shared the news that Rose was pregnant.

"I'm sorry. I didn't mean to upset you."

Dragging herself from the vision of her sister's joyous face, mouth wide open as she sang with her long dark hair whipping around her head in the wind, she found Nate's concerned eyes scanning hers.

Elaine bit her teeth together and internally swore at herself. What was with her lately? She'd casually referenced Rose on the phone last night with Brent before almost oversharing about her past. Yesterday at work, Leslie could see she was upset after blatantly offending Nate in the cafeteria. Hiding how she really felt was a life skill she'd learned early and practiced often.

Putting a believable self-deprecating smile on her face, she said, "You didn't. Sorry if it seemed that way. I was just remembering how awkward I was as a teenager teaching myself to swing dance in my room."

Another song started, all brass and saxophone. She didn't remember the name of it but recognized its familiar melody.

The corner of his mouth picked up slowly like he wasn't quite sure he believed her but wasn't going to press. "Everyone has those bumbling phases of their life, especially in high school."

She felt her shoulders lower as she playfully twisted her lips. "I'm grateful there's no photo evidence."

Nate's easy laugh preceded, "Unfortunately, mine's *well-documented*."

She sucked a breath through her teeth. "That's unfortunate."

His broad smile was aimed at the countertop before he set down his mug and outstretched his hand. "Swing is just a rock step, right?"

Her instinct was to wave off his offer, but instead, she set her coffee down on the island and gave him her hand. Nate pulled her into an easy embrace and led her through a basic swing step before sending her into a spin as a clarinet soloed over the song.

"So you know how to dance?" She tried to keep the surprise out of her voice.

He wore a shy grin as she returned to him. "My mother insisted her sons know how to dance. We were forced into lessons when we were teenagers. I think it was the final nail in the coffin of my brother's rebellion against my parents."

She chuckled as they took a series of side steps. He effortlessly led her through the dance as he said, "I'm the opposite. I usually did what I was expected to."

This simple statement somehow explained so much.

Something pinched in Elaine's chest, and she swallowed to clear it. "You're a good dancer. You can report back to your mother that the lessons were worth it."

"She'll be pleased to hear that." He sent her into another spin.

The song was coming to a close, and he placed a firm hand between her shoulder blades easing her into a quick and simple dip to finish the song. The first few notes of Sinatra's "The Way You Look Tonight" played into the kitchen and instead of dropping her frame, Nate continued the swing step.

"My father always played Sinatra records in the den, where he'd escape after dinner. My brother usually took off to his room, but I'd help my mom clean up, and we could hear the music from the kitchen."

"Thus the playlist," she said.

He nodded.

Unlike the previous song where the dance had felt light and friendly, Nate's fingers on her back had widened, and a slight pressure brought her closer to his body. He didn't let her out for any more spins or turns.

Elaine noticed for the first time the soft texture of his navy T-shirt over his firm deltoid, the warmth of her other hand encircled in his, and the subtle scent of cedar and soap that radiated from his body at this proximity. Swallowing at her observations, Elaine took her gaze from the dip between his collarbones and lifted it upward.

Nate's focused eyes met hers and then skittered over her face as a slight furrow knitted his brows. Before she could say anything, Addie and Colton burst through the doorway to the kitchen.

"We made a fort!" Addie squealed.

Nate dropped his hands as he turned to his daughter. "That's awesome."

"Ya, it's got—you're dancing. I love dancing! Can I dance, Daddy?"

"Of course, sweetheart." He pulled his daughter into his arms and began swinging her goofily around the kitchen.

Addie's giggles filled the room and momentarily distracted Elaine from the strange sensation of loss prickling under her skin.

Colton pulled at her hand and asked softly, "Can we dance, Mama?"

"Sure, bud." She pulled her lips into a grin before lifting him up. Her son's eyes brightened, and he threw his weight back against her arms as she twirled him around.

When the song ended, both kids lost interest and ran back upstairs.

Nate rubbed the back of his neck. "Are you hungry? There are some muffins left." He moved a metal tray from the oven to the island. What looked like homemade strawberry muffins with raw sugar on top stared back at her.

"Did you make these?" She picked one up and took a bite.

His shoulders bounced toward his ears. "Addie likes strawberries."

Cinnamon, nutmeg, oats, and strawberry hit her taste buds with an explosion of flavor. A satisfied hum sang over her full mouth. He grinned at her obvious approval, and her stomach relaxed seeing his smile again.

Before she could determine why she'd had that reaction, Nate grabbed a muffin, ripped two paper towels off the holder, and gestured to the kitchen table. "Do you want to sit down?"

They became lost in parental chatter about the kids for a half hour. Elaine had asked for advice from Leslie and other coworkers with kids before, but being able to share the minutiae of parenting with someone whose child was at the same stage as hers felt like being able to finally exhale.

Colton quietly arrived in the doorway to the kitchen, clinging to the wall.

Moving to crouch in front of him, she asked gently, "What's wrong, bud?"

"I got poop in my undies," he whispered as he looked at his feet.

"That's okay." She kissed his hair. "I'll get another pair from the car."

His sweet eyes rose to meet hers. "I was trying to wipe myself like Addie does."

Gathering his small body in her hands, she pulled him to her chest. "I'm *so proud* of you. Remember when we learn something new, it's okay to mess up. You'll get better every time you try. Why don't you wait in the bathroom, and I'll be right back."

"Can we use hers? There's dinosaurs on the walls."

"Sure, bud. I'll meet you up there." She grabbed her keys from her purse on the kitchen counter as Colton walked uncomfortably up the main stairs. "I'll be right back," she said quietly to Nate. "Potty emergency."

Nate nodded his understanding before she headed to the car. The emergency bag she kept under the passenger seat of her car was just a plastic bag filled with extra pairs of Colton's underwear and pants. He'd been potty trained for a while, so she was pretty sure the undies in this bag were probably a size too small.

After finding the bathroom upstairs with dinosaur decals covering the otherwise pink walls, she helped Colton out of his clothes. She was in for a bigger cleanup than she'd anticipated. Her poor boy had gotten it all over his pants and legs too. Luckily, there were flushable wipes on the top of the toilet. She dumped the contents of the bag on the ground, and three pairs of undies, but no pants, fell on the floor.

"I'm going to need to get you cleaned up, okay?"

"Kay, Mama."

After getting him cleaned and washing everyone's hands twice, she gathered up the bag filled with soiled clothes. "I'm going to see if we can borrow some pants from Mr. Nate, okay?"

Colton bobbed his blond locks.

Knowing he would stay in the bathroom out of embarrassment, she shut the door behind her. She also knew they would have to go home if Nate didn't have anything Colton could wear. Her muscles pulled tightly as she descended the front stairs. A better mother would have a change of clothes *and* the right size undies. As much as she tried, there was always something she missed. Once they got home, she'd replenish her emergency bag so this wouldn't happen again.

She walked back into the kitchen, placing the contents in her hands on top of her purse. "Are there any pants of Addie's that Colton could borrow? I 'parenting failed' and don't have a spare pair for him."

Nate hopped up from his chair. "Yeah, she has some soccer shorts that should fit him."

The breath that escaped her lips was involuntary. "That would be great."

"Let me get them for you."

Addie burst into the kitchen again. "Where's Colt?"

"He's just going potty, sweetheart. He'll be out in a minute," Nate said, walking toward the front stairs.

"Then you have to play with me while he's busy." Addie pulled hard on his hand toward the playroom.

"I can grab them," Elaine offered.

Nate let out a measured breath. "Sorry. Top left drawer in her dresser."

Addie dragged Nate to the playroom stairs as Elaine climbed the main stairs. She found the room with walls painted the same pink as the bathroom and opened the top drawer of the dresser. Neatly folded socks, undies, and shorts were lined up in rows. As with everything else in his house, it seemed that even his four-year-old's dresser was orderly.

Elaine picked up a pair of mesh shorts from the left. When she closed the drawer, something made her freeze. Her heart jumped, suddenly racing in her chest. Sunlight passed over the top of the dresser and illuminated a slight layer of dust atop it.

The image brought her back to a matching view in a much dirtier house, in a much dirtier room, fourteen years ago.

She never liked going into her mother's room. Especially since it was never clean and stank of the alcohol her mother left in discarded glasses on her nightstand. But Elaine's feet were cold. It was always cold in the apartment—her mother opting to pay for drugs instead of heat. Chuck was over, and the door to the bedroom she shared with her sister was closed—music and their voices softly floating up from the crack underneath.

No one was in her mother's room when she peeked in. She hadn't seen her mother this morning, but that was nothing new. Sometimes, she'd leave for days, and they never knew where she went. Elaine searched her mother's dresser until she found a pair of socks and closed the top drawer just as Todd, her mother's boyfriend, pushed into the room. Usually, he came over late when she and Rose were already asleep in their room with the door locked.

"Well, lookie here. I was hoping for Rita, but I guess you'll do." Todd stretched his body in the frame of the door, blocking it.

"I've got to study." She looked down, hugging her mom's socks to her chest and taking a step toward the door.

"Oh, you're not going anywhere." He lunged toward her.

Before she knew what was happening, rough hands were roaming all over her body, and she was pushed hard onto her mother's unmade bed. He was heavy, stank of beer, and his stubbly face scruffed against her neck as she felt wet, slimy lips on her skin.

The beginning of a scream escaped her lips before he covered her mouth with one grubby hand, using the other to unbutton and unzip her jeans. She struggled against him with all her might, but he was so much bigger and stronger than her. He started to pull the right side of her pants down, and instantly she was free.

The space above her opened to nothingness.

The smutty water-stained ceiling occupied her view for a breath before Rose's face and dark hair swept over her own. Her sister's arms pulled her up and rushed her toward the door. Turning her head as they escaped, Elaine saw two things—Chuck's body straddled over Todd's as he repeatedly punched him in the face and her mother standing in the doorway to the en suite bathroom, looking over the room through glassy eyes.

"Did you find them?"

Elaine spun to find Nate in the doorway of the room, and for a split second, she panicked. Hugging the tiny soccer shorts to her chest, she took a step back.

The casual smile fell from his face. "Elaine?"

She didn't answer but started working her mind back as fast as she could. Pink room. Dinosaur toys. Baby powder smell. Nate, not Todd. She was okay. She was safe.

Still, her mind remembered the strain of her arm being tugged as she'd stumbled barefoot behind a running Rose to Chuck's car. How her sister's shaking hands had pulled up her zipper and re-fastened her jeans. How Rose and Chuck had had a wordless conversation in the rearview mirror before his bloodied hand had gunned the engine. How Elaine had sat extremely still in a state of shock as Rose gently buckled her in before gripping her tightly and weeping.

She blinked her vision back to Addie's room. A ringing pulsed in Elaine's ears, but she managed a "Hi" in Nate's direction. Her voice felt dry in her throat, and she swallowed before raising her trembling lips into what she hoped was a smile and holding up the shorts. "Found 'em."

Nate stepped slowly and cautiously over to her. "Are you okay?"

His voice was so soft that Elaine cursed herself for letting her emotions show for the second time in less than an hour. She was stronger than this. She *had* to be stronger than this.

Once Nate was standing a foot in front of her, searching her face for answers she'd never give, something in her wanted desperately to lean forward. To surrender herself into his arms again. Her whole body ached with the last tendrils of fear that were slowly dissolving from her veins as her heartbeat slowed.

"Mama?" Colton called from the bathroom outside Addie's room.

Her son was waiting for her. Colton first. Colton always first.

"Colton needs me." She sidestepped Nate and his question, heading to the bathroom to help her son.

·CHAPTER 14·

A slight breeze sifted through Nate's hair as he watched Addie play soccer with the older kids in the large grass field beyond the paver patio. The thick smell of smoke and roasting meat made his stomach squeeze and growl as his index finger pushed lines into the condensation on his cold can of Coke.

Though he was supposed to be paying attention to Addie as she intermittently looked up and waved from the field, Nate's mind kept tearing back to Elaine's terrified face when he'd seen her from the doorway of his daughter's room. Her eyes had darted all around as if she'd been surprised to find herself there, as if she'd been expecting something or someone else.

He could almost see each layer of protection slide over another until she'd regained the strength she usually exhibited. That was until he'd been standing before her. When he'd been standing close enough that he could have gathered her to his chest again, her face faltered. He got the impression that she'd wanted him—maybe even needed him—there.

Nate rubbed his chest against the squeezing sensation that lingered and took a large gulp of his soda. He was swallowing thousands of tiny searing bubbles when a strong hand slapped his back.

"Nate. Glad you could make it." Tyler nodded to the can in Nate's hand. "Good choice of drink."

Wiping his other hand across his mouth, Nate said, "Hey, Tyler. Thank you again . . . for last night."

His friend's eyes did an appraising sweep before his lips pulled into a smile. "Anytime. I'm here whenever you need me." His head tilted toward the large banquet table filled with dishes. "You should go grab some food before Chloe tries to get you to eat something she made."

Over the last two years, since Chloe had joined Tyler in hosting his monthly backyard barbecues, it had become painfully obvious though Chloe *thought* she was a gifted chef, she was truly helpless in the kitchen.

"Okay, I will." Nate didn't take a step away from his friend. He was working through the words to tell Tyler thank you for allowing him to set down the biggest weight in his life. Nate knew it would take time for the knowledge that it wasn't his fault to fully register, but for the first time in years, he'd woken up this morning without his shoulders straining at his neck.

"You better move, or Ma will harass you next." Tyler raised his eyebrows.

At that second, the woman herself appeared talking rapidly to her son. All Nate got out of the conversation was "Tyler" before she turned, folding her arms in his direction.

"You're not eating?"

Over her head, Tyler tried not to snicker.

"I'm heading over there right now," Nate assured her, giving her a quick hug. "Good to see you, Elna. That's a lovely dress."

"Thank you." She allowed a satisfied grin before pushing him away. "Go. Make a plate."

As he headed toward the food, Tyler went back to manning the grill with this father. Nate was putting a healthy portion of kebabs, chicken, and grilled corn on his plate when Chloe came up to the table with a large wooden bowl.

"Afternoon." She beamed at him. Chloe was always beaming. She looked extra bright today in a sunset-orange, long-sleeved blouse over white jeans, her long blonde hair free around her shoulders.

"Here, have some kale salad. I made the dressing myself with herbs from the garden. Can't get any more earth-to-table than that."

Before he could protest, she was spooning a portion onto his plate. "Thanks."

"How are you?" She tilted her head to the side as she observed him. "Your Ajna chakra is congested." She shifted the bowl into the crook of her left arm and pressed her right thumb firmly between his eyebrows. "What are you worried about?"

Based on the fact that she hadn't asked about last night, he assumed Tyler had kept their conversation private.

Nate was used to Chloe's lack of personal space by now, but the first time he'd met her, he'd been surprised when she'd done something similar to this. As the owner of one of the most popular yoga studios in Virginia Beach, she was usually talking about energy, using words Nate wasn't familiar with.

"I'm worried about a friend," Nate said, knowing it was better not to lie to Chloe because she'd eventually badger the truth out of him.

"Not Tyler?" She released his forehead and put the bowl she was carrying on the table.

"No, someone else."

"I hope everything works out for them," she said, as if she was willing it from the universe. "Did Addie eat?"

"Yeah." He'd fed her a PB&J, cheese crackers, and strawberries in the car, knowing she'd only want to play once she got here.

"She is magical." Chloe was always saying offbeat but accurate things like this.

Nate followed her gaze to where the children were now playing tag between the line of oak trees and the goat pen. Chloe kept pygmy goats for her popular goat yoga class.

A smile lifted his lips. "Addie's the light of my life."

After placing a napkin under his sagging paper plate, Nate made his way down to the edge of the paver patio behind Tyler's farmhouse-style home. Finding himself at an empty table, Nate tried to pay attention to the delicious umami flavors rolling over his tongue, but his mind kept replaying his morning with Elaine.

He wished that she had talked to him but supposed since they were just starting to get to know each other, it made sense she hadn't explained herself when she'd returned to the kitchen after helping Colton change. They'd made casual small talk for another hour before she'd told her son it was time to go.

Even though she'd been polite throughout that hour, she'd also seemed guarded. Part of him wondered if it was because of him. If he'd gotten too close in Addie's bedroom or maybe overstepped the parental playdate boundaries by asking her to dance.

In the moment, he'd told himself he just wanted to show her that he had indeed gone through a solid year of dance lessons, but really he'd been acting on an impulse that had thrummed under his breastbone ever since her eyes had watched his smile in his backyard.

When she'd put her hand in his this morning, awareness had slowly engulfed him. Like how she'd fit perfectly in his arms; and that generally, she emanated a floral scent he couldn't name, but her hands smelled subtly of menthol; or how the dark strands of her hair tickled over his cheek whenever he brought her back from a spin.

It had already been difficult to file away Elaine's obvious beauty up until that point, but he'd reminded himself that she was the mother of Addie's closest friend. An incredible mother who was tender and protective and always there for Colton.

But when his favorite song had filled the warm kitchen and he'd pulled Elaine closer, this newfound knowledge of how she *felt* kept picking at his brain until he'd relinquished himself to it. Yes, she was a mother, but she was also a smart, confident, amazing woman.

Then she'd swallowed and gazed up at him, and he'd only felt one thing—a resounding urge to kiss her. The impulse had come on so strong and fast, he'd been completely overwhelmed by it.

To his gratitude, the kids had interrupted then. For all he knew, Elaine had a boyfriend and their parenting encounters were just that—platonic. If nothing else, she was the only single parent he knew, and having a friend who understood what it was to be both mom and dad was invaluable.

Still . . . something in his brain wouldn't let go of the sensation of her ribs expanding as she breathed under his hand.

"I'm going to let the kids into the enclosure with my goats. Is it okay if I bring Addie along?" Chloe interrupted his thoughts as she stopped by his chair.

After swallowing his mouthful of chicken, he said, "Of course. She'd love that."

Chloe moved off the patio but stopped to call back to him. "Elna just put out malva pudding. You should get some before it disappears."

That had Nate standing quickly. "Thanks for the head's up."

She grinned and continued down to collect the kids. When she asked if they wanted to see the goats, Addie screamed and hugged Chloe so hard she nearly knocked the grown woman down. Nate couldn't help but laugh long and hard.

As he headed back to the main serving table, he wondered if Colton liked animals and if he'd enjoy playing with the pint-sized goats. That thought was all it took for Nate's mind to find its way to Elaine again.

·CHAPTER 15·

Elaine pushed her nails firmly against her scalp as she slowly massaged the shampoo into her sweaty hair, savoring the satisfying feeling that came with washing away the efforts of a hard workout. The almost too-hot water cascaded over her body and eased the tension in her sore muscles. After rinsing, she lingered in the water, rocking back and forth. The translucent droplets dangled from the tips of her fingers before plunging to the shower floor below.

There were days when being in the shower was her only refuge. There were days, especially after Rose's death, when the shower was the only place she could let down all her barriers. Here, she could weep big, messy tears without scaring Colton. At two years old, he'd been so fearful and unable to understand what had happened that he'd zeroed in on Elaine's emotions, reflecting whatever she portrayed. The calmer she seemed to be, the better he was. It had been exhausting pretending everything was okay when it clearly wasn't, but that was what he'd needed, and she would do anything for Colton.

She was twisting a towel around her hair when her phone lit up on the countertop with a text from Brent.

Brent: *Hey*

Elaine: *Hi*

Brent: *How's my girl?*

She snorted at his presumption before it occurred to her that they'd been texting for two weeks. Sure, they'd only seen each other in person twice, but she'd definitely communicated more with him than anyone she'd dated before. Maybe that endearment was accurate.

Her stomach rolled involuntarily. Being *his girl* had implications tied to it, expectations—like sharing full histories.

She thumbed out an answer, giving her head a little shake. Nothing was changing tonight. He was just asking about her day.

Elaine: *Tired and sore again*

Brent: *That's right. It's Tuesday*

Warmth flushed through her muscles at the realization that he'd remembered her schedule. Was it sad that his attention to this tiny thing impressed her?

Brent: *I have an idea. How about a long-distance phone date? Do you have time now?*

Colton was asleep, and other than going through the kindergarten prep packet she'd printed at work to see what Colton needed to know before next year, she had absolutely nothing going on.

Elaine: *Now works. Give me a few minutes and I'll call you*

She pulled on the sweatpants and shirt from the bathroom countertop and began moisturizing her face before she slathered a thin layer of menthol over her aching hands.

Brent: *Pour yourself a glass of wine*

After responding with a thumbs up and a wine emoji, she dragged a brush through her thick hair and looked at herself in the mirror. The droning fan was working away at the steam that had clouded it a moment ago. A blanket of fatigue covered her face, but it was flushed from the hot shower and dewy from the condensation of the small bathroom.

She shrugged at her reflection. "Doesn't matter what I look like for a phone date."

Elaine stretched out on the couch with a glass of cheap red blend and clicked the call icon.

Brent picked up on the first ring. "Hey." It sounded like he was smiling.

She grinned as a buzzing singed under her skin. "Hi."

"Have you got your wine?"

She lifted the glass, even though he couldn't see it. "Yup."

"Good."

"What were you up to today?" She lifted her hair off her shoulders where it was starting to soak through her shirt and tied it into a ponytail.

"I was networking with gallery owners who've already shown my work, seeing if anyone wanted something more recent." As he spoke, she heard a clicking in the background that sounded like a car turn signal.

"Any luck?" she asked, before taking a sip of wine and nestling deeper into the couch cushions.

"Unfortunately, no. Which normally would send me into a tailspin, but I'm still holding out hope that my interview Friday will go well."

She kicked down a throw pillow and propped her feet on it. "That's right, the elusive photography gig. If it even exists," she teased.

"Oh, it exists," he countered quickly. "It's just abstract right now."

"I thought artists love abstract things."

A huff sounded through the phone. "Normally, yes. Right now, I'd like the name recognition and respect that comes with a job like that. That kind of publicity drives people to look you up. The more interest I get, the more likely I will be to have gallery owners calling *me* to get my work in their locations."

Elaine glanced at Jodi's artwork on her walls understanding that being sought out was an artist's dream. "That makes sense."

Part of her wanted to prod more, but she'd kept so much of herself hidden for so many years, it wasn't fair of her to press.

He offered more on his own. "The job isn't abstract. I'd be taking the photos of the hosts and musical guests on NYCLive."

She nearly spat out her wine. "NYCLive?" Her ab muscles whined as she sprung up quickly, setting her wine on the coffee table. "You're kidding!"

"No." The pride in his voice was evident.

"Oh, wow." It was hard not to get excited. Elaine had watched the live sketch comedy show since Chuck had gotten her and Rose hooked on it. "That's amazing."

"I know. It will be so good for my career," he said before hesitating. "But . . . can you keep this quiet? You're the only one who knows, and I'm a little superstitious about sharing good news before it's finalized."

"Oh, sure." She smiled, delighted that she'd been let in on the secret.

"How was your day?" Brent asked.

"Boring, compared to yours." Nothing was as exciting as working for NYCLive.

"That's not possible," he said. "I bet you made more of a difference in people's lives today than I have in the last week."

She tilted her head to the left, considering his words. "I didn't think it was a competition."

"It's not, but you were comparing us." He had her there.

"I guess," she said.

"Hey, I have to run a quick errand. Can I call you back in ten minutes?"

The swift change of topic surprised her. "Uh, sure. No problem."

"Thanks, gorgeous," he said, and the call cut out.

Elaine blinked at her phone for five full seconds before she tossed it onto the banged-up coffee table and picked up her wine. She was only a third way through the glass, but she decided to chug the rest.

Her toes clenched before she swung her restless body from the couch. She aggressively washed and dried the wine glass before placing it back in the cabinet. Taking bread, carrots, and jelly out of the refrigerator, she started making Colton's lunch for tomorrow. Just another rote thing that had to be done every day. Just something that couldn't possibly interest a sexy, enigmatic photographer who was about to have the breakthrough of his career.

Elaine shook her head as she spread peanut butter on bread. "This is why we keep our distance."

Finishing his lunch, she packed two chocolate kisses instead of his usual one and wrote *Mama loves you* on a sticky note. Colton's Hulk lunch box hit the fridge shelf with a thunk as a frustrated exhale passed through her nose.

Three quick raps sounded at her front door. The last thing she needed right now was to pretend to be pleasant. After reluctantly cracking the door open a few inches, her mouth fell wide open.

Brent's stubbly, devilish smile only deepened upon seeing her shocked expression. "I thought we could finish this date in person." His arms were pulled behind his back, leaving his bomber jacket gaping to reveal a tight, black T-shirt stretched across his firm chest.

She pulled the door open wide, but fell into old habits, schooling her features and allowing a coy, "I don't know."

His brown eyes danced mischievously from underneath his flop of curls as he revealed a bottle of wine in one hand. "I brought wine . . ." His other hand pulled forward an artisanal box of candy. "And these amazing hand-painted dark chocolates from one of the best chocolatiers in the city. You said dark chocolate was your favorite dessert, and I promised to make up for Saturday."

Even though sunshine beamed in her chest, she still kept a wry twist on her lips. "I suppose I should let you in, then."

·CHAPTER 16·

As Elaine stepped deeper into her apartment to let him in, her incredible jasmine scent slapped him across the face. It only took a second to realize her wet hair pulled into a ponytail was the source. With no makeup, dressed in grey sweatpants and a loose henley, she was still unthinkably captivating. Brent could have taken twenty shots of the twist of her lips alone; the dim light from her apartment was playing perfectly with the curves of her face.

"I like your apartment," he said, pulling his focus away so he didn't immediately give into his desire to crush his weight against her.

To the left was a couch, a coffee table, and a TV on a stand, and to the right was a galley kitchen that ended in a small table with two chairs. Beyond the compact living room, he could see three doors. The door on the left was closed, with kid's drawings taped to the outside; the middle was open to the bathroom. The door on the right must lead to her room. He tried not to let his eyes linger too long on the bed through partially open door number three.

"Whose work is this?" His feet brought him to the detailed drawings on her main wall. He settled himself in front of one that was unmistakably Elaine with her son when he was about two years old.

She arrived at his shoulder carrying two wine glasses and a bottle opener. "My friend Jodi's."

Placing the wine bottle into her outstretched hand, Brent never took his focus off the portrait in front of him. "She's really good."

"I know." The pride in her voice drew his gaze.

"So I'm not the only artist you know?"

A wry smile traced her lips as she started pouring wine into the first glass. "Not quite."

Something dawned on him. "Wait. Had you been to that gallery before? Art Culture?"

Her damp ponytail slipped over her shoulder when she bent to get the second glass. She stood, pouring and letting him dangle in the wind for a moment before responding. "I might have."

Brent couldn't help himself. He let out a huge laugh. He had been trying so hard to impress her he hadn't even asked basic questions like what kind of art she liked or if she'd been there before. And she'd coyly played along. She was quite possibly the first person who had ever caught him at his own game.

Her eyes went wide, and she brought her index finger to her lips while the other four held a full glass of wine. *Another amazing shot.* He ignored the itchiness behind his eyes and quickly quieted his laugh.

Relieving her of the glass, Brent made sure to gently graze her fingers with his. "So I didn't impress you by introducing you to my artist life."

"I enjoyed meeting Umi and seeing her collection," she offered.

He pulled his lips down enough to take a sip of his wine. As the exquisite flavor exploded in his mouth, he was glad he'd splurged on the expensive bottle.

"Perhaps these will impress you, then." He rounded the table and sat on the old couch.

After untying the ribboned box of chocolates, he offered them to her. Each chocolate truffle was a unique shape, hand-painted a solid color with artistically placed accents in other shades to indicate their flavors.

"Wow. They're almost too pretty to eat." She sat and took her time looking over the assortment before picking up a robin's egg blue chocolate with a Jackson Pollock-style fuchsia drizzle.

He gave her his best smile and raised an eyebrow. "So I did something good?"

She took a bite of the chocolate, humming her approval before licking the blue paint off her lips. "*These* are good."

Satisfaction thrummed under his collarbone. "I wanted to make up for missing you last Saturday."

Elaine took a big sip of wine and picked up another chocolate. This time selecting a bright, sunny yellow with a forest green X artistically painted on the center. "*And* for hanging up on me earlier."

He was trying to come up with a witty retort to that, but all he could focus on was how her lips were the ideal shade of dusty-rose and how the color balanced perfectly with the yellow-painted chocolate. The image was so flawless he had to blink away the fierce impulse to get his camera from his car and ask her to hold the chocolate in her teeth.

Instead, he brushed the edge of her bottom lip to free it of the yellow paint before sucking his thumb clean. The look in her eyes as she watched his mouth was devastating. He should receive a medal for having the restraint not to pick her up like a fireman and carry her to the bedroom.

Brent cleared his throat and focused. "And for canceling again this weekend. That's actually why I'm here tonight. I fly out for my assignment with Mark first thing tomorrow, and afterward, I need to return to the city for my interview with NYCLive.

"I don't know if that's going to hold me there over the weekend, so I might need to cancel our second date—again. Knowing that . . ." He took a deep breath and let the words fall from his lips. "I knew I had to see you one last time before I left."

She swallowed the last bite of her chocolate slowly. "So you drove down here."

"Yeah."

Elaine took her time sipping her wine with her eyes on his. As she swallowed, a smile tugged one corner of her lips. "Because you had to see me?"

"Aren't you happy to see me?" He made a playful pout.

She lifted a slender shoulder. "The wine and chocolates are nice."

This woman will be the death of me.

Brent had never been so singularly distracted by another person in his entire adult life, and he'd been with a lot of women. As excited as he was for this new opportunity and all the implications it had for his career and life, the time away from her was going to be painful.

"That's the only nice thing about tonight?" he pressed.

Her eyes flicked to his with an alluring gleam. "So far."

"What can I do to make it nicer?" he said, setting his wine glass down and leaning toward her.

"Hmmm." She placed her index finger along her jawline as if thinking. The action exposed the side of her neck.

Brent inched forward slowly, placing a light kiss at her collarbone before working his way up toward her ear, allowing his hot breath to coat her skin.

"That's not terrible." Her words were raspy.

"*Not terrible,*" he whispered hoarsely into her ear before softly kissing the edge of her jaw toward her mouth. "Let's see if I can work my way to 'acceptable.'"

A sassy "you can try" escaped her mouth before he covered it with his own. Their tongues swiped at each other with quick, fervent motions—her mouth tasted like the heavenly combination of good chocolate and great wine. His arms gripped her body until she slipped her hands up and pushed at the collar of his bomber jacket.

He tilted back to shrug out of it before returning to her,

this time pushing her onto the couch. She leaned back, allowing him to lie on top of her as her lips continued to devour his. When she pushed her hands firmly through his hair, he couldn't help the moan that escaped his mouth. Skirting a hand up the side of her body, he barely grazed the edge of her braless breast. The grip on his scalp tightened with his motion, but then Elaine froze unexpectedly.

When he pulled up to look at her, wondering what had gone wrong, she tilted her head away to the side, as if listening. He found himself following her gaze and straining to hear a neighbor's door close. At the sound, she exhaled with a soft laugh, dragging Brent's focus back to her. Elaine was even more stunning with a sensual flush to her skin and her lips swollen from his kisses.

Brent slowed his pace, gradually returning his lips to hers in teasing fractions. He lazily explored each part of her mouth and focused on every little sensation—the feel of her tongue touching his, her intoxicating scent, and how her breath went ragged when he held her bottom lip in his teeth.

He wove his hand under her head, applying enough pressure to expose her neck, so he could trail kisses up to her ear. "Any progress?"

"Better." She breathed the word against his shoulder and lifted her hips firmly against his.

Brent wasn't made of stone. As much as she probably enjoyed this teasing game he'd started, with that movement, she'd destroyed any ability he may have had to hold back. He pushed his body hard against hers, nipping her ear as she moaned.

Fuck. Actually, that was exactly what he wanted to do now.

He roughly took possession of her mouth as his hand flew over her body. No teasing, no side sweeping, but fully and firmly grabbing her gorgeous breast. While one of her hands tightly gripped the base of his neck, the other impatiently pulled at his shirt over his torso. He leaned back, pulled his shirt off quickly, and was heading straight back to her lips when a knock sounded loudly at her front door.

Pausing, they both looked at it. Silence followed and his gaze returned to her, his fingers teasing at the flat belly under her shirt. Her eyes rolled back in her head before the knocking started again.

This time it continued, insistently.

"Let me see who it is. If they keep knocking like that, they'll wake Colton."

As much as Brent didn't want her to move from her position under him, the last thing he wanted was for this to stop. The sooner Elaine could dismiss whoever was at the door, the sooner they could move this make out session from the couch to her bed.

"Yeah, okay." He exhaled, shifting off her.

Elaine cracked the door a few inches like she'd done when he'd arrived and assessed the person on the other side. Even watching her back, he could see her demeanor change as he heard an older woman's voice say, "Hello, Elaine."

"Mom." She sounded startled.

Before Elaine could open the door fully, he found his shirt and put it back on.

"Can I come in?" He heard from the door.

"I, uh . . ." Elaine quickly glanced at him.

Brent gave her an encouraging smile, letting her know it was okay if her mom needed to come inside. Maybe her mom was here to drop something off. You'd think she would've called or texted first, but they had been so fully occupied that perhaps Elaine had missed the message.

"One minute," she said to her mother and then closed and locked the door.

That action struck him as odd.

"She can come in for a minute if she needs to. I'm great with parents if you're worried about me."

Elaine's sagging shoulders still faced the door, her hand on the deadbolt. When she turned around, all the color had drained from her face. "It's not . . ." Her fingers shook as they pushed over her forehead.

Immediately rising from the couch, Brent had his arms around her in four large steps. "What's wrong?"

She stood stock-still in his grip. "I haven't seen my mother in ten years."

"Oh." He didn't know what to say to that.

Her mother's voice called from beyond the door. "Elaine?"

Elaine's muscles felt insurmountably rigid. Tightening his grip with one arm, Brent loosened the other to gently rub her back. When her cheek finally fell against his breastbone, he found himself exhaling.

"I should probably let her in." She didn't move.

"Do you want me to stay?"

"No." Her jaw stiffened. "I can take care of myself."

"I didn't mean—"

"I know." Uncertainty filled her eyes. "I'm not upset at you. It's just . . . never mind."

She pulled away, and he reluctantly released his arms.

"Are you sure you don't want me to stay?" he asked, gathering his jacket from the floor.

Elaine was obviously not happy to have her mother waiting on the other side of her door.

"No." She ran her hand over hair, straightening her shoulders. "Thank you."

"Okay. I'm flying out first thing, but text me if you need me. I'll be eight hours ahead of you, but I'll answer when I can. I won't be out of cell service this trip, so you'll be able to reach me whenever."

She gave an absent nod and opened the door. Her mother's hand was raised to knock again. The woman's eyes wandered from him to Elaine as she lowered her arm.

"I'm sorry. I didn't know you had company."

"I was just leaving." Brent exited as her mother took a step out of the way. Once he was behind the woman, he mouthed "text me," and Elaine subtly bobbed her head in confirmation.

"I guess you should come in." She stepped back, letting her mother walk inside.

Elaine met his eyes one last time before she closed the door. The insecurity in them made his throat tighten. Now more than anything, he wished he wasn't flying overseas in just a few hours.

·CHAPTER 17·

As Elaine shut the door behind her mother, a range of emotions whipped through her body. A persistent sourness, tinged with the flavors of wine and chocolate, lingered at the back of her throat as she looked at the woman she hadn't seen in a decade. The woman she'd written out of her life when she'd left California.

The woman who was now barging back into it.

"Thank you for letting me in." Her mother stood a respectable distance away, a small cross-body purse over her slim frame.

Elaine noticed her mother's hand fiddling nervously with the strap of her purse. She'd learned young the importance of being hyper-aware of body language. It had been essential to her survival knowing what version of her mother she'd encounter in any given moment.

After gathering all the items from the coffee table, Elaine set them on the kitchen counter, using the physical movement to try and gain control over the pitching feeling in her stomach. "Why are you here?" she asked, folding her arms across her chest.

Her mother didn't stutter or try to give any excuses. "I came to find you and your sister. I wanted to see you both. I've been sober for two years, four months, and sixteen days." As if to punctuate the sentence, she pulled a sober coin out of her jeans pocket and set it on the kitchen counter for Elaine to examine. "I'm working again, and I've really got my life back together. I wanted to find you girls and let you know some important information. But I also wanted to see if I can be a part of your lives again."

Her mother paused, and Elaine tried to absorb the details she'd just been given. Her head hurt as she tried to process everything, but anger pulled hard at the top of her chest, stalking back and forth just below her collarbone like a caged, feral cat who wanted release.

"How'd you find me?"

"I was planning on using some money I saved for a private investigator, but when I searched the internet for your name, your picture came up on the website for the hospital where you work," she explained.

Elaine remembered sitting for that headshot last year. The website had a link below her picture to make an appointment with her at the clinic, but that didn't explain how her mother was standing inside her apartment right now.

"But how did you find out where I live?"

"I called the number on the website asking about you, and the scheduling lady gave me to your manager . . . Glen, I think.

When I told him I was your mother, he gave me your home address."

Disbelief smacked her in the chest. Leave it to Glen to give away private, *personal* information. Her mother wouldn't have found her if he'd abided by hospital policy and not given out her address.

Although . . . then her mother might have shown up at the clinic.

She felt a strange gratitude that she was having this conversation in the privacy of her home instead of at work.

"I know this is a lot to take in, but I have information I need to share with you, and I promise that I'm being honest about my sobriety," her mother said with a determined set of her jaw, her body stilling.

Elaine examined her mother's eyes, trying to discern if she was telling the truth. Remembering how she'd been fooled before—the time when she was a sophomore, again her junior year, and right before she'd graduated. How her mother had sworn she'd been clean, and they could all be a family again, but every time it had been nothing but lies. How much it had hurt to be disappointed over and over again.

Her mother took a long, deliberate inhale, as if sensing Elaine's resistance. "My back pain isn't an issue anymore . . ."

That was all it took for Elaine's mind to fling her back to eighth grade when her mother had hurt her back moving a filing cabinet at work. Since she hadn't been able to afford the surgery to fix the misaligned disk, the doctor had given her oxycodone to help deal with the pain and a referral to physical therapy. Elaine had gone to those afternoon PT appointments with her mother, learning the exercises to help at home. It was working with those therapists and seeing the difference it made in her mother's pain that had cemented her career choice.

But when her mother had exhausted her allotted therapy appointments, she had done the exercises less and less and relied on the pain medication more and more. Eventually, her mother had added alcohol to make it through between the pills. By the time Elaine had started high school the following year, her mother was usually drunk at night but had somehow managed to get to work every morning. Over that year, though, she lost her job, and began getting her pills from drug dealers. That's when the house had never been warm and the cabinets never full of food. That's when random men had begun coming around, forcing Elaine and Rose to lock themselves in their room at night.

Rita's voice pulled her back into the room. ". . . and I'd like to earn your trust back. Yours and Rose's."

The mention of Rose's name released the fury Elaine had been struggling to hold. Her skin vibrated with the heat as her toes gripped the cheap linoleum.

"Rose is dead." She spat the words through her teeth.

"What?" Her mother's eyelashes fluttered in uncoordinated blinks before her gaze fell to her trembling fingers. "She can't . . ."

It was then that Elaine saw how old her mother really was. Rita was only fifty-one, but she easily looked ten years older. Her light brown hair was heavily streaked with grey, and her skin sagged from years of neglect and misuse. Elaine had been watching Rita's light brown eyes for signs of alcohol or drugs the second she'd walked through the door. Though they now brimmed with tears, her mother's eyes remained focused and clear.

"But . . . when?"

"She died two years ago," she said coldly.

When Rita crumbled into one of the kitchen chairs, a flicker of guilt over not breaking the news more gently washed over her. But then the vision of her mother standing in the bathroom doorway as Rose pulled her off the dirty bed, leaving Chuck to pummel the man who'd tried to rape her at fourteen, flashed fresh in her mind. Her teeth ground together.

Wiping away tears, Rita asked, "How?"

Elaine rattled off the information almost robotically like she was watching herself say the words. "Intracranial aneurysm."

"W-What?" she stuttered. "What does that mean?"

"It means one minute Rose was sitting on a park bench alive, and the next minute she was dead."

Elaine had learned that her sister had been out at the park with her moms' group when she'd died. They'd all been chatting and drinking coffee from their reusable thermoses that sunny morning with their children happily playing in front of them, when Rose had collapsed facedown into the mulch.

Rita pulled a travel-sized tissue container from her purse and then did the strangest thing. She *apologized*.

"I'm so sorry, Elaine."

Her mother had never, not once, apologized. Even when she'd been wrong. *Especially* when she'd been wrong.

Everything inside Elaine froze, and her breath sat trapped in her lungs.

"I cannot imagine how hard that was for you. She wasn't just your sister—she was your mother when I couldn't be."

The hot liquid hit her face before she realized tears were streaming down her cheeks. Elaine swiped at them, furious at herself for crying in front of the woman who had already hurt her so much. Turning to get a paper towel, she held it over her closed eyes.

Rita's words hurt so much because they were true.

Even before her mother had started using opioids and alcohol, she'd been a struggling single mother raising two girls on a kindergarten teacher's salary. Though Rose had only been four years older, she'd often picked up the slack when Rita was busy keeping them all afloat.

Elaine drew a staggered breath as memories assaulted her. Her sister's childhood laugh as she pushed Elaine high on the school playground swing, their mother inside finishing her lesson plans. A preteen Rose's dark-eyed wink as she insisted Elaine tag along with her friends, always making her feel included and wanted. Rose's body gripping her impossibly tight in the back of Chuck's car promising Elaine that they would never go back to that apartment, that they'd figure something out, that she was never going to let something like that happen to Elaine again.

"That means I just have you." Her mother's quiet voice startled her.

Elaine spun around with a heated glare. "You don't have me. I'm not yours anymore. I haven't been yours since I was fourteen."

"I know." Her mother stared at her aged hands. "I'm sorry. I just meant . . ."

She let the sentence evaporate into the tense air between them. Neither of them spoke for a long time, and the ticking of the clock over the small table was starting to dig into Elaine's brain.

"I think you should go." Her words dropped like ice on steel.

Rita nodded as her shoulders caved. "I'm sorry for bursting in on you late at night, but I honestly couldn't think of a good way to come back into your life."

"You're not back in my life." She clenched a fist.

"Elaine . . ." Her mother's tear-streaked face lifted. "I know I've wronged you and Rose. I'm here to atone for those sins. I will have to live with the fact that I'll never be able to apologize to Rose, but I'm here to show you how I've changed. That I want to make up for all those years I mistreated you."

Rita took a piece of paper out of her purse and set it on the table. "Even if you don't accept any of that, I need to talk to you at least one more time. There are things you need to know. This is my cell number, my sober coach's cell, and the phone for the house where I'm staying. It's a dry house through AA. You can call the house any time to ask about where I've been. My sober coach is available to talk and confirm what I've told you about myself." She paused and let out a long breath. "I hope that you'll call me, and we can arrange a time to talk."

Elaine glanced at the table but didn't move an inch.

Her mother stood, adjusting her purse over her shoulder before walking toward the door. Elaine followed and opened the door, standing as far away as possible.

As her mother crossed through the threshold, she caught Elaine's eyes. "I really am sorry about Rose . . . about everything."

Elaine held completely still, only moving to shut the door and let the bolt slide with a satisfying click once her mother had stepped onto the concrete slab outside her door. She wanted to collapse against the door, drag her knees to her chest, and weep like she had after Rose's death, but the buzzing of her phone pulled her to the kitchen counter.

Her phone sat two feet away from the sober coin her mother had forgotten. She stared at the metal circle, internally refusing to move or touch it. When her phone buzzed again, she tore her gaze away and picked it up.

Brent: *You okay?*

Brent: *I'm worried about you*

It was then that the tears she'd stopped before flowed vigorously. There was no way she could answer his innocent question. No way Brent could understand all the injustices she'd experienced. No way she could explain that with one swift knock, her mother had uncovered parts of her she'd long since buried.

She couldn't respond. Just. Couldn't. Instead, Elaine went to her room and gave in to her deepest desire at the moment. She sobbed like a small child, curling herself into a ball on the bed. Only *one person* could have understood her now and she was dead.

Every single muscle in Elaine's body ached as she cried, her chest heaving erratically. She didn't hear Colton's door open or see him walk into her room. Only when he climbed onto her bed and patted her hair with his small hand did Elaine realize he was awake.

She almost went to wipe her eyes, but it was futile. Even though he hadn't seen her cry since he was too young to remember it, there was no way she could hide her tears from him now.

"It's kay." He gently wiped at her face before he kissed her cheek. "It's a dream."

Her son was repeating the four-year-old version of the words she'd said to him every time he'd had a nightmare since he was two. Elaine couldn't help the raw wail that ripped from her body.

Here was the goodness of Rose in the body of her son—even at four, Colton was as nurturing as his mother had been.

"It's kay," he repeated. "I'll stay with you."

He laid in front of her, folding his hands under his cheek, his blue eyes watching hers.

She pulled him into her arms, hugging him tightly. "I love you," she whispered into his hair.

"I love you, Mama."

They lay like that for a long time, until Colton fell asleep in her embrace. Elaine's mind raced over everything—everything that had happened in her childhood, and everything that had happened when Rose died. It was a long time before his soft breathing, his clean lavender scent, and the solid warmth of his little body snuggled against her eventually lulled Elaine into her own fitful sleep.

·CHAPTER 18·

The staticky voice of the captain welcoming them to Terlenitsi broadcasted over the sounds of people shifting in their seats, gathering their belongings after the flight. Like everyone around him, Brent's fingers pushed over the rough airplane seat, picking up the various items he had dispersed in his small area.

When the captain announced the local time, Brent did the math, determining it was a little after 1 p.m. Eastern Standard Time. Three hours ago, when he'd switched planes in Istanbul, he'd finally received a response to the question he'd texted Elaine yesterday evening. Just a quipped "I'm fine." No explanation as to why her mother was stopping by late at night after ten years of separation. Nothing.

He found himself pulling up her text screen as he turned off airplane mode. The woman next to him rose from her seat, and Brent readjusted his backpack on his shoulders as he followed her, shuffling out of the plane.

Brent: *Just landed*

Once he was free of the aircraft and its stale air, Brent quickly found the customs line. While he waited, he sent off a few other messages. The first was to Mark, to let him know that he was on the ground, and to firm up the time and location for their meeting with the source tomorrow.

Elaine: *K*

Brent stared at her short answer—a letter—not even a full word and blinked to try and clear the irritated sensation at his temples. If he hadn't accepted this last freelancing assignment for *The Washington Post* with Mark, he wouldn't be in this tiny Central European country. He'd have been able to talk to Elaine without five thousand miles between them.

Taking a deep breath, he reminded himself they'd barely been on two dates. Things were going to have to change on both ends before they got to more intimate stages of a relationship, like meet-the-parents.

Brent: *How's your day?*

He waited for a reply for a few seconds before he flipped the screen and started responding to emails. The producer's assistant at NYCLive wanted him to confirm their three-thirty appointment on Friday. His flight out of Terlenitsi Thursday night would get him back to Manhattan just before noon. He'd be incredibly jet-lagged, but it's not like he hadn't done this a hundred times before. Brent knew how to run on empty and still impress everyone with his work.

Elaine: *Busy. In between appointments right now. My one o'clock just canceled. Trying to catch up on charting.*

The overbearing fluorescent light stung his eyes as he reread her words, once, twice. He probably shouldn't ask, but his fingers ended up typing the words. Some part of him needed to know, to understand why Elaine looked like she'd swallowed ash as she'd closed the door last night.

Brent: *How did everything go with your mother?*

Three dots hovered and blinked incessantly while he waited for the lengthy response.

Elaine: *It was fine*

A short breath left his lungs. Okay. Fair. She obviously didn't want to talk about her mother, and she probably was having a crappy day. Noticing he was nearing the front of the line, he decided to give her an out.

Brent: *Okay. I'm about to go through customs, and then I'm going to try and knock myself out with alcohol and Benadryl to acclimate to the time change. Talk to you later*

Sliding his phone into his front pocket, he handed his passport over to the customs officer. Once he was through the line and walking toward the baggage claim, he felt it vibrate.

Elaine: *Night*

His lips kicked up at the message. Maybe not all was lost. He just needed to give her some time. He'd initiate again when he was stateside, after hopefully crushing his interview Friday.

Brent exited the busy terminal, and the scent of exhaust and garbage assailed his nose. The sound of taxi drivers forcefully vying for his business forced him to close his eyes for a beat. Once he'd haggled for a fair price and was settled into one of the cars, his phone buzzed again.

Mark: *This is crap. Meet me at the bar when you get here.*

Thumbing back a quick confirmation, he told the driver to take him to the downtown Radisson. A quick ten-minute drive brought him to the hotel where *The Washington Post* was putting him and Mark up for the night. He smiled at the friendly doorman and quickly located the dark, wood-paneled bar off the lobby. Mark was slouched over a small table with two shot glasses and what looked like a bottle of local vodka.

"Hey, Mark." He took the seat opposite his colleague.

"Brent." Taking a quick shot, he wiped his mouth with the back of his hand. "I've got bad news."

Grabbing the bottle to fill the empty second glass, Brent laughed dryly. "So I gathered."

Mark's eyes were a bit unfocused in the dim bar lighting, but he drilled them in his direction. "There's no tie back to D.C."

A dropping sensation like they'd just lost altitude in a plane hollowed out Brent's stomach. "None?"

Mark shook his head solemnly.

"Shit."

His colleague moved to fill his glass again. "Exactly."

So he'd flown halfway around the world to help Mark report on *local* corruption occurring in a country with no political ties to the United States. This story would be buried, *if* it even ran, and likely wouldn't warrant a photo. He was here for nothing.

And . . . he could have been with Elaine instead of exhausting himself before the biggest interview of his life.

Damn it.

Mark watched Brent's face contort. "That's how I feel too. I switched jobs because I wanted to focus more on politics at *home*. If I'd wanted to fly around the world chasing stories, I would have stayed where I was."

After taking his full glass in hand, Brent quickly swallowed the clear liquid. A slight burn smoothed down his chest.

Brent turned the bottle, reading the label as he poured himself another shot. "Okay. We can handle this. We're professionals. It's not what either of us hoped for, but we'll do the best we can with what we have." Mark groaned at his optimism. "And in the meantime, we'll get shit-faced on great vodka."

"*That* I can get behind," Mark said, lifting his glass.

They sat in stony silence, letting the liquor soften the edges they both felt. The exposure and the payoff for the trip seemed to evaporate into the warmth flushing over Brent's arms and legs.

"I'm sorry you're not going to get paid." His friend broke the quiet.

Brent ignored the pulsing behind his left eye. "Don't worry about it. It's not your fault."

Mark chuckled to himself. "Hell, I might not even get paid." He poured another shot, and half of it ended up on the table.

Brent pulled the bottle away from Mark, signaled the waitress for glasses of water, and asked if the kitchen was still open. After ordering himself and his friend something greasy, he poured his last shot.

"When is the interview tomorrow?"

"Early afternoon. That should give us enough time to get it done before we leave. I already changed my flight to the one scheduled to leave a few hours earlier. You should do the same."

That was a good idea. The faster he could get back to NYC, the better.

"Okay," Brent said. "Where are we meeting?"

"They want to do it in their home. Meet me here for lunch tomorrow, and we'll go over story details and head over together. I have a translator meeting us there, but I understand the deputy speaks fluent English." Mark leaned back in his chair.

The arrangement struck him as odd. Usually, if they were talking to a whistleblower, they did the interview in a safe location in order to not draw attention to the fact that they were conducting an interview in the first place.

"Won't it raise flags with fellow parliament members when two Americans show up at his house?" he asked.

Mark snorted. "I thought so, too, but apparently this guy's just waiting for the story to go public with the press so he can launch his own version on social media. He wanted the legitimacy of a world-known publication behind him." He swung his hand sloppily between the two of them. "I guess that's us. This guy figures he's safer telling the world because if something happens to him, everyone will know who's to blame."

Brent let out a low whistle as Mark bobbed his head in agreement. When the food arrived, they dug in like starved men and finalized their plans for the following day. It was agreed— the quicker they could get this story done, the quicker they could both get back home.

·CHAPTER 19·

It had been more than two hours since Brent had asked about her mother, but Elaine still felt a suffocating constriction circling her chest. She'd honestly never expected to see Rita ever again, and naturally, the woman had shown up at the worst possible time.

Elaine had finally found a man who was interesting, attractive, and incredibly sweet. The fact that he had driven all the way from New York to Virginia to spend the evening with her before he'd left for his assignment was undeniably romantic. Even if the underlying motivation was the chance of seeing her naked, she wasn't going to lie and say that the feeling hadn't been mutual.

She'd barely gotten a glance at his toned chest and abs before her mom's knuckles had hit the wood of her front door like a sledgehammer. Though Brent hadn't seemed phased by Rita's arrival, the best course of action was to set up a wall between them to keep her mother's craziness separate from him. It'd been hard enough to concede the parts of her true self that Brent had already experienced—her full past was too much to share.

Elaine blinked at the computer cursor over the note she was supposed to be making in the chart as unease snaked through her muscles.

Her coworker, Finn, plopped down at the computer beside her and started vigorously typing. "Elaine, do you have a minute?"

Giving herself a little shake, she glanced at the time. "I have to grab my next patient, but I've got a sec."

She closed the computer chart, reminding herself to finish her note later.

"You've been here a while and seem to have a good relationship with Glen. I've had the request in for time off for my race since before I started working here. When I was hired, I was told I'd get it off, but he still hasn't approved my PTO. I already have plane tickets purchased and my weekend planned out." He took a large breath with an audible exhale through the nose. "I need to know I'm not going to get in trouble for going on a trip that was supposed to be guaranteed upon my hiring."

Finn was a former college baseball player turned long-distance runner and a new-grad PT at their clinic. He'd also been training for, and incessantly talking about, the New York City Marathon—not that Elaine minded. Most athletes were like that with their sport of choice.

"I'll see what I can do," she said.

She'd need to call her mentor, Cora, after her shift and see what her perspective was. Glen should have already approved Finn's PTO when their workday schedule went out at the beginning of the quarter. Fixing the treatment schedule after the fact was one thing, but Elaine didn't think she could approve PTO. *Not yet, anyway.*

"Thanks. It means a lot," he said before turning back to his computer.

She rolled her shoulders as she stood to leave.

"I know I'm not supposed to say anything." Finn spoke in a low voice. "But you'd be a better supervisor than Glen any day of the week."

She suppressed the surprised grin tugging at her lips. "Thanks."

He nodded and got back to his chart as she headed to the waiting room to call back her next patient. She'd been treating Ava for radicular pain and nerve compression for the last three weeks. Her symptoms of back pain and near full numbness down her left leg were caused by her being thirty-eight weeks pregnant with twins.

"Hey, Ava. How are you feeling today?" Elaine offered a supportive smile and her hand to help her patient stand. The poor woman could barely fit her belly between the armrests of their waiting room chairs.

"Every day, I get closer to the end." She pushed up with one arm while the other one pulled at Elaine's. "Scheduled C-section in five days."

Doing a quick calculation in her head, she said, "Monday. You must be excited."

Ava hadn't let go of her arm as they walked down the hallway to the gym. "Excited . . . scared . . . happy beyond belief . . . terrified . . ." she joked in a sing-song voice.

"I'm sure everything will go smoothly," Elaine reassured her.

If Elaine knew anything, it was that you should always compliment and encourage a pregnant woman. They were incredible beings, undergoing tremendous feats in the creation of another person from their own flesh and blood. Or in Ava's case, two people.

Her patient took one look at the crowded gym, and her eyes pleaded with Elaine. "I'm feeling particularly heiferish today. Could we do the therapy in one of the back rooms?"

"Sure." Elaine steered her toward an empty treatment room. Luckily, there was one. "Let me just grab a fitness ball, and I'll be right back."

Bringing a cushioned mat with her as well, she put it on the floor and helped Ava slowly down to her knees. Elaine placed the fitness ball in front of Ava, so she could use it to brace her body.

"Let's start with the pelvic tilts, ten of them, and then take a break with a backwards stretch. We'll do three sets. Then we'll switch to glute strengthening."

Ava huffed playfully. "Well, you've got me where you want me. I'm obviously not going to make a break for it."

A chuckle escaped Elaine's lips as her patient tucked her head and started the pelvic tilts. "How's the numbness today?"

"Better. I've been doing the exercises at home too. Turns out I already had one of these balls in a closet leftover from some abandoned New Year's resolution."

"I'm glad it's helping," Elaine said, placing her hands around Ava's hips and helping her into a fuller tilt.

"I'm having boys," her patient said out of nowhere.

"What?"

Ava had told her when they first met that she didn't know—and didn't want to know—the sexes of her babies.

"I couldn't wait. They did a placement ultrasound and since both of them are still breech, they went ahead and scheduled me on Monday. They were wiggling around on the screen, and all of a sudden, I couldn't wait any longer. I *had* to know. My husband still doesn't know." She paused slightly out of breath from the movement and sat back on her heels. "Am I terrible?"

For a second, Elaine's brain froze. "Uh, no. It's your body and your children. If you want to know, then you should know. As far as your husband goes . . . I can't help with that."

Ava lifted a shoulder, exhaustion evident on her face. "I think it's one of those deathbed confession things. I'll tell him when we're eighty, and he's too senile to be mad about it."

Dual emotions ran through Elaine's body. First was empathy for her patient who was physically and emotionally drained from the strain of her pregnancy. The second was unexpected jealousy over the fact that Ava had someone who would be with her into her eighties.

Elaine maintained her neutral expression and said, "That sounds like it could work."

"I don't know what to do with boys." Ava had a three-year-old daughter who was in preschool right now so she could come to this appointment but knew that Elaine had a son. "Tell me what to do with boys."

Elaine's mind rapidly ran through the first few months of taking care of Colton. Of all the times she and her sister had been unexpectedly overwhelmed in caring for him, one memory whipped at her ribs like a hot, smoldering branch.

Her sister had just taken a shower for the first time in two days and decided Colton could use a bath too. After Rose had carefully undressed him, she'd lowered Colton onto the soft blue bath sponge in the warm water. As soon as his back had touched the pad below him, he'd started peeing in a high arc that had soaked Rose's clean shirt. Elaine had been playing the part of photographer for Colton's first bath and caught the whole thing, including Rose's face as she'd started laughing so hard her eyes watered—then sobbed hard, ugly tears because her husband would never see any of these little moments.

"That bad?" Ava's eyes widened.

Elaine glanced at her patient and quickly schooled her features. "No. It's just . . . make sure to cover their privates when you bathe or change them unless you want pee everywhere. That's probably the biggest thing with baby boys. Everything else should be the same."

Ava visibly relaxed. "Oh, pee." She giggled. "I can handle pee."

"You can handle anything, Ava."

Every woman needed to hear that as often as she could.

A knock sounded at the treatment door and Madison, their scheduling assistant, stood in the hall. "Elaine, I'm sorry to bother you, but I still have two patients scheduled for you next hour. What do we do with this?"

Elaine had been dealing with issues like this all day. In an unprecedented display of laziness, Glen had taken the day off unannounced, shoving his appointments onto her schedule—unfortunately, not every patient could reschedule.

Resisting the urge to roll her eyes and groan, she held up a finger to Madison before leaning back to instruct Ava, "Continue alternating between these two exercises, and I'll be right back."

Ava gave a thumbs up mid-pelvic tilt.

Elaine softly closed the door, though she wanted desperately to slam it. "Let's look at the charts. I might just have to double treat if no one can help."

◊◊◊

This was the only good part of today, and it was completely serendipitous—Elaine was actually grateful to her fellow spin instructor for needing a sub at the last minute. Now, she could put all her frustration and anger to good use, pushing hard against the pedals of her bike. Exiting the women's locker room, she strode straight to the water cooler to fill her bottle before class.

"Hey," came a familiar voice behind her.

Her toes scrunched in her shoes. She didn't want to talk to anyone. She just wanted to ride hard and fast until all this tension left her body.

"Hi," she said, watching the water level rise in her clear blue bottle.

"Are you teaching for Kim today?"

"Yup."

"Can I ask you something?"

She took a long quiet inhale as she lifted her torso. "What's up, Nate?"

"You seemed upset this morning at drop off when Colton mentioned having a coin that was mine. My mom likes to give Addie quarters for her piggy bank. If Addie gave him one, then he's free to keep it. I don't want you to think he took it or anything. I'm sure she gave it to him."

First thing this morning, Colton had immediately found her mother's sober coin where it had remained, untouched on the kitchen counter. He'd been curious and asked about it. Making a groggy, pre-caffeine decision, she'd told him it was Nate's coin. Telling Colton it was play money or a pirate coin or basically anything else would have been better than what she'd said. And because the universe had decided to see how much strain she could take today, they'd run into Nate and Addie at drop off, and of course, Colton had mentioned it. Only Addie asking Colton to go trick-or-treating with her had derailed the conversation enough that Elaine hadn't needed to explain herself.

Until now.

Elaine pulled a deep breath into her lungs and turned to face Nate. She was prepared to lie. She was prepared to allow Nate to think that her son had taken money from his house, but then as she glanced up at his kind eyes, the weight of the last twenty-four hours sank like lead in her stomach.

She was so *incredibly* tired—tired of lying, of skirting around the truth, of hiding how she really felt about things all the time.

And then she understood something.

Right now, she needed a friend.

Today had felt like one of the longest days since Rose's death. She hadn't had time to fully process what had happened last night or discuss it with Jodi, and she didn't want to explain things to Brent because she didn't want her family drama to taint her first attempt at a dating relationship, but Nate was right here, patiently waiting for her response.

Elaine exhaled her shuddering breath, and Nate's gaze seemed to soften even more.

"Colton didn't take anything from your house. He found my mother's sober coin on the kitchen countertop this morning, and I lied about it. She came by last night and accidentally left it at my apartment. It was a super fun surprise since I hadn't seen her in ten years." Saying the blatant, honest truth out loud felt strange, like instead of real words, she'd spat out incoherent syllables.

His only reaction was a slight twitch of his left eyebrow. Elaine hadn't realized she'd been holding her breath as she spoke. She'd been keeping oxygen trapped in her lungs as the barely banked rage simmered millimeters under the surface of her skin.

"Oh," he said.

"Yup." She borrowed Colton's word again while her chest strained, as if there was no way to exhale.

Those same kind eyes that had prompted her honesty now seemed to be seeing all of her torn, lashed, *ugly* wounds. The gentleness in them was too much for her to bear. She spun around and started power walking toward the cycling room.

He was by her side in a second. "Okay," he said. "That sounds like a lot."

The bikes in the room were already beginning to fill, and Nate aimlessly threw his bottle and towel on one to reserve it before following her to the podium in the front.

Elaine let out an irritated noise. "Just a little bit." She was aggressively adjusting the handlebars of her bike as she heard his next sentence.

"You're going to kill us today, aren't you?"

His spot-on assessment surprised her, as if someone had splashed her with a bucket of water. An unrestrained laugh bubbled from her stomach, tickled up her esophagus, and sang out of her mouth. The transition from pure, indignant anger to shocked joy was so striking she stopped her motion to glance at him.

A look of pride skirted across his face before he tucked it away. "If you want to talk about it, I'm here."

"Thank you." She moved to the back of the bike to adjust her seat. "But right now, I just want to ride."

"Okay." Nate nodded and walked away to start setting up his own bike.

After adjusting the mic and plugging in her most aggressive playlist, Elaine mounted the spin bike and gave her intro before adding, "Buckle in, folks. You're going to be sore tomorrow."

·CHAPTER 20·

One of the reasons Brent loved working with Mark was that the man was always professional. No one would have guessed that he'd been completely hammered the night before. Sitting casually a few feet away from the deputy, Mark asked questions through a reliable translator. The deputy did speak adequate English but kept switching back to his native tongue when he became irritated, which had, so far, been the whole interview.

Brent kept his camera mostly over his face. First, he gathered overall shots of the lavish living room before focusing in on small details, like the way the dust gathered between concentric circles of the intricate lace overlay on the end table.

As Mark continued his interview, Brent started gathering close-ups of the man's face and of his wife's nervous hands wringing in the lap of her primly folded legs. On a coffee table before them, the bribe lay on a tea towel. A huge diamond necklace, a ruby bracelet, and a sapphire ring. Brent sat patiently knowing he couldn't capture posed photos, that these images had to be organic.

Trying to keep his mind from the hollowing fact that none of these photos would ever see the light of day, he began creating artistic layouts in his mind. He would have the young, beautiful wife hold the large ruby bracelet over her eyes with her lips pressed tight. Or maybe he would pose the husband, wide eyes staring directly into the camera, with his wife's manicured hand covering his mouth, the enormous sapphire ring on her finger. It would have been so poetic to visually display the silence the prime minister was trying to buy with the bribe.

Brent's focus returned to the room when the deputy became increasingly agitated by the interview. He was saying how disgusted he was that the prime minister had attempted to bribe him, stating he had only taken the jewelry so he could notify the press of his corruption. The couple said they weren't going to hide their identities, and they hoped once the story was blown open, others under the thumb of the prime minister would step forward.

Mark asked questions directly to the wife, and as she spoke about how the bribe had been given, she picked a piece up. With the diamond necklace dangling from her delicate fingers, Brent first snapped a close up of her hand then quickly moved and adjusted the focus to grab her in the frame from below with her eyes focused on the jewelry.

Perfect.

Back at the hotel, they settled outside the lobby coffee shop to work, their bags already behind the desk awaiting their evening departure. After uploading all the pictures to his laptop, Brent wrote details on each shot for the photo editor. Mark's keyboard clicked at lightning speed as he documented all the information from the interview. Like Brent, Mark never took notes in front of a source but instead came back and jotted them all down as soon as the interview was over.

When Brent finally had all the digital images looking the way he wanted, he sent the photos directly to *The Post*. Hopefully, they would like one enough to use it, even buried in the back with the story.

Brent shut his laptop. "I'm set. You want to grab dinner?"

Mark continued typing for several seconds. "Huh?"

"I just submitted the photos to your photo editor. Do you want to take a break and eat?"

The sky had pinked as the sun set beyond the city buildings outside the large lobby doors.

Mark looked up from his computer. "Thanks, but no. I'm going to work through. My flight leaves in two hours, and I want to make sure this story is filed before I leave. I'll grab something at the airport."

Unfortunately, Brent hadn't been able to get onto the earlier flight out.

"Okay." He held his hand over the small table. "It was good working with you again."

"Yeah, it was." Mark paused to shake hands. "Sorry again about this. If you decide you want to freelance again, I'll put in a good word for you."

"I really appreciate that, but I've got to try something different. At least for now." He may have mentioned wanting to focus on his art last night over their final shots of vodka.

His colleague nodded. "See you when I see you."

Brent grinned. "Same."

Since the table was right next to the lobby doors and there was a long line at the check-in desk, Brent simply carried his backpack with him into the street. If he was forced to spend extra hours in a foreign country, he was at least going to enjoy the local cuisine instead of eating hotel food again. The sounds of the city engulfed him as he trekked up the sidewalk. Well-dressed professionals stepped around him before a couple entered a restaurant to the left.

Following them, he was quickly seated at a small window table. After ordering a glass of wine and using his phone to translate, his gaze roamed over the restaurant. It was busy, but he liked being surrounded by other people, even if he couldn't understand them. Now that he was officially done with his assignment, he picked up his phone and clicked back over his text screen.

Overnight, he'd received another text from Elaine. She'd apologized for being short earlier in the day, saying she'd had a really hard day at work. When he'd woken late for his meeting with Mark in a slightly hungover haze this morning, he'd thumbed out a quick "no prob" before he had to shower, pack, and checkout.

His fingers hovered over the screen as the waiter arrived with his food, and its delicious scent completely distracted him. After tucking his phone away, he began cutting into the savory dish with zeal.

"I'm sorry to bother you, but I heard you thank the waiter. Are you American?" A lovely twenty-something brunette woman with blue eyes stood at the edge of his table.

"Yeah." He noticed her lack of an accent. "You too?"

"Yes," she said, surprising him by pulling back the empty chair across from him and sinking into it. "I hope you don't mind, but I need to talk to someone from home. I've been working here for a few months, and I miss the sound of unaccented English. Can I please eat with you . . ." She paused expectantly, awaiting his name.

"Brent." He offered his hand over the table.

"Kristy." Her lips curled as they shook hands. "Are you here for work too?"

"Yeah. Homesickness getting to you?" Brent remembered the familiar ache of longing for home from his early years shooting on location.

"It really is." She deflated as she exhaled.

Sympathy pricked at his temples. He was going to have to eat anyway; it didn't hurt to share the table with this young woman if it made her time away from home a little easier.

"Why don't you stay, and we can talk about whatever you want."

Kristy perked up with a sweet smile. "Really?"

"Sure."

The waiter arrived, and Kristy ordered a few things, speaking the local Slavic language in halting sentences.

The two of them had a surprisingly enjoyable dinner. He found out that she was from the Midwest, worked in IT, and that her company was expanding internationally. After breaking up with her college boyfriend, she thought trying something new would be just the thing to get over him.

"It's been a good adventure, but I'm always happy whenever I run into someone from home," she said.

"I would think you'd be able to find a bunch of expats here." He took another bite of the dessert she'd insisted they share.

"I suppose I should try harder," Kristy said. "At least I found *you*." Her foot tapped against his shin.

By this point, it was evident she was flirting with him. Normally, he would have relished a one-night stand. Especially a no-strings-attached one with a woman in a foreign country, but when the check came, he insisted on paying it and was ready to wish her good night.

"Why don't you come back to my place?" she said from under her dark eyelashes. "I've got an apartment a few blocks from here."

"Actually, I'd better get back to my hotel." He stood and immediately felt woozy. The room spun around quickly, and he had to close his eyes and grab the back of his chair to keep from crashing to the ground. Once he felt steady enough, he inefficiently reached for his backpack and jacket.

Two cold hands touched his forearm, and her voice sounded muffled and far away when she spoke. "Hey there, let me help you."

Kristy led him outside, and the brisk air slapped his face, clearing some of the fuzziness he felt. He hadn't put his jacket back on, and his fist balled around its soft leather to keep from dropping it on the sidewalk. Kristy had his backpack, containing his laptop and camera, slung over her shoulder. A nervous uneasiness followed the fatigue snaking through his veins.

Something's wrong. I need to get back to the hotel. Now. He stumbled a block until he realized Kristy was pulling him in the wrong direction.

"No! I need to go that—" He pointed in the opposite direction and, in that action, lost his balance and crashed to the ground. Blinking his eyes rapidly, he saw brown hair in the periphery of his vision and blue eyes over his as he blinked once, twice, and then everything went black.

◊◊◊

Brent woke up lying on a mattress on a low-bed stand staring at colorful green and yellow fabric hangings on the wall in front of him. Light sliced in through the open window, alerting him to the fact that it was probably mid-morning. *Shit.* He'd missed his flight. He was supposed to be in New York. Where was his phone?

His head was pounding, and as he put his hand to it, his arm hurt with the movement. His sweater sleeve was rolled up and his right elbow was wrapped in gauze, like he'd given blood. He was fully clothed, and it felt like he was weighed down with lead skin. *What the hell happened?*

Once he pushed himself to sitting, he swayed a bit without the bed to support him. There was a small, purple bedside table containing a glass of water and an old lamp. Just as he was reaching for the water, Kristy came into the room wearing a nude cami, lace underwear, and nothing else.

So many questions raced through his mind, but all he wanted was to drink water. Picking up the amazingly heavy glass, his hand dipped a little, and she quickly supported his hand with hers.

"Here. Let me help," she said with a sweet smile.

After he had drunk the full glass, he could finally manage speech. "What the hell happened?"

"Not much." A teasing frown traced her lips. "You passed out. Too much wine."

Panic surged through his veins again—his inhales becoming short and ineffectual. *No. That doesn't make sense.*

"Shh. It's okay." She leaned over and kissed his forehead. "Why don't you sleep it off?"

No. He needed . . . He needed to . . .

Exhaustion hit his eyes, his throat, and sat heavily on his chest. He felt his body start to sway as he fought to keep it upright. Kristy's hands applied gentle pressure on his shoulders as they pushed him back into the pillows. His eyelids fell closed against his will. Words reverberated as if spoken underwater the second before he blacked out. "Sweet dreams, Brent."

·CHAPTER 21·

Elaine's toes wiggled in her boots—the only part of her body she'd allow to fidget because no one could see it. The metal cafe chair had not yet warmed in the midday sun, and its coldness seeped quickly through her jeans. She'd chosen this counter-order restaurant with a large outdoor seating area on purpose. The idea of meeting her mother was already making her feel like the walls were coming in on her. At least now she didn't have physical walls exacerbating the sensation.

Wednesday, after fully pushing all her frustration into the pedals of the gym's spin bike, she'd gone through her evening routine with Colton with one lingering thought on her mind. What if her mother was actually telling the truth? After her shower, she'd found her fingers dialing the numbers for Rita's sobriety coach and the owners of the sober house.

Both corroborated her mother's story, and that left Elaine with two possibilities. Either her accomplices were very good liars, or her mother was being honest. The second possibility baffled Elaine.

Crossing and then re-crossing her legs, Elaine looked down at the timestamp on her phone.

Her mother was ten minutes late.

She allowed herself a petulant sigh before opening her text screen. Brent still hadn't responded to her last message. All that stared back at her was his "no prob" to her apology for being short with him.

Friday morning, she'd sent a text wishing him good luck on his interview. Technically, it was one of those texts that didn't warrant a response. But it was surprising he'd never answered. Maybe the interview had gone poorly, and he needed time to process it before getting back to her. Or maybe . . . maybe he was blowing her off. Maybe he'd seen the craziness that was her life and decided he didn't want to be part of it. Everything was going fine until—

"Hello, Elaine."

Her teeth clenched together.

Elaine squared her shoulders as she looked up, sliding her phone from the table into her lap. "Hello."

Rita tentatively took the seat opposite her. "I'm glad you wanted to meet with me."

Elaine crossed her sweater-covered arms, fully letting ice seep into the tone of her voice. "You said you had some important information for me. That's the reason I'm here."

Elaine ignored the woeful sigh coming from across the table.

"I do. It's about your father."

All she knew about the man was that he had abandoned them before she'd turned two. "What about him?"

Her mother sighed again. "Unfortunately, he died a year ago."

It was like hearing news that a complete stranger had died. She'd never even known her father's name. Rita had only referred to him, in the rare moments she had mentioned him, as *your father*—said as if that particular conglomeration of letters tasted like sewage.

Elaine assumed she'd feel nothing hearing this news. It was hard to have emotions for a man she'd never met, but there had always been the idea that there was another person she belonged to. Someone other than her mother, especially now that she didn't have Rose. With him gone, an oppressive emptiness settled deep in her belly.

"His wife was the one who found me and told me about his death."

Rita set a glossy four-by-six photo on the table between them. A man with dark hair and dark eyes held a swaddled newborn baby, a four-year-old Rose beaming next to him. The two girls were both spitting images of the man.

"At the time, I didn't trust in my sobriety enough to try and reach out. I wanted to make sure that I would never go back to pills or alcohol before I saw you girls again. My coach mentioned that you called him to confirm what I told you, and I'm glad you did. I want you to know how much I am trying to do the right thing here."

Elaine scrutinized her mother's eyes, looking for signs of falsehood.

"His wife wanted me to know that he'd passed away from complications related to early-onset Parkinson's Disease. He'd been diagnosed in his mid-thirties." Her mother paused, as if gathering her strength. "In his last few months, he mentioned you girls. His wife apparently hadn't known about us. Once she knew he had children, she felt it was her duty to inform you because there's a potential hereditary component."

A long pause settled over the table, and it was only then that Elaine registered the sound of Rita's charm bracelet clinking as her fingers fidgeted with the zipper of her purse.

"When she searched for you, she couldn't find you. She could only find me." Her mother paused again, looking in her lap. "The reason she couldn't find you or Rose is because your father didn't know your names."

Her already sore muscles from holding such a rigid posture tightened. "How did my father not know my name?"

A long exhale preceded her mother's words, "Because your name at birth was Elizabeth Davis."

"What?" Surely, she had not heard that correctly.

Her mother straightened, but that tinkling sound still struck Elaine's ears. "Your birth name was Elizabeth Davis. Your father's name is Michael Davis. When he left us, I changed your names to my maiden name, Ritter. I figured if I was changing your last name, I should change the whole thing. . ." She trailed off, then recovered herself and continued.

"You have to understand. I was so young, and I was so angry with your father for abandoning us. It consumed me, that anger. I had a friend who worked for the court, and she fudged the papers a bit for me. I figured if your father didn't want us, we didn't want him or his name." The cadence of her mother's speech had picked up, and she took a deep breath before starting again. "I learned in recovery that not only was it wrong what I did to you and your sister while I was high or drunk, but taking your birth name from you was wrong as well."

Elaine's mouth had fallen open, and she closed it, swallowing over the sawdust lining her tongue. Of all the crimes her mother had committed, she wasn't sure where on the spectrum to place this one. Not only did Elaine not know her father, but she didn't even know her own *real name*.

Thoughts zinged through her mind, but only one question came out of her dry throat. "What was Rose's name?"

"Rachel. Rachel Davis." She reached across the table. "Elaine. I'm sorry. I should have told you sooner."

Elaine drew back rapidly as if her mother was a noxious chemical. "And our middle names?"

"They are the same as your birth ones. You were both given middle names after my aunt." She returned her hand to her lap and played with the charms on her bracelet again. Elaine had heard that growing up, both hers and Rose's middle names had come from their great aunt.

"So my name is not my name?"

"No. Yes. Legally, your name is Elaine Nora Ritter. I changed it to that when you were a year old, so all your paperwork is in that name. You were just born to a different one." She reached into her purse and pulled out an embossed blue paper. Setting it gently between the two of them, she unfolded another and placed it beside the first.

Elaine stared at the two birth certificates. She'd never seen her birth certificate before. She'd never needed it. For identification when she'd applied for jobs, she'd used her social security card and driver's license. Reaching down with an unsteady hand, her fingers brushed a feather-light touch over the letters of her sister's name.

Rachel.

The rush of bile from her stomach to the back of her throat was swifter than she expected, and she swallowed hard to force it down. This was all too much—her mother being here, the fact that she now knew her father's name, learning her and Rose's birth names.

"I know this is a lot to take in," her mother began, "but I felt it was important to let you know about your father's diagnosis once it was brought to my attention. And the truth about your birth name."

Itchiness rolled over her muscles as they twitched like they were trying to crawl out of her skin. The cool breeze that pushed over her face and hair did nothing to settle her, only pricked at the tension in the corners of her eyes. She blinked, realizing the collection of hot liquid there was tears.

She couldn't stay here a second longer.

Rooting around in her purse, she found the two-year sober coin and put it on top of her birth certificate. "This is yours."

Her mother looked at the coin and the papers between them, saying nothing.

"I need to go." She rose swiftly from the table.

"Elaine . . ." Her mother stood and then sighed. "Okay. Can we talk again another time?"

She bristled at the question. That familiar flush pulled and tugged just beneath her skin, searing rapidly through her entire body. Everything in her flashed hot, tight, and Elaine only felt one thing—relief.

"You already told me the information you needed to share. I don't see a reason for us to speak ever again," she bit out through clenched teeth.

Rita opened her mouth but then closed it.

Elaine spun away and stode to her car, never looking back.

◊◊◊

Within minutes, Elaine was stepping through her front door, her head swimming with the information that'd been dumped on her.

"Mama!" Colton ran over to her and gave her legs a hug before looking at her face. "What's wrong?"

She should've driven around, she should've cooled down before bursting through her door like a madwoman, but all she wanted to do was be somewhere that brought her comfort. Someplace that didn't make her feel like everything she was barely holding together was coming apart.

"I have a headache." Even as the words left her lips, her stomach rolled and squeezed.

Lies. *So many lies.*

She didn't want to lie to Colton, but at that second, she couldn't think of a child-friendly way to explain what had just happened to her. Even as that rationalization sang through her mind, her heart squeezed.

A deep, shocked inhale filled her lungs, and she staggered back onto the closed door behind her.

I'm as bad as my mother.

Colton hadn't asked much about his dad yet, and she'd always told herself that when he did, she would tell him who his parents really were. When Rose had died, he'd been so little and insecure that she'd wanted him to understand *she* would always be there. That no matter what, even though she hadn't given birth to him, he was her son—legally and in her heart.

Now, all her good intentions seemed deceitful.

In trying to help Colton feel secure, she'd erased Rose from his life, like her mother had erased her father. There were pictures of Rose all over her apartment, often holding Colton as a baby, and when he asked questions, she'd told him Rose was her sister who died.

It was the truth, but it was also an omission.

She never wanted Colton to feel the way she was feeling right now. Like the entire axis of her world was being realigned, and she was stumbling to keep up with the changes.

Jodi looked up from the soapy plate she was washing, her face contorting in concern. Immediately abandoning her task, she rushed over. "Hey, it's okay. It's going to be okay."

It was then that Elaine noticed she was shaking, vibrating with an intensity she couldn't control. Colton leaned his body on her legs, his eyes wide and worried.

Jodi tugged at her shoulders, pulling her until they were both seated on the couch. Colton repositioned himself on the ground, leaning on her lap.

"Cutie, can you play with your trucks in your room for a minute, so I can talk to your mommy?" Jodi asked.

Her son didn't move.

Elaine tried to still her limbs, but a residual trembling lingered in the tips of her fingers. "Just for a minute, bud." She ran a shaky hand over his silky hair.

"Kay." His little frame kept hugging her knees.

"I'll let you watch your favorite show on my phone," Jodi said, encouraging him along.

Only after Jodi had pulled Colton's hand away and led him to his room did a large, hot tear dot the dark denim of Elaine's skinny jeans. She pushed impatiently at her face with the sleeves of her sweater, trying to regain some semblance of control before Jodi sat beside her again, handing her a full glass of wine.

"It's past noon."

Elaine took a grateful gulp. "Thanks."

Jodi delicately asked what had happened, and Elaine detailed the conversation she'd just had with her mother.

Letting out a low whistle, Jodi said, "What a mind trip."

She dragged another long sip of wine down her tight throat before responding. "Yeah."

"What are you going to do?"

Elaine had been staring into the space in front of her, but her head turned to Jodi as her eyebrows bunched. "Nothing. This doesn't change anything. I might have been born with one name, but I've only ever known the name I have now. I have an answer to the question of who my father is, but he's dead and gone, just like everyone else so it doesn't matter."

"Hey." Jodi's hand was warm over her knee. "You're not alone. I'm here whenever you need me."

Elaine grabbed for her friend's hand and squeezed it. "I know. Thank you."

Jodi's smile was soft before she took a sip of her own wine and asked cautiously, "Are you going to see you mom again?"

That bloom of heat pulled over her chest again. "I don't see why I would."

Jodi was quiet for a breath. "Why not?"

"What do you mean 'why not?'"

Her friend leaned back on the couch. "Think about it. What do you have to lose? I know that your mom was a completely awful person when you were a teenager, but what if she's changed, and you miss out on the opportunity to have a relationship with her now?"

Elaine forcefully pushed a breath through her nose. "I don't want to have a relationship with her."

"I understand, but that's because you are thinking about all the bad years. What about when you were little? You've told me stories of fun things the three of you used to do together before everything went bad. What if you could have that mom back?"

Elaine *did* remember good times. She remembered that even though they hadn't had much money and there had been no father figure in their lives, their mother had been a beloved kindergarten teacher at their school. Kids would stare in awe when they learned that *they* were Ms. Ritter's daughters. It hadn't mattered that they'd sometimes shopped in the "lost and found" after everyone had gone home for the day or that her mother had snuck milk and crackers from the cafeteria when they were doing their homework in her classroom after school.

But those good years were often blocked out by the many poisoned with opioids and alcohol.

She shook her head. "I don't think . . . no. It's been too long. I've got my own life. *Colton's* life to worry about. I don't need her here making everything worse."

"Okay." Jodi stopped pressing and took another sip of her wine. "Just something to think about."

They sat with the quiet between them for several long moments, silent except for the chatter of the characters from Colton's favorite cartoon.

"There's something that seeing her has made me realize," Elaine paused. "I need to tell Colton about Rose. It's time he learned the story of his past, so he doesn't feel blindsided when he gets older."

"You didn't tell Colton because he was too young to understand. He still might be too young. It's not like you were planning to never tell him. These are two entirely different things." Jodi leaned down to catch her gaze. "You're *nothing* like your mother. You are just like Rose."

Her eyes welled with tears again. Being compared to her sister was the best compliment she could receive, especially since Jodi had *known* Rose. Her friend's words filled a corner of the uncertain void that Elaine always felt about her ability to be a good enough mother for Colton.

Jodi leaned over and held her in a firm hug for a long while. They finished their wine before Jodi said goodbye to Colton and left to walk across the complex to her own apartment.

Elaine found her son sprawled out on the floor of his room with a bucket of small cars dumped on the carpet before him as he made the sound effects of driving and crashing.

"Hey, bud." She sat on the carpet next to him.

"Is your head better, Mama?" he asked, driving a small truck over her foot.

"It is." She kissed the top of his head. "Thanks for asking."

The photographs she'd collected from her bedroom were clutched tightly in her hands. Younger faces looked back at her. Her and Rose when they were older teenagers. The two of them with Chuck. Rose and Chuck at their courthouse wedding. Chuck in his dress uniform next to a barely showing pregnant Rose. Rose with a full belly already at seven months pregnant. A red, screaming newborn version of Colton in Rose's exhausted but elated arms. Celebrating his first birthday, just the three of them.

Elaine swallowed the sadness that always welled up when she looked over these images and settled her eyes on her son. "There's something I want to talk to you about."

After she'd explained his past as best she could in a way he would understand, he sat holding the picture of Rose and him right after his birth for a long time before his eyes lifted to hers with a slight twinge of his golden brow. "So I came from her tummy?"

"Yeah, bud." Elaine tried to keep her voice from cracking.

His blond eyelashes, so thick they made you want to run your fingertips over them, fluttered. "But you're still my mama?"

She immediately gathered him to her chest with a snug grip. "Yes. No matter what, I will always be your mama."

His hair tickled her chin as he nodded. "Kay."

"Do you have any other questions?" she asked, releasing him to see his eyes.

He silently shook his head.

"Well, if you ever have questions or want to know anything about her or your dad, you can always ask me, and I'll tell you."

Colton looked at the picture again and then handed it back with a small smile. "Kay, Mama."

A lightness flowed through her veins at not having to keep the memory of her sister to herself anymore, of being able to share the truth with Colton and have it not shatter him. "Okay," she breathed, wrapping her arms around him again for a long, tight hug.

·CHAPTER 22·

A staggered breath drew into Brent's lungs as consciousness quickly returned to him. Blinking his eyes open, his vision flicked over the familiar surroundings. Light streamed from the small basement window above his mattress, contrasting against the grey cement ceiling beyond. Though the high window was covered in a film that obscured the view outside, sunlight still permeated.

The beams illuminated the diminutive particles in the air. In a way it was beautiful—the sun glinting off bits of dust that otherwise would've gone unnoticed—each miniscule piece dancing and flowing to its own rhythm. In another way, it was cruel. A taunting vision of something normal—something he'd seen before and taken for granted many times. Now, it was going to be the most enchanting thing he'd see all day.

His entire body ached as he swallowed a groan, turning on his side. An errant metal spring pushed hard into his ribs, almost encouraging the air trapped in his lungs to fall from his lips in a desperate sigh. Brent's eyes landed on the crude scratches on the wall. Seven. It had been a week. Or that was roughly how long he assumed it had been. The first few days, he hadn't thought to make hash marks, and he didn't know how many days he'd lost to whatever drugs Kristy had given him.

His right eyelid began to twitch, and he brought his hand to his forehead, trying to stifle the emotion squeezing at his throat.

Panic.

Every morning brought panic. In the daylight, he saw his situation for what it was.

That first day, after he understood where he was, he'd gone a little crazy. The instinct to flee had been so strong that only bashing his body against every surface in search of escape had soothed it. But the concrete walls were impenetrable, as was the barred prison-style door to the eight-by-eight room. On the second day, he'd methodologically searched for any weaknesses in the structure that surrounded him. A bolt wasn't completely fixed at the door, and he'd used the ceramic lid of the toilet to try and smash through it with no success.

That day, he'd learned if he stood at the metal door and pushed his body hard to the left, he could just see the edge of a staircase. He'd spent the rest of that second day screaming until two men trudged down the stairs carrying a water bottle and a disposable food container. When they'd heard him shouting, they'd only laughed—heartily. Brent understood that wherever he was, it was too far away for anyone to hear him scream.

Initially, Brent had refused to eat the food that was in the container or drink from the large bottle of water. He'd assumed it was laced with something like the water on Kristy's nightstand had obviously been. After a few days, hunger had eventually won. He'd found that after ingesting a small amount and waiting for the sickening, dragging sensation to overtake him, that the food and water they'd given him were clean.

This time, when Brent rolled over to face the empty room, he let out the moan that wanted to escape from his mouth. He'd been tempted to fill the small space with his own voice but hadn't yet permitted himself. Partly because that meant he'd have been here long enough to warrant being his own company, and partly because he needed something to save if his days stretched out longer.

He pulled his one comfort object—a moss-colored wool blanket—over his shoulders until it brushed against the scruff of his face. Itchiness met itchiness, prompting him to rub at his jaw.

It was then a door slammed shut above and stomping feet told him that they would soon come down the stairs. Deep anxiety pulled at his collarbone and refused to let his lungs accept a full inhale. Though he anticipated the same routine he'd experienced every day now for a week, he was never quite sure what would happen. As he lay perfectly motionless, surges of adrenaline punched at his organs.

The acrid scent of cigarette smoke preceded the heavy steps nearing the cell door. Brent's trepidatious eyes watched A1—or Asshole One, as he mentally referred to him—slide a disposable food container and a liter water bottle through the slot at the bottom of the door.

The man's whiskered face twitched into a sneer as he took a drag from his cigarette. "Eat, healthy American," he said in broken English.

A2 flicked his cigarette butt into the cell with a laugh before they both turned to climb the stairs.

It was always the same two men. Usually one at a time, but sometimes together when they were talking to each other in their heavy native tongue like this morning. Normally, Brent enjoyed the sound of other languages, but their inability to speak English only exacerbated the desperation that pulsed behind his eyes.

They never spoke to him except to say the same sentence every morning. He'd tried, unsuccessfully, to bargain with them—telling them that whatever they wanted, he'd find a way to get it for them. To tell whoever was in charge that if he could get word to his parents, they'd pay whatever it cost to release him. Whatever it was, he would find a way.

The men had just shaken their heads and laughed, the coarse barking sounds falling from their peeling lips. Neither of them were particularly distinct—both of average size with dark brown hair and eyes, sparse facial hair, and a yellowy complexion. They wore pants and jackets, so he couldn't identify any tattoos or other markings, but Brent started memorizing their faces. He wanted to be able to dictate each downward slope of a lip or slightly uneven eyebrow with extreme accuracy.

The terrifying thing that kept jolting through his mind was that he'd known colleagues who had been through something like this. It was far too common that journalists were taken hostage. As confident as the deputy had been about his safety, Brent should have been more concerned about his own. He wondered, not for the first time, if Mark was being held somewhere as well or if because he'd stayed behind at the hotel, he'd made it out.

Brent waited until he heard the door close to the house before moving to pick up the carton he knew held cornmeal mush and two hard boiled eggs. His jeans hung a little loose on his hips when he stood. Sitting back on the mattress, he took his time running his tongue over the insipid but slightly abrasive, sticky corn dish before each swallow. This morning, the eggs were even slightly warm in the middle, and an unexpected rush of emotion brought tears to his eyes. Using the sleeve of his now-filthy sweater, he rubbed away the hot liquid.

He set down the container before pressing the heels of his hands into his eyes and taking a deep extended breath. After seven more, he was calm enough to finish his meal with the attention it deserved. Though he'd already grown tired of eating the same thing every morning, it was paramount for him to focus on anything that was positive, to take pleasure in what he could.

Tiny semblances of control were what kept his brain from fully fraying at the edges. He couldn't leave this room, but he could choose where he sat. He could regulate the pace at which he ate his two meals, how he held his tongue in his mouth, the speed at which warm air left his lungs.

Brent lavished the last bite of food over his tongue before swallowing it and taking a rationed swallow from the water. Then he slowly and neatly folded the cardboard box down on itself and placed it through the door slot. The sight of its spent form lying beyond his room brought a twinge of sadness. It would be a long, lonely day before the Assholes returned with dinner tonight. At least his evening meal varied, and he could spend the rest of the day fantasizing about what he'd receive later.

He took the scratchy wool blanket, folded it until it resembled a cushion, and placed it on the floor closest to the stream of sunlight. The uncertainty of what would happen was the hardest thing to wrestle with. Tension crawled and clawed at the back of his throat. Brent took a controlled inhale and slowed his exhale as he closed his eyes. He needed to stop his brain from spinning in an anxious circle within his skull.

Though he'd never been one for affirmations, it seemed like a perfect time to start. Initially, he hadn't known what to send out into the universe and started with *I will survive this*. But survival could come after months, years. Then it transitioned to *I will be released*, but his brain nagged at the fact he hadn't specified a time, so now the cadence was *I will be released soon*.

He pressed his fingers onto his knees to ground himself as he repeated the words in his head. Saying that sentence to himself over and over allowed him to edge away from the nagging sensation that had started to wash over him when something different didn't happen each day. As afraid as he was every morning that something would change, he felt a strange feeling every time it was the same.

Comfort.

Being drugged had been terrifying. Not understanding what was happening those first days had been devastating. He'd mourned so many losses so quickly in those first few days—his freedom, his dream job, his relationships. It was then that the steady rhythm of his days had begun to bring him an odd sense of peace. How, as time ticked on, it almost seemed commonplace to be locked here. Normal. How it took a surprising little amount of time to get used to an eight-by-eight room.

A rippling shiver ran down Brent's spine.

No. You won't be here forever. You'll be released. You'll see the sky again.

He tilted his head back and opened his eyes to the cracked ceiling. Pressure mounted at his collarbones, as if someone had placed a hand there and was squeezing. He sprung from his spot and allowed himself to pace for a long while until the restlessness abated.

Head bowed, he moved to the dirty mattress, wrapping himself snuggly in the blanket before he lay down facing the wall. That one repetitive thought nagged at him again, the one that reminded him how he'd always prioritized himself and his work above others. Now that he was utterly alone, he realized how often he'd recklessly taken his relationships for granted.

A halting breath left his lungs. The more he stared at the grey concrete in front of his eyes, the more his vision lost focus. He began calling images of those he missed to his mind. The faces of his family flew through his brain initially, but then his body relaxed fully as flirty umber eyes, dusty-rose lips, and soft, silky hair dominated his experience.

·CHAPTER 23·

No matter how hard he tried not to, Nate kept thinking about what a perfect foursome they made walking the streets of his neighborhood. Colton was holding Elaine's hand but also trying to keep up with Addie, who was sprinting excitedly from house to house shouting "Trick-or-Treat!" at anyone who would listen. Colton wore a dinosaur costume like Addie—his a Stegosaurus to her Tyrannosaurus. As Elaine was dragged in front of him, Nate attempted to limit the time his eyes focused on her, but her outfit made that nearly impossible.

A homemade headband held green spikes starting at her forehead and ending at the ponytail at the nape of her neck. It was the perfect accent to her grey sweatshirt. The word "Mamasaurus" was screen printed inside the body of a green stegosaurus. Like him, she was wearing jeans and comfortable shoes to keep up with their excited children.

"Nice hat." Elaine grinned when she returned with the kids from the house they'd just plundered.

"Thanks." He'd purchased a ball cap with eyes on the top and teeth over the rim, making himself look a little bit like his tyrannosaurus daughter. "The headband and sweatshirt are a nice touch too." He grinned back while accepting the extended pail from his daughter.

Nate liked that they'd both independently made the decision to mirror their children's costumes.

"It's our first time trick-or-treating, and I wasn't sure if the parents dress up too." She looked uncertain as she glanced down, tugging at the hem of her sweatshirt.

You look absolutely perfect.

"I don't think you can ever go wrong with dressing up on Halloween," he said, a slow smile pulling at his lips.

Elaine blinked at his mouth, and he felt a sharp tug on his fingers as Addie ripped the thin jack-o'-lantern handle from his grip.

"Come on, Colt!" Addie grabbed her friend's arm next and dragged him toward a folding table set at the end of the next driveway.

Elaine's gaze followed the children, and he let a deep inhale of chilled Halloween air fill his lungs. It was the perfect night, cool but not too cold, the air lightly charged with the laughter of children happily in pursuit of sugar.

Now that they were alone, Nate wanted to ask her how she was doing with her mother being back in town. It'd been a week since she'd taken that staggered breath and confided in him. Her vulnerability had hit his chest, ripped the oxygen from his lungs, and left him empty. The impulse to gather her in his arms had been so overwhelming that forcing himself to stay still had been physically painful.

The only thing stopping him from asking now was the memory of how she'd rapidly transitioned to anger as she took off like a rocket, striding away from him. Nate didn't want to ruin the serene smile on Elaine's face as she watched their children run hand-in-hand.

When they caught up with their children, he asked, "Addie did you say 'thank you?'"

His daughter spun around with an "Oh ya," her fluffy tail whacking Colton in the shins as she said her thanks.

The older woman at the table called out, "I've got mulled wine for the adults if you want."

An unrestrained laugh broke free of Elaine's mouth, and Nate had to control the rate of his inhale. God, she had an amazing laugh.

"Sure." She took the outstretched steaming cup of wine the woman had just ladled from a slow cooker. "Nate?" She grinned at him, and he was unable to tear his eyes away from her upturned lips. "Do you want some wine?"

His answer was instinctual. "You don't have to ask. The answer's always 'yes.'"

Her lips raised higher at his words before she turned back to receive a second cup. The setting sun lit the sky in subdued pinks and oranges. Everything looked different than the bright, noisy mornings when he usually saw her, surrounded by reminders of work and responsibilities.

Nate tried not to jerk at the electricity crackling up his arm after his fingers brushed Elaine's when she handed him the disposable cup.

"Thank you," he said to the older woman. "Happy Halloween."

"Happy Halloween!" she replied. "I love your family costumes. It's so cute when everyone dresses up."

Nate had only known Elaine a month, but he didn't correct the woman. As he took a swallow of the cinnamon and clove spiced red wine, his body warmed from her assumption—of the four of them being a family.

"Oh, we're not—" Elaine began before the sound of crying stopped her speech.

Turning around, they saw Colton lying backward in the street, a teenage boy in a skeleton mask standing over him.

"Watch yourself, dino." He laughed and then stepped over Colton, leaving him sprawled out on the pavement. Two other teenage boys chuckled along with the skeleton as they sauntered off.

Elaine ran the short distance to Colton, dropping her orange paper cup in the grass on the way. She picked him up quickly, pulling down the headpiece on his costume and examining the back of his head as best she could in the dimming light of the evening.

Nate was at her side after setting his wine on the curb. "Is he okay?"

Colton held Elaine's neck tight, sniffling and rubbing his face into her shoulder.

"I think so." She rocked Colton, her hand firm on the back of his head as a fierce look crossed her face. "Can you hold him for a sec?"

"Of course." Colton wrapped his small arms around Nate's neck in the transfer.

"Daddy, is Colt okay?" Addie rubbed Colton's dangling foot in a sweet four-year-old attempt to make him feel better.

"I think so, sweetheart." He glanced at his daughter as the woman from the table came over.

"I've got Band-Aids in the house if you need them."

"Thank you, but I think it was just a bump," he said before noticing that Elaine was nowhere near them.

Searching the crowded street teeming with witches, Avengers, and princesses, Nate found the very angry mamasaurus. She was standing directly in front of the three teenage boys and had her pointer finger in the middle of the skeleton's chest.

"Addie, come on." He walked as fast as he could, holding Colton and dragging Addie over to Elaine.

"Who do you think you are that you think it's okay to knock over a four-year-old boy? You didn't even apologize or check to see if he's okay. What's wrong with you? What's wrong with all of you?" She was nearly shouting at the trio.

The skeleton grumbled, "Geez, sorry, lady."

"You think that's an apology?" Elaine swiped the mask from the boy's face and threw it on the ground. "Look at me when I'm talking to you!"

Several other groups of trick-or-treaters stopped to watch the altercation. Elaine was right in talking some sense into these miscreants, but she seemed to be losing her cool.

"Give her and her son an honest apology," Nate said sternly.

"I'm sorry," the teenager mumbled before looking at Colton. "I'm sorry."

"Don't pull that crap again." Elaine jammed her hands on her hips.

The skeleton grabbed his mask off the ground, and the three boys skulked off quickly, looking back over their shoulders periodically.

"Oh, bud." She took Colton back in her arms, hugging her son to her chest. "I'm so sorry. Do you want to keep going, or do you want to go home?"

Colton wiped his nose with his forearm. "I want more candy . . . but can I hold your hand the whole time?"

Elaine kissed her son's head and held him tighter. "I'll never let go." When she set him down, she adjusted his costume and took a firm hold of his hand.

After they started walking back in the direction they had come from, Nate remembered the wine on the curb and went to grab it. "Here." He pushed the cup into Elaine's free hand. "Have mine."

A slight lift pulled at her mouth, but it didn't reach her eyes. Her gaze flowed over Colton, darting from his head to their entwined hands and back. Nate's neck muscles pinched watching her obvious concern for her son, prompting him to rub at the back of his head.

They walked silently for a few houses, Addie bolting to the door and getting candy for both her and Colton. Colton held back, nervously clinging to Elaine's leg at the base of each house's front steps. At the fourth house, Colton pulled his mother to the door and smiled as he received a full-sized chocolate bar. Once that grin laced her son's lips, it was as if Elaine's whole body sighed. Nate felt her exhale as she finally relaxed, taking a sip from the paper cup in her hand.

Over the next block, Elaine relaxed even more, recounting an entertaining story about seeing a patient who'd dislocated his shoulder trying to jump over a low cinderblock wall. The man had been participating in a popular zombie race the previous weekend and had been attempting to evade a brain-sucking monster at the time of injury. The scheduling assistant had put "zombie attack victim" in the complaint section of their paperwork instead of "dislocated shoulder," which had made everyone in the clinic laugh.

When the kids' buckets were near overflowing and the sky had darkened fully, they headed in the direction of Nate's house. The few scattered stars peeked through the remaining stratus clouds dotting the sky as they walked home.

"I'm sorry." Elaine's voice quickly changed from the conversational tone she'd been using to a more serious one.

When Nate glanced over, her eyes were already on him. "Why?"

Her gaze flitted to Colton, but he was busy chatting with Addie about which type of candy they were going to eat first. Lowering her voice, Elaine said, "For blowing up at that kid.

He's just a teenager. I'm the adult. I shouldn't have behaved that way."

Her shame unexpectedly kicked him in the gut. "Elaine, you had every right to take him down a notch."

"I know. He shouldn't knock over a small child . . ." Nate watched her jaw clench tight before she exhaled loudly. "But I shouldn't have touched him. Sometimes . . . I just get a little overprotective of Colton."

Nate already knew this. He remembered distinctly a response just like this when they'd first met.

"It's okay," he said.

"I have to take care of him." Her eyes held a pleading quality, like she needed him to understand, like she needed someone else to validate her experience.

Nate's arm twitched at his side, but he pushed his free hand in his jeans pocket. "I know."

The skin around her eyes relaxed a little bit. Her lightly mascaraed lashes beat twice before her jaw loosened, and he heard her nasally exhale.

Perhaps it was inappropriate, but a sense of accomplishment flooded his veins, pushing to the pads of his fingertips and soles of his feet. His presence, his words, had made her feel better. It was probably completely false, but in that moment, he was going to live in the span of that fabrication. He was going to hang curtains, put a rug under the couch, and comfortably rest as long as he could in the idea that he could be good for her.

As they stepped up the sidewalk to his front door, the kids tore away running toward the porch.

Elaine stopped, and he felt his body mirror her motion.

"Thank you." She transferred Colton's plastic jack-o'-lantern to her other hand and lightly rested her fingertips on Nate's upper arm, watching her hand as she did so.

His throat squeezed at the motion, and he swallowed, unable to give the polite answer that was expected. He nodded instead as her eyes swept from her hand to his face and let him go, turning to follow the kids up the stairs. As Nate watched her walk away, he lingered with the sensation of connection that accompanied her touch and wondered if she'd noticed that slight pull too.

Nate firmly shook his head.

No. She was upset and thanking him for understanding her position as a single parent. That's all. It was just a friendly, grateful gesture. This was a platonic evening playdate, nothing else.

Digging his keys out of his pocket, he set a playful tone to his voice. "Who's ready for candy?"

"Me!" the kids yelled in chorus, jumping up and down until Nate could get his door open.

·CHAPTER 24·

Elaine tried to ignore how it felt as if she'd applied an active e-stim electrotherapy pad to the tips of her fingers when she'd touched Nate. Fortunately, her phone plunked out its text notification sound, giving her an excuse to lag back in the hallway as Nate followed their jubilant kids into the kitchen.

Curling her hand around her phone after she tugged it from her back pocket, unease surged through her belly. It had been more than a week since Brent had texted her, but karmically, it would make sense for him to finally respond to her now that this unexpected energy was rushing up her arm.

The message was from Jodi. She'd sent a bathroom mirror picture of herself dressed up and ready to go out for Halloween with the single crew. For someone who generally didn't like to stand out, she made a very attention-grabbing Jessica Rabbit. Elaine thumbed back a quick but emphatic message of approval before pausing and tabbing to the screen from Brent.

Radio silence.

After communicating at least every other day for weeks, he was obviously ghosting her. The drama with her mother must have been too much. Elaine let out a resigned sigh before archiving the conversation and continuing to the kitchen.

Both kids flitted around Nate's kitchen table as they waited for their parents to sort through the candy. Once the okay was given, Addie dug into her chocolate first as Colton opened a full-size sucker and happily popped it in his mouth.

Elaine smiled at her cheerful son, enjoying his lollipop-distorted grin. No matter what, she always had Colton.

Nate was settled in his spot leaning against the end of the island, watching the kids with a mirrored smile. She could have easily stayed near the table but found herself gravitating to his side.

They watched the kids in companionable silence for a few moments before she leaned over slightly, asking in a hushed voice, "How much candy are we supposed to let them eat? It's Thursday. They're going to have to go to bed soon."

She felt his body still before he answered just as quietly, "It's your choice. I usually try to keep it to about four or five pieces tonight and then have her set aside two to pack in her lunch for tomorrow."

"Good idea," Elaine said before moving to gather a handful of Colton's spilled candy, putting it back into her son's pail. "Pick out four more of your favorites to eat with Addie, and we'll save the rest."

"Kay." Colton selected the pieces he wanted to keep.

"You too, sweetheart," Nate told Addie.

Addie grumbled but did as she was told. Once the buckets of sugar had been removed from their tiny humans, Nate settled back against the island.

"Other than treating a zombie attack victim, did you have a good week?" The question was given in Nate's light and friendly way.

A laugh bubbled up before she said, "Yes, pretty good overall. Yours?"

"Same old, same old." He shrugged, moving to the far end of the kitchen. Though she'd often shared anecdotes from work, Nate never elaborated on his workday. "Would you like coffee? I'm going to brew a pot."

She felt her lips kick up with a teasing twist. "I thought we'd been through this. The answer's always 'yes.'"

That slow smile spread across his mouth as he searched in the fridge for the milk. He placed the plastic gallon jug on the island before stepping away to gather a spoon and a sugar bowl. Elaine examined the unfamiliar little ceramic jar filled to the brim with sugar, certain she hadn't used it last time.

The coziness of the kitchen, the promise of coffee, the sounds of children chattering away, and Nate remembering how she took her coffee without asking eased the remaining tautness from her muscles. A contented grin crossed her face before she heard the *plunk plunk* of her phone.

Sliding it out of her jeans, she anticipated another picture from Jodi. As much as Elaine missed getting all dolled up for Halloween, she was having a surprisingly good time doing the kid side of this holiday tonight.

Unlisted: *Elaine, hi. This is your mother. This number was on my dry house's caller ID, and I thought I'd try to get a hold of you this way. I'd like to be able to talk to you again if possible.*

Her teeth ground together as her grip tightened on her teal phone case.

Nate's cedar and soap scent preceded his presence at her side. "Everything okay?" His voice was low.

Elaine flipped her phone over and slapped it harder than she'd intended on the shiny counter surface. "Fine."

Nate didn't flinch, just silently took a step away and turned his attention to the coffee machine.

Suddenly her "fine" left a sour taste in her mouth, like she'd shouted an expletive at a bunch of toddlers. She wasn't fine— nothing had been "fine" since her mother walked back into her life.

Elaine pressed her hands firmly onto the cool granite to ground herself and allowed her eyes to close. She wasn't sure how long she stood there with her shoulders pitched forward, only that when she opened her eyes, Nate was wordlessly sliding a steaming mug in front of her. When he let go of the cup, she impulsively grabbed for his fingers, catching only three of them.

"I'm sorry," she began. Maybe her mother wasn't the problem. Maybe it was her. Her short, closed-off responses had evidently pushed Brent away, and now she was responding the same way to Nate.

Taking her gaze from the golden flecks dotting the hard surface, she raised her head and released his hand. "I didn't mean to snap."

His careful focus flowed from her eyes to her frowning mouth and back. "You don't need to apologize—"

"No, I do. It's just . . ."

She felt that if she finished that sentence, the muscles that held her ribs together would disintegrate. Then she'd be left without structure—open for all to see. Pushing her hand against her sternum, she dragged a breath into her lungs and forced the words out.

". . . my mother texted me."

Nate was silent as he waited, hip leaning on the counter, his soft eyes watching her.

"She wants to meet again, but I already met with her Sunday, and I didn't even want to do that. She needed—"

"Daddy. Can I have one more piece of candy, please?" Addie drew the last word out in her begging way.

"Absolutely, sweetheart. Have Colton get another piece too," he said, never taking his steady gaze off Elaine.

Somehow, she registered the kids' joyful cheers from behind her, but her attention was transfixed on the sunburst golden-brown part of Nate's irises.

He gave an encouraging nod.

Right, she'd been talking.

"She wanted to tell me about some family medical history that might be important for me and Colton." Elaine exhaled, letting her hand drop from her chest. There. She was still in one piece.

Nate allowed for a pause before adding, "I guess that's good information to know."

"It is." She nodded, moving to put a large spoonful of sugar in her mug. The metal clinked against the ceramic at irregular intervals as she stirred.

Nate took up his mug, blowing across the top.

"We just . . . we didn't have the best relationship when I left. It was more of a tense agreement between her and my older sister." She glanced to see him watching her again before she focused on pouring the right amount of milk. "I never emancipated, but I lived with my sister and her husband as a teenager."

Rose and Chuck had coordinated with her mother if something legal was ever needed and assisted Elaine in getting her driver's license when the time came.

The words kept coming as she stirred. "My mother tried to get her life together off and on for the next few years, but she always went back to the pills and alcohol. The last time she said she was sober was near the end of my senior year of high school, but she showed up to graduation drunk. When Chuck was given orders a month later, the three of us moved here, and I haven't seen my mother since."

"I'm sorry. I had no idea." Nate's warm, solid hand settled on her shoulder.

Moisture sprang to the edges of Elaine's eyes, and she pulled her gaze wide to prevent them from spilling. She set her spoon on the counter next to her mug, watching the bubbles swirl in slowing circles and memorizing the comforting touch of Nate's hand.

"It's okay," she whispered to her cup. It wasn't, but her brain couldn't think of anything else to say.

Nate gently removed his hand. "Is there anything I can do?"

At the motion, that same strange sense of loss she'd experienced after their dance around the kitchen returned, but this time it intensified to the point where she wanted to rub her back to try to alleviate the sensation. Everything in her felt itchy and tight, and she fought to control her inhale through her nose.

"No," Elaine said, picking up her mug with an unsteady hand before using her other one to secure it firmly. She pinned her shoulders back. "Thank you."

Addie ran up to them. "Daddy, can I have another piece?"

"No. You've had enough," he said. "You can pick out two pieces, and I'll pack them in your lunch tomorrow."

Elaine used the interruption to take a long draw from her coffee mug. The almost too-hot coffee singed her tongue, but right then the sting was welcome. It gave her something else to focus on. She inhaled the bitter coffee scent, holding the gulp in her mouth longer than warranted before its heat slid down her throat. Her eyes fluttered closed as she exhaled.

Finally feeling composed, she turned to face the table. "Colton, you can pick two, and I'll do the same for you."

Colton and Addie launched into a discussion about which candies they had, trying to select the same two pieces, so they would match at daycare tomorrow.

Elaine drank another large swallow of coffee and set down her mug before walking to her son. "Why don't you go potty, bud. We're going to have to head home soon." She unfastened the top to his costume.

"Kay." Colton half-ran/half-waddled with his Stegosaurus costume falling around his ankles on the way, fully revealing his blue striped undies.

"Hold up your—" The bathroom door slammed. "Never mind," she mumbled.

Addie stood giggling uncontrollably in the hallway, her hands over her mouth.

"Sweetheart, can you blow out the candles in the pumpkins on the porch?" Nate called from the kitchen.

"Did you see mine, Miss Elaine? It's a dino-sa-nor!" The little girl bounced in place.

Elaine had seen the Tyrannosaurus-carved jack-o'-lantern next to a traditional triangle smiley face pumpkin on the porch steps. She knew Nate must have carved both. Colton's help in carving the one in front of her door had been limited to seed removal.

"I did." She put on her excited mom voice and gushed, "You did a great job."

Addie's smile was luminescent. She flung open the front door, lifted the stem to a pumpkin, and blew furiously. Elaine's lips lifted as she watched. The zeal with which Addie took on a task always succeeded in making Elaine feel lighter.

Nate's low voice as he stepped close startled her. "I just wanted to tell you that if you ever need anything, I'm here for you. If you need me to watch Colton or if you ever need to talk . . . you can always call." His eyes reflected the good intent of his words.

Not trusting her voice, she nodded.

The bathroom door opened, spilling light into the hallway.

"Anytime." His gaze remained fixed on hers. "Really."

She pulled her eyes from Nate's to fasten the back of her son's costume as Addie came skipping back to them. "This was the best day ever," she squealed.

The kids did their jumping-holding-hands thing that always accompanied their excitement, and Elaine found herself smiling again.

When she glanced up at Nate, his gaze was already steady on her, and the look in his eyes made her breath catch. Awareness flushed quickly under her skin, warming her from within. Time stretched and yawned as if it could now expand in ways previously impossible.

Elaine was jolted from her reverie by the sound of two small bodies hitting the hardwood floor in laughter. Using the diversion, Elaine immediately crouched to help her son and Addie get up—their large fluff-filled tails made it harder for them. She stared at the stained oak hardwood floor for a beat before rising. "We should be going."

When she hazarded a glance, Nate looked just like his normal, friendly self.

"Of course." He grabbed Colton's plastic pumpkin and walked them to the door.

As the kids were doing their dramatic goodbyes, he said, "Thanks for coming out with us tonight. We had a great time."

"Yeah, so did we. Thanks for suggesting it."

"No problem." He handed her the candy bucket.

"See you later," she said, suddenly feeling awkward.

"Goodnight."

The kids shouted goodnight repetitively to each other as she and Colton walked down the front steps. When they reached the bottom, she glanced over her shoulder to find Nate still watching her before he quickly switched his attention to his daughter.

"Come on, Addie. Let's brush all that sugar off your teeth," he said, walking back into his house.

·CHAPTER 25·

"No, Daddy. You have to drink it like this." Addie lifted her littlest finger to display the proper way to sip the air that filled her plastic teacup.

"A thousand apologies, m'lady." Nate lifted his pinky away from the tiny purple cup.

Saturday mornings usually meant an unfairly early wake-up call from his bed-headed daughter but a traditionally lazy morning thereafter. They stayed in pajamas until they decided to go somewhere, which generally happened sometime midday.

After breakfast this morning, they'd settled into the playroom for Addie's high tea service.

"That's better." Her little lips smiled in approval. "Don't forget to eat your donut too."

Nate picked up the plastic toy donut and pretended to take a bite. "Did you make these yourself?"

"No." Addie giggled at the absurdity of his question. "Seratops did." She pointed to the stuffed triceratops seated next to him.

Some time this morning, Addie had crammed the dinosaur into one of the pink frilly dresses meant for a much smaller baby doll. Nate was about to comment on the reptile's cooking ability when his cell phone rang in the pocket of his sweatpants.

It was a local but unfamiliar number. "Hello?"

"Nate?"

The panic in Elaine's voice struck him first. Everything in him seized up as his breath sat trapped in his chest. "What—"

The words spilled out of her. "I need your help."

"Of course, anything." He bolted to his feet, unease rippling down his spine. "Are you okay?" Hearing the anxiety laced in his own words, he forced himself to exhale. She was probably fine. He was being reactionary. "Or do you need me to watch Colton for you?" He glanced at the clock in the playroom—just after eight o'clock.

Hearing her friend's name, Addie stopped feeding her stuffed dinosaur and asked excitedly, "Colt's coming over?"

Nate put a finger to his lips, listening for Elaine's response.

A ragged inhale came through the phone. "No. Not me . . . it's Colton. We're at the hospital. I need help here."

Before he knew it, he was up the playroom stairs and in his bedroom, pulling off his dirty T-shirt. "What's happening?"

"I don't know . . ." Her voice sounded like it was about to crack.

Nate's chest squeezed as he pulled a sweater over it.

"They took him to surgery, and no one is telling me anything." The end of that sentence came out in a growl.

Nate pulled at the base of his neck. "Where are you?"

She sighed. "In the surgery waiting room."

"Okay. I'm coming. I'll be there as soon as I can."

Elaine's "thank you" sounded defeated as she ended the call.

Nate quickly switched his sweats for jeans and was pushing his feet into a pair of shoes when Addie came bounding into his bedroom. "Change of plans, sweetheart. You're going to play at Nana's." He picked his whining daughter and carried her straight to the garage.

◊◊◊

Nate jog-walked down the hall to the second floor surgery waiting room. Elaine was pacing back and forth in front of the large floor-to-ceiling window like a caged animal. She had her thumbnail in her teeth and a deep frown creasing her forehead. When he started across the chair-laden room, she glanced up.

"Nate," she breathed his name as relief flooded her face.

She ran the last few steps and hit his body harder than he expected, almost knocking the both of them over.

As much as the force of her hitting his body was a surprise, shock ran through him when she curled into his chest. Things must *really* be wrong; he'd half expected to find her yelling at the hospital staff.

Immediately, he wrapped both arms around her, holding her as tightly as he could. "It's okay. It's going to be okay," he soothed—not knowing what was happening, or if it was, in fact, going to be okay.

Elaine's ragged breath warmed the skin beneath his sweater.

"Tell me what's going on."

She lifted her head to meet his gaze. "He woke up early this morning saying his stomach hurt. I thought it was my fault because I let him have carte blanche with the candy last night, figuring it was Friday, and we didn't have to be anywhere today. But when I touched him, he was hot with a fever. He kept crying about his stomach and wouldn't move, so I brought him here.

"The doctors did a bunch of tests and said he had appendicitis, which doesn't make sense because that's something that happens to teenagers, not little kids. They said they needed to take it out, so I signed all the paperwork, and they took him. That was two hours ago." At the last sentence, her voice broke. Her haphazardly pulled back ponytail made her dark brown eyes even more striking and vulnerable as they brimmed with tears.

"Okay." He rubbed the soft fabric of the navy pullover hoodie covering her shoulders. "Let me find someone to tell us what's going on."

"There's no one here." Her voice pitched with exasperation. "There used to be a woman at that computer, but I kept telling her to get me some answers. She said she would go check and didn't come back."

Nate assumed the woman was probably hiding from Elaine. "That's okay. I can—"

"I just want to see Colton." She trembled slightly in his arms, and a single tear dropped from her right eye. Elaine ducked her chin as she swiped at it, as if its presence on her face was painful.

Nate watched her struggle with the worry any parent experiences when their child's safety was out of their hands. He just needed to grab his phone from his front pocket, make a call, and he could get her the answers she needed. But she was clinging so tightly to him—the cables of his cream fisherman sweater were tangled between her fingertips.

And then there was the undeniable part of him that didn't want her to let go. Didn't want the vice grip of those slender hands to release. All he had wanted for weeks was to hold her in his arms, and now that she was there, his selfish body only hugged her tighter.

"Maybe since you're a doctor, can you go and find him? See if he's okay?"

Her innocent questions sent ice flooding through his veins.

Suddenly, all he heard was his father's voice in his head. *His* own voice in his head. Voices that haunted him for years—ones he was now working hard to quiet.

Failure. She needed you and you failed.

Where Elaine touched him suddenly felt as it was freezing to the point of pain. All of the expanded lightness he'd felt previously, that this incredibly strong and capable woman had chosen him to help, abated. Instead, an agonizing sensation seeped straight through his clothing until he could no longer stand the torment. He had to let go and step back.

A perplexed Elaine blinked at him, her hands still slightly curled as they slowly lowered to her sides.

"I'm not a doctor." Weariness pulled at every bone in his body. He'd failed Sarah because he didn't have the knowledge or skills to understand what had happened to her, but he could help Elaine find her son in *his* hospital. "But that doesn't mean I can't do something to help."

Nate turned away from her and strode toward the window, pulling his phone from his pocket. In two seconds, he found the contact for the medical director of pediatric surgery.

The man answered on the second ring. "This is Tanner."

He took a deep breath and switched to his professional self. "Tanner, it's Nate Brennan."

"Nate. Little early for work on a Saturday, isn't it? I'm on the links myself."

The sounds of others laughing and wind filtered through the phone. "Sorry to interrupt your game, but I was hoping you could do me a favor. I have a friend who's son is in surgery right now after coming through the ER, and she's not getting any answers as to what's going on. Could you see if there's another doc in your service in-house who could come answer some questions? I assume your on-call is operating right now. I'd really appreciate it."

Tanner didn't hesitate. "Sure thing. I'll check the schedule and find out for you. Are you in the surgery waiting room?"

He let his gaze fall over the sunny courtyard beyond the chilled pane window. "Yes."

"What's the child's name?"

"Colton Ritter."

"His last name is Myers." Elaine's voice said.

Nate spun, not knowing she was immediately behind him, and nearly knocked into her. Her eyes pinched in a mixture of confusion and hope as she searched his face.

He met her gaze and held it. "Colton Myers."

"Colton Myers, got it. I'll text you once I know who's headed your way. Hope your friend's weekend gets better," he said.

"Thanks again, Tanner." He hung up the phone and pocketed it. "A surgeon should come by and tell us what's going on soon. He's going to text me their name in a minute."

Elaine's face slacked. "Who's going to text you? Who were you talking to?"

"The director of pediatric surgery." His phone buzzed in his pocket, and he pulled up the text screen. "Abigail Nugent should be by to talk to us soon."

Nate's body blocked the sunlight from beyond the window, casting Elaine in shadow.

"So if you're not a doctor . . ."

"I'm a hospital administrator," he finished for her.

Nate waited and watched for the eventual disappointment to seep into her eyes. He was so used to seeing it that he'd like to think he didn't even notice it anymore. The way you stop noticing the paint color of the walls in your bedroom. But that was a lie. He noticed every time. Every time he saw it because for years he saw that same disappointment in his own eyes when he looked in the mirror.

"Of course." A snorty chuckle escaped her. "The *suits*. It all makes sense now." Her mouth pulled into a broad smile as she said a sentence that pinched Nate's brows. "That's even better."

"What?" The question escaped on its own.

"It's even better that you're an administrator. You can help me find him. You've already found someone to talk to me." Her hands opened in front of her as if her answer was obvious.

The next question slipped through his lips like the previous one. "You're not disappointed I'm not a doctor?"

She tilted her head. "Why would I care if you're a doctor?"

His mouth dropped open, but before he could formulate an answer, his name was called by a redheaded woman in a white coat. He was still processing Elaine's question when she spoke for him.

"Over here." Elaine waved to the surgeon.

By the time the woman with glasses was next to them, he'd collected himself enough to extend his hand. "Thank you for coming so quickly."

"No problem. I'm Dr. Nugent." She briefly shook his hand. "Tanner told me you needed some answers regarding a patient."

Elaine interjected again, "Yes. Colton Myers, my son."

"I didn't have a chance to check the chart before I came over. I thought I'd come talk to you first. Why don't you follow me over here. . ." She gestured to the open computer. "I'll see what I can find out in the system before I talk to the surgeon in the OR."

Dr. Nugent was typing her password into the hospital's electronic charting system when another doctor in green surgical scrubs began walking toward them.

"Mrs. Myers?"

"Yes." The word was an anxious breath dropped from Elaine's lips

Dr. Nugent looked up from the computer. "Oh, Simon, did you just finish on Myers? Tanner called me about getting the family some information."

The man in scrubs leaned against the high counter separating the computer from the rest of the waiting room. "Yeah, I just closed," he said before extending his hand to Nate and Elaine. "Dr. Bates. Pleasure to meet you. Let's have a seat, and I'll tell you how the surgery went."

When they were seated in the pale blue chairs across from the surgeon, Dr. Bates explained that by the time Colton got to surgery, his appendix had ruptured. The surgeon had needed to flood his belly with fluid and irrigate it to make sure it was fully cleansed.

"He also had a little bit of unusual anatomy in that the terminal portion of his ileum and cecum were slightly rotated. I tacked those so he wouldn't end up with a malrotation in the future," Dr. Bates continued.

"What does that mean?" Elaine asked.

"It just means that his intestines were a little rotated and potentially could cause a blockage in the future, so while I was in there, I fixed it. Had his appendix not ruptured, it might never have caused him problems, but once I found it, I needed to repair it.

"Overall, surgery went great, and they were starting to wake him up as I came out to talk to you. Once he's out of the PACU, he'll get a room on the peds floor. He'll need to stay overnight and finish the course of IV antibiotics, but if he's eating, walking, and not showing any signs of complications, you should be able to take him home tomorrow."

"Okay." Elaine's previously tense hands unfurled in her lap. "Thank you, doctor."

Dr. Bates leaned forward and rested his elbows on his knees. "You're welcome. Feel free to move to the pediatric waiting room, and the unit assistant will notify you when he's been transferred to the floor. I'll be here for the rest of the day, so if you have any questions, you can have the nurse page me."

He stood, prompting them to do the same.

Two other families filtered into the waiting room, speaking in hushed voices among themselves as Elaine turned to Nate. "I don't think I'll be able to relax until I can see that he's okay."

Even though the surgeon had just given her great news, Nate understood. Had it been Addie, he would want to see her breathing. "I can take you into the PACU if you want, but as the surgeon said, Colton might not be fully awake."

Elaine straightened, rolling her shoulders back. "I need to see him."

"Okay." He pulled his hospital badge from his pocket. "Then let's find him."

·CHAPTER 26·

A strong, crisp gust blew over the long grass, pushing the viridescent blades down in rippling patterns. Stiff brown leaves followed each blast, tumbling against the ground and then up again in sweeping circles. Elaine tilted her chin slightly up and to the left to catch the warmth of the sun's rays.

It was the prototypical perfect fall day. Cool enough to wear jeans and her favorite snug hoodie, but so gorgeously sunny that you just wanted to spend all of it outside. The remaining leaves clinging to the trees added an earthy music that mingled with Colton's giggles as he called for her.

She looked all around but couldn't see him. Where was he? Her heartbeat galloped under her breastbone as all of her muscles twitched.

"Mrs. Myers?"

Elaine's eyes flew open wide as a loud, halting breath rapidly drew into her lungs. Gone was the soothing scent of grass and soil, and replacing it was the ubiquitous smell of hospital-strength antiseptic. She stared at the ground, taking in the buzz of the halogen lights overhead with their harsh critical glow and the stick of her sneakers against the vinyl composition tiles.

Tightly gripping the armrests of the plastic chair, nausea rolled from her stomach and soured the back of her throat. Her breath only escaped her mouth when she found Colton's small body in the hospital bed beside her. A long plastic tube was still connected to the catheter in his arm, but otherwise he was sleeping soundly.

"Mrs. Myers?" The black-haired woman in a white coat tried again.

"What information do you have, doctor . . ." A grumbly half-asleep voice came from her left.

"Dr. Russo. Good morning." She held her hand out to Nate.

Elaine blinked at their interaction, speechless. Nate's crumpled body straightened as he leaned forward to shake the doctor's hand.

Numbly, her exhausted brain began functioning again, sluggishly running over the last twenty-four hours. She rubbed her forehead and then dragged her hand over her left cheek, feeling the impression Nate's sweater had left on her skin. It was his warmth that she'd felt in her dream.

He'd been here all night?

"I wanted to talk to you about Colton." The doctor's words fully woke Elaine.

"Is everything okay?" She'd have bolted out of her chair had she not been able to see her son's chest rising and falling evenly with every breath.

Nate's hand covered her tense one, his fingers fully blanketing hers, the tips resting lightly on the armrest. The tension in her toes slacked first, followed quickly by the fine muscles in the back of her hand. A flushed, overwhelming sensation flooded beneath her collar bones as she flipped her head to see his reassuring gaze catch hers. Elaine felt her body sag with an exhale before the doctor's words drew her focus.

"Colton's doing great. I wanted to talk to you about him going home today. He did a good job eating last night and walking around. If he continues to do that today, I can send him home after his last dose of antibiotics this afternoon.

"He's going to be in some expected discomfort from the surgery, so I'll be sending you home with some pain medication and a recommended dosage schedule. He's also going to have some antibiotics to take as well. The nurse will come in to go over the wound care with you, and our office staff will call tomorrow to schedule a follow-up to check on the incision. He'll need to take it easy for the next two to four weeks, but generally kids his age bounce back pretty quickly," Dr. Russo finished with a gentle smile.

"That's so good to hear," she said as a squeeze gripped her left hand.

"Do you have any questions?" The doctor tucked her hands in her coat pockets.

Elaine sat dazed, unable to come up with an answer. Too much had happened in such a short amount of time. All she wanted was to be able to wrap Colton in her arms— disconnected from a medical device—and take him home.

"Can she call the office if she thinks of any questions in the future?" Nate asked.

"Absolutely." The doctor nodded. "And one of us is always on call, so a page can be sent through the answering service after hours, though when in doubt just head to the ER."

"Okay," Elaine managed to say, though the idea of taking Colton to the ER again sent a tremor through her muscles.

"I'll check back this afternoon," the doctor said, before stepping out of the room.

Colton stirred, and Elaine leaned over the bedrail, stroking his hair as his eyelashes fluttered. "Hey, bud," she whispered, liquid collecting at the edges of her vision.

Colton's soft blue eyes opened. "Hi, Mama," he said as he rolled toward her and winced.

"Are you hurting?"

He nodded to the bed rail. "Uh-huh."

"I'll get the nurse," she said, before she felt Nate's hand gently grip her upper arm.

"I'll get her. Stay with Colton." His voice was so soft Elaine couldn't have formulated a "thank you" without spilling tears.

After a dose of pain medication and a little time, Colton felt good enough to eat another simple meal for breakfast and walk around the pediatric unit. After lunch, the nurse gave him his last dose of IV antibiotic and removed the catheter from his arm. He started looking more and more like her active little boy instead of a hospital patient. Soon, Elaine was receiving discharge instructions and dressing him in the pajamas he'd worn to the ER.

As the transporter pushed Colton's wheelchair to the hospital exit, Nate asked, "Are you okay to drive home, or do you want me to drive you?"

"I can drive." She shifted the large paper bag filled with medications and dressing supplies in her arms.

"Then I'll come with you to get him settled." He took the surprisingly heavy bag from her.

Exhaustion raked through every fiber of her being as she tried to think of the appropriate response. To tell him that it was too much trouble after he'd already helped her so much, or that his car would be left parked at the hospital if he came with them, or that she was fine on her own, that she could handle this herself. In the end, she said nothing and nodded instead.

Colton was quieter than normal on the ride home, and she could only imagine how exhausted he must be from the whole ordeal. She kept flitting her gaze between his face in the mirror and the road. She wanted nothing more than for Dr. Russo to be right—for him to heal quickly so he wouldn't feel this pain for very long.

After she parked her car in her assigned spot, she collected their things, and Nate gently picked up Colton and carried him to her apartment. Silently working in tandem, she took Colton to his room for a nap while Nate unpacked the bag from the hospital. Colton hadn't napped since he was three, but he snuggled against her as she wrapped her body around his and almost instantly fell asleep. After listening to his steady breathing for a few minutes, Elaine gently slid off his twin bed and quietly closed the door behind her.

Nate was pouring coffee into cups for them, but she was distracted by what he'd set out on the counter. He'd used the grocery list paper to write out the prescribed dosing schedule for Colton's antibiotics and pain medication. Little check boxes drawn beside each time were organized under every day of the week in Nate's neat handwriting. She picked up one slip of paper as he placed a mug of coffee in front of her.

He pointed to the list. "I wrote out all the dosing times for you. You can come up with your own system, but I found this one works for me. Addie had a lot of ear infections when she was younger, and I learned you have to stay on a schedule with the antibiotics."

"That makes sense. Thank you for doing that. Colton's never had to take any medication before, except Motrin for a fever here and there, so I wouldn't have thought of this." She ran her free hand over her forehead as she set the list next to her mug.

Caramel-colored coffee swirled in an ever slowing circle in the pink "Best Mommy Ever" mug Jodi had helped Colton buy last Mother's Day. Wrapping both hands around it, she brought the liquid to her lips and sampled it. The bitterness of the coffee had been softened with the addition of milk and the perfect amount of sugar. It tasted as if she had made it herself.

As the small sip rolled over her tongue, flowed down her throat, and warmed her stomach, it dawned on her that Nate had been the person she'd called first when her world had turned completely upside down. Not only had he helped her navigate the hospital system, he'd slept in an uncomfortable chair overnight to make sure Colton was okay. To be there for *her*. Even now, after perfectly preparing her coffee, he was sorting her son's medications on her kitchen counter.

"Let me know if you need help persuading him to take them. I came up with some pretty good tricks over the years, though I doubt he'll give you any trouble. He's such a good kid." He lifted a bottle to examine the label. "And it looks like they already flavored these. That helps."

Setting down her coffee, she turned to face him. "Nate."

He placed the bottle on the counter, glancing at her before seeing the solemnity on her face and stilling.

"I can't thank you enough for what you've done for me and Colton." She paused. "I can't start to think of how I can make it up to you. I mean, where's Addie right now? Who's watching her? You took so much time to be with us—"

"Addie's fine," he interrupted, fully turning to her. "She's with my parents. They spend weekends together all the time. Don't worry about her. And you don't need to make it up to me. I was happy to help. Happy to be able to help. There's nothing you need to do except take care of Colton."

She nodded, staring at the notches and whirls of the fabric over his chest. "I don't think I could have done this without you." Her words were a whisper.

"Yes, you could have." His voice rang with certainty. "You'd have been fine. I was only able to get you a little bit of information a few minutes before you were going to be told it by the surgeon anyway. And by the time we got to PACU, Colton was ready to be transferred to Peds."

Elaine shook her head. "You knew the right questions to ask and thought of them when my brain couldn't function. I mean, I work in healthcare, and I froze up."

"You were trying to process your son being hospitalized for the first time. Everything you did was exactly what I would have done had it been Addie instead of Colton," he countered.

Elaine felt something open inside of her, like how the first petals of a flower cautiously press away from the center, causing the rest of the delicate layers to follow suit.

"And then you stayed," she said, her voice low again.

A quiet expanded between them, and she watched his chest rise and then fall before she lifted her gaze.

His eyes darted over her face. "You seemed like you needed . . . that you wanted . . ."

She heard the word he didn't say—"me."

"I did," she said, pausing. "I do." The truth sounded clear as it rang through her throat, out of her mouth, and into the silent air of her small kitchen.

Elaine felt the shift instantaneously as her gaze dropped from his eyes to his lips to the notch between his collarbones. He stepped ever so slightly closer to her, and she felt herself leaning forward, her breath quickening.

"Elaine?"

"Yes." The word came out in a raspy, half whisper.

"Can I kiss you?"

When her eyes flitted to his, he didn't have the furrow in his brow like when they'd been this close before. Instead, his gaze held an intensity that made her skin flush under its attention.

Her nod set a slight upward tug on the corner of his mouth before it slacked when she sucked her bottom lip between her teeth. His nose unhurriedly skated down her face, and she tilted her chin in anticipation. When he brushed his lips against hers, the movement was so slight it could've almost been mistaken as an accident. A sharp inhale pulled oxygen into her lungs as her hands found and clung to his biceps.

Normally, this would be when she would push, where she would take control, but as much as that needy pulsing in her wanted to discover the taste of his mouth, a quieter part of her whispered, *Wait*.

His hands gripped her waist as he pushed firmer against her mouth before retreating to barely touching again. When the air from the room tingled her wet lips, her soft sigh was an audible protest. She felt his smile before his tongue dove into her mouth with all the pressure and possession her body craved.

A pliable moan escaped her as Elaine softened into his demanding kiss. It was familiar and novel at the same time. He tasted like coffee and smelled undeniably like Nate, but the heat from his fingers seeping through the thin fabric of her hoodie sent a new, aching awareness crackling through all her muscles. The pleasure of his lips on hers made all the stress over the last two days evaporate until she felt boneless.

Her knees unexpectedly dipped on their own, and his firm grip caught her weight.

Nate gasped as he pulled his face away from hers, resting his forehead at her hairline. His breath was hot over her lips. "I'm pressing you too much with everything you've been though. I've just wanted— I'll stop— I'm sorry." His eyes were pressed tightly together.

Disappointment crept into her husky words. "You're sorry?"

Raising his head, his eyes flickered open, scorching her with their simmering heat as they flowed to her mouth. "Actually, I'm not."

Electricity quickly radiated from the base of her spine, up her back, and down her arms until her fingertips stung with it. She'd decided her move before a single muscle fiber twitched. The placement of the parts of her body against his would be similar, but the intent behind it would be completely different because Nate wanted *her*. Not the super sexy version of her that he'd never seen, but the ordinary, everyday version.

"Good, because neither am I." Elaine's hands roughly drove up over his shoulders, weaved into his short hair, and squeezed his scalp as she brought his mouth quickly to hers.

A small surprised breath escaped his lips before he gave into the needy flick of her tongue. The hesitant grip that held her waist tightened to a greedy one as his hands splayed wide. She could feel his breath growing more urgent, the speed of his kisses becoming more ardent. Clutching the nape of his neck, she pushed her body firmly to his, and a groan met her lips. Only one word reverberated through her bones as a response to that sound—*Yes*. Nate's hands found her hips with a hard grip and she leaned again, pulling and pushing at the same time.

Then he surprised her by kissing her with an unrushed stroke of his tongue as his fingers applied a gentle pressure, slowly separating their bodies. Her eyes fluttered open under a twinged brow. Questions burned in her mouth instead of the sensation of his tongue touching hers.

His chest heaved as he spoke. "A lot has happened in the last forty-eight hours. With all the stress you've been through, maybe this isn't the best time. I don't want you to think I'm taking advantage of you."

"I don't think that." Her breath was ragged as it escaped her lips.

"Good." His gaze was intense again.

Elaine suddenly wanted nothing more than to wrap her legs around his firm torso. She'd never had a man stop kissing her because he was worried about her. She'd never had anyone care like this.

She'd just decided she was definitely going to jump into his arms when she heard a muffled call from Colton's bedroom.

Nate turned his head at the sound, delicately releasing her hips. Not ready to untwine her hands from behind his head, she let out a quick sigh before she called over his shoulder, "I'll be right there."

Her gaze flowed to his radiant hazel eyes before she exhaled all the oxygen in her body, nestling her forehead between his neck and shoulder.

Nate hesitated only for a second before his arms wrapped around her.

"I need to take care of Colton," she said, sliding one hand down to his chest, tracing the woven pattern of his sweater. "Can we try this another time? Maybe not right after my son's appendix has just burst?"

Her hand rose and fell erratically as a low, throaty chuckle escaped Nate's mouth. She tilted her face up, a silly zing of happiness radiating through her body.

Then he stole her breath with that slow smile of his. "You don't have to ask. The answer's always 'yes.'"

·CHAPTER 27·

Nestling herself at the middle computer between Leslie and Finn, Elaine logged into the hospital system. It was her first day back after she'd taken ten days off to care for Colton. The last two days when he'd been almost back to his normal self, he'd begun begging her to go back to daycare. This morning, as he'd half-run through the glass double doors, her heart had felt like it was beating outside of her chest.

While the slow computer booted up the hospital charting system, Elaine went to the break room in search of a second cup of coffee. Opening the fridge, she pulled out the small paper milk container she'd bought from the cafeteria before filling her travel tumbler from the office carafe. The sight of caramel coffee swirling brought a smile and the memory of coffee-flavored kisses.

Since the surgery, Nate had texted every day to see how Colton was doing and to ask if she needed anything. So used to doing everything by herself, she'd initially answered "no" before letting him bring some additional dressing supplies and Addie to see her BFF Wednesday after work.

When she'd opened the door, her hands had spontaneously flexed and then extended at the sight of the strong line of Nate's jaw softening into that smile. She'd wanted nothing more at that moment than to press herself to him, but Addie briefly hugging her knees before looking for Colton reminded her they weren't alone.

Luckily, they *had* been able to sneak a sweltering kiss after he'd brought these incredibly delicious gourmet sandwiches for lunch on Saturday while Addie and Colton played in his room. For the first time, Elaine found herself the one always wanting more. Nate had fed her incredibly well, bringing all sorts of easy-to-reheat but delectable dishes each time he visited, but she had an insatiable hunger for something else entirely.

Elaine's fingertips traced her lips as she stared blankly at the large tea tin Leslie always kept on top of the microwave. Blinking hard, she let out a firm exhale to regain focus and made herself return to the therapy office.

Swallowing a large gulp of coffee, she glanced over her schedule for the day and froze.

There must have been a mistake.

Listed for her first appointment was patient Rita Ritter. Quickly, she checked the DOB to confirm that it was, in fact, her mother.

Dx: Low Back Pain. Evaluate and Treat. New Patient Intake.

Adrenaline shot through her veins as a building pressure constricted her ribs.

A humming Glen leaned his head into the room with a "Good morning, everyone" before continuing down the hall.

"Uh, Glen." She chased after him as he continued toward the small supervisor office.

He turned with a grin. "What can I do for you, Elaine?"

Internally, she yelled "Your job!" But honestly, she didn't want him to do his job. She wanted him to leave so *she* could do his job officially instead of squirreling away fixing things after he'd left a complete mess.

Drawing in a steadying breath, she asked, "Why is my mother on my schedule this morning?"

"Why wouldn't she be?" He seemed genuinely confused. "You're the spinal specialist, and she has back pain."

The sound of her forceful nasal exhale bounced off the walls of the hallway. "Because treating family members is a conflict of interest and against Edwards Memorial Hospital's policies," she said, struggling to keep her tone professional.

"Uhh . . ." His mouth gaped open.

This is ridiculous.

"You know what? Never mind." She spun around. "I'll ask someone to swap with me."

Luckily, she found Leslie in the therapy office dipping a tea bag into steaming water. Finn's computer was empty, a half-eaten bagel resting on a paper towel.

"Oh good, you haven't started." She slumped into the chair next to her coworker. "I need your help."

Leslie gave an exhausted look. "What did Glen do now?"

"He scheduled my mother as my first appointment."

"Okay, yeah, conflict of interest. I've got it. My first one is a rotator cuff surgery rehab. What's she here for?" Leslie clicked open the clinic schedule for the day and opened Rita's chart.

"Back pain." Elaine tried to keep her voice even, but it cracked slightly.

Leslie's concerned eyes flitted over her shoulder as she lowered her voice. "What aren't you telling me?"

Elaine wasn't going to do this. She wasn't going to get into this at work. Her mother had thrown her entire personal life into jeopardy, but Elaine was not going to let her ruin her professional one. Especially not now when she was so close to being able to interview for the supervisor position.

Elaine smoothed her voice out. "We're not close."

"Okay." Leslie surveyed her face again before attempting at humor. *"Thanks, Glen."*

"Tell me about it," she scoffed with an eye roll.

Because her mother was scheduled for an intake appointment, Leslie had Rita back in a treatment room for most of the hour. Meanwhile, Elaine had the most pleasant older gentleman as a patient. He was a retired university music director who now conducted a local concert band. Unfortunately, his surgery had been on his dominant arm.

After they completed his therapeutic exercises in the gym, she set him up in a treatment room to relax with a modality. She decided to use ice because she had really tested his strength and range of motion during his session.

Stepping from the treatment room, Leslie caught her in the hall.

"Hey," her colleague said softly. Elaine braced herself for whatever would come out of her mouth next. "I don't think your mom needs to be here. I know you aren't close, but I think she's only here to see you."

Rita had texted a few times and called even more often, but Elaine had ignored every message. In her mind, things between them were done.

"She said she was willing to stay in the treatment room until you're ready."

Elaine clenched her teeth. Her mother was going to take up space that was needed for people who actually required treatment. Naturally, all she could think about was herself. Nothing had changed.

"I'll take care of it," she clipped out.

After quietly shutting the treatment room door behind her, Elaine rounded on her mother. "You need to leave. Now." She kept her harsh voice low.

Rita was perched on the edge of the blue padded treatment table with her purse in her lap. "Elaine—"

"No," she interrupted. "There's a reason I didn't call you back. I don't want anything to do with you. I don't care that you're sober *now*. You weren't when it counted." Her throat tightened against her will.

Rita sighed, looking at her hands. "I know. I know I failed you in many, many ways. I know I didn't take care of you. I know I didn't keep you safe. And there's not a day that goes by that I don't feel incredibly remorseful for what I did to you . . . for what I did to your sister—"

"Good," she spat out, feeling her shoulder's rise.

Her mother chuckled.

She *chuckled*.

"The ironic thing is that I didn't get the back surgery because I didn't want it to ruin us. I didn't want the bills to get over our heads and for us not to be able to pay for rent, or food, or for you girls to have to switch schools to live in a cheaper neighborhood. I dealt with the pain because I thought I was doing the best thing for you and Rose. I always wanted to do the right thing for the two of you, but then it all went horribly wrong.

"I'm not going to try to rationalize my addiction and all the ways I failed you. I know that means nothing. I just want you to know I'm never going back to being that person again, and I'd like to have a place in your life." She paused. "And in your son's."

Elaine felt like someone had thrown a forty-pound dumbbell at her chest—all the air left her body.

"Your apartment is covered in children's drawings," her mother explained. "And there was a portrait of you and him on the wall."

Why hadn't she thought of this? Her house naturally looked like a four-year-old lived there because he did. His drawings were taped to the walls, his kiddie cup was always waiting on the kitchen table, and his toys were scattered around the living room.

"*No.*" Venom infused through the word as her body trembled.

Her mother deflated with an exhale.

"You're not to come anywhere near him. Do you understand?" Her pointing finger shook.

"Elaine—"

"We're done here." She flipped to open the door.

"I got the back surgery."

Those words had her pausing, hand hovering over the door knob.

"After being sober for a year, my sponsor and my pastor at church crowd-funded the money for it. I've been pain-free ever since. I even did the recovery with just the physical therapy and ibuprofen. I'm never going to be that woman again. I'm here because I want to make up for what I lost, and what I did to you. I hope that you'll give me a chance."

Elaine found herself waiting a beat before silently turning the doorknob and letting herself out of the room.

◊◊◊

It had been difficult for Elaine to mentally put away the interaction with her mother and finish out the work day. Her mind kept flashing back between her younger years, feeling loved and safe even though they hadn't had much, and the undeniable fear and uncertainty she'd experienced in her teenage years. By the time she finished with her last patient, indignation had won.

For the first time in a long time, things were finally right—Colton was healing quickly and getting stronger every day, her career goals were on track, and she was spending time with an incredible man who cared about her *and* her son. Elaine wasn't going to let her past or her mother poison the good things she had now.

As she helped Colton out of the car, nervousness threaded through her that her mother might be waiting outside her apartment, wanting to talk to her again. Fortunately, she only found her neighbor, Walter, shuffling around their sidewalk porch.

Elaine stopped massaging her tired hands and watched as the older man leaned onto his cane, placing his hand on his lower back.

His wrinkled face brightened from under his grey flat cap when he saw them. "Well, if it isn't my favorite neighbors."

A chuckle escaped her. "We're your only neighbors."

"That's not true. The hooligans who live above me, I do not particularly care for." He glared at the second story of their building. It was not the first time she'd heard him complain about his upstairs neighbors. Luckily, she had two light-footed flight attendants who were rarely home above her.

"Hi," Colton said quietly.

"Hello there." Walter winked at her son before wincing slightly.

Elaine fully assessed her neighbor. The fact that he had kyphosis hadn't escaped her, but she'd never seen him hurting before. As he hunched over his cane, he rubbed his back again. "Does your back hurt?"

Walter straightened with effort. "No. I'm fit as a fiddle." His eyes crinkled as he smiled. "Fit as a seventy-five-year-old fiddle."

Elaine gently laid one hand on his thick flannel shirt in front of his shoulder and the other on his mid-back. "Do you know what I do for a living?"

"Can't say that I do. Do you know what I did for a living?" He attempted to gruff, but his words landed softly.

Another unexpected chuckle escaped her lips. "No, I guess not. I'm a physical therapist. I can give you exercises to help with this . . ." She patted the top part of his spine that was an exaggerated curve. ". . . which will help with your pain here." She delicately touched his lower back and then stepped away.

Walter was silent for a moment, shifting his cane from one hand to the other. "Nothing wrong with exercise."

Elaine assumed this was as close as she was going to get to a "yes."

"Why don't you come in, and I can show you some posture techniques and strengthening exercises you can do that will help relieve your pain." She unlocked her door.

"I suppose I have a few minutes." He took out his own keys and locked his front door. "You can never be too careful."

Colton headed inside and put his backpack on the hook by the door. The scent of creamy roasted chicken reached her nose, and she was grateful she'd started dinner in the slow cooker this morning.

When her son picked up his figurines and splayed himself on the carpet like there had never been an incision on his belly, radiant joy bathed her tired muscles, and she took a deep, satiated breath.

Turning, she found Walter hovering just inside her door. "Come on." She urged him over. "Sit down and let's get started. We're going to check your alignment first."

·CHAPTER 28·

Nate tossed his jacket and tie on the empty backseat before releasing the rigid grey clips to free his bouncy daughter from her car seat. "Stay next to me while I grab dinner."

"Yes, Daddy." Addie hugged her stuffed triceratops and spun in tight circles between his 5-Series BMW and the adjacent minivan.

After retrieving the lasagna pan from the passenger floorboard, they walked up the sidewalk pathway. Addie bounded excitedly as he tried his best not to do the same.

"Would you knock for me, sweetheart? Daddy's hands are full."

Addie beamed at him, knocking hard on the door four times with no intention of stopping.

"That's enough," he said.

Elaine opened the door a crack before pulling it back wide. "*Nate.*" The way her face lit up made his entire day. "What a great surprise."

Addie immediately bolted inside searching for Colton, and Elaine grinned at her as she passed.

"I brought dinner." He noticed the scent of chicken and rosemary coming from inside her apartment. "Unless you already made dinner. In that case, I brought tomorrow's dinner."

"What is it this time? Rack of lamb with all the trimmings?" A flirty twist pulled at her lips.

"No, just lasagna."

Elaine raised her eyebrows. "I'm sure it's not 'just lasagna.' If it's like everything else you've brought, it's probably the best lasagna I've ever tasted."

A grin tugged at his mouth. His version included mandoline-sliced roasted vegetables and a Béchamel sauce, which did make it a little more involved than the typical recipe.

Elaine's gaze fell to his lips, and she leaned in as if she was going to kiss him but bumped into the pan in his arms. When her chest made contact, she tilted her head back to laugh at herself, and Nate savored the lightness streaking through his veins.

All of a sudden, she took a deep inhale like she'd forgotten something. "I'll be right back. I left Walter on my bed."

All the light in him extinguished as he coughed out, "Who?"

"My seventy-five-year-old neighbor who I'm treating for back pain," she said in an entertained tone. "It's easier for him to do shoulder flexion lying down."

He exhaled. "Oh."

As Nate was setting the lasagna down in the kitchen, Elaine walked past with an elderly gentleman using a cane. The man noticed Addie on the floor with Colton before he saw Nate in the kitchen. Elaine made introductions, and when Nate clasped the older man's hand, he had the feeling that he was being deeply scrutinized.

Once she'd closed and locked the door, Elaine found him trying to make space in her refrigerator for the large pan. "I didn't think I'd see you until tomorrow's class." Her smile was so large it made his brain sing with triumph.

"I thought we'd surprise you with dinner and some company. I hope that's okay." He finished rearranging things and closed the refrigerator.

Elaine glanced over at the kids who were playing with Colton's plastic dinosaurs by the couch before her eyes fixed deviously on his. Placing both hands on his chest, she pushed him against the wall next to the refrigerator, efficiently blocking them from their children's view.

When she raised her face, he met her halfway, wrapping his arms around her waist and enjoying the first kiss they'd snuck since Saturday. As they deepened the kiss, her hands reached up and pulled hard on his shirt collar. Resisting the urge to slide his hands down over her slacks and pick her up, he tightened his grip around her body. When she eventually pulled away, she straightened his collar and slithered her hands slowly down in a way that made him want to shiver.

"I'm glad you're here." Her flirty eyes glinted up at him.

He loosened his arms a little but didn't let go. "Me too."

"Daddy."

Both of them quickly dropped their hands as Elaine stepped back.

"Yeah, sweetheart." He ducked his head around the refrigerator.

"I'm hungry." She jumped to her feet.

"Me too." Colton got up, but slower and with intention.

"I'll have dinner ready in five minutes," Elaine said.

Addie grabbed Colton's hand and pulled hard toward his bedroom. "Let's play in your room." His little body jerked with her movement, and a slight grimace flashed across his face.

"Addison Grace," Nate said sternly. "Be gentle with him. Remember he's still recovering."

"Oh ya," Addie whispered. She looked down before giving Colton a soft hug. "Saw-dee."

"It's kay." Colton hugged back. They smiled at each other before heading to his room, quickly moving on with their play.

"I'm sorry about that." He looked back at Elaine who was taking a steam-bag of broccoli out of the freezer and putting it in the microwave. "She gets overexcited at times."

"Nate." She punched in the numbers. "I know who Addie is. You don't have to apologize for her. It was a simple mistake. Besides, Colton is happier when he's with her."

Nate waited for that statement to be applied to him, but she turned back to the refrigerator and grabbed a gallon of milk to pour into the two plastic cups on the counter.

Unbuttoning and rolling up his shirt sleeves, he asked, "What can I help with?"

After dinner, the kids went back to playing in Colton's room, and the two of them lingered over empty plates and a bottle of Chardonnay that had paired surprisingly well with weekday creamy chicken and broccoli.

"I was thinking about Saturday—" Elaine began.

"Yeah, me too." Nate liked that she'd also assumed that they would be together this weekend. "Do you think he'd be up for a trip to the zoo? Or would that be too much walking? I could always put him on my shoulders if he got tired."

A burst of giggly laughter floated from Colton's open door and Nate grinned. It was good to see Colton getting back to himself so quickly.

"I was thinking more that we should have our first date, and maybe Addie should spend the night with your parents." Elaine's voice was so sultry that all the hair on his arms stood up as his head snapped back in her direction.

The smile on her face could only be described as delicious, and he wanted nothing more than to taste, savor, and run his tongue over those lips. God, she was so incredibly sexy. Every once in a while when they were alone, this sensual confidence radiated from her that nearly short-circuited his brain.

When he was once again able to form a coherent sentence and have it logically come out of his mouth, he said, "Saturday. I'll make it happen."

"Can't wait." The temptress that she was, she stood, casting a flirty glance over her shoulder as she walked away from him.

She'd barely set the dishes she was holding in the sink when he pinned her against the kitchen wall. A quick gasp filled her lungs before he finally got the taste he'd been craving. As her incredible scent overwhelmed him, his usual order, logic, and restraint all fell away. He was demanding in a way he'd never been, but Elaine pushed back just as hard.

Her fingers weaved through and tugged his hair, and the sensation was immeasurable. The heat and pressure of her body against his was another incomprehensible topic altogether. His imagination worked in overdrive, picturing what it would feel like to finally make love to her.

Only her shoving at his shoulders pulled his mind back to hear hard little footsteps coming their way. Nate released her just in time.

"Colt says his tummy hurts," his daughter said when she came around the high kitchen counter.

A muffled curse word dropped from Elaine's lips as she strode past him.

Colton leaned against the doorway to his room with his hands on his belly.

"I'm sorry, bud." Elaine pushed back the hair on his forehead. "Let's get you your medicine."

Nate told Addie to start cleaning up the toys in Colton's room and took over cleaning the kitchen. When Elaine returned, he was finishing the last of the dishes.

"Is Colton okay?" He put the slow cooker bowl on the drying rack next to the sink.

"Yes." She let out an exhale and leaned against the counter beside him. "He takes Motrin every night when we get home, but I got distracted and forgot."

"It happens." He dried his hands on the towel in front of him.

"It shouldn't happen." Her jaw was tight. "I should be better. He shouldn't be in pain because of *me*."

"Hey," Nate said gently, placing both hands on her shoulders. "You missed a dosage by a few minutes, an hour tops. He's going to be okay. He *is* okay."

"I should be better," she muttered, looking at his feet.

His knuckle found her chin and lifted it until she looked him in the eye. "Elaine, you are amazing. The way you handle yourself and take care of Colton is incredible. The only thing you could stand to improve on is not beating yourself up when you make a mistake."

She blinked at him but said nothing, and he found himself wrapping his arms around her. He took a deep breath and kissed her forehead. "We're going to head out and let you guys relax."

"You don't have to." Her eyes closed as a serene look washed over her face.

Nate could have spent the rest of his evening in the easy, intimate space they'd created. The comfort he felt next to her was one he hadn't felt in so long that his body was weary from longing for it. Stepping back with great difficulty, he let go of her.

"I'll see you Saturday. What time can I pick you up?"

"How about six?" She grinned slowly at him, a little of her fire sparking back into her eyes.

"Perfect."

Once Addie had been gathered, Elaine pulled open her front door to let them through. On the threshold stood a brunette woman with her hand raised to knock.

"Oh . . . hi," she said, eyes wide.

"Hey," he said, stepping past her while holding Addie's hand.

"Hi, Auntie Jo." Colton gave a small wave with his smile.

Everything clicked. This must be Elaine's sister. The one that she lived with when her mother was too high and drunk to take care of her as a teenager. The one whose husband's job had moved them here.

His friendly grin widened as he held up his right hand. "I'm Nate."

The woman's face lit with recognition. "*Nate.* So nice to meet you. I'm Jodi."

Internally, he cheered that she had heard of him. His eyes flicked to Elaine's as an unusually shy smile tugged at her lips.

Jodi clasped her hands together in front of her cream blouse. "Well, I just wanted to check on my cutie now that I'm back in town." Her eyes shifted to Elaine as a shadow of sincerity weighed on her features. "I'm sorry I wasn't here to help you when he was in the hospital."

Nate realized in that moment that Elaine had called him for help because her family had obviously been out of town. It made sense she would call family first, but coming to him second had to mean something.

"Don't worry about it," Elaine said to her sister before grinning at him. "We were in good hands."

The look in her eyes took the breath from him. It was more than gratitude. It was trust and complete faith—like nothing bad could happen to her when he was around. Even though he already towered over both women, he felt like he was two feet taller.

"We'll let you two catch up," Nate said. "It was nice to meet you, Jodi."

"Same." She smiled warmly before dropping to crouch in front of Colton and give him a gentle hug.

"So, I'll see you . . . later." He left out the day in case Addie would figure it out, assuming Jodi would be watching Colton that night.

Elaine's eyes flickered as she nodded. "Later."

Nate swallowed hard. Saturday could not come fast enough.

·CHAPTER 29·

"They'll be here any minute. Maybe they had car trouble. You know Two seems like the type to forget to fill the tank until the last minute." Brent rubbed his upper arms, trying to produce some warmth against the damp coolness of the dank basement room.

By his estimate, he'd been awake for three hours. It was difficult to truly approximate the time since the light was even more subdued today. The sun outside must be hiding behind a clouded sky. It had been three weeks, roughly, since he'd seen the sky, and at this point, he missed it almost as much as he missed human interaction.

Brent hadn't understood how much he'd relied on his morning routine. How he'd depended on them bringing his early breakfast with the same heavily accented sentence for a sense of normalcy. The abrupt change this morning had brought tears to his eyes.

"It's okay," he said, rubbing the remaining hot liquid out

of his developing beard. "They'll be here soon."

For the first few weeks, his brain had wallowed in the understanding that he wasn't going to be released quickly. As soul crushing as that had been at the time, the sudden change today was completely unraveling him. He missed his routine so much his bones ached.

A desolate sigh broke over his wrists as his palms cradled his forehead.

He had to keep this hollow feeling of emptiness from pulling his mind into wild circles.

Closing his eyes, he envisioned a large grass field on the cusp of spring. He mentally watched clouds change shape above him, allowing the flexible, effervescent quality of each evolving design to soothe his soul. As the vision became more vivid, he almost smelled the earliest blooms of the daffodils and the sting of wild onion.

At the abrupt sound of a slamming door and stomping feet, Brent let out a shaky exhale. His forearms twitched as he lowered them to his knees, and it took everything in him not to rise from his folded blanket and wrap his hands around the bars in anticipation. When his captors' faces arrived behind the cold metal, he felt his eyes fully relax. They were in a good mood today—laughing, conversing, smoking—and Brent fought a smile.

One was wearing his blue jacket instead of the black one, Brent noticed. The blue one suited his personality more. He slid the food carton and water bottle through the slot.

"Eat, healthy American," he said.

Two blew smoke through the bars with a "Yeah" that sounded like "Jah."

Brent deeply inhaled the cigarette smoke. It was a scent he'd hated in his previous life, but now he cherished the two times a day he smelled something other than stale, moldy dampness.

Two's hair seemed shorter. Brent's gaze focused on the dark hairs over his ears and the back of his neck as he turned his face to say something that made One laugh. Yes, he must have recently had it cut. He tried to stop *It looks nice* from sounding in his brain but failed.

As One and Two receded from the barred door, Brent memorized the patterns on the bottoms of their shoes. *Goodbye* sang through his mind, but he forced his teeth to trap the word inside his mouth.

Though he was ravenously hungry, Brent made himself wait until the front door slammed before crawling to the disposable container. Forcing himself to take his time with each bite was so much harder today, and halfway through he gave up, shoveling food in his mouth with a crazed ferocity he hadn't felt in weeks. He drained the last of the bottle from last night before he took several large gulps from the one they'd just brought him.

He was mid-swallow when the change clicked in his brain, and he spewed the water across the grey cement floor.

No.

He looked at the cap in his right hand and the half-empty bottle in his left.

"No. No. No. No."

Setting the bottle on the ground, he frantically crawled

backward until his back hit the windowed wall with a thud. His knees pulled tightly into his chest as he began to rock. The bottles were always sealed. There was a rewarding cracking sound they made as he opened a new one. In a room devoid of sound, he noticed each change in decibel.

This morning, there was no clicking sound as tiny plastic teeth were forced away from each other. There was no extra force that his hand had to apply against the lid of the bottle. Trembling fingers sifted through his too-long hair and pulled at it.

His mind flew wildly through possibilities, but in his gut, he knew the answer—there were drugs in the water.

"But why?" The words tore from his lips as the hollowing feeling of betrayal dropped in his stomach.

Why would they drug him again?

Irregular heaves filled his lungs as his hands gripped his curls.

"They have to be moving me." The stark realization had him lifting his head with wide eyes.

Yes. That was the only logical explanation. They had to be moving him, and maybe that wasn't the worst situation. What if he was being released? What if a ransom had finally come through? If they wanted him dead, they could have easily shot him. It hadn't escaped his knowledge that each of his captors had a handgun tucked into the waistband of his pants. They could fire at him through the bars, and he'd have no way of defending himself.

Brent scrambled on his knees to the bottle, poured the rest of it down the toilet and flushed it. His hands were shaking, but he neatly put the empty water bottle and container back through the slot in the door like he did after every meal.

"Maybe I didn't drink enough of it. Maybe I won't pass out entirely . . . Yeah. I'll be fine. I'll be okay."

With his new delusion firmly seated in his mind, Brent forced himself to stand, pulling up on the bars of his cell. His knees buckled almost immediately, and a loud, desperate sob racked from his body. He staggered back a few unsteady steps until he collapsed onto the mattress.

He was going to black out.

As an oppressive sense of dread rose in him, his gaze drifted to the cracks in the ceiling. They intersected at different points, and he'd mentally tried to draw a different constellation every day—to find beauty in his limited surroundings.

Unconsciousness pulled slowly at his toes through his calves and up his legs as he traced a familiar image. His fingers twitched as his forearms pushed against the protruding mattress springs, trying and failing to fight the dragging sensation of weight snaking through him. When it reached his chest and firmly pressed his shoulders back, Brent accepted his fate. His blurring vision traced the outline of a raven-haired face tilted back in laughter one last time before his eyes closed.

◊◊◊

The first thing Brent noticed when consciousness returned to him was the smell. It was a mix of a metallic scent and something burning. As awareness returned to him in degrees, he recognized the smell. It was something he'd encountered on a formative assignment, early in his journalistic career—blood and burning flesh.

There were no sounds of a war zone to accompany the smell, only a rhythmic electronic beeping, a constant hissing, and men speaking foreign words in the distance.

His brain told his eyelids to tear apart, and surprisingly, they obeyed the command. Bright light directly above him nearly blinded him. Turning his head to one side, he saw medical machines beyond his outstretched arm, which was strapped to the table. Rapidly turning to the right, he saw his other arm was fastened in the same way. Beyond his fingers lay a tray of surgical tools, and beyond that, a doorway in which two men in scrubs stood arguing.

The chilled air of the room pricked at his naked, exposed skin as he began to pull at his restraints as hard as he could. His heels rose off the cold table causing elated joy to sing through his feet as they flipped up, trying to get leverage against his secured arms. Pain seared through his shoulder as his twist wrenched his body, but his right wrist remained securely in place.

A guttural groan pulled from him, and either that or his movement alerted the men to his consciousness, because they both ran to the surgical table. One dove over his legs, trying to restrain his forceful kicks, and the other covered his screaming mouth with a gloved hand. Biting as hard as he could, Brent heard the man's painful shout as he continued to thrash on the surgical table.

"Help! Someone. Hel—"

The first man, now straddling him, fumbled with a breathing mask and struggled to hold it over his shaking mouth. The second man held Brent's face steady with a rough hand over each ear so the first man could secure the mask. He tried not to inhale the gas hissing toward him, but in his aggravated state, he was breathing hard, and soon his vision began to blur.

Under the command of medical sedation, his body slowly stopped listening to his mind's instructions to fight. His muscles twitched as the voice inside his head shouted but everything decelerated. A pulsed ringing settled in his ears over the incomprehensible words of the two men who loudly quarreled over him. As his movements became weaker, the first man climbed off his torso and returned with a scalpel. Brent's scream ricocheted against the rounded bones of his skull.

Against every fiber of control left in his body, his eyelids closed in short, uneven degrees.

Open, he commanded them. Once again, they split apart, and a blurry image filtered through his retina. The first man held the scalpel poised over Brent's torso, but his face was turned toward the doorway. More shouting collected in his ears as the voices around him seemed to multiply.

Cold, searing pain pushed against the skin at his waist, and his eyes winced shut automatically. With his last effort, they fluttered apart a crack, taking in only the surgical light. The pressure on his right side released as he heard several loud pops that he knew from experience were gunshots. The surgical table jostled once before all the sounds dimmed and everything went black.

·CHAPTER 30·

Colton flipped the page of the colorful instruction manual. "We need a grey one."

Elaine glanced at the book, seeing the next Lego piece was a two by four grey block. "Okay, how many circles are on the long side?"

Her son counted under his breath, touching each little circle on the picture before saying, "Four."

Running her hand over the small plastic blocks, she picked up and held out the appropriate piece. "Is this it?"

"Yup!" Colton beamed as he clicked it into place.

The police car they were building was finally coming into shape. Colton was a little young for a regular set, but with everything that had happened lately, she figured it was a good time to spoil him. Especially since tonight, she'd be leaving him for the first time since his surgery.

Waiting in her closet was the snug green mini dress she was going to wear along with her highest heels. They would nicely close the distance between her mouth and Nate's. Elaine wanted to be able to reach his lips whenever she felt like it, which she expected would be often.

Tonight, she was going to let Nate see the sexy, polished version of herself that she brought out at night. The poor man had no idea what was coming his way—he was going to lose his mind.

Even as this thought passed through her mind, it felt a bit reductive. She *did* want Nate to lose his mind. She wanted to see the orderly version of him fall away like it had the last time they'd kissed. She craved him wanting her more than she'd craved anything in a long time.

But she needed to be careful with him. He wasn't a toy for her to play with. He was an incredibly caring man who knew and seemed to like the side of her that was an insecure, sometimes over-defensive mother. Who seemed to like *her*.

Normally, that would have scared her to the point where she'd close up completely, but there was something gentle in the way Nate's eyes watched her that made her feel like she could let her guard down. Something about him made her feel less alone—that she could depend on him, that she could trust him.

Her phone rang from its place on the kitchen counter, and she hopped up, anticipating Nate's call.

Seeing Brent's contact, her brows twitched together. Before she knew what she was doing, she swiped open the call with a suspicious, "Hello?"

A loud exhale sounded in her ear. "*Elaine.* Thank God. I'm so glad you picked up. I need to see you. Can you . . . can you meet me at the airport? I'll be landing in an hour." Flight announcements echoed over his words.

He's just getting back now? It'd been weeks. Maybe he hadn't blown her off. Maybe her family drama hadn't scared him away.

Did it matter? She was supposed to be going out with Nate in a few hours.

"I don't think that's a good idea."

"Please," he begged, his voice taking on a more desperate tone. "I *need*— I can explain everything, but it'd be better if I told you in person. Please come. Please say you'll come. *Please*."

The way he pleaded sent a shiver down Elaine's spine. Something was wrong. She wasn't sure what, but something was *very* wrong.

"Okay," she ended up saying. "Okay. I'll come."

"Thank you." He almost sounded tearful.

After taking down the flight information, she called Jodi to see if she didn't mind coming over for a bit now in addition to later. Jodi assured her it would be no problem, and even Colton was surprisingly okay with her leaving on short notice. Elaine fed Colton a quick lunch but wasn't able to stomach anything herself. Strange uneasiness continued to pulse through her as she drove to the airport.

As she reached the end of the hallway to the terminal exits, a large glass-ceilinged atrium opened before her. The bright sun filtered through the glass and bounced off the pearl floor tiles. The three terminals exited into this space, wide open with the exception of small seating areas and potted plants scattered throughout.

Straight ahead was Brent's airline, and passengers were already coming down the hallway. As she crossed the large room, she scanned each face. After intently watching about eight people, Elaine saw Brent walking slowly down the declined hallway. She might not have noticed it was him except she recognized his brown bomber jacket over his thinner frame. An unkept beard hung under hollowed eyes that carefully watched the floor beneath him. What used to be playful curly brown locks just looked shaggy.

Elaine froze mid-step, shocked at the difference between the man across the atrium and the memory in her mind.

What happened?

Brent glanced up unseeingly, and she forced her feet to continue in his direction. All around her, people flowed through the now busy atrium—finding their loved ones, giving hugs, laughing. Elaine only moved silently and slowly toward the shattered-looking man in front of her.

"Elaine?"

The familiar voice pulled her from her trance, and she flipped around to find herself face to face with Nate.

"Nate. What are you—" she started before she heard loud sobbing and spun back around.

A very put-together woman in her early sixties was hugging Brent and weeping. After the woman finished hugging Brent, a man in slacks and a tailored blue jacket over a crisp white collared shirt took his turn, slapping Brent's back while in his tight embrace. The woman pulled a fabric handkerchief from her expensive purse and started dabbing at her perfect eye makeup.

When he was finally released, Brent took a step closer to her but turned to put his arms around Nate. "Nate, you have no idea how good it is to see you."

Nate hugged and held Brent. "You too."

Elaine's gaze bounced as if at a tennis match, silently between the two men.

Brent eventually turned his exhausted eyes to her. "Elaine, thank you for being here." He captured her in a fierce hug, much like the ones everyone before her had received.

As he held her, she watched Nate's face contort from joy to confusion. Brent buried his nose in her neck and took a deep breath before he released her. "I missed you."

"How do you know Elaine?" Nate directed his question at Brent.

Before he could answer, the older woman rushed in front of him, fussing with his jacket sleeves and laying a hand on his chest. "Let's get you a wheelchair so we can go to the car. I want to get you home."

A small movement lifted Brent's lips. "I'm not as bad as I look, Mom. I want to walk."

So she was his mother. That probably made the man his father, but why was . . .

"Nathaniel, take your brother's bag," the woman instructed.

As Nate's fingers closed around the small carry-on Brent had over his shoulder, Elaine's throat closed around a trapped inhale. The ground felt as if it went from under her as she grabbed for something, anything, her fingers only gripping tightly on each other. The light in the room was suddenly too bright. She blinked rapidly, but her vision couldn't seem to focus. Nausea swelled in her stomach as her brain slowly did the calculation.

"He's your brother?"

Both men turned at her shocked words. Two sets of similar brown eyes looked at her, and she started to notice the similarities in hair color and build. Elaine actively swallowed the vomit at the back of her throat. Only their faces were completely different, and Nate's now surveyed hers like he did when he was worried about her.

Though the question was meant for Nate, Brent answered it. "I'm sorry. I haven't talked to anyone in a long time. It's still odd being around so many people. Elaine, meet my brother, Nate, my mother, Margot, and my father, Henry."

When the older man stepped in front of her, she numbly accepted his outstretched hand before doing the same with the woman. Nate moved forward, his jaw working soundlessly, and Elaine came to a staggering halt.

Awkwardness flooded her body. She couldn't shake hands with the man whose mouth she'd been fantasizing about less than an hour ago, for whom she'd strategically planned an outfit to maximize the amount of access she'd have to his tongue.

"You folks wanted a wheelchair?" An airport staff person in a uniform pushed a wheelchair into their group.

"Yes, thank you." Margot gave the employee a large tip while Henry encouraged Brent to sit.

With both of his parents aggressively insisting he not walk to the car, Brent conceded and sat. Henry started pushing the wheelchair while Margot held Brent's hand, keeping pace beside him. Elaine found herself walking side by side with Nate.

He slowed his pace to allow for several feet to pass between his parents and them.

When they'd lagged back far enough, he asked in a low voice, "How do you know my brother?"

Elaine could feel his gaze on his face, but she kept her eyes fixed on the back of the wheelchair. It was a simple question with a simple answer, but the words were stuck in her throat. She opened her mouth and nothing came out.

She swallowed hard and tried again. "We went on a date before he left . . . Two, technically."

Her face flushed thinking about it. Did the night Brent came over and they made out like horny teenagers count as a second date? She was pretty sure that evening would have ended in sex had her mother not shown up out of thin air.

"Oh."

The coolness of Nate's word drew her gaze. His hand gripped into a tight fist as he released a pent-up breath through his nose. Naturally, he was angry. Who wouldn't be if they found out you'd been with their brother first? An involuntary shudder shivered down her spine.

"It was long before . . ." she whispered. "I mean he's been gone for weeks. You and I . . ." She let that sentence drop off. "I didn't know."

"I know." His tone softened as he met her gaze.

"Nathaniel," his father bellowed. "Talk some sense into your brother."

Reluctantly, Nate's eyes pulled from hers as he jog-walked the few steps to the wheelchair. Not moving from her spot, she watched as they discussed Brent's need to be seen by a doctor.

"They sent someone to check me out when I was received by the Embassy," Brent was saying.

His father scowled. "Like I'd trust a foreign doctor." It was weird to see his father's face frown with disapproval. It was the same stern face Nate had made when she'd first met him.

"Do you want me to call the emergency department medical director? I can see if she can come in and examine Jay herself." Nate pulled his phone out of his front pocket.

"Yes, make the call. I just want someone here to set eyes on him," his father answered.

Nate nodded and started clicking through screens on his phone. He stopped when his father put his hand on his shoulder.

"Thank you, son."

Nate looked surprised to see the grateful expression on his father's face before the older man rotated to answer his wife's question. A small shake tossed Nate's head before he turned away, putting the phone to his ear.

As the group began moving again, Elaine's feet dragged slower and slower. She felt like an interloper, not a person who was supposed to be interacting with the family before her. The distance increased between them, and she actively stifled the overwhelming impulse to run.

·CHAPTER 31·

All Brent wanted was to be done. He wanted to sit outside on his parents' back deck and watch the river. Now, he was going to be dragged through another medical examination—*inside*. Probably in a small hospital room. It had been hard enough stifling his anxiety on the plane.

Only the first-class drink service had helped. The glasses of wine he'd consumed had made him slightly less apprehensive about being trapped in a metal tube.

The fact that the plane had been crowded had also helped. Plus, the elderly woman next to him hadn't seemed to mind that he'd "accidentally" pushed his forearm until it was touching hers. She'd only smiled to herself and continued with her crossword. Brent had been so overcome with her kindness, he had to open his eyes wide and stare at the ceiling to prevent tears from falling.

But now, they wanted him back in another small space. Visions of the ceiling, the concrete floor, and the specific flaking paint patterns on the walls flowed through his mind and he swallowed roughly. A pressure just below his Adam's apple squeezed as an irregular twitchiness tore at his body, like a fox trapped and scratching to get out.

He blinked up to the glass ceiling, trying to center himself. The sky was right there—blue, bright, beautiful. His mom's pervasive hairspray scent was to his left, her small, cold hand gripping his. His father's authoritative presence as he pushed the wheelchair was, for once, comforting. Even the sound of Nate's professional voice as he made a work call soothed Brent. But someone was missing.

"Elaine?" he called, turning his head.

She was several feet behind and sped her pace to walk next to the wheelchair. "Um, yeah?"

The look in her eyes was one of shock and confusion, and Brent realized he hadn't explained anything to her. His parents had been notified almost immediately after he'd been rescued and had arranged for his quick return to the states—he assumed they'd explained everything to Nate.

He must be a horrible sight. He'd showered and been given new clothes along with what remaining belongings the police had retrieved, but he wasn't the man she'd known from before. Maybe he should have waited a few days before he called her, but when he'd landed in Dulles, he'd called on impulse. He wanted to see the woman who had made his days a little less lonely, see her beautiful dark eyes in person, not just in his head.

Brent turned to his parents. "Could I talk to Elaine alone for a minute?"

The movement of the wheelchair stopped as a look passed between them.

"Of course," his mother said.

His parents stepped back a few feet next to Nate who was still on his phone call.

"I'm sorry. This must be a lot." His gaze flicked to his lap before returning to her face.

Her eyes regarded him steadily. "Are you okay?"

He fought the automatic shake of his head while silence expanded between them. Only for the first time in weeks, it wasn't silence. It was saturated with airport announcements, foot traffic, and voices—it was beautiful music.

"What happened?" Her whispered words rose about the noise.

He blinked, feeling the skin below his right eye twitch as a shaky exhale left his lungs. "I . . ." He stopped. "What happened was . . ." A wince accompanied his words as they dropped off.

Suddenly, his mother's hand was pushing over his forehead and through his hair like she'd done when he was a child. "Let me tell her."

Brent's eyes flicked to hers with a tiny nod.

She took a deep breath and squared her shoulders in Elaine's direction. "There's no easy way to say this. Jay was abducted and held captive in a cell until the police raided the compound late Thursday. When the U.S. Embassy called us yesterday, we immediately arranged for his flight home."

The pulse in Brent's throat felt like it was going to press out of his skin.

Elaine's hand gripped the wheelchair as if to steady herself. "What? Why?"

A single tear trickled down his steel-spined mother's face. "He was targeted by organ traffickers."

Brent closed his eyes tight at his mother's words, but all he could see was the last frame he'd witnessed before he went under sedation, so he flew them back open again.

He'd come out of unconsciousness at the central police station in Terlenitsi. Once he was fully awake, he'd joined two other Americans in a conference room, neither of them journalists. The police had given them blankets and sour coffee as they'd explained that the country had a very extensive and lucrative organ trafficking ring. A task force had been trying to shut it down for more than a year and a half.

Fortunately for the three of them, the raid had happened before their organs had been harvested. The heavily accented police director admitted that a fourth person had not been so lucky. Brent had sat in stony silence next to his fellow hostages as the woman had sobbed openly, and the man had dry-heaved into a waste basket.

"Oh my God." Elaine's words drew him back to the airport. Her dusky-rose lips were pale, and she looked as if she was going to drop to the floor.

His father was swiftly at Elaine's side, holding her steady by the elbow. Nate dropped his phone from his ear, taking a large step forward before the voice talking through the phone grabbed his attention. His brother watched the three of them warily as he gave answers to the voice in his ear.

The whole scene forced Brent's gaze to the polished tiles as he muttered. He shouldn't have done this to her. He should have recovered first and then contacted her, but she'd been such a specter for the last few weeks that as soon as he touched down on U.S. soil, the need to see her in person had itched under his skin until he'd found himself dialing her number.

"I'm sorry." The words ripped out of his lungs as his eyes found hers.

Elaine straightened, and his father tentatively let go of her. "I didn't have to live through it," she murmured. "I'm sorry this happened to you."

He nodded. There was nothing else he wanted to say about it. Brent knew he probably should talk about everything that had happened to him, but right now, he couldn't.

"I thought about you a lot while I was gone." That sentence was too honest and too vulnerable, but he needed to say it.

Her chest rose with a deep inhale.

"We've got to keep going, Jay," his mother said gently while his father began pushing the wheelchair again.

"Okay," he said as his mother took his hand again before returning his focus to Elaine's face. "I don't want to ask you to come to the hospital with us, but could you come over tomorrow for dinner? I need to talk to you about something."

The more he'd thought about it during his endless hours alone, the more he knew that he was making the right decision. There was so much to tell her, but he needed time alone with her to explain everything.

Elaine's eyes rounded. "Tomorrow? Don't you need to . . . recover?"

"No," he said, knowing he did need time, but knowing that he needed to fix this now. "My mom hosts a family dinner every Sunday. It wouldn't be any trouble to add one guest for tomorrow, would it?"

Surprise barely glinted in his mother's eyes before she answered, "We'd be happy to have you."

"Are you sure?" Elaine's gaze flitted over his face. "You don't want to, uh, rest for a while? We can always catch up later." She took three tiny steps farther away.

"I'm sure." He gave what used to be his best smile, not knowing if it held up with a full beard.

Elaine hugged her ribs. "I don't think so. I'll have my son with me. My friend who's watching him now is driving to South Carolina to visit family tomorrow."

That's right, her son.

"He can play with my brother's daughter." Brent abruptly noted that Addie wasn't here. No little fireball yelling "Unky J!" and jumping into his lap. "Where is Addie?"

"She's with a friend of mine," his mother answered.

Brent nodded. It was probably better that she wasn't here; it might have been too confusing for her.

As the automatic double doors to the parking garage opened, the cold November breeze drafted against his face. He would no longer take for granted the feeling of fresh air on his skin. It was such a little thing that he usually never noticed, but from now on, he would cherish any minute he got to be outside. Any minute he wasn't confined.

Elaine pulled away from them. "I parked a flight down."

"*Wait.*" His father stopped the wheelchair, and Brent stood, quickly covering the distance to her. "Thank you for being here," he said, hugging her tightly. "You have to come tomorrow. You're coming, right? Please tell me you're coming." He hated it, but his voice broke on the last sentence.

He felt her tense up in his arms, but she said, "Sure."

As soon as he released her, she strode rapidly toward the stairwell. Nate disconnected from his phone call, and Brent watched their eyes catch before she descended the steps.

Nate turned his gaze to their parents. "The ER director is coming in to personally see Jay. When we get there, he'll go straight in. They'll do all the intake information in the department. He's been assigned room twelve."

"That's wonderful." Their mother gripped Nate's hand before kissing it. "Thank you."

"Yes. Thank you, Nathaniel," his father chimed in.

Nate's eyes quickly darted between his parents before resting on his. "Jay, why don't you come in my car, so I can take you directly where you need to be. Mom and Dad, just use the ER valet when you get there and call me. I'll bring you back."

"Yes. That makes the most sense," his father agreed.

After Brent was buckled in the passenger seat of Nate's silver BMW, his brother drove out of the parking garage. A quiet hung between them, and he wondered if Nate wanted more details about what had happened to him. While he waited, Brent leaned toward the dashboard and turned on music to block out the silence. After about three minutes, his brother started asking questions.

·CHAPTER 32·

"I thought you were still dating Sloane?" That was the first question Nate asked his brother.

As soon as the words had passed over his lips, he'd internally chided himself. He'd just found out *this* morning that his brother had been held captive in a foreign country. Their parents had apparently known Friday when they'd coordinated Jay's flight, but had decided not to relay that information to him until Jay was safely on a plane home.

His mother's panicked call had brought him and Addie to his parents' house immediately. While his mother's friend had distracted Addie in her room, his father had relayed all the information they knew while his mother had wept openly on a settee. The whole situation was so strange that halfway through hearing it, he'd pinched the inner side of his arm just to make sure he wasn't dreaming.

After that, Nate hadn't thought of anything but Jay. He couldn't imagine the terror Jay must have endured. The despair his brother must have felt not knowing what was going on, being held for such a long time without anyone to talk to, and being rescued under such violent circumstances.

The saddest thing was that no one in their family thought twice when they didn't hear from Jay for weeks. His brother often went out of communication for his job, and he wasn't the best at keeping in touch even when he was stateside. The last time Nate had talked to him was at the dinner at his parents' house after Addie's birthday. Nate didn't know how much time would've had to pass before they would've even thought to look for him.

But now, sitting next to Jay in his car, all Nate could think about was that Elaine had been at the airport to see Jay.

A long, ragged exhalation filled the car. "We haven't been working for a while."

"But you're still together." God, he was being an asshole. He should be asking Jay if he needed anything, not interrogating him.

"I didn't want to say anything last time I saw you at dinner because I didn't want to get into it with Mom and Dad. You know if Mom had known, she would've called all her friends with single daughters, looking to set me up." His brother was looking out the passenger window.

Nate knew that was *exactly* what his mother would have done.

Silence settled between them again except for the melodic strumming of a bass guitar.

"So who was . . ." He wanted to say her name so badly but left it to the air.

"Elaine?" His brother picked up where he left off, the tone of his voice brightening. "I met her before I flew out. She's amazing."

Nate gripped the steering wheel so tightly his knuckles paled before he forcibly encouraged his hands to loosen. He shouldn't have asked about her. That was stupid. He didn't want to hear about Elaine from Jay's lips. Didn't want to think about the fact that his brother had probably kissed her. Maybe had even—

"Do you want to swing by any place before we go to the hospital?" Nate said quickly to interrupt his own thoughts.

A smile curled on his brother's mouth. "I'd love a hamburger and fries."

Nodding to the road, he said, "Then let's get you one." It was time to be the helpful big brother he'd always been.

When they got to the hospital, Jay was happily sucking fry grease off his fingers. Nate took him straight back into the emergency department and thanked the doctor for coming in to help his family. His parents arrived at the same time they did, so he did a quick double back, taking them to Jay's assigned room.

The ER staff buzzed around the room like bees in a hive for thirty minutes before things calmed down. While his brother was being examined, Nate saw the long, thin cut on his right flank. The doctor stated that it was very superficial, basically a scratch. Jay did seem to be medically fine, all things considered, barring unusual levels coming back in his blood work. Since they were just waiting on lab results, Nate excused himself to step outside to speak to the staff.

After thanking the ER director again, Nate found his feet walking down the hall to his office. He let himself into the darkened space and sat behind his desk. Taking the first deep breath of the day, he rested his head in his hands.

Nate was incredibly grateful that Jay was okay, but this disparate pulsing kept tugging at his shoulders. His fingers slid over his head to grip the base of his neck as an exhale pressed from his lungs.

What were you supposed to do when the woman you really liked—the woman who'd been lighting up your days—dated your brother first? What etiquette did you follow when the first brother was out of the country being held captive and otherwise would have been with her?

Nate felt like he was stuck in some sick game of "dibs."

A bitterness swelled in his mouth, and he swallowed against it.

When his phone buzzed with a text, he rose to go back to the ER, expecting it to be his parents. He straightened the collar of his grey oxford under his heather-blue half zip as he took a deep breath. It was time to go back to taking care of everyone else.

Elaine: *How are you?*

A blend of emotions ran through Nate's body at lightning speed. He was happy that she'd contacted him, that she wanted to talk to him, that she cared enough to ask, but a deep, stabbing guilt immediately shadowed his elation. He couldn't ignore the fact that while he had been having some of his best days since Sarah's death, Jay had been suffering immensely.

Nate: *Okay. Getting Jay checked out at the ER.*

It was so weird to text his brother's name to Elaine.

Elaine: *Can I call?*

Instead of answering, he pressed the phone call icon.

"Hi." Her voice was soft in his ear.

"Hey."

The air hung silent for several seconds before she broke it. "What do we do?"

Acid rose at the back of his throat again as his stomach twisted. "It's up to you. What do you want to do?"

"I don't know." Elaine sighed. "The whole situation is so strange. I want you to know that when we kissed, I thought he'd ghosted me. We hadn't texted since he left. I wouldn't have kissed you if I was also dating someone else . . . I wouldn't have done that to you." Her last sentence was quieter than the preceding ones.

"I know," he whispered.

The quiet grew between them again. When she spoke, her words slashed further than the wound he'd seen on his brother's side. "I think with everything he's been through, it wouldn't be a good idea to tell him about us."

Us.

She'd used the word "us."

Was there an "us"? Their first date was supposed to be tonight, but that obviously wasn't going to happen now.

For him, there had already been an "us." For him, this was more than just casually dating. She and Colton were already so intertwined with his and Addie's lives. He'd been ready to jump in with both feet and see what happened.

As much as Elaine had seemed to enjoy time with him, maybe she didn't feel the same way. Maybe for her, this was casual. Or maybe now that she had a better alternative, she'd rather be with his brother.

Nate hit his office chair before he realized his legs had dropped from under him.

He took a deep breath and let out a shaky exhale. "Okay," he forced himself to say.

"I'm just worried that he'll break or something," she said, her tone steeped in concern. "He looks so . . . so fragile."

As much as he wanted to commend her for sympathizing with his brother, who undeniably had been through hell and back, Nate couldn't help feeling crushed that she didn't think her words would be hurting *him*.

"I don't know what's the right thing to do," she sighed.

Nate wanted to scream "choose me" but kept silent. He ran his hand through his hair. She was right, and he was an asshole for only thinking of himself.

"He's been through a lot," he agreed.

"Are you okay with me coming to dinner at your parents' tomorrow?" she asked quietly.

It was if somebody had thrown ice water over him and then punched him in the face. Hard.

"What?"

"O-oh . . . um," she stuttered. "He asked me to come over tomorrow and seemed really unstable about it. I tried to say no, but I felt like I couldn't."

"Oh."

Elaine probably felt cornered and didn't want to say "no" to a man who'd just come back from weeks in solitary confinement. Nate shouldn't be upset with her for having a compassionate heart. If anything, it made him like her even more, which hurt like hell.

"I can just make up an excuse that Colton is sick or something," she offered.

Forcing himself to use his neutral administrative tone, he said, "If Jay asked you and you want to come, please feel welcome."

A quick pause was followed by, "You're sure?"

"Of course," he lied.

A part of him shattered in that moment. He'd never wanted to lie to Elaine. In his mind, he had set the intention that during their relationship, he would always tell her the truth to any question she asked. She deserved that much after having her mother lie to her time and time again.

"Okay." Her voice sounded so small.

Nate's phone beeped in his ear, and looking at the screen, he saw that his mother was calling him. "I have to go. My mom's calling me."

"Oh, sure." She paused as if to say something else, but all he heard was "Bye."

"Goodbye, Elaine," he exhaled as he swiped on his mom's call and disconnected from hers.

·CHAPTER 33·

Elaine stared at the phone in her hand as if she didn't recognize it—its weight heavier than usual in her fingers.

What had she done?

She'd been trying to save one brother from harm and unintentionally injured the other. Her chest squeezed as breath almost refused to filter in and then out of her lungs. The pain she'd heard in Nate's voice as he'd said goodbye still echoed in his ears.

Her phone dropped to the floorboard of her car, tumbling next to the brake pedal, and it was only then she noticed that her fingers were trembling. Reaching down to get it, she unintentionally honked her car horn. A frustrated growl ripped from her lips.

"Enough!" she yelled before repetitively slamming her hands on the steering wheel. Why was there always a mountain of obstacles against her? Why couldn't she have one good thing without something else tainting it? A familiar sensation pinpricked over her skin, but it brought her no relief this time.

"Enough," she whispered as her forehead met the steering wheel, her hair blanketing the sides of her face. Her chest heaved in a sob as tears tore down the side of her nose, dangling suspended for a moment before splashing on the scratchy fabric of the driver's seat. Her hands clenched at the air of her lap, her muscles flexing as skin gripped skin.

After a long cry, she pushed her wet hands through her hair. She couldn't imagine the horrors Brent had seen, but she understood how a single traumatic event could haunt your life forever. She wasn't going to be the one to shatter him after he'd survived so much. Nate would understand. They could just press pause for a while. She just needed to call him and explain what she'd meant earlier.

Elaine was unlocking her phone when three loud raps on her driver's side window startled a shout out of her.

"Are you okay?" Walter's frame cast a shadow over her.

She pressed a hand against her sternum, gathering her breath before she answered, "Yes. I'm fine. Everything's fine." She winced at the lie.

Leaning over, she gathered her purse, pushing dark sunglasses over her eyes.

Walter moved back as she opened the door. "You're sure?" he asked when she stepped out.

"Yes. Thank you," she said probably too crisply as she strode away from him.

Only once she was inside her apartment, exhaling against her closed front door, did her eyes well again. The pop of Trouble's bubble dice through Colton's bedroom door sounded over his favorite kid-music soundtrack. Elaine put her purse away as she heard Jodi reading him the number and letting him count the board spaces.

Her body moved until it was standing in the doorframe.

"Hey." Jodi looked up with a smile that fell almost immediately once she'd tracked Elaine's fragile state.

It only took a minute for her friend to get Colton settled with animal crackers, apple juice, and a cartoon in the main room before closing the bedroom door behind her.

Elaine stretched out on her mattress, sweater-covered arms flopped over her eyes.

"What did Brent want?"

A groan escaped her mouth before she spit it out. "He wanted to tell me he hadn't blown me off. That he'd been captured and held by organ traffickers in Europe. That he'd just gotten back today."

Her friend crawled up on the mattress next to her. "That's some story."

"No." Elaine pulled her arms away to see her friend's light brown eyes. "I saw him. He was thinner and had a full beard and he looked emotionally shaken . . . maybe even broken. He wasn't lying. His parents were there and . . ." She swallowed the thick lump in her throat. ". . . and so was Nate."

"Nate?" Jodi asked. "Why was Nate there?"

The heater hummed as its forced air warmed the room, but Elaine still shivered as she spoke the next words, "Nate is his brother."

Her friend's eyes grew wide. "Nate? Nate who was with you for Colton's hospitalization. Nate who you've been gleefully playing house with for the past two weeks. Who you were supposed to go out with tonight? He's Brent's brother?"

Elaine couldn't answer, just covered her face with a sigh.

A string of expletives filled Jodi's mouth with a ferocity Elaine had never heard before, especially since Jodi didn't swear. "Wow," Jodi whispered, lying beside her. They could hear Colton singing the theme song to his favorite cartoon.

"Do they know about each other?"

"Nate asked while we were at the airport and I told him." She shuddered involuntarily at the memory of the incredibly awkward conversation.

"I'm assuming Brent doesn't know about Nate."

"No." She was starting to feel sick to her stomach again.

Jodi turned to face her. "And you're not going to tell him."

Elaine pivoted to her friend, lying on her side. "How can I when he looks like he's one tiny push from completely crumbling? It would be cruel. You didn't see him, Jo. He was unstable. It was strange, and scary, and incredibly sad to see a man broken down like that."

She expected Jodi to nod and say something thoughtful about the trauma Brent had lived through, so what she said instead was surprising. "But what about Nate? You were happy with him. Like really happy. Happier than I've ever seen you."

Elaine exhaled slowly and rolled her gaze back to the white popcorn ceiling. One of the soft-footed flight attendants was in residence this weekend, and she could hear her stealthy movement above.

She was happy with Nate. Little things he did always caught her off guard: like how he'd bring her dinner without her expecting it, how he'd give her that slow smile when she was trying to exhaust him in her spin class, or the way he always seemed to know if she was stressed and could always comfort her with his touch.

And she'd been really looking forward to tonight—more than she had looked forward to anything in a long time. Not just to see where the flirtation between them went or to feel his naked skin under her nails—though she'd been excited about that too—but she wanted to spend time with him without parenting or hiding from their kids. To get to know him on a deeper level.

Heaviness pushed at her chest. Again, she was presented with a situation where what she wanted didn't matter. She had to do the right thing. "I think we should just take a break until Brent recovers."

"That's ridiculous," her friend scoffed. "You're already hiding from your kids. Just keep it from Brent too."

She found her head shaking. "It's too much deceit, Jo." Her friend swung off the bed causing Elaine to sit up. "What?"

Jodi's face pinched before she let out an exhale. "Do you want me to tell you the truth, or do you want me to agree with you?"

Elaine picked at the seam of her jeans. "Can't you do both?"

"No." Her friend's raspy voice was stoic.

"Fine." She flopped up her hands. "Hit me."

Jodi's usually gentle eyes bore into her. "You really like Nate, and you know he's good for you, so you are going to allow Brent to interrupt what you have going with Nate because you're scared you don't deserve him."

Elaine's mouth worked at words that didn't make sounds for several seconds. Jodi had never once called her out like that. Some self-preserving side of her deflected, as she said, "Brent's not an interruption, Jo. He's a human being who was locked in a room against his will for nearly a month. It's not his fault he wasn't around."

Jodi's gaze didn't relinquish. "I know. And what happened to him was horrific, but that doesn't mean he automatically gets what he wants because he went through a trauma."

She felt her brows raise. "How can you say that?"

"Sorry." Her friend held her hands up in surrender. "I should have left my work-self at home today. Pretend I never said anything. It's your life, not mine." Jodi took a step back.

Elaine leaned forward. "Look. I don't want to fight."

Jodi spread her hands out in front of her. "We're not fighting. You're fighting yourself. I don't want to upset you when you've already had a long day, so I'm going to head out."

With that, her friend left, kissing Colton on the way, as Elaine sat stunned in her bedroom.

·CHAPTER 34·

Brent's forehead wrinkled as his brows pinched against the light that was streaming across his face. When he opened his eyes, it took a minute to acclimate to his surroundings. The light was the first thing he noticed, piercing his retinas with its steady beam. The second was the comfort of the cushions he lay on and the softness of the Egyptian cotton duvet that covered his body. The third was the scent of coffee filtering into the room from the kitchen nearby.

Turning his head away from the large pane windows, his gaze rested on the ceiling of his parents' living room—perfect creamy white with artfully patterned drywall brush strokes. A long, uneven exhalation escaped his lungs as the surge of adrenaline he felt every time he woke up abated.

You're back. You're okay.

Brent threw back the blanket and faced the sunlight again. A wall of seamless windows, that with a push of a button accordioned back and forth on each other to completely open, stood in front of him. Walking to the single door on the left, he let himself out into the brisk morning air.

A mist rested over the river, and the early dew settled on every surface. It wet the soles of his bare feet with a reassuring chill as he padded onto the deck. Brent watched the daybreak sun reflect off the water as birdsong filled his ears.

Sleep had been elusive last night as he'd tossed and turned until the early morning hours. His mother had offered him a sleeping pill, but the idea of drugging himself when it had been done against his will so many times made him vomit in the back of his throat.

Finding he couldn't relax in the guest bedroom upstairs, he'd padded down in his cotton pants and long sleeve shirt and made a bed on the couch facing the backyard. Even though the room he usually occupied when he was in town was spacious with a large window that he'd left open, he'd still felt confined.

The glass door behind him opened with a whisper, and his mother silently came to stand next to him. She was wrapped in a long cashmere robe over her silk pajamas. It had been so many years since he'd seen his mother in bed clothes. She usually never came downstairs without being perfectly coiffed.

Wordlessly handing him a steaming cup of black coffee, she delicately sipped her own mug. The companionable silence of her presence, the smell of good coffee, and the beauty of being outdoors was so soothing that Brent found his eyes watering. A halting exhale left his body.

His small mother wrapped an arm around his back and laid her head against his side. The warmth of her body against him was everything. Lowering the hand clutching the mug to his side, he pushed at the hot liquid that flowed down his face. His mother simply squeezed her arm tighter, staring straight ahead into the sunrise as Brent cried hard, ugly tears.

◊◊◊

After a long, very hot shower in which he was able to shave the beard from his face, Brent eventually started feeling better. The mirror in the en suite bathroom was heavily fogged when he got out, and a sigh racked his chest. He wasn't ready to see his weakened body just yet. The wardrobe in his room held his old clothes, all of which were too loose on him, but he used a belt to cinch in the pants until they would stay up.

Though after the breakfast he'd had, it wouldn't take long to regain weight. When he and his mother had returned inside this morning, his father had been sitting in the kitchen reading the paper while his parents' chef had prepared all manner of breakfast items. It looked like there would be fifteen people for breakfast, not three.

Only after his parents were convinced he'd eaten enough was he allowed to leave the breakfast table and find refuge outside. He'd spent the rest of the morning and early afternoon on an Adirondack chair near the river, memorizing the sights, smells, and sounds of nature.

Brent opened the door to his bedroom and moved down the hall. Though his parents' house was usually quiet, soft orchestral music played throughout the speaker system as he descended the stairs.

The second his feet hit the floor, Addie accosted him, gripping his legs like a python squeezing its prey. "Unky J! I missed you!"

Brent pulled the little barnacle from his shins and smothered his face into her tumbling hair, compressing her slight body as strongly as he could without harming her. "I missed you, too, princess."

Leaning back, she said, "Did you bring me some-ting from your trip?"

Sickness washed over him as he heard her question. Too many images started pushing their way into his vision. All he wanted to see was his adorable niece in his arms.

Nate entered the hallway, answering for him. "Uncle Jay was too busy this last time to get a present for you."

Her eyes darted from her father's back to his. "Let's go play with my bear from last time." She wiggled out of his embrace and pulled hard on his hand.

Before he could get dragged up the stairs, Nate wrapped him in a hug almost as fierce as the one Brent had given Addie. Letting go, his brother's eyes flowed over his face and his sweater and chino covered body. "You look good."

"I feel better," he admitted.

"I'm glad." His brother's hand clapped his back, pulling him into another tight hug.

Their father appeared, asking for Nate to join him in his study while Addie continued her tug-o-war with Brent's arm to get him upstairs.

"Actually, princess, do you mind if we play soccer instead? Outside." He hated the pleading sound of his voice.

"Oh ya. Let's play soccer." The fireball took off in the direction of the backyard.

After a half hour of soccer, they switched to leaf collecting. Since the gardeners had already taken care of the leaves and there were none left for her to jump in, Brent settled her on his shoulders and they pulled brown, orange, and red ones from the trees.

The back door opened, and a familiar boy came sprinting across the lawn to them. Brent had to catch Addie mid-dive from falling in the grass. Once she was on secure ground, she hugged the little blond boy, and they took off toward the water's edge. Addie was picking up sticks and throwing them into the river, encouraging her friend to join.

Brent's gaze whipped to the deck, looking for Elaine and finding her with a relieved exhale. Standing next to his mother on the deck, Elaine looked beautiful in a flowy navy day dress that ended mid-calf, with a camel blazer and matching ankle boots. Her hair was loose around her shoulders in an effortless but gorgeous way, and all he wanted was to touch it. His fingers aimlessly rubbed together at the thought.

His mother went back inside, and Elaine smiled nervously across the lawn. Striding to her at twice the pace she advanced, Brent gathered her into his arms. She smelled the same as yesterday—the same as in his memory—lightly and heavenly of jasmine.

"Hi," she said to his shoulder.

"Hey." He held her a fraction longer than a hug warranted. "Thank you for coming. You look amazing. You have no idea."

Her gaze quickly appraised his face and body. "You too. You look . . . better."

"Thank you. My mom made me eat two breakfasts today. At this rate, I'll look like Santa by Christmas." Sending her his best smile, he hoped it landed like it used to.

Elaine's eyes regarded him steadily, but a corner of her mouth gave a slight tilt. "But you just shaved off the beard."

Her lips fell as her eyes darted toward the deck before returning to his chest. Brent turned to find Nate walking from the back door to one of the outdoor deck chairs with a highball glass in hand. His mother was behind his brother but continued down the grass toward where the children were still throwing things into the water.

"Dinner will be in thirty minutes, Jay," she called out on her way.

"I meant to ask yesterday, but why is everyone calling you that?" Elaine asked.

His vision left his mom and went back to the beauty in front of him. She was too far away, so he reached for her waist. "It's my nickname. My legal name is Jacob Brent Brennan."

Her eyes flicked away again as he spoke but then focused back on him. "Oh."

"When I started doing photography in high school, I used my first and middle names in reverse to thumb it to my dad. We weren't always on good terms like we are now. He didn't approve of what I was doing, and I didn't want his last name on anything I created. After that point, everyone knew me as Brent Jacobs. It's sort of my artistic pseudonym. Only my family calls me Jay."

She winced at the word family. "Brent . . ." She began leaning slightly away from his grip. "I think . . . I think maybe we should talk."

"I agree." He wrapped his other arm snuggly around her waist. "There's a lot more I need to tell you . . ."

·CHAPTER 35·

As his brother put his second arm around Elaine's waist, Nate watched her eyes flick to his for a brief second. In the short span that their eyes met, time stopped. She looked exceptionally breathtaking today, and all he wanted was to be the sole focus of those dark brown eyes.

When her gaze quickly returned to his brother, all the air left Nate's lungs. What was left was a stinging sensation that vibrated over his whole body. To numb the discomfort, he took a deep draw from his brimming glass of bourbon.

He'd poured himself the drink after casually talking to his father in the study. It had been a weird yet enjoyable conversation because it had been the first time his father had asked questions about and seemed genuinely interested in Nate's work at the hospital.

When the doorbell had rung, reality had descended upon him. He hadn't forgotten that Elaine was going to be here today—to see Jay, not him—but he'd managed with great difficulty to push it from his mind. At the sound of her and Colton being led to the backyard, Nate had found himself generously pouring a glass of bourbon from his father's small bar before excusing himself to "get some air."

Nate didn't even taste the bourbon, just swallowed down the burning gulp so it could mix with the irritation swirling violently in his veins. He was a complete asshole for feeling this way, but it was impossible to avoid.

A better man would be happy for his brother. Nate *was* happy that Jay was home and safe . . . but he couldn't be happy about this. Not when it was so appallingly unfair. And he of all people understood. Nate *understood* that life was not fair. Life had taken Sarah from him, and now it was taking Elaine.

No, that wasn't right. Life wasn't taking Elaine. She'd *chosen* Jay. She just didn't want him.

When Nate returned the drink to the armrest of his chair, Jay started lazily rubbing his thumb against Elaine's lower back. Nate's grip tightened so strongly around the base of the highball that his knuckles turned white. The glass would have shattered in his hand had his mother not invested in the finest, thickest crystal.

"Daddy!" Addie surprised him by being right next to him. She was usually as stealthy as a horse falling down stairs. "Can I show Colt my room?"

Nate turned away from his brother to look at his daughter. Her hopeful, joyful face nearly freed him from the twisting vines of indignation that had been successfully overtaking him.

"Sure, sweetheart. Just clean up after yourself before dinner."

As soon as this meal was over, they were leaving. He didn't want a reason to have to stay longer than he had to. If he was forced to watch Jay put his lips on her, Nate wasn't sure what he would be capable of.

Colton rushed over, his blond hair flopping and stopped next to his daughter.

"Daddy said 'yes!'" Addie turned to leave, as Colton asked, "What's wrong?"

Nate had noticed that Colton was particularly good at reading adult emotions before, but he'd never been on the receiving end of his gentle scrutiny. It was a little bit like being caught naked.

"Nothing, little man. I'm fine." He reached to tussle Colton's hair as if to solidify the lie he'd just told the thoughtful boy.

Colton gave him a tiny, wary look, but relinquished because he was four and Nate was an adult. As Addie pulled his hand into the house, Colton glanced back at him before disappearing. Nate was still watching the kids when he lifted his glass to his mouth. Misjudging the amount of bourbon in his next large gulp, brown liquor spilled down the front of his collared shirt. He cursed and leaned forward to brush himself off as he heard the door open again.

"What the hell?"

Nate swiveled his head toward the voice and recognized the person standing in the doorway. Sloane's gaze was fixed in the direction of Jay in a murderous way.

What is . . .

"What in the actual hell, Brent?" She spat out each word out like they were distasteful in her mouth. Sloane pushed her long blonde hair out of her face as she stomped over in high-heeled black knee boots. Nate sat up in his chair and noticed Jay drop his arms from around Elaine's waist.

His mother walked from where she was standing near the water toward the threesome. Using her most diplomatic voice and folding her hands in front of her, she said, "Sloane, what a surprise. Good to see you, as always."

Sloane completely ignored his mother and set her angry eyes on Jay.

"What is going on? You leave for weeks on a no-cell service assignment, and then all I get is a text saying not to worry but that you aren't coming back to the city because you were hurt overseas. That *your mother* is taking care of you. I was worried sick, so I hopped on a plane to make sure you were okay. You look pretty okay to me, Brent. Especially with your body draped all over . . ." She paused to do a devastating sweep of Elaine. ". . . *this*."

"I am recovering here," Jay said.

"He is," his mother corroborated. "I don't know if he told you, but he's been through a lot in the last few weeks."

Sloane scoffed and tossed her hair, "I wouldn't know. All I got was a text that my boyfriend was suddenly 'too weak' to fly home—"

Elaine took a step back. "Boyfriend? Wait. Flew?" She turned to Jay. "You don't live here?"

"Of course not!" Sloane answered for him. "He lives with *me* in New York. Like he has for the past two years."

"Two yea—" Elaine began, brows tight.

"That's right, slut. So I suggest you get lost." Sloane sneered as she flicked a wrist in a dismissive manner.

"Maybe we should—" His mother began, trying to diffuse the very uncivilized situation in front of her.

"I am not a slut." Elaine coldly enunciated every syllable.

Nate watched anger light like a fuse beneath Elaine's skin as her muscles tensed and her jaw tightened. He was familiar with this look, though he usually only witnessed it when she was defending Colton. In a millisecond, he was on his feet and moving swiftly toward the two women.

She took a step toward Sloane, setting her hands on her hips. "I'm in the dark about this, same as you."

Sloane towered over Elaine as she got directly in her face. Nate was a few steps from them as he watched both Jay and his mother warily back away.

"Like I'd believe you, you dirty whore." She put both her hands on Elaine's shoulders and shoved hard.

Elaine stumbled backward, almost losing her footing from the powerful push. Nate caught her before she fell and spun her around, using his body as a barrier between the two women.

"Are you okay?" he whispered into her ear.

She leaned back a fraction of an inch into his chest and gave a curt nod. The brief moment of her in his arms shouldn't have been as gratifying as it was. Nate wanted to do more than make sure she was steady on her feet. He wanted to hold her until the tight line of her jaw relaxed, but first, he had to deal with his brother's lies.

Reluctantly, he let go of her and turned to Sloane. "Jay told us you broke up before he left. Your anger needs to be directed at him."

"Broke up?" Sloane laughed viciously and swiveled her attention to his brother. "So living together and having sex the morning you leave is us being 'broken up'?"

"Sloane . . ." Jay blew out a heavy sigh. "We haven't been working for a long time. You have to have known that. You have to have felt it. It's just . . ." His eyes dragged to the grass. "I texted to let you know I was okay because I was tired of lying. I was going to explain everything later." He swallowed with difficulty and raised his face. "But I'll do it now."

"What are you talking about?"

Jay let out another extended breath. "I'd used your theater connections to get an interview at NYCLive."

"What?" Sloane's question was breathless.

Jay winced but continued. "I spoke to your producer who put me in contact with the NYCLive people. It was an asshole move but I was desperate. I wanted something bigger and better . . . something different." His gaze traveled to Elaine, and Nate had to consciously stop himself from fisting a hand. "I told you I was going to be out of contact, but really I was flying back to New York after my freelance assignment for an interview. I just . . . I just didn't want to sever things between us until after the interview. I didn't want you to sabotage it."

"Are you freaking kidding me?" Sloane's nostrils flared.

"No, and I'm sorry. I had a lot of time to think things through over the last few weeks. I shouldn't have used your connections. Honestly, we should've ended things months ago, but I had so much riding on that interview. And when you initiated sex that day, I didn't want to say no to you and jeopardize anything."

"Wait." Elaine held a hand out. "The night my mom showed up, you said that you were flying out early the next morning."

His brother turned. "I did fly out the next morning," Jay said. "I flew out of ORF at five forty-five the next day."

Elaine closed her eyes tightly before opening them and pointing to Sloane. "She just said that you had sex with her the morning before you left."

Sloane leaned back, folding her arms across her chest.

Jay's mouth opened and closed before opening again. "I did. I did and told her I was going to the airport, but then I drove here."

Elaine's jaw tightened. "To bring *me* wine and chocolates and try to sleep with me."

"Elaine . . ." Jay began reaching out to her.

Hearing her name on his brother's lips was the last straw, Nate pulled his hand back and punched him square in the jaw. Pain rocketed through his fist as he made contact with his brother's face, but it didn't touch the outrage surging through his chest.

·CHAPTER 36·

His mother's loud gasp sounded as Brent staggered back, grabbing his throbbing cheek. A ringing echoed in his ears as pain radiated over his face. "What the hell, Nate?"

Shaking out his fingers, Nate shouted, "You are such an asshole! You've *always* been such a self-centered asshole."

Brent's hand rubbed at the impact point. "Look, I know what I did was wrong." The fact that his mild-mannered older brother, with whom he'd never come to blows with in their lifetime, had just punched him in the face was shocking, but it was taking a strong second place to his need for Elaine to understand him. "I was going to come clean to both of them. That's why I asked Elaine here. I lied to everyone, okay? I lied to myself . . .

"It's just . . ." He took a step toward Elaine but she backed away. "You're different from anyone I've ever been with. You've always seemed to see through my charms. I know we started off on dishonest terms, but I feel like I was stripped to my core in that cell, and now I just want to start over. Be better. No more manipulation. No more lies. No more deceit. No more games."

Brent ignored his brother's heaving chest and Sloane's eye roll as she stormed toward the house, his mother chasing after her. He needed to make things right with Sloane, but right now he needed Elaine to believe him.

Elaine was slowly rocking her head back and forth.

"I'm serious. You have no idea how important to me you've been over the last few weeks." He stopped with a thick swallow. He needed to get this out. He *needed* her to know. "It was you who kept me sane when my brain started going to dark places every day. It was your image that I traced and then retraced in my mind to keep from going crazy. *You*, Elaine. You helped me survive."

From the corner of his eye, he saw Nate blink rapidly and then take a slight step back.

Elaine's gaze darted between his eyes for a long, silent moment before her expression smoothed a fraction. Brent took it as a small victory. "No one deserves to go through what you did, and I'm glad thoughts of our time together helped when . . ." She didn't finish that sentence. "I'm glad you're safe and that you're going to work on bettering yourself. I hope you get your life sorted out, but . . ." She took a deep inhale. "I can't be part of it."

No. Everything inside him felt like it was shattering. Everything that he'd barely held together over the last few weeks was crumbling all around him. This wasn't how this was supposed to go. This couldn't be happening.

"Please," he begged with a desperation he hadn't known he was capable of.

Her eyes were glistening, but her head shook gently again. "No, Brent."

The loud, painful exhale he heard had come from his own mouth. "You have to think about it. Please just think about it. I think we'd be good together."

His eyes swung to the left and caught the pity in Nate's gaze.

Then Brent lost all self-control, grabbing hopelessly at her waist. He drew her hard into his body and took a deep breath of her sweet scent. "But . . . I need you," he breathed into her hair. Didn't she understand that? Didn't she know that without her, he'd have been lost long ago?

Elaine pulled her hands up and pushed against his chest with tight fists. "Brent, stop."

"Jay, let go of her." Nate's voice was a warning.

Had that whiny "no" come from his lips? None of this was making sense. None of this was going the way he'd thought it would. After living in his head for so long, real life was harder to acclimate to than he ever thought it would be.

Elaine's breath quickened as she struggled, pushing harder against him, but his body wouldn't—couldn't—relinquish its hold on her.

All at once, a stiff grip grabbed his wrists and wrenched both arms firmly behind his back. Pain seared through each shoulder joint, but the right one ached with a tearing sensation. Surgical lights flashed over Elaine's terrified face as she backed away. Blinking once and then twice, all he could see was the operating room.

The scent of blood and burning flesh overloaded his nostrils to the point of suffocation. He snorted, shaking his head violently to try and clear his airway, but it didn't help. A burning built in his chest as his body was being deprived of oxygen.

Out of nowhere, a soft female voice said, "Let go. He's scared." And Brent immediately felt like he was floating through space as he was instantly untethered. He heard his brother's whispered curse, as though it was far away.

Dragging air into his lungs, he doubled over, put his hands on his knees, and focused on the ground. Grass. There was grass there. Not hospital tiles splattered with blood. Brent tried to shut his ears against the pounding in his head. What was that noise? Why wouldn't it stop? The incessant rushing sound only intensified as his vision swam.

His lungs couldn't seem to cooperate with the air around him. His breaths only shortened, grew more frantic. The pressure built exponentially, and he felt as if his heart was bursting in his chest.

He was dying.

He'd made it home only to die.

Just as Brent was about to collapse, he felt a firm hand on his shoulder. His eyes darted up to see Nate next to him.

"Jay. I'm sorry. I didn't mean to . . . You were . . ." His brother's lips downturned in a firm line.

Elaine stepped forward with a delicate touch to his forearm, but Brent winced as if she'd stung him. "Easy. You're okay. Breathe in. Breathe out." She made a show of taking a breath and exhaling it through pursed lips.

Brent found himself following her repeated instructions. Once he'd successfully mimicked several rounds, Nate's grip on his shoulder loosened a bit. Vibration still rushed throughout his body as exhaustion swiftly replaced the menacing feeling of imminent death. His hands found his chest, searching for a hole or wound of some sort. Seeing that it was solid, he looked up to find Elaine observing him with mournful eyes.

"What just happened?" His mouth felt filled with sand.

She stepped back as her lips parted momentarily. "You had a panic attack."

"I've never . . . I don't . . . Is that—" Brent gripped at his sides, doubling over again.

Instantly, his brother's hands were on his body, supporting him under his arm before guiding him to the house. "Let's sit down and get you some water."

"No!" His head snapped up. "No water. Anything but water."

Elaine and Nate exchanged a look.

When they reached the base of the deck stairs, Nate eased him to sit on the lowest rung. His mother came outside and was quickly sent back into the house for a glass of milk. Breaths still heaved in and out of his lungs as his eyes flitted from the ground to his brother's face, and then back to Elaine's umber eyes.

"It'll get better," she whispered, gaze locked with his. "They come less often with time."

Nate's neck snapped in her direction.

As Brent wondered what she meant by that, his mother pushed a glass of cold milk in front of his face. His father sat next to him, a plush tea towel for wiping the excessive sweat from Brent's forehead in his hand. His parents' steady presence, as the cold milk slipped into his stomach, settled the lingering anxiety coursing through his veins.

When he'd finished the glass, he realized everyone but Elaine was watching him. It took several slow seconds to remember that he'd physically restrained her in his attempt to make himself feel better. *Confined* her. Her hands were clasped together in front of her dress, but that didn't fully hide the slight tremor in her fingertips.

"I'm sorry," he rasped. "I shouldn't have . . . behaved like that."

Elaine watched him silently before she nodded her head slightly and her shoulders lowered. The brisk mid-November breeze pushed her hair halfway in her face before she tucked it away behind her ear.

Clarity washed over him in gentle, pulsing waves. There were so many things he had to fix. He needed to fix his relationship with his brother and parents. He had to figure out how to be able to exist indoors without that pervasive itchiness running through his body. But first, he needed to let Elaine go.

Though the memory—the *idea*—of Elaine had been an anchor and had kept him sane for the many hours he'd spent alone, he understood that he was asking too much to expect her to be his savior now. They'd barely known each other before his abduction, and most of the time he'd spent with her, he'd been lying to her.

Brent opened his mouth to say as much when they heard Addie's high-pitched screech.

·CHAPTER 37·

Looking back on that moment, somewhere in her mind, Elaine had registered the loud splash before she'd heard Addie's panicked "Daddy!" Through the whole afternoon—the incredible awkwardness of being there in the first place, Sloane's confrontation, learning the depth of Brent's lies, even the horrifying feeling of Brent holding her against her will—Elaine had remained in control of her body. But the second she saw Addie on the edge of the boat dock above the frothy disturbed circle of water below, Elaine completely shut down. She simply froze.

Colton.

The sight of Nate sprinting toward his daughter finally forced Elaine's muscles into action. Her breath squeezed in her lungs as she ran after him as fast as she could, the whole time feeling as if she was struggling against something outside herself. Nate was at the end of the dock and in the water before Elaine's feet even hit the start of the wooden boards.

Somehow seeing his body plunge into the water sped things up because before she knew it, Nate resurfaced, Colton tucked into the crook of his shoulder. Her sweet boy's lips were slack as water ran freely from them. His lashes dewed together on his cheeks. Rivulets of liquid trickled from his sweater and jeans as Nate hurriedly climbed the dock ladder with one hand.

"Colton!" The unearthly scream passed her lips as something deep inside her cracked. Her knees hit the hardwood as Nate laid Colton down, turning his head to listen for breath. Her hands grabbed for her son's legs, but her brain recognized that Nate was starting CPR, so she fought the overwhelming urge to gather her son to her chest to feel his little body next to hers.

Nate's mouth twisted into a deep frown before he tilted Colton's head, pinched his impossibly small nose, and covered his mouth with his own, breathing two steady breaths. The oxygen in Elaine's lungs sat trapped and useless as she watched Colton's chest rise, but then nothing happened. Nate swore under his breath and breathed for her son again.

"Come on, bud. Breathe. *Please*." Tears clouded her vision. "Please breathe."

Somewhere in the background, Nate's parents took Addie from the dock. She heard someone say "911," but her entire life was lying soaked on a plank of pine. Seconds seemed to freeze as the sounds of distant wind chimes, rustling leaves, and lapping water fell away. Her existence was the steady exhalation of Nate's breath into her immobile son.

At the third breath, Colton spit water from his mouth, his body bouncing with a cough, and she couldn't fight the need to hold him anymore. Pulling him to sit, she wrapped her arms around him as water seeped into her clothes. As his lungs expanded and contracted under her hand, she rained kisses on his hair, this face, and his eyes.

"Mama?" His voice was garbled.

At the sound of her name, her chest hitched as she let a deep heaving wail rip from her body.

Three breaths.

That's how long it had taken for her son to regain life. If someone had been timing Nate's response, she was sure it had been in the seconds, but never in Elaine's life had time been so pliable. It shifted and stretched and burned her heart with its suspension.

Elaine tucked her chin into Colton's face and rocked him. His hand-me-down argyle sweater stuck to his frame as she pulled flecks of mud from his jeans, trying to erase the fact that he'd been in the river. Her world was the pressure of his small body in her lap, his reassuring breath, and the salt on her lips, as she tasted her tears.

Eventually, she registered a paramedic kneeling beside her with a gear bag. Elaine loosened her arms just enough for the woman's stethoscope to listen to the sound of Colton's lungs. When Elaine couldn't let go of him, the kind woman suggested she climb onto the stretcher with him on her lap.

Somewhere in there, she heard the loud slam of an ambulance door. Somewhere were the sounds of sirens and beeping machines as they examined Colton. There was the thin sensation of plastic tubes laid over her arms as they snaked into her son. That all happened in the periphery. Her focus was settled over where Colton's miniscule intercostal muscles seesawed with regularity.

Then it was an all too familiar scene, all too soon. The green curtains of the ER screeching on their metal rings as they slid open and closed, people shouting commands and answers echoing through the vinyl tiled halls, the heavy smell of antiseptic and human odor stinging her nose. A nauseating feeling of deja vu rolled through her as she stood next to the hospital gurney, squeezing Colton's hand as they put in another IV, did an X-ray, and returned him to oxygen.

At first she answered for him, but they explained softly that they needed to assess if his brain was fully functioning. She bit her lip so hard she tasted the salty metal of blood before she told her shy boy to talk to the doctor. As Colton answered question after question, his tired blue eyes kept vigil on hers like they were the only two people in a room of ten.

Sitting in the chair next to him, she leaned her elbows on the stretcher and intertwined her fingers with Colton's small ones. "I'm so sorry, bud. I never wanted you to be here ever again."

"It's kay, Mama." He blinked at her from over the blue hospital gown covered in smiling sea animals. The sight of him wearing that particular piece of cloth again brought bile to the back of her throat. "It's accident."

Her forehead hung so fast and with so much shame that the muscles at the back of her neck protested. Colton was too young to understand that this wasn't an accident. This was entirely her fault. Had she been paying attention to where her son was instead of being distracted by two men, this *never* would have happened.

Her head shook back and forth.

A familiar cedar and soap scent preceded the warm hand on her shoulder. "Elaine? I didn't want to ask the doctor without your permission. Is Colton okay?"

Elaine didn't want Nate's voice to send a soothing sensation from his slight contact at her shoulder down to the balls of her feet but it did. As she struggled with her body's response, her mouth failed to create words.

"Hi, Mr. Nate." Colton's gaze blinked up.

"Hey, little man." Nate's voice pinched with emotion and that sound almost did her in. He cleared his throat before asking, "Are you feeling better?"

Colton slowly nodded his head. "I'm tired."

"I bet."

A doctor stepped into the small room, pulling Elaine's attention. She stated that Colton had been very lucky in that his lungs looked free of fluid, but they were going to observe him for a few hours, just to be safe.

"Okay." Elaine numbly nodded. Though she'd let her gaze flow to the woman's eyes for a moment, she quickly returned it to Colton.

"Humor me for a couple of hours, and we'll get you home soon," the doctor said as she left.

Her sweet boy yawned as Elaine began finger-brushing his dry and frizzy hair. "You can sleep. I'm right here. I'm not going anywhere."

The warmth of Nate's hand left her shoulder as he found a chair and set it next to hers, silently existing in the same space, demanding nothing. This man had lived through the trauma of reviving her son with his own breath and was still unwavering in his support of her. Elaine was uncertain of how much time had passed before the words formed in her mouth and passed over her teeth.

"Thank you for saving his life," she whispered, her gaze never moving from her son's peaceful and sleeping face.

An open mouth exhale preceded his words. "Elaine, I'm so sorry."

Nate's defeated breath was the one that broke the sturdy resolve she'd just reclaimed after hearing her son's positive prognosis. Her shoulders slumped as she curled in on herself, hands fisting in her lap.

"This is my fault. This wouldn't have happened if Colton was with . . ." She let her sister's name drop from her lips.

Her body ached into one tight, muscular clench. She'd always known she was a poor substitute for her sister, but in the past few weeks, she'd proven that time and again. She kept screwing things up. Making the wrong choices. She was *failing*, and Colton was paying the price.

I'm sorry, Rose.

"This wasn't your fault." Nate's fingers tucked away a strand of her hair with searing gentleness. "This was a terrible accident. There were five adults outside at—"

A near silent moan broke free of her. "But *I* didn't know my son was on the dock. I didn't keep him safe."

Nate's hands were warm over hers, and she reluctantly allowed him to gather her tight fingers in his. "Addie was on that dock too, and I didn't know she was there. It was just an accident. It wasn't you. You're an amazing mother."

Elaine watched Colton's eyelids flicker as she shook her head.

No. The beeping of the heart rate monitor in the corner was proof enough that she wasn't.

A good mother would have *known* where her son had been at all times. A good mother wouldn't have been wrapped up in another family to the detriment of her own. A good mother always put her child first.

For the first time since he'd arrived, her eyes found Nate's. The golden-brown center whirled by the green of his irises bounced between hers, worried. He was still wearing the same clothes he'd been wearing when he jumped into the river—grey slacks and a thinly-striped white oxford, now dotted sporadically with algae.

Even when he'd come down the deck to catch her after Sloane's push, his clothes had already looked disheveled. They were wrinkled as if he'd slept in them, and there'd been a caramel bourbon-scented stain down the buttons of his shirt. Two days growth studded his otherwise sharp jawline, and exhaustion ringed his eyes. It was the first time she'd seen Nate without his air of order and control, and it was immediately unsettling.

The look of him had made it feel like she'd snapped all her tendons. Bone and muscle had severed from each other in an excruciatingly painful way. Brent had been wrapping her in his arms, but her own limbs only wanted to soothe Nate. In that moment, all she'd wanted to do was rewind time and have the conversation she should have had with him yesterday.

She was brought back to the room by the feeling of Nate

gently gathering her in his arms. The peace she felt was immediate. She'd never wanted anything more than she wanted to let Nate comfort her in that moment. Being in his embrace felt safe, felt like finally coming home. A ragged breath fell from her lips as she let her face rest on his sturdy chest, surrendering.

When her cheek hit the cool, damp fabric of his shirt, a painful shock ran through her muscles as she realized she was wrong—

What she wanted more than anything was for Colton to be safe. Was for him to live when Nate had breathed oxygen into his tiny lungs on the sodden dock. Visions of her son's slack body swam in her consciousness.

The shaking started at her fingertips and settled into her shoulders as an inhalation tore into her lungs.

"Elaine?"

She could feel Nate's gaze on her but couldn't pull her eyes from her son's sleeping body.

Her head shook on its own.

Nate had never once brought stress into her life—if anything he alleviated it. He didn't deserve this, but she had to do this for her son. Her decisions of late had heavily and negatively affected her son.

She had to keep Colton safe, even if it cost her own happiness.

He had to be the most important thing.

Elaine blinked her oncoming tears away. "I think you should leave," she whispered.

She felt Nate still. "Okay." He took in another breath as he released his arms. "I drove your car here so you wouldn't be without it." He slid warm metal keys from his pocket over her clenched fingers.

When his fingertips grazed hers, a sharp intake of air filled her lungs. This was going to be so much harder than she thought.

"I'll call you tomorrow," he continued, brushing a fleeting kiss to her crown. "Can you please text me when you get home, so I know you made it safe?"

An errant tear rolled down Elaine's cheek as she squeezed her eyes shut. "No."

"No?" She heard the surprise in his voice, but like a coward, she refused to look at him.

"I think . . ." She sniffed, her voice shaky. "I think it would be best if we didn't see each other anymore."

"Elaine, don't—" In her peripheral vision, she watched his hand reach out but then fist and find its way to his side.

"It would be best," she whispered. "For everyone."

"Oh." The short word left his mouth as if she'd punched him.

Elaine winced. She'd never meant to hurt him. He was a good man, and he deserved so much better than a mess like her.

"I'm sorry." Her words came out cracked.

A heavy exhale preceded his response, "Me too."

When he rose, he stood for a long time before eventually exiting through the glass door. Only when the soft whoosh of the door sighing into its creases punctuated the rhythmic pinging of the medical machinery around her did she let the last torrent of tears finally fall.

·CHAPTER 38·

Nate raked his hand over his hair as he walked down the hallway to the ambulance bay. Short, inefficient breaths drew in and out of his throbbing chest. Once he'd exited the automatic double door, he stumbled past the two parked ambulances and only made it another forty feet away from the ER before his legs went out from beneath him. Crumbling to the curb, he leaned his elbows on his raised knees as his hands bracketed his head.

Nate had been strangely operating on autopilot until this moment, when the cold scratchiness of the concrete sidewalk underneath him finally grounded him. Sensations filtered into his consciousness, immediate and overwhelming—the stench of river water on his still-damp clothes, and the stale taste of bourbon at the back of his throat. He drew a staggered breath into his lungs as his shoulder muscles tautly contracted.

It had all happened.

His mind flashed to a hundred different scenes, but the one that forced itself to the front was the green tint of the brackish river water as sunlight tried to permeate it. It had only taken a millisecond for his brain to register that finding Colton by sight would be nearly impossible in the murky water. As held air had burned in his throat, he'd groped feverishly around the slimy riverbed, and, fortunately, his fingers had felt the boy's narrow ankle on the second swipe.

Then it was a blur of getting Colton on the dock and starting CPR. The whole time a strangely calm voice instructed him at each step—check for breathing, tilt the head and lift the chin, give one-second rescue breaths, pause and assess for breath. When Colton sputtered to life, Nate doubted the reality in front of him. For half a second, his brain didn't want to believe what he was seeing. It wasn't until Elaine had pulled Colton into her arms and his garbled "Mama?" reached Nate's ears that he understood.

It had worked.

This time it had worked.

He *hadn't* failed. He hadn't been able to save Sarah, but he'd saved Colton. While Elaine had been placed on the stretcher with her son, Nate's face had fallen into his hands as he hyperventilated. *It had worked.* A few moments later, he'd waved off a concerned EMT and strode into the house to find Elaine's keys. The only thing that had mattered then was making sure Colton was okay.

Hearing the sweet boy's voice say "Hi, Mr. Nate" in the cramped ER room had threatened to break the last of the control Nate had been narrowly harboring. He'd almost lost it until he'd seen Elaine's face. Nate didn't have the vocabulary to properly describe how devastated Elaine had looked in that moment. Instantly, he had straightened his spine, determined to be the support she'd desperately needed, hoping his presence would make a difference.

But somehow, it hadn't worked like it had before. She'd melted into him only to stiffen, pull away, and ask him to leave.

His brain kept running through the events of the day, trying to figure out what he'd done wrong.

Nate's ears brushed his shoulders before he let his hands fall from his head with a defeated exhale. He barely registered the pain of his knuckles hitting the hard curb.

"Nate?"

He blinked up at the scrub-clad person shadowing his face but couldn't answer.

"What are you—" Tyler dropped next to him, his car keys scattering on the cement. "Are you okay?" His friend's hands quickly and efficiently roamed his body checking for damage, but Nate couldn't open his mouth to tell his best friend that the wreckage was inside. "What happened?"

He silently shook his head.

"Come." Tyler tugged on Nate's forearm, trying to pull him to standing. "I'm taking you inside."

"No." The word that escaped him was so etched with pain that his friend froze.

"Okay." Tyler folded his legs beneath him as he took the spot next to Nate on the curb. "Okay."

The cold wind from the harbor infiltrated his damp clothes, and Nate shivered as he let the weight of everything that had happened in the last two days bend him in half over his legs.

Tyler never spoke again. He simply sat and waited until, at last, the words spilled free.

◇◇◇

Nate used one hand to give Tyler another strand of white Christmas lights while stabilizing the ladder with the other. Normally, he wouldn't be helping his friend put up his Christmas lights, but over the last ten days, Nate had found he needed distraction every chance he could get. Luckily, Tyler understood and didn't seem to mind the extra hangout and gym sessions.

As they worked silently, Addie's shrieks of laughter made it all the way to the house. Keeping two hands firmly on the extension ladder, Nate turned his head to watch Chloe put some more animal feed in Addie's open palms. His daughter laughed again as six miniature goats jockeyed for access to her fingertips.

Tyler descended the ladder. "I meant to ask earlier, but Addie was in earshot. How are you doing today?"

Every day since his friend had found him crumpled on the sidewalk outside the ER had been difficult for Nate. Today, he'd really wanted to work the whole day, to keep busy, but every one of his staff had taken a half-day since it was the day before Thanksgiving, so he followed suit.

"Okay," he hedged.

"Are you ready for tomorrow?" Tyler asked, as he began collapsing the ladder.

An exhausted breath escaped Nate's lips. "No, but I can't keep avoiding Jay forever. I know he's going to need a lot of support to work through everything that's happened to him. I just needed a little time to get my mind organized before I talked to him."

He'd been avoiding his brother's calls and texts while still helping his father arrange various doctors for Jay. Surprisingly, after Nate had answered all his father's queries, his dad had continued to ask him other questions about his life and work in general. For the first time in years, they'd been regularly conversing.

"Nate . . ." Tyler stopped his movement. "You don't always have to help everyone else, you know. It's okay to just be there without fixing."

He gave a slow nod, picking up the empty plastic storage bin. "I'll try that."

Tyler's gaze swept to Chloe and Addie. "Has she contacted you?"

"No." The word sent a chilled frost shuddering through his muscles.

"I'm surprised," his friend mused, hoisting the ladder and walking toward the garage. "I was sure she would have called you by now."

Tyler was convinced that Elaine had simply been overwhelmed and hadn't meant to break up with Nate in the ER. That she would approach Nate once she'd sorted out the emotional strain of almost losing her son.

"I don't think it's a good idea to keep holding onto hope." Nate felt a pinch in his shoulders as he raised the bin in his arms.

The truth was he'd already given up on the idea that she wanted him, and that knowledge made his skin feel like it was frostbitten all the time. He'd only known Elaine two months, but it hadn't mattered. In his mind, he'd already knit their lives together, even though they hadn't even had a chance to share a solo meal.

The way he felt about her and the way she responded to him said more to him than the words that could have been exchanged on a first date. Everything had already felt as if it fit. The way Elaine lit up and laughed at Addie's antics, never getting frustrated with his exuberant daughter. The way Colton seemed to come out of his shell around them and trusted Nate as much as he did his mother. The way Elaine's eyes watched him with such affection it seemed her gaze radiated its own energy.

Without Elaine and her gentle boy in his and Addie's lives, everything felt dull. He'd been sustaining himself on microwave meals and toaster waffles because he couldn't see the point of making anything delectable if he couldn't taste it. Sleep was elusive and fitful and always short-lived. His responsibilities were still there, and he was still functioning but barely.

"If she wanted to be together, we would be." Nate consciously instructed his shoulders to lower, even though it felt like his heart was incinerating. He glanced at the goat pen to see Chloe still engaged with Addie before changing the subject. "Is everything organized for Saturday?"

Tyler anxiously eyed the pen before lowering his voice. "Yes, but . . . I'm so nervous."

For the first time since he'd arrived, a smile lifted Nate's lips. "It's going to be perfect. Chloe will love it."

Tyler had planned to propose to Chloe after her Saturday evening candlelight restorative yoga class. The same one Tyler had attended at the recommendation of his physical therapist after pulling his back at the hospital—where he'd first met Chloe years ago.

"There's no way she'll refuse you, Tyler," Nate said, reading the worried crease in his friend's brow. "She loves you." As the words came out of his mouth, his chest did that squeezing, breath-stealing thing it'd been doing for the last week and a half.

"Yeah, you're right. It'll be fine, right? It'll be fine."

Nate couldn't help but chuckle. His steadfast friend was more untethered than he'd ever seen him. "It'll be fine." He gripped Tyler's shoulder.

Addie came running over to them, her face flushed above her pink puffer jacket. "Mr. Ty, did you see me feed the goats?"

His friend chuckled at the straw dotting Addie's hair before plucking out a piece. "I sure did. Did you have fun with Miss Chloe?"

"So much fun!" Addie squealed with a bounce.

Tyler's face fully relaxed into a smile. "Are you excited for Thanksgiving tomorrow?"

"Yup."

His daughter nodded her head like Colton used to do and Nate's neck pinched, prompting him to rub it. "There are no less than five turkey crafts on the fridge right now."

Tyler's grin grew. "Impressive."

Addie twisted back and forth with pride as the bleating of tiny goats could be heard in the background.

Chloe caught up to them, waving her glowing phone. "Very Vegetarian Pizza just texted that a driver is on their way. Let's get washed up for dinner."

Tyler clapped and rubbed his hands. "Great idea."

"Colt's favorite pizza is cheese and so is mine," Addie said, taking Chloe's free hand.

"Is that so?" Chloe's eyes jumped cautiously to Nate's as she followed Addie through the back door.

His body froze as he pushed a hand against his sternum. He might not have seen Elaine since she'd asked him to leave the ER, but Addie still saw Colton every day. Up to this point, it had been challenging to stave off the playdate requests from Addie.

Every time she mentioned her friend, Nate felt as if he was cut and bleeding. "I'll be there in a minute," he coughed out.

"Sure thing." Tyler's hand gently clapped his back on his way past.

Nate rubbed his forehead and swallowed against the sour flavor in his mouth. Time. This all was just going to take time. Fortunately for him, time was now something he possessed in abundance.

·CHAPTER 39·

Brent returned from his mid-morning run sweating and exhilarated. He'd never been a runner before, hadn't really seen the point of slogging from one point to another, but now he completely understood its allure.

There was power in covering a distance propelled only by the force of your feet. Running took everything else out of the equation, leaving only you and your will to move forward. Brent found incredible solace in that. If he chose to go straight from the house and back, he could, or he could loop around, or he could stop or start anytime he felt like it. Even as his body throbbed from the stress applied to it, his heart only felt one thing—freedom.

Instead of going through the house and dripping sweat all over his mother's fine furnishings, he looped around the side of the house and stopped running only when he'd reached the deck. Climbing the stairs, he ran the hem of his shirt over his brow. A deep, satisfied exhale left his body as Brent clasped his hands behind his head, and a slight breeze pushed over the exposed parts of his body.

"Did you have a nice run?" His mother came outside carrying a tall glass filled with ice and lemonade.

"I did. Thanks," he said, accepting the proffered drink.

Brent took a long draw of the perfectly sweet, fresh-squeezed lemonade and resisted the urge to hug his mother. Had he not been damp and she not been impeccably dressed, he would have. She'd brought him the tart beverage because he still couldn't bring himself to drink water. It felt like water would forever be linked with being drugged and held captive. Maybe time and therapy would help with that, but for now, he couldn't separate the two in his mind.

As if she could read his thoughts, she said, "I confirmed your appointment for tomorrow afternoon to talk to Matthew. Are you sure you don't want me to go with you?"

After wiping his hand on his shirt to make sure it was clean, he set it on her shoulder. "I'm sure. Though I appreciate you and Dad arranging everything for me."

He'd been looking forward to doing more normal things like driving a car. He knew nothing that happened to him had inhibited his ability, but with what happened the weekend Elaine came to dinner, Brent was afraid he'd have another panic attack behind the wheel and hurt someone. Since he hadn't had another episode since then, he began to wonder if it was Nate holding his arms back that had triggered his panic. Perhaps Matthew could confirm that tomorrow.

His mother squeezed his hand, and a smile lifted the corners of her mouth. "You better get showered and dressed. Your brother will be here soon."

Brent had a lot of things he needed to talk to Nate about, and his mother knew that.

"Yes, ma'am," he said, gulping down the rest of his lemonade and heading into the house.

◊◊◊

Brent was clean, presentably dressed, and sitting outside again when Addie came running through the back door an hour later. The skirt of her orange long-sleeved dress flapped against her purple striped leggings as she dashed toward him. After weeks and weeks of grey, every time color hit his retinas, Brent's brain sighed with satisfaction.

"Unky J!" She climbed onto his lap and put both hands around his neck for a firm hug. Crossing her forearms on his chest and using them as a pillow for her chin, her blue eyes sparkled at him. "Happy Thanksgiven."

"Happy Thanksgiving to you, princess," he said, giving her forehead a light kiss.

"Wanna play?" She pushed against his sternum, propelling herself backward.

A smile tugged at his lips. "Always, but I've got to talk to your Daddy first. I think I heard Nana saying she was setting up tea and cookies in the playroom."

Addie didn't answer, just squealed and bolted in the direction of the house. A chuckle left his body as his delighted niece slammed the door shut behind her. Inside the house, the smell of roasted turkey and stuffing pleasantly emanated from the kitchen. He began searching for Nate and found him talking with their father in the study.

Upon seeing Brent, his father stood. "I need to check the wine cellar and make sure we have enough champagne for dinner. Excuse me."

He knew it was an unnecessary errand and so did his brother, but Nate didn't look like he was going to punch him or leave, so Brent sat in the leather armchair his father had vacated. "Happy Thanksgiving, Nate."

"Happy Thanksgiving." His brother's eyes were drawn to the large purple bruise on his face.

Brent rubbed his left cheek. "You've got a mean right hook, if I never complimented you on that." Nate opened his mouth to speak and Brent interrupted him. "Which I completely deserved, by the way."

His brother closed his mouth and leaned back in his chair. Brent took his brother's silence as permission and continued. "I've been a complete asshole to pretty much every person my life and—"

"Finally, we can agree on something," Nate interjected.

"I deserve that too." Brent paused. "I just wanted to apologize for being a shitty brother to you for years. I was always trying to see what I could get out of any given situation; I never really cared who got hurt in the process. You, on the other hand, only ever looked after me and treated me well."

A regretful exhale left Brent's lungs. "I'm sorry. I'm sorry for being a huge ass. I'm sorry for not defending you when Mom and Dad were always down your throat. I'm sorry for not being there for you more when Sarah died. That was supremely shitty of me. I mean, you were a grieving husband and new father, and I couldn't even be bothered to visit." His head hung on its own as tension pulsed around his eyes.

Nate listened with an unchanging expression but didn't interrupt again.

Brent looked back up. "I'm also sorry about how I treated Sloane. I should have ended things when I felt it wasn't working. She and I talked, and she was more gracious to me than I could have ever expected. Knowing Sloane, I half expected her to light my things on fire on the sidewalk and dare NYPD to try and stop her."

Nate's lips slowly tugged up. "Yeah, that sounds like Sloane."

His eyes found his intertwined fingers as he said, "I'm also sorry how I treated Elaine." It was still difficult for him to concede the fact that the vision that kept him sane in that eight by eight concrete room wasn't going to be his future, but every day that passed, he was able to understand better the difference between real life and fantasy. His mind had created that fantasy to help him survive, but the reality was she didn't want anything to do with him, and he had to accept that. "I didn't realize you knew each other."

Nate half-coughed/half-cleared his throat. "Excuse me?"

"I should have figured it out by the way Addie was so friendly with her son, but I assumed she was just being her normal outgoing self." His shoulders bunched up as he stretched out his palms.

"How did you figure it out?"

"When you left to go to the hospital, Addie mentioned that it was unfair that the boy—"

"Colton." Nate's voice held an unusual gruffness.

"Right, Colton. That he had to go to the hospital again because he'd just had surgery. Mom put the pieces together—that he must have been the little boy you helped while she watched Addie a few weeks ago."

Nate slowly rose and crossed the room to their father's small bar in the corner. A sleek, glass-doored mini-fridge had recently been installed beside the mahogany, hand-carved dumbwaiter. "Drink?" he asked, facing the wall.

"Just a short scotch, thanks."

Silence hovered in the room, and his brother was oddly stiff as he pushed a highball glass into Brent's palm.

"But anyway, what I'm trying to say is I'm sorry for basically everything up until now." He paused to take a sip of the amber liquid as Nate twisted the bottle cap from his miniature glass bottle of Coke. "But I want things to change. I'm going to be staying here with Mom and Dad for a while. I want to have a better relationship with you, with Addie—"

"You already have a great relationship with Addie."

He pinched his face dubiously, raising his free hand. "Yeah, but that's because she's four and a terrible judge of character. She'd hang out with Ted Bundy if he was giving out cookies in the shape of a dinosaur."

Nate almost spat out his soda he started laughing so hard.

Satisfaction roared through Brent as he allowed himself to chuckle along. "See, we need more of this. More time laughing and less time arguing—or worse, being cold and stilted. We've wasted too many years like that. This is how I want us to be when we talk to each other. I want us to be able to laugh at the brutal honesty of Addie's inability to see anyone's faults."

Nate's face fell to a frown mid-snicker, and he cleared his throat again. "If you want honesty, then there's something you need to know. Something that is going to upset you."

"Okay . . ." Brent racked his brain in the impending silence, but after all the times he'd steamrolled over other people's lives, he couldn't imagine Nate saying anything of magnitude.

A slow, deliberate inhale led to a controlled exhale. "The night you came home, Elaine and I were supposed to go on a first date."

It was as if Nate had stood and punched him in the face again. Actually, that statement fully explained the first punch.

"Oh . . . damn."

His brother's gaze swept to the bottle in his hand. "Yeah."

Brent fought the urge to place his hand over his chest. "But you didn't."

Nate's eyes flashed up quickly. "Obviously not. I was here with you. Making sure you were okay."

"Right," Brent said, his mind trying to process this new piece of information. Even though his right lower eyelid twitched, something in him knew the right answer before it fell from his lips. "Well, I'm fine now. And there's nothing between Elaine and me. You should reschedule."

This would be his first big step toward becoming the person he wanted to be. He'd sworn he'd be a better man, and not getting in the way of his brother's happiness was an ideal way to start.

Nate's eyes rounded before a small grimace flashed momentarily across his face. "She doesn't want to."

"Because of me?"

"No." Nate exhaled and swallowed the dregs of the bottle. "I think she didn't want me. Not really, anyway."

He waited until his brother's gaze found his face again. Nate was obviously upset, and for the first time in a long time, Brent pulsed with a need to lessen his brother's heartache instead of standing aside as Nate handled it on his own.

"I didn't see that coming." He twisted his face in a *Well, shit* look. "Both turned down by the same girl. I thought we'd left that kind of thing in high school."

Nate snickered, and a flashbulb of lightness radiated through Brent. "That never happened in high school."

The smile on his lips felt luminescent. "I guess we were due, then."

Nate's mouth turned slowly upward. "I guess," he agreed.

Brent finished the last sip from his highball. "I'm still sorry," he said. "For that, and for being a general asshole."

A smirk rested on his brother's lips. "Based on how bad your face looks, I'd say we're even."

Brent simply laughed. This fledgling feeling of warmth between them was something he hoped he could nurture and sustain. "That's nice of you to let the score go. You were always a better man than me."

"Yet another thing we can agree on," Nate said, standing and outstretching his hand to help Brent up. "Come on. Let's go see what your bouncy niece is up to."

"Deal." Brent clasped his brother's hand and then pulled him into a hug. Nate allowed the embrace to last as long as Brent needed, and for that, he was incredibly grateful.

·CHAPTER 40·

It was so much harder than Elaine had thought it would be not to fidget as they waited on the doctor. She'd clenched her toes, teeth, and fingers and still found her knee slightly bouncing. To distract herself, she looked around the colorful exam room.

The white floor tiles were interspaced with random solid colored ones, and a mural of an osprey holding a fish filled the wall beside the two bright chairs where they sat. Even the exam table was a vibrant blue. Colton wasn't on the table but securely in her lap, head nestled under her chin.

Two quick raps sounded before Colton's pediatrician pushed his way into the room. Elaine had always liked this man—he had a warm, fatherly vibe that surprisingly put her at ease, even though she'd grown up without a father.

"There's my favorite patient," Dr. Caruso said with a wink in Colton's direction.

Her son just looked down and rubbed his forehead into her collarbones.

Normally, she'd instruct Colton to "Say hi to Dr. C" but with the way he'd been behaving lately, she found it hard to ask him to do anything.

"Feeling shy today?" the doctor asked softly with raised eyebrows in Elaine's direction.

"Yes," she said with a weary sigh.

"What can I help you with?" Dr. Caruso leaned back against the exam table, crossing his ankles.

Usually, it was hard to talk about Colton in front of him, but Elaine felt like a pressure gauge had been broken as the words spewed out of her.

She detailed every single one of her worries. That she'd thought Colton was recovering well after his emergency appendectomy, but then he'd fallen in the water and been unconscious for a few agonizing seconds. How the emergency doctors had said that he'd been lucky to not sustain an injury in the water, and he'd been like his old self before they'd even left the ER. He'd been fine for a week or so, but then he'd started acting differently.

"I'm worried that maybe there are some latent negative effects from the . . . the . . ." She couldn't bring herself to say "drowning."

"From being unintentionally unconscious," Dr. Caruso supplied in a gentle tone.

She swallowed the acid in her mouth, as a cracked "Yes" left her lips.

"I understand." He nodded as he sat in the empty chair next to her, pulling his stethoscope from his neck. "Colton, buddy.

I'm going to listen to your lungs and heart while Mom gives you a big hug."

Elaine helped move Colton slightly one way or another as Dr. Caruso delicately examined him. When he was finished, he leaned against the chair back.

"The good news is that he sounds good, but I saw in his chart that he's lost a little weight. That's to be expected after surgery, but by this point out, that usually rebounds. Does he still not have much of an appetite?"

"He was eating well until the week after . . . it. But now he says 'food doesn't taste good.'"

"Is that true, buddy?" The doctor tried, but Colton didn't raise his head. "What about sleep?"

"He won't unless it's in bed with me."

"Mom's super snuggly, huh, Colton?"

Silence filled the room, leaving only sounds of the muted cries of babies in other exam rooms and nurses walking the hallways.

"Okay. It seems to me that maybe Colton is having a hard time recovering emotionally from the two medical episodes," he began. "It's not uncommon for a child to exhibit signs of depression after going through something like this. It's completely normal for him to be scared to be alone because he's worried that something bad will happen again."

Elaine nodded as the doctor spoke. That actually made a lot of sense. What he'd been through had been truly terrifying—of course, he wasn't acting normal.

"Focus on things that bring him joy and support him in knowing that you'll be there for him and he's safe." Dr. Caruso took a pensive breath. "Is there anything that makes you really happy, buddy?"

To her surprise, Colton lifted his head and locked his blue eyes with the doctor's. "Addie."

"Addie, huh?" The doctor flicked his gaze briefly to Elaine.

"His best friend at daycare," she supplied.

"She used to be my BFF all the time, but now I can only see her when Mama works," Colton whispered.

Elaine had to consciously refrain from squeezing Colton when all her muscles seized at her son's answer.

"Okay," the doctor said with an encouraging smile.

"And I miss Mr. Nate." Her son's face pushed back against her sternum, and it felt as if the bone was breaking under his golden locks. All the air in her lungs was sucked into the suddenly too bright room. Her eventual inhale was halting, throbbing, and painful when it came.

The observant doctor's eyes took one look at her face, and a quiet "Oh, I see" left his mouth, taking her in for the first time.

Elaine knew her eyes were haggard and the concealer she'd applied didn't begin to hide the circles under them. She knew her muscles refused to hold their normal posture and defeat sagged in her shoulders. That the sheen of tears threatening at the corners of her vision was visible to Dr. Caruso.

The doctor reassuringly patted her knee twice before rising. "I think Colton just needs some time to adjust to your new circumstances. Once he does, this episode should pass."

Elaine tried to keep her son's words out of her mind as they drove from the pediatrician's office to the hospital but failed miserably. These past two weeks had been so incredibly hard—

being scared for Colton as he seemed to deteriorate and missing Nate with a physicality that had genuinely shocked her. She'd wanted to call him so many times, but then a hot poker had slowly pushed into her side as she remembered she couldn't. That she had to stay away from the man who made her feel safe and truly wanted because stability for Colton came first.

But what if this wasn't what was best for him?

Her mind kept circling over and over on one idea, and eventually, the question pushed itself from between her teeth. "Colton, are you not feeling good because . . ." She took a deep breath, squeezing her hands around the steering wheel. "Because we aren't spending time with Addie and Mr. Nate?"

She watched his eyes as he nodded in the mirror. "I'm not scared, Mama. I'm sad."

The anguish that ripped through her muscles at that short sentence vibrated outward until each cell of skin resonated painfully. A quick car horn beep from behind them alerted her that the light had changed, and for the rest of the short drive, an unfamiliar and uncomfortable silence filled her car.

◊◊◊

An oppressive ache had infiltrated Elaine's bones after she dropped Colton off at daycare. Especially since Addie had run over and hugged her legs tightly through the half-gate. Exhaustion pulled at the skin of her face as she pushed through the glass door to the clinic. At least she only had six appointments to get through today.

She was crossing behind the intake desk when an unwanted voice called her name from the waiting room.

"I thought I told you—" Elaine hissed quietly, her eyes darting to their scheduling assistant, Madison, as her mother rose from a teal chair.

"I know." Her mother kept her voice low and held her hands in surrender. "I *am* listening to you, Elaine. I just wanted to stop by one last time and tell you that though I'm not ready to give up, I understand you need time."

Everything in her vibrated with anger, but she forced herself to sit calmly next to her mother to keep from making a scene.

"I brought these." Her mother searched through her reusable shopping bag and held out two gift bags. "One is for you and one is for your son. For Christmas."

Elaine stared at the outstretched gifts, unmoving.

"I'm returning to California. I have people there who support me, and my job is waiting for me." Her mother lowered the gifts but didn't return them to her bag. "I want you to call or text if you ever feel like it. I will always answer, and I hope that in time you might want to talk. I understand it might be a long way in the future . . . if at all."

She wanted to scoff that she was correct, but instead, she said, "Okay."

"I hope you know how sorry I am." Rita held her gaze. "And I hope you know how much I love you."

Knowing she couldn't respond in kind, Elaine held her hands out. "Thank you for the gifts."

Her mother's lips curled in a small smile as she handed them over. "I hope you like them, but I understand if you don't. That's something I learned in recovery. You can try and do the best for your children as a parent, but you will always fail in some way. It's impossible to always do the right thing. Sometimes, you have to do what will bring you the most joy. For me, that's giving you these."

Elaine's fingers felt numb as they gripped the satin bag handles and pulled them to her chest.

"Merry Christmas, Elaine."

Instead of saying "goodbye," she found herself murmuring, "Merry Christmas."

Clutching both gifts in one hand, Elaine rushed to the therapy office to stash them under her computer. Her head was under the desk when Glen's voice startled her to the point of smashing it on the underside.

Holding the back of her head, she took a deep breath before rising to stand. "How can I help you, Glen?"

"Today, it's about how *I* can help you." Her supervisor's smile was wide as Elaine watched Finn, Leslie, and Madison crowd behind him in the doorway. "I know you all are sad that I'll be leaving at the end of the year." He paused, and Leslie rolled her eyes behind his back. "But I'm happy to say, Elaine, that I'll be leaving this clinic in your capable hands."

She'd interviewed for the supervisor position the previous Monday with Sherrie, the director of physical therapy for the hospital system. Elaine hoped she'd interviewed well, but it had been incredibly difficult to push away all that had happened the week prior during those forty-five minutes.

Her eyes widened as her hand dropped. "I got it?"

"Of course, you did." Glen tucked his thumbs in his pockets. "It was stiff competition, but you've more than proven yourself over the last eight months. Congratulations! You are the new clinic supervisor starting January 2."

Leslie pushed past Glen and pulled Elaine into a tight hug. "We all called Sherrie to endorse you," she said.

"Really?" She glanced around the faces now crowding the small therapy office.

Everyone nodded in agreement, even Glen.

"Wow." She exhaled. "Thank you. Thank you so much."

"You put in the work," Finn said, leaning against the door jab.

"Yeah," Madison piped up.

"Congrats again." Glen smiled. "Now, I'd better make myself scarce because you've got a retirement party to plan."

Elaine grinned in spite of herself. "Yup. Let us work on that."

Glen winked at the group as he moved down the hall.

"Okay, so we'll obviously have to do something for him, but we'll worry about that later," Leslie started. "I wanted to let you know that I'm taking your last patient, so you can leave a little early to celebrate." She squeezed Elaine into another hug.

As Leslie's shoulder hit her chest, Elaine felt an echo resonate in the emptiness beneath. She had pushed away the person she wanted to celebrate this news with the most.

She sucked in a quick, uncomfortable breath. "Thank you."

"No problem." Her coworker released her with an uptick of her lips.

The next few hours flew by as the clinic was busy, as usual. After another round of hugs, Elaine grabbed the two gifts and took three steps toward the daycare center before flipping around to the parking garage. It'd be better not to pick up

Colton holding gifts she wasn't even sure she wanted him to have.

Standing over the open trunk of her car, she looked under the tissue paper of the largest bag. All it contained was a very cuddly and soft teddy bear—nothing nefarious. The smaller bag contained a colored cardboard box nestled in the center of green tissue paper. Inside was a delicate chain of rose gold with a dainty pendant anchored in the center. When she saw the flower pendant, her eyes clouded with tears as she ran her fingers over the metal shape.

Rose.

Taking the necklace from the box, Elaine fastened it around her neck before laying her hand over the pendant.

Rose had seen the same pain and hardship Elaine had experienced, but she had always approached the world with an openness that Elaine could never muster. She'd always been too afraid to take that chance, to truly trust another the way her sister had wholeheartedly put her trust in Chuck. Only Nate had ever gotten close to her, and in the end, she'd found some excuse to push him away too.

"Enough," she whispered, closing her eyes.

She might not always succeed, but she was going to try to hold onto what made her happy and trust that her decisions would only make her life—and Colton's life—better, not worse. As Elaine strode back into the hospital, she hoped that after two weeks, she still had a chance.

·CHAPTER 41·

Nate rubbed his neck as he softly closed the door to Addie's room. She'd been so wound up when he picked her up from daycare, he thought she'd never settle down for the night. Jay had met him at the hospital after work and pushed him for a hard and fast six-mile run. After the run, making dinner, and Addie's extensive bedtime routine, all Nate wanted was to take a hot shower and then veg out in front of the TV.

As he was walking from Addie's room to his, a quick punch of the doorbell sounded. Telling himself it was probably a delivery, Nate took his T-shirt off and continued to his room. When three sharp knocks met his ears, he leaned his head back with an exhale before pulling his shirt back on. Whoever was on the other side needed to go away. He wasn't about to go through Addie's bedtime routine a second time.

The tightness around his eyes vanished as his brows lifted at the sight of Elaine on his welcome mat. Her dark jeans and black sweater were topped by a red peacoat, and she looked perfectly festive, even though Christmas was weeks away. As his gaze took in the nervous grin tracing her lips, his chest squeezed involuntarily.

All the anguish that he'd been assiduously attempting to ignore over the last few weeks intensified. To divert his attention from the torment, he focused on the object in her hand. At least ten different candy bars were wrapped together with a large blue bow. The collection roughly resembled gathered flowers.

"Hi," she said.

"Hey." He managed when his breath returned to him.

"I . . . um. I didn't know your favorite candy bar, so I asked Addie this afternoon, and she said the one with the orange wrapper, but then changed it to yellow." Elaine's words tumbled out, her slender fingers spinning the "bouquet." "So I bought Peanut M&Ms, Butterfinger, Reese's Peanut Butter Cups, KitKat—"

"Are these man flowers?" Part of him wanted to laugh at the absurd sight of Elaine nervously chatting about candy on his doorstep, but he bit the inside of his lip.

Her dark brown eyes were earnest when they met his own. "These are *apology* man flowers."

Warmth radiated through his bloodstream before he quietly told himself to simmer down. She might be apologizing, but that didn't mean she wanted anything else to do with him. Even so, the remorseful turn of her brows and the gesture was so sweet, he couldn't help the slow smile spreading across his lips.

"Reese's Peanut Butter Cups," he said.

Elaine's eyes were centered on his mouth, and he had to fight the overwhelming urge to seal his lips over hers.

"What?" she asked, slightly breathless.

He couldn't control the cough that escaped him. "Those are my favorites," he clarified.

"Oh, good." She blinked and then held the candy out to him. "I've got two of those in there."

When her fingers brushed his in the transfer, he fought the new torturous impulse thrumming through his body and instead listened to the commands from his brain.

"Can I come in?" she asked softly, sweeping a strand of hair behind her ear.

"Of course." He stepped back to let her in. The slight scent of her floral shampoo reached his nose, and he had to intentionally stop himself from inhaling deeply.

Setting the candy on the kitchen counter, he thought about offering to start a pot of coffee but didn't want to presume she'd be here long enough to drink it. Instead, he settled himself at the end of the island and waited. Elaine stood in the space in front of him much like she had the first time she'd come into his house to drop Colton off.

"I have . . ." She paused. "I, um. Wow. This is hard." An uneasy chuckle escaped her lips before she rolled her shoulders back. Nate recognized the change as determined Elaine overtook the vulnerable version who had stood on his doorstep.

"I want to thank you again for saving Colton's life. I don't know what I would have . . ." She took in a shaky breath, and it took all of his resolve to keep his body glued to the granite island. "But you were there, and you saved him, and I will forever be grateful to you."

Nate opened his mouth, but she quickly continued.

"I'm also sorry for pushing you away that day. I was worried about Colton. He's always been the most important thing. I *have* to keep him safe."

"I know," he said softly.

Her gaze drifted to the floor as she took a breath. "You see . . . he's always come first, and I noticed when I was with you, I wasn't thinking about him." Her vulnerable eyes darted back up. "I was only thinking about you."

His muscles twitched as his brain screamed at him to gather her to his chest. Even though his body and mind were now in agreement, he was going to wait for her explicit invitation.

A pained expression crossed her face. "I'm a mess, Nate. Like, a huge mess—"

"No, you're not." His answer was gruffer than he'd intended.

"You don't . . ." She exhaled. "There's so much." She paused and placed a hand over her stomach. "Okay, here goes. My mother, Rita, raised my sister, Rose, and me. She was a single mom but took good care of us until she hurt her back. Then she became addicted to opioids and alcohol and didn't keep us safe. When I was fourteen, her boyfriend tried to rape me in our home and Rose and her boyfriend, Chuck, rescued me—"

"Oh my God, Elaine—"

She held up her shaking palm, and Nate wanted nothing more than to kiss those trembling fingertips.

"After that, the three of us lived in a little apartment until I graduated. Rose and Chuck got married. When he received orders, we all moved here. I went to PT school and Rose became pregnant . . ." She paused again, looking at him with a pleading gaze. "With Colton."

He felt his brow furrow.

"Chuck died in active duty combat while Rose was pregnant, and I moved in with her. After Colton was born, we co-parented until shortly after he turned two . . . when . . . when she died suddenly one morning."

Pain rippled over Nate's breastbone as tears welled in her eyes.

She took a shaky breath and continued. "I took Colton from the social worker that day and adopted him as soon as I could afterward. It's been just the two of us ever since. That's why I have to keep him safe. I have to take care of him for Rose."

She touched a pendant he hadn't noticed before just below her collarbones as a fat tear dropped down her cheek. Unlike before, she didn't move to push it away, she let it sit in between them with her words. If he'd been waiting for an invitation, she was basically begging him.

Nate stepped closer and paused when he was inches before her. In the short suspension of his movement, she did what he hoped she would—she leaned forward. Wrapping his arms around her, he felt her hot breath on his chest as she exhaled. Her arms reached around his waist and held him tight as she rested her cheek against his thumping heart.

"You *are* taking incredible care of Colton because you're an amazing mother." His words were raspy.

He felt her shoulders rise. "I try so hard, but there are times I feel like I'm never enough."

A deep breath pulled into his lungs. "I understand what it feels like to think you're completely failing as a parent."

Elaine lifted her face with a frown pulling at her lips. "What do you mean?"

"When Colton fell in the river . . . that wasn't the first time I'd done CPR." The words escaped with his breath.

Elaine's eyes widened, but Nate forced himself to keep his gaze on hers.

"The first time was on my wife after she'd died."

A gasp tore between her lips as her fingers curled around his grey T-shirt at the base of his spine.

"I didn't know she was already gone. I thought I could have saved her, but . . ." He let his gaze lift over her head, seeing the same images that populated his brain whenever he thought of that day. ". . . I couldn't remember my CPR training. I did everything wrong. For years, I thought it was my fault that she'd died. That it was my fault Addie didn't have a mother."

"Nate." Elaine's soft voice pulled his eyes down. "I'm so sorry."

Her eyes were wet with unshed tears as she delicately pressed her hands to the sides of his face. The sensation of her gentle caress allowed him to close his eyes, to surrender. Her hands flowed to his shoulders, tightly bringing him to her. A loud, halting exhale left his lungs as she gripped him steadily and held him.

"I'm so sorry," she whispered.

For the first time in a long time, he allowed himself to simply be held. Minutes stretched into one another as the kitchen clock ticked over the sink.

"I'm sorry for adding pain to your life when you've already experienced so much." Her voice cracked as she spoke.

When he raised his head, Elaine did the same. A single tear blinked from her eye, and he chased it with his thumb.

"We both have."

Understanding bloomed between them as their gazes held.

"Do you think . . ." She softly cleared her throat. "Would you consider starting over?"

He knew the answer she wanted to hear, but he had to be honest with her. "No."

"Oh." She blinked, looking away.

His knuckle found her chin. "I don't want to start over. I would be okay with continuing, but our past is what makes us who we are. I want to know these kinds of things about you, and I want to be able to share these parts of myself. I've kept so much of how I've felt inside me for so long, and I can't do that anymore.

"I'm not perfect. I've made mistakes. You should know that there was a point in time when I depended too much on alcohol to deal with my emotions. To deal with the grief and the guilt I felt over my wife's death." He sighed, resting his forehead on her crown. "I'm ashamed to admit that the day Colton fell in the river, I'd poured myself a large bourbon before I came outside because I was upset that you chose Jay over me."

"I didn't—" Their faces were so close that her words exhaled moist, warm air on his lips.

"I know," he whispered.

He pressed his eyes closed for a beat before he lifted his face. "I know that now. And as excruciating as these past two weeks have been, I haven't drank to numb my emotions even one time. I realized that day at my parents' house that it wasn't helping me. That it wasn't a good way to deal with how I was feeling."

Her eyes watched carefully as she listened.

A heavy breath pulled at his chest. "I'm trying to be better. I can't promise I'll always do the right thing, that I won't fail in some way in the future, but I *can* promise I'll always be honest with you.

"But now that you know that about me . . ." He swallowed against the lump in his throat as his heart rate jackknifed. "Now that you know about my past and the mistakes I've made, would you still want to be with me?"

Her gaze never wavered from his. "Yes," she breathed.

His thumb found her bottom lip and gently rubbed across it. Even though Elaine's lashes fluttered closed at his touch, residual doubt still brewed in his chest. "You're sure?"

The lip touching his thumb lifted into a soft smile as her eyes opened. "Haven't we been through this? The answer's always—"

Before she could finish the sentence, he crushed her lips with his own. Consonants and vowels dissolved into a soft sigh and a slight moan as he wove his hand into her loose hair. When her tongue searched for his, her hands interlaced around his neck, drawing him even closer, holding him to her.

Her fingers digging into his scalp helped him feel less frantic about his overwhelming need to touch every inch of her. He wanted to take this slow, he wanted to be tender and gentle, but something about Elaine simply drove him out of his mind. His hands found the lapels of her coat and roughly pushed. For a breath, slender fingers broke from his neck as she pulled her arms back. A second later, the sound of wool fabric hitting the tile floor resonated in his silent kitchen.

As if a fuse had been lit and was rapidly accelerating down a line, he could feel her breathing become more ragged and her need becoming more intense, mirroring his own. When he captured her hips, flipped her body, and pinned her against the counter, the deep, resonant moan filling her mouth had his tongue chasing after it. Her lips broke from his with a hoarse gasp. "*Nate.*"

A string of expletives tore through his brain at the way she said his name because now he wanted to hear it screamed from her throat.

She pushed him back far enough for her to jump and wrap her legs around his torso. A strangled groan escaped his lips as the heat, scent, and pressure of her completely short-circuited his brain.

"I hear"—her words escaped with a rough exhale before her tongue wove around his again— "first dates are overrated."

He hummed some non-committal agreement against her lips before she broke away. When he opened his eyes and saw the naked intensity in hers, his breath caught.

"We've already done everything else backwards." A vulnerability filtered into the slight turn of her mouth. "I yelled at you before I even said 'hello.' I met your parents before we've even gone on one official date." Her fingers gently traced the cords of his neck. "Technically, we've already slept together in hospital chairs, but right now I'd really like you to take me upstairs . . . if that's something you want."

Taking a large step forward, he settled her on the island. "Elaine. I want that more than anything," he exhaled. "But first, let me do this backwards too. Before our first date, before our family, our friends, or our kids find out that we're together, you need to know that I love you."

A silent gasp parted her lips. As her eyes darted over his face, uneasiness pinched Nate's shoulders until she grabbed the sides of his head. "I love you too," she said, on an exuberant exhale before crushing her mouth to his.

Radiant light and heat swept through his chest, racing down each of his limbs, until a vibrating tingle spread over his skin. Boundless pleasure rushed through him as one of her hands gripped his back and the other wove through his hair again. Their lips never disconnected as his fingers roved wildly over her shoulders until they gripped firmly at her waist.

Then he felt a shift as she pulled back just enough for him to feel her smile at his lips. Palming the back of his head, she slowly kissed her way to his ear. "Nate," she rasped and he involuntarily shivered. A satisfied hum followed her lips as they made their way down his neck until he felt a little nip of teeth in the dip between his collarbones. "You have no idea what you're in for." Her sultry whispered words sent fire to the base of his spine.

Picking her up, he possessively claimed her mouth as he marched them up the stairs. Once he'd closed and locked his bedroom door behind them, he tossed her onto his bed with a growl. "Then show me."

·CHAPTER 42·

Elaine splayed her hand wide in the warm pool of mid-morning sunlight on the countertop as Dean Martin softly crooned in the background.

"How'd you sleep?" Nate's voice murmured in her ear as he slid a prepared coffee mug in front of her, brushing his chest against her back.

A smile pulled on her lips as she leaned into his radiant heat. "Good. All things considered."

Jodi had given Elaine a happy and knowing smile when she'd walked into her apartment late last night after her and Nate's incredible first date.

Nate had been a perfect gentleman, picking her up, opening doors, and treating her to dinner at the nicest restaurant downtown. During the date, they'd laughed and talked with an openness that made her whole body feel free. Afterward, she'd convinced him that instead of going dancing as he'd planned, they should dance in his kitchen. They'd made it through half a song before moving upstairs to fall into the perfect balance of pulling and pushing, of gentle affection and absolute abandon.

On Monday night, she'd initially taken the lead, and Nate had lost his mind as she'd expected, but after, he'd held her more tenderly than she'd ever experienced. Then that slow smile had lifted his lips as he moved over her, and she'd felt herself completely let go, completely trust, for the first time in her life. Her heart had felt as if it was beaming outside her chest as the touch of Nate's body echoed the whispered "I love you" he husked in her ear.

Nate's arm cinched around her waist, eliminating the space between them. As she tilted her head and rested her cheek on him, his lips brushed her hair. "I wish I didn't have to drive you home last night. I missed you this morning."

The slight growl at the end of his sentence sent fire crackling over her skin. Elaine's eyes blinked slowly closed as Nate's other hand slid to her jaw, tilting her lips toward his.

At the sound of little feet pounding down the playroom stairs, Nate let out a resigned sigh, stepping back and dropping his hands.

"Daddy, I'm hungry," Addie announced, a flowy green princess dress covering her tunic and leggings.

"Me too, Mama." Colton's hand slid into hers as he came to her side.

"Why don't you two sit down, and we'll have a snack. There's something Miss Elaine and I want to talk to you about." Elaine caught his slight smile as he opened the pantry.

Before long, the kids were giggling to themselves at the kitchen table, making their pretzel sticks into walrus tusks and slurping apple juice from their plastic cups.

"What do you think about the idea of me and Miss Elaine spending more time together?" he asked Addie.

"Like sleepovers?"

The question was innocent, but it almost made Elaine spit out her coffee. Since Addie had been at her grandparents' last night, there was no way for her to know that Elaine had already spent a good portion of the evening here.

Nate chuckled at her reaction and reached for her hand under the table. Elaine loved how warm his touch was every time, even when it was occasionally demanding—*especially* when it was demanding.

"Like having her and Colton around more *and* maybe sleepovers." His hazel eyes radiated with affection as he squeezed her hand.

"Colt, you get to sleep here!" Addie stood, doing her happy, jumpy dance next to her chair.

Elaine was caught up in Nate's gaze when she heard Colton's question. "Mama, would that make you happy?"

As always, her observant, considerate child pulled on her heartstrings.

Focusing on her son's sweet face, she let the truth fall from her lips. "Being here makes me really happy."

"Me too." He nodded, and his blond hair flopped. "I like Mr. Nate."

She and Nate shared a quick, private smile. "I like Mr. Nate too."

Addie grabbed Colton's hand. "Let's get my sleeping bag and put it on the floor next to my bed. We can play sleepover right now!"

Colton allowed himself to be pulled from his chair. "Kay."

"That went well," she commented as they ran from the room.

"I don't think they understand the concept, but now I can do this whenever I want." Lacing his fingers under her ponytail, Nate brought her lips to his.

The kiss was sweet, passionate, and satiating at the same time. Elaine found herself leaning into the corner of the table that separated them and wrapping her hand around his tricep to bring him closer.

"I can't find my . . . eeewww!"

They broke apart to find Addie and Colton standing in the doorway to the kitchen. Addie's face was pulled into a look of disgust, but Colton's lips held the biggest smile.

"You're kissing," Addie pointed out.

Elaine stifled a laugh as Nate answered his daughter. "That would be part of Miss Elaine spending more time here."

Addie dropped her face and turned to Colton. "Adults are weird."

"Yup," he answered but kept grinning.

"Come on. We'll use blankets instead." She sprinted down the hall.

"Kay." He followed close behind.

Once she heard the sound of both kids at the top of the stairs, Elaine let out her restrained chuckle. Her eyes glinted to Nate's, expecting the same reaction, but the corner of his lower lip was caught in his teeth as a heated intensity saturated his gaze. The sound of chair legs scratching against the tile floor entered her consciousness in the periphery as they both shot up from their spots and into each other's arms.

This kiss was needy and exacting in a way that made her core ache. Nate's coffee-flavored tongue wove around hers in the most flawless way as his hands gripped her possessively. His strength and intoxicating scent dominated her experience for several blissful minutes until they heard their children stomping again.

Nate rested his forehead to hers, his heaving breath hot over her lips. "I've never been so grateful for Addie's lead feet."

She laughed softly as they listened to the two children return to Addie's room instead of coming down the stairs. Lifting her head, she gently slid both hands to frame Nate's face before bringing his mouth to hers. He let her kiss him slowly, sweetly, as she tried to express the happiness that radiated in her muscles through her lips.

"Nate, I—" she breathed when she finally broke the kiss.

"Me too," he whispered against her lips.

A smile tugged at her mouth at his presumed end of that sentence. Elaine couldn't fault him, because that was the exact sentiment she'd been trying to convey with her kiss. Nate leaned back, crossing his arms at the base of her spine. She let her hands fall to his chest, playing with the woolen swirls of the cream sweater he'd been wearing when he'd helped her with Colton at the hospital.

"I want to ask you something," she began again, letting her focus drift to her fingers. "I've been perusing housing listings this week. Actually, I've been doing that for a long time, but Thursday I found an opening in a townhouse complex I've had my eye on about two miles from here."

She glanced up to watch his reaction. Nate's gaze was open, the green whirl of his irises patiently waiting for her to continue.

"I've never bought a house before, and I was wondering if you wouldn't mind going with me to see it. I have an appointment with Leslie's realtor this afternoon at two."

Her breath sat trapped in her chest as she waited.

Nate's right eyebrow twitched as he opened his mouth, closed it, and then opened it again. "Why don't yo—"

Elaine's body blushed with warmth, because a small part of her had expected this reaction from him. "We don't know where this"—she gestured between them—"will go, and though I deeply hope it lasts, owning my own place is something I've wanted for a long time. This is something that I've wanted to give to Colton since I became his mother. I want him to have his own room in his own house that he can paint whatever color he wants. I need to do this for him . . . for me." She drew in a breath. "But I'd still like you and Addie to be a part of it." Her eyebrows twisted. "I don't know if that makes sense."

He brought a hand to frame her face, his thumb caressing the corner of her jaw. "It makes complete sense. I'd be happy to go with you."

"Really?" she rasped.

"Yes." A smile lifted his lips before he brought them to hers.

"They're doing it again," Addie whined. Apparently, his heavy-footed daughter was also capable of stealth.

This time when his face lifted from hers, Nate's warm laugh bounced off every cabinet in his kitchen, and Elaine's muscles simply resonated with joy.

·EPILOGUE·

One year later

"Do you have any jellyfish?" Addie's blue eyes peered over her cardholder. She had almost all of her cards stacked precariously on the left side and one single card on the right. Her hair was still a mess of tangles over the reindeer Christmas pajamas Elaine had bought for her and Colton.

Glancing at the colored Go-Fish cards in her hand, Elaine did have one jellyfish. "What number is a jellyfish?"

Addie carefully examined a card, her little bare feet tucked under her on the carpet. "Eleven."

Elaine handed over the card before stealing a sip from her coffee mug on the small kid's table next to them. The scent of cooking waffles joined the sound of Christmas music wafting up the playroom stairs. This morning, Nate had decided that he and Colton were going to make breakfast for her and Addie.

"Do you have any sevens?" Elaine's hand muffled a yawn at the end of her sentence.

They were all a little weary from last night's event—both her and Addie's hair still held the remnants of their curled updos from being part of Tyler and Chloe's wedding party. The whole affair had been the perfect combination of rustic charm and boho-chic as they said their "I dos" under one of the large oak trees on their property. The outdoor reception afterward had been as energetic as the couple themselves, making Elaine grateful she had a day to rest before joining Leslie for a sixty-mile ride tomorrow.

Addie finished placing the new card next to the one on the right side of her cardholder. "Go fish."

Elaine's phone *plunk plunked* next to her as she picked up a card from the draw pile. She'd given Olivia, the newly hired PT, her cell number in case she needed anything on her first Saturday shift. Elaine found that even though she'd had to reduce her treatment hours by a quarter to complete the administrative duties required to run the clinic, she loved the new responsibilities of her job as supervisor. Her favorite so far had been training Olivia—who was already proving herself to be a valuable asset.

Looking over the screen, Elaine saw the message was actually from her mom, double-checking that they were going to talk later that evening.

"Let me answer this real quick," she said, thumbing out her confirmation before setting the phone down.

A lot of time had passed before Elaine had finally texted her mom and asked for her email. In the beginning, she'd felt more comfortable emailing than talking. A few months after that, they'd started scheduling calls. Part of her was perpetually waiting for her mother to relapse, but at more than three years sober, Elaine found herself softening to the idea of maybe Rita could be more involved in her life. Each time they spoke, some of the hurt and anger that was wrapped around her heart gently loosened.

"Do you have any jellyfish?" Addie's lips were curled in a smile.

A laugh escaped her. "Go fish."

Elaine loved these lazy mornings together. Almost every Friday night after her and Nate's first date, they'd started having "sleepovers," alternating between her place and his. The second time they'd stayed over at his house, Elaine had found a set of bunk beds in Addie's room instead of her usual twin frame.

The sound of Nate singing off-key to Perry Como's "It's Beginning to Look a Lot Like Christmas" in the kitchen brought a smile to her lips. "Do you have any—"

"I almost forgot." Addie put her cards down face up and jumped to her feet.

"Addie, cards down," she said, covering her eyes with her palm.

"Oh ya." Addie flipped the cardholder. "Saw-dee."

"It's okay." Elaine lowered her hand. "What'd you forget?"

"I found an ornament we need to add to the tree." The little girl bounced on her toes.

Over Thanksgiving break, they'd taken turns decorating a tree here and one at her townhouse. Nate had even helped his "little man" string white lights all over the Hulk-green walls of his bedroom, highlighting Colton's numerous taped up drawings.

"Are you sure?"

Elaine couldn't imagine there could be any forgotten ornaments. The tree downstairs was nearly bursting with various decorations, tchotchkes, and kid's art. With the kids' Kindergarten Christmas party next week, she and Nate would each be receiving another handcrafted ornament soon.

"You'll see!" Addie bounded up the stairs and quickly came back carrying a thin, red satin ribbon with something silver attached to it.

"I found it in Daddy's drawer." She held out the ribbon.

Elaine's breath caught as her hand grasped the "ornament" and recognized that a ring hung from the ribbon loop. A white gold band held a two-carat diamond flanked by a smaller blue stone to the left and a pink stone to the right.

"Waffle time!" Colton clamored up the stairs with Nate behind him.

"Come get them while they're hot." Nate's broad smile fell as he saw the ring in her upturned palm.

"What's that?" Colton bounced over and plunked down on the carpet.

"It's an ornament," Addie answered as Nate crossed the room and lowered himself to the ground.

"I . . ." He ran his hand through his hair and gripped the base of his neck. "Uh, you were supposed to see that on Christmas morning."

Soundless air escaped her mouth as her eyes flicked from his face to the ring and back.

"I found it," Addie said, pride apparent in her voice.

"Thanks, sweetheart." He glanced at his daughter for a second before focusing all his attention on her.

Nate reached for her hands, and she let them be ensconced in his, the ring secure in the center. The warmth of them pulled at her first, radiating up her arms and settling in her heart, which pulsed slowly, surely, already knowing what he wanted to say. Everything seemed to slow—even their bouncy children silently stilled.

"Elaine, this past year with you has been one of the best of my life. I cannot imagine my life without you, without Colton. I know in that time you've built a home of your own, but I want you to know that to me . . . you are home." He swallowed audibly. "I was wondering if you'd consider building a life with me that we can all share." His breath left his body in a short burst. "I love you, Elaine. Will you marry me?"

A brief pause hung in the motionless air before the corner of her mouth lifted. "You don't have to ask. The answer's always 'yes.'"

"Yes?" His hazel eyes bounced between hers.

"Yes." She rose swiftly to her knees. "Of course, yes!"

Nate gathered her into his arms, covering her mouth with his in a deep and thorough kiss. Only when their kids' protests reached their ears did they break apart, the ring still clutched in her fist behind his neck. Leaning back on his haunches, Nate gathered the ring from her and untied the bow in the ribbon with slightly shaky hands. After he slipped the perfectly sized ring on her finger, his eyes lifted from her hand as that slow smile spread across his mouth.

Elaine felt the air leave her lungs. "Nate, you're—

"Does this mean Colt and I are getting married?" Addie's question caused Elaine and Nate to erupt into surprised laughter.

"No, it means that when we get married, Colton will be your brother," he answered.

"Really?" Addie shot up from her spot on the ground. "I'll be your BFF *and* your sister!"

"Yiphoo!" Colton stood and grabbed Addie's hands.

"Brothers and sisters," the kids sang repeatedly while dancing in a little circle.

"I love you." Elaine pulled Nate's face to hers as he wrapped his arms snuggly around her waist. When her lips were an inch from his, she whispered, "You're home for me too," before sweeping his mouth into a kiss that promised forever.

ACKNOWLEDGMENTS

Words cannot describe how important Rachel Garber is to me, and that means a lot because words are my business. You are the best editor/proofreader/cheerleader a writer could ask for—infinite thanks. Thank you also to my line editor, Emily Poole, and copy editor, Rebecca Jaycox. I am grateful to Karri Klawiter for her amazing cover design. I want to thank April Kirkner for sharing your insight into the world of physical therapy so I could write Elaine's work life with accuracy. Thank you also to Jackie, Chelsea, Alison, and Stephanie for reading an early beta copy of this book.

I couldn't have done this without the unwavering support of my family and friends. I'm grateful for my two cuties for always being so happy to help when I got stuck, and for my husband for his unparalleled love and encouragement. Also, a huge thank you to my wonderful parents, extended family, Jackie, and Chelsea for their endless support.

Thank you to my readers for picking up this book and spending time out of your life reading my work. I truly hope that you enjoyed A Guarded Heart—that it surprised and entertained you, and tugged at your heartstrings.

When I wrote the first draft of this book in the fall of 2019, I named the hospital Edwards Memorial Hospital after my incredible Uncle Eddy. He was a man that always went after his dreams and encouraged everyone else to do the same. He died in May 2020, long before I announced to my family that I was writing and the publication of my first novel. I'd like to think he'd have gotten a kick out of his inclusion in this book and is cheering me on still.

ABOUT THE AUTHOR

Laura Langa strives to write stories that pull at her readers' heartstrings and create relatable characters you can't help but root for. As a former medical professional, she uses her experience in the field to inform her writing. Laura loves trees and all things green, hates flossing but forces herself to do it every night, drinks tea—not coffee, and believes that salt air can often cure a bad mood.

Visit her website at www.LauraLanga.com
Subscribe to her newsletter for the latest details at www.LauraLanga.com/Newsletter
Follow on Instagram and Facebook @LauraLangaWrites

Made in the USA
Middletown, DE
08 December 2021

54683105R00222